THE XANOTEK STRATAGEM

A NOVEL BY LAURENCE SMITH

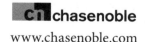

www.chasenoble.com

First edition published 2014.
Second edition published 2014.

Copyright © Chase Noble Ltd, 2014.

Published by Chase Noble Ltd.
Registered office Audley House, Brimpton
Common, Berkshire RG7 4RT.

Designed by Rita Sexton.

Cover by Simon Collins.

Printed by Hobbs The Printers, Hampshire

British Library Cataloguing in Publication Data. A catalogue record
for this book is available from the British Library.

ISBN 978-0-9575092-3-8.

Dedicated to Harry

Keep right on

STARRING

Craig Richards	The strategist
Marcelle Williams	Troubleshooter
Dimala Naidu	Marcelle's protégé
Jeremy Barker	Materials scientist, Xanotek CEO
Nobuyuki Hino	Corporate financier
Katherine Foster	Secretary of State for Defence
Hugo Cunningham	MOD permanent secretary
Adrienne Dodier	Xanotek finance director
Mike (Neil) Ward	Mercenary
Thomas Pohl	Recluse

AND ALSO FEATURING
(in alphabetical order)

Rebecca Cunningham	Hugo's wife
Monsieur Daviau	Restaurant owner
Kim Drahem	Xanotek scientist
Marco Elderfield	Adrienne's deputy
Nicola Everill	Corporate lawyer
Daniel Fricke	Chad's deputy
Chuck Gral	Lincoln Leaders coach
Frank Griffiths	Oil refinery worker
Fred Humphreys	Exchange supervisor
Jhavier	Mumbai police superintendent
Joakim	Pohl's assistant
Victor Jones	Xanotek scientist
Dr Kwong	Drydock director
Mrs McDermott	Retired headmistress
Ted Milner	Oil refinery worker
Roger Neilson	Foreign Secretary
Nripendra	Orphan
Paulo	Mugger
Adam Peralter	Xanotek scientist
Mr Phillips	Night watchman
Riccardo	Waiter
Natalie Richards	Craig's daughter
Patricia Richards	Craig's ex-wife
Mr Ryu	Detective
Quentin (Neil) Shaw	Ward's accomplice
Chad Spillane	Xanotek head of production
President Tshuma	Leader of East Phoenicia
Martin Thorpe	Special constable
Brent Tuxworth	Voast Motors CEO
Elsie Underhill	Personal assistant
Stella Weseldine	Chandansar orphanage manager
Secretary Zavrazhov	Russian foreign minister
Suiren Zhi	Architect

Prologue

Located in:
Malkin Castle, Norfolk

It was as if the battery in a child's toy had just sputtered its last.

After sixteen intense hours, exhilaration had turned to exhaustion. The day spent arguing and conjecturing was finally taking its toll. Jeremy Barker glanced at his watch with exaggerated surprise. Marcelle Williams and Adrienne Dodier, who had been engaged in a heated debate about the prospects for the global economy, waved away the waiter offering to replenish their glasses. Chad Spillane tapped the edge of the oak table with his knuckles. In the corner of the room, the Victorian long-case clock lingered on the final note as it completed its elaborate midnight chiming sequence. Chronologically as well as emotionally, the first day had run its course.

Barker coughed audibly, clearing his throat to signify he had some post-prandial comments to share. Briefly, he thanked the group, the six men and three women, for their "fulsome input" and "honest thoughts". His bony right hand was in perpetual motion as he spoke, running his fingers through the thinning hair around his temples, pushing at the reading glasses that were balancing on the tip of his nose, and fiddling with a lapel pin badge in the shape of the logo from the 1980s cult series *Blackadder*. High above, dark shadow obscured the top half of Gainsborough's portrait of the Duke of Argyll, but the Duke's eyes pierced through the blackness, undimmed by the gloom.

"In particular," he said, turning to the individual seated on his immediate right. "I'm sure we can agree Craig Richards' contribution has been invaluable."

Across the table, Dodier nodded aggressively.

Barker then turned his remarks to the day ahead. In a pointed and mischievous tone, he said he was looking forward to another "early start" and "packed agenda", phrases which cued an outbreak of nervous smiles.

"I'm not sure exactly what Craig has in store for us. But I've no doubt whatsoever about one thing. The journey won't be dull."

Barker coughed again, out of habit not infection, gathered up his papers, straightened his jacket, and rose to leave the room. For him, as for most of the group, the day's proceedings were now concluded. Even Daniel Fricke finally abandoned his attempts to digest the amorphous mass he'd created by blending his three mini-deserts into one concoction. It was time for the party to make the short walk along the narrow stone corridor that connected the Malkin Castle banqueting hall with the keep, which had been converted around thirty years ago into guest accommodation. And then to rest and recharge in the comfort of its world renowned luxury.

For Craig Richards, however, work had barely begun.

The strategist had exuded a relaxed charm ever since taking his seat. Two of his dining companions, including Spillane, remembered him from his monthly Management Tomorrow column, back in the 1990s. The goatee remained, clipped as in the masthead photograph; his light blue eyes still as piercing. And not a single grey strand was detectable amidst his ample chestnut hair to mark the passage of time.

On the surface, Craig seemed to be loosening up, unwinding after the exertions of the day had now passed. His conversation was light-hearted and unthreatening. He had engaged every participant in delightful repartee, enquiring casually of their family circumstances, and sharing inoffensive anecdotes from his long and colourful career. But a scrupulous observer might look beyond these superficial signals. Craig's posture was always a few degrees more erect than his companions'. He blinked less often. His gaze was more focused. And during momentary breaks in the exchanges, he would tense up, clasping together his hands, taking advantage of the fleeting seconds to filter out the surrounding distractions and undertake vital mental processing. For Craig, all material, however inconsequential, was potential evidence, to be analysed, sifted and weighed.

As the group dispersed, Craig contemplated the hours ahead. Since the break-up of his marriage, he had more than ever revelled in the magnificent period when the rest of the world slept. With the night at its darkest and most silent, he often felt consumed with an electrifying thrill. He tingled with the euphoria of making discoveries and connections while others were out cold. Like an outlaw sneaking past dozing, oblivious guards to execute the perfect heist, there was something exotic about breaking through while everyone else lies comatose.

Before departing, Craig swapped courtesies with Barker, Spillane and Dodier, and crossed the room to acknowledge another member of the party, a wiry silver-haired businessman from Tokyo. Nobuyuki Hino had flown into the country by private jet two days previously, especially for the occasion. Hino leant forward, his skeletal fingers pressing into the back of Richards' hand and he shook it forcefully.

"A very interesting day," he said, expressing each word with precision. "Much to consider."

The majority of guest rooms were on the far side of the keep, up a restored spiral staircase. As they ascended, Craig lagged behind his companions. He paused to peer through a narrow arrow slit and survey the surrounding Norfolk countryside, allowing his imagination to wander. He transported himself half a millennium back in time, into the body of a medieval archer defending the last bastion from insurgents and marauders. Strategy, capability, motivation, execution – all coalescing in the perfect moment at which the bow is raised and drawn, and the arrow released, to soar through the still air, and skewer with a satisfying bullseye the scalp of an enemy. Precious the modern day plan whose success can be so emphatically judged.

At the top of the stairwell, Craig took his room key from his inside pocket. The key was unmistakable in its size and weight, befitting the grandeur of the location; he had been conscious of its presence for most of the evening. Not for Malkin Castle the plastic card keys popular with nondescript hotel chains, that need simply to be waved across a tiny panel to release the lock. The wrought iron key in Richards' hand was serious business. It required conscious will to force it into the keyhole and twist. The pins resisted gamely, and then released with a thump, causing the stud-encrusted door to swing open under its own enormous weight.

Inside his stateroom, Craig readied himself for the task. He was now in his element, surrounded by information and insights from numerous sources. A few hours beforehand, when he had checked in, the room could have been lifted from the centrespread of an upmarket lifestyle magazine, bathed in an opulent purple and gold hue which cascaded from the elegant damask wallpaper with its frenzy of gilded peacocks. Dead centre had been an imposing antique four-poster bed, bedecked with hand-embroidered, pure linen sheets smelling of lavender oils, and a shimmering thick velvet quilt. To the near side had stood a Chippendale camelback sofa, with a tight, serpentine back and high rolled arms, almost submerged in scatter cushions, next to a well-stocked walnut drinks cabinet. And across by the window had been a nineteenth century rolltop desk, complete with traditional rotary telephone, blotter and fountain pen, from which one could gaze across the castle courtyard as one composed correspondence. All lit by a menagerie of side lamps, floor lamps, table lamps and a commanding cut-glass chandelier.

For Craig, lavish soft furnishings were as welcome as radio static. They interfered with the clarity and rigour of his thinking. During a break in the afternoon session, he had sneaked a moment to rearrange the room in a manner more conducive to his state of mind. Pillows and cushions had been tossed into a heap in the corner, alongside the superfluous lamps, and the mattress had been pulled off the bed, and now leant against the wall in the manner of a mutated flip chart. Over the next fifteen minutes, Richards plastered both mattress and wall with almost a hundred separate pieces of paper until it was a kaleidoscope of analysis – extracts from reports on polymer technology, meeting notes, personnel profiles, and bullet point summaries of the key issues which he and Marcelle, his adviser and confidante, had made at the end of every session since the early morning kickoff.

At the centre of his kaleidoscope, he attached to the wall a Financial Times cutting from twelve months beforehand, with the headline: "Barker returns to Japan for additional fund raising."

When Craig had finished creating his display, the designer wallpaper, once so domineering was barely detectable beneath the maze of foolscap sheets and post-it notes. He took a pace backwards to survey his work, and stood, arms crossed, studying the contents. Occasionally, he moved a piece of paper from one area of the wall to another. When he was finally satisfied with the organisation of the materials, he took from his case a ball of coloured string, which he cut into different lengths and used it to highlight links between different areas of his display, in particular a page torn from a classified Ministry of Defence report on troop deployment. He checked the time on his mobile phone, and grimaced to see the background setting had somehow defaulted to a photograph of Patricia and their daughter Natalie, taken in a different era, an era when contact between them did not require lawyers. With a swipe of his finger, the photograph was erased, and the background returned to a generic pale azure. Almost one o'clock, time to start mapping out the programme for the second day with Barker and his team.

The next hour would be crucial to a successful outcome for the event. Craig always felt a frisson of excitement when he reached this stage, and in addition now felt a slight moistening at the nape of his neck as a couple of beads of sweat bubbled out from a pore. He needed to be fully alert; nothing could be overlooked if he was to justify Hino's trust. There was no margin for casual error or misjudged conclusions.

Craig was particular about the environment that best released his creative imagination. The lights needed to be slightly dimmed; an eighteenth century symphony needed to be playing in the background (today, he had chosen Haydn's Maria Theresia). And one thing more. In his en-suite bathroom, Craig draped a towel across the floor tiles, and knelt down next to the basin. Briskly, he wiped some tissue across the glass surface of the vanity cabinet to ensure it was dry, and then tipped out two hundred milligrams of white powder, which he inspected carefully, removing a small section where the particles had clumped together. Using a hand mirror, he arranged the powder into two lines, each a few inches in length, and continued adjusting the contours of the lines in pursuit of perfection, long past the point of practical effect. The product was remarkably fine. The lines glowed with beckoning purity, and seemed to dance like desert sand dunes in a light breeze. Finally, he used a cut straw to ingest the cocaine, yelping uncontrollably and wide-eyed as the drug was sharply absorbed through the lining of his sinuses.

The effect was like an adrenaline surge; every moment of time came alive with power and significance. For a moment, Craig imagined he was an Olympic sprinter, revelling in the adoration of the spectators, lifting his arms in the middle of an eighty thousand seat stadium as every man, woman and child in the crowd rose to their feet in thunderous applause. He was the renowned Craig Richards, no less, the Usain Bolt of the corporate strategy world. As he plotted and schemed, the multitudes gazed on, expectant, dazzled, overawed.

Pumped up from his ingestion, Craig brushed the residue of powder into the sink, and headed back into the stateroom to contemplate his kaleidoscopic display. But as he turned the corner, a sixth sense told him something was amiss, moments before his ears caught the light drubbing on fingers against fabric, and his eyes made out a darkened figure seated on the camelback.

"How the…" began Craig.

"Be quiet and sit down," said the stranger, motioning towards an exposed section of hard wood floor.

"Who are you? What are you doing?"

"I'm not going to ask again. Be quiet. Sit down."

Craig ignored this entreaty and instead marched toward the rolltop desk. He had overcome his initial astonishment at the intrusion, and was now intent on seeing the perpetrator ejected with menaces from the premises. Grabbing the receiver, he was about to dial the receptionist, when the stranger rose purposely from the sofa. He was pointing a Browning 9mm pistol directly at Craig's temple.

"It's got a suppressor. So I suggest you forget about playing the hero, and do as I say. Which is to sit down," he said.

10

Craig returned the receiver to its cradle, and raised his hands to indicate compliance with the instructions. Finally, at the third time of asking, he sat cross-legged on the floor.

"I'm pleased we have an understanding," said the stranger. "Head shots can be so messy."

"What's this all about?" asked Craig, cautiously.

"All this nonsense you've been taping to the wall," said the stranger, looking across the room. "It all looks very elaborate. And I suppose you brainiacs need to do your stuff to justify your fees. But from now on, it's not your way any longer. From this point, you'll be doing what I say."

At which point the stranger eased the stopper from the whisky decanter, and poured himself a generous measure of 25 year old single malt Macallan.

Chapter One

Located in:
The Angola, on Grand Union Canal
and
London City Airport

NINE WEEKS EARLIER

The first burst of canal water erupted through the gate paddles, propelled outwards in a frenzied dance. Within moments, the surge was unstoppable. Each new jet spewed more forcefully into the chamber, arching through the early afternoon air, before crashing ten feet down into the lower reach of water. The sudden explosion of noise overwhelmed the prevailing light breeze.

In the gardens of the nearby *Fox and Hounds*, an elderly lady looked up from her plate of roast beef, and peered quizzically in the direction of the lock. Elsewhere, a rambler struggled to restrain a Labrador that was barking madly in the direction of the deluge.

As the water level rose, Craig Richards perched at the end of the balance beam, dangling his legs over the towpath, and making a gentle circular pattern in the dry soil with the sole of his boot. The elderly lady caught his eye; she raised her wine glass in his direction, and he nodded in acknowledgement. It would take around ten minutes for the chamber to fill, and he was content to use the time in silent contemplation of his surroundings. He had purchased his narrow boat, the day after a district judge had granted Patricia her decree absolute, precisely so he could enjoy rare moments of serene and indulgent reflection.

The boat itself was a restored vessel from the late nineteenth century. In its earlier days, it would have been horse-drawn, with around fifty of its sixty foot length used for transporting cargo, and the rear portion set aside for a small, functional boatman's cabin. Few of these features now survived. Before Craig made the boat his permanent residence, he had commissioned an enthusiast to complete an overhaul to his meticulous specifications. Horse power had given way to a vintage diesel engine. The hull was reinforced with steel. And the living accommodation was extended to almost the full length of the boat, leaving at the stern just a small deck and steering area beyond the rear doors. The internal structure comprised three rooms, all centrally heated, and – given Craig's occupation – fitted with secure high-speed digital connectivity. Craig had insisted that the ornate paintings of rose bushes in full bloom must be retained on both the port and starboard sides. He had always enjoyed the juxtaposition of emblems of tradition with hallmarks of ultra modernity. It appealed to his worldview.

The chamber was now almost filled, so Craig smiled a final time towards the *Fox and Hounds* onlookers, and prepared to resume his leisurely progress westwards. With a practised manoeuvre, he disengaged the iron key from the axle of the lock's winding gear, closing the paddles and blocking off any further egress of water. With the water level equalised on either side of the upper gate, he was now able to push the gate ajar, securing it into position. He slipped the iron lock key back into his rucksack, and dusted down his trousers. Another faultless procedure completed. Would that his recent engagement with the Sagar Corporation had proceeded quite so smoothly.

Having released the moorings, Craig stepped back aboard *The Angola* – on the day he named the boat, the homage had seemed eerily appropriate, and he had been sufficiently fired up with bravado to insist upon the most gaudy, prominent nameplate allowable under British Waterways guidelines. He had not set out that morning with a prescribed schedule or route, and he remained content to follow his instincts as the day unwound.

But as the *Fox and Hounds* disappeared from view behind the sprawling branches of a silver birch tree, he detected a faint sound inside the cabin that, he feared, might herald other plans: the sound of a mobile phone ring tone – a mobile whose number was known to just four other people.

The oncoming stretch of river was wide and empty of traffic, so Craig calculated he had time to retrieve his mobile while leaving the boat to drift alone for a few moments. He had left the phone on a plastic tray on the nearest berth, alongside a cereal bowl and a resealed bag of coke. The 'caller ID' headshot flashing on the display panel confirmed his suspicions. The penetrating brown eyes. The full, no-nonsense lips. Hair the colour of an eagle's wings that spilled the length of her neck and then looped under her chin rather than rest on her shoulders. The distinctive and purposeful mien of Marcelle Williams. She was streetwise enough only to call at the weekend if the situation warranted.

Craig pressed a green icon to accept the call. "I'm here."

"Where's here? I've left three messages."

"*The Angola*. Somewhere near Aylesbury. Is there a problem?"

"Can you make it to London City Airport in the next two hours?"

Craig paused. "I'm not really in the mood for another overseas jaunt so soon."

"Not for a flight. It's to meet someone. A gentleman by the name of Nobuyuki Hino. He comes by way of personal recommendation from Brent Tuxworth."

"And what can you tell me about Mr Hino?"

"Apparently a highly successful financier who started out in the early 1970s using family money. But also reclusive and low profile. Over the years, his name has appeared in the small print of a few prominent flotations on the Tokyo stock market, but otherwise there's remarkably little of public record. Not much on the blogs either. It seems he prefers to operate in the shadows."

"Any indication about the brief?"

"He only wants to speak with you. He'll pay twenty thousand pounds for a thirty minute meeting, no strings attached, no commitment on either side. But he wants to meet you today."

"Why London City?"

"That's where his Gulfstream 550 is parked. He's flying back to Japan shortly, but will delay his departure slot once you've confirmed."

"And how am I meant to get to the far side of Stratford?"

"He seemed pretty confident you'd agree. A chauffeur has already been despatched to bring you in. I just need to pass on the satnav details."

"Seems presumptuous, but such people are used to getting their way. I'll need you at the meeting, Marcelle?"

"I guessed as much. I'm flying to Mumbai just before midnight to clear up some loose ends you left after the Randhawa assignment. So I'm already in the aviation mood. There's plenty of time to swing by City Airport."

With the call concluded, Craig steered *The Angola* towards a wide section of the canal where he moored the vessel unobtrusively and texted the coordinates to Marcelle for onward transmission. One of the earliest works in his repertoire had involved a client from the Land of the Rising Sun, and it had not ended happily; it had been one of those penny drop moments, the time it became clear beyond contradiction that operating alone was neither feasible nor effective. While he waited for the driver, he unwound the elastic band from the neck of the plastic bag, and fortified himself with a short, energising blast from within.

The entrance to the VIP lounge at London City was discretely set back from the main thoroughfare, where it was unlikely that waylaid travellers would stumble across it by mischance. Inside, it had been furnished in a manner befitting its clientele of billionaires, celebrities, dictators and corporate powerhouses. Its buffet counter invited patrons to succumb to temptation, indulging themselves in a liberal range of hors d'oeuvres sourced from every continent, and quaffed down with industrial quantities of aperitifs.

The maitre d' welcomed every newcomer by flinging open his arms in exaggerated, slightly effeminate fashion, and escorting them to the two tiers of burgundy Chesterfields overlooking the apron. He prided himself on never forgetting the names of any guest. But when he spotted Craig and Marcelle wandering towards the lounge, he narrowed his eyes slightly and clenched his lips in an effort to place their faces. The lady had a similar bearing to one of the members of the Danish royal family; her hair was the colour of a rich chardonnay, parted at the front to expose her high, unlined forehead, and at the back weaved into a complex braid that stretched down beyond her shoulder blades. And such divine posture, such purposeful strides. But no, he concluded, like her companion, she was a first-timer.

"We're here to meet a Mr Hino," said Craig. "Nobuyuki Hino."

"Aha," said the maitre d', nodding vigorously. "Mr Hino has been expecting visitors. He's in the private suite."

He gesticulated towards a padded, windowless door, on the far side of the lounge.

"Please follow me. And do help yourself to some refreshments on the way. The smoked salmon is exquisite. Wild, not farmed, and delivered fresh every morning from Formans of Fish Island."

Craig's assumption, from his previous Tokyo adventures, was that Japanese businessmen usually hunt in packs, so he casually expected that, lying in wait, was a party the size of a World Series squad. In fact, as they entered the private room, it was evident their host was alone. Yet more evidence, to add to the burgeoning compendium, that this was no ordinary encounter. Mr Hino had been tapping gently on a tablet device, and sipping from a tumbler that contained more ice than water, but he set aside both items as he rose to greet his guests. By Japanese standards, he was almost a giant, a touch over six feet, taller than Craig when at full stretch, but stooping slightly as he advanced towards them. He was dressed immaculately; his crisply laundered brilliant white shirt and tailored dark grey suit betraying no hint that he might use his imminent longhaul flight for recreational down time. He welcomed them individually with full, firm handshakes.

"Mr Richards, thank you. And to Miss Williams," he gestured for them to sit. "My friend Brent Tuxworth spoke very highly of you."

"We have been pleased to work with Brent over a number of years," said Craig.

"He said you're the best at what you do," said Hino. "He called you The Strategist."

"I've heard him use that term," said Craig. "I think it's meant as a compliment."

"Oh, you can be sure of that. He told me it was your work that turned around Voast Motors. You identified the models whose time was up. And for the lines that remained, you rejuvenated them with new features for a more aspirational customer base. Brent says it was the most dramatic renewal of an automobile manufacturer since Lee Iacocca took the helm at Chrysler. And the trebling of the Voast's share price in 18 months suggests he wasn't alone in that assessment."

"Voast does tend to land in my credits column," said Craig.

"The Voast tale is largely public domain information," said Hino. "But I have other sources that speak with equal praise of your, shall we say, less widely reported work."

Craig returned Hino's poker stare, as he wondered silently, and not for the first time, where the discussion was headed.

Hino continued. "I've heard that Voast's return on investment was as trivial as the death pangs of a fruit fly compared with the impact you had in Africa. Clifton Oil. Turner Mining Enterprises. Each one was racking up costs to perilous levels before you intervened. They were too far invested to walk away, but had exhausted the cash runway that enabled them to persevere. In each case, just before the banks pulled the rug, the chief executives pivoted in a different direction and achieved that elusive, longed-for breakthrough. That's true, isn't it?"

Of course it's true, thought Craig, *but how can you possibly be aware of my role?* His involvement with both Clifton and Turner Mining had been shielded from public view by obsessive management teams, paranoid lest they frighten the markets with any news that could be interpreted as lacking confidence in their publicly announced plans, and who shortly afterwards claimed fulsome credit and generous retention packages for the sharp upturn in results. Marcelle sensed Craig's surprise, and fidgeted restlessly.

"Many of the brightest lights in the corporate firmament – and especially western interests – have flickered and floundered in Africa, Mr Richards," continued Hino. "Your work there was most impressive."

"I'm sure you'll understand the strictures of client confidentiality," Marcelle intervened. "You're right in general terms about the track record. But in many cases, it's not possible to confirm the details."

"The Turner Mining story really caught my eye," said Hino. "So many lessons. A high calibre team of engineers, including a Nobel prize winner. Revolutionary technology to extract minerals from inaccessible seams. But adrift, woebegone and at sea, when it comes to navigating an alien culture and commercialising their ideas. A chief executive who looked backwards and repeated the old mistakes in distribution and application. Who couldn't discern opportunities over the immediate horizon, ones presented by the changing nature of the surrounding world. Yes, you are indeed worthy to be known as The Strategist. It is most apposite."

"Mr Hino," said Marcelle. "Your comments are flattering, but I understand you're short of time. Perhaps you could share a bit more about what's led to this urgent summons."

"Thank you, Miss Williams. You are true to your reputation. Fearless and canny. Forgive me if I've been overcome at finally meeting the legendary strategist. I do appreciate that, with Mr Richards' streak of maverick brilliance, he needs someone to control access, manage his priorities, smooth ruffled feathers, and of course handle the issue of fees."

"You've clearly done your due diligence," said Marcelle, who felt it was probably best in the circumstances to overlook the passing jab about feathers.

To Hino's right was an opulent candelabra mounted atop a tall gold plated cabinet. A sleek attaché case was resting against the furniture's base. Hino hooked the case's handle with his forefinger, and he passed it unopened across the table.

"I do find banking so bureaucratic and pedantic," he said, a hint of contempt in his tone. "Inside you'll find the twenty thousand pounds. No strings, no obligations. And I still have twelve minutes remaining, and I'd like to use that time to talk with you about the affairs at Xanotek."

Marcelle flicked open the clasps of the attaché case, and inspected the contents for a few seconds, long enough to confirm that, within an acceptable margin, the contents were as described.

"You bought it, you got it," she said, and eased back in her chair so that Hino could once again focus his primary attentions upon Craig.

"I'm listening, Mr Hino," Craig added.

"This is a photograph of a gentleman called Jeremy Barker," said Hino, swivelling his tablet so Craig had a clear view of the screen.

The image was of a wiry middle-aged man in a lab coat, gawking nervously in the awkward manner that can transform someone who is simply camera-shy into a shifty renegade in a police line-up.

"I doubt you've come across him, so allow me to flesh out the story."

He swiped his finger across an icon in the top corner of the display and a summary of Barker's CV flashed into view.

"Barker is widely regarded as one of the most accomplished materials scientists of his generation," continued Hino. "Doctorates from Oxford and Yale. Dozens of peer-reviewed articles published in the world's most distinguished scientific journals. In the nineties, according to some measures, the quantity of his output ranked him among the top ten academics worldwide.

"Before his thirtieth birthday, his work on polymer technology was already ground-breaking; as seminal as any research in the field since Hermann Straudinger first proposed the concept of the polymer in the early twentieth century. Barker's Yale thesis described a revolutionary method, that can be adopted in any well-stocked laboratory, for synthesising molecules into covalently bonded chains, or networks, using a range of chemical catalysts. The new macromolecular structures which are formed can be harnessed to create new products with unique physical properties."

"So what happened to Barker circa the turn of the millennium?" asked Craig. "Looking at this resumé, he seems to have dropped off the map."

"The usual scenario. Family pressures, the mortgage, young children. His salary as an academic was pitiful. The published papers were respected by his peer group, but the bank had no use for them when making decisions about credit-worthiness. So he went to lead the research and development team at the food processing giant Rumixit. And that's where I found him."

Hino paused for dramatic effect. He had reached a crucial milestone in the narrative, so he stood up, sauntered over to the drinks table, replenished his glass with spring water, and drank deeply. He seemed lost in thought. Craig wondered if their presence had been forgotten, and after a couple of moments felt the need to interrupt the silence.

"So what happened next?"

"Ah yes," Hino snapped back into focus.

He returned to his seat with the bottled water and offered to pour for his guests. Both nodded in acceptance.

"For the last thirty years, almost all my corporate financing activities have been limited to the Asia Pacific region. Of course, that's not really been a constraint. Economists tell us the region has grown twentyfold in that time. There have been opportunities to earn great wealth, and I've been fortunate to benefit from my fair share. But a few years ago, I grew restless. I wanted to expand my horizons. I started to think about my legacy, and I wanted that legacy to be global not regional. I looked towards Europe."

"Rumixit is one of the top twenty employers on the continent," said Craig. "I've had some dealings with them. Catalan by origins, but now with operations in every major market south of Oslo. It wouldn't have taken long before you came across them."

"My first transactions were nothing to do with them," said Hino. "I had been investing in undervalued assets in Turkey. So beautifully poised between east and west, and about to overtake Germany as the country with Europe's largest population. I reasoned there was money to be made. Within a couple of years, I had purchased commercial property in central Istanbul and a shipping line. And a food wholesaler which I later flipped to Rumixit, who had also been eyeing up the territory. Barker flew into Kütahya Province as part of their technical due diligence team."

"I'm guessing you tempted Barker away from Rumixit."

"My greatest investments have been when I've backed exceptional people. In Seoul, I plucked a software designer away from some forlorn outpost of Sony, and helped him become the fifth richest person in South Korea. I saw in him this rare spark, this vision. That was enough."

"And now you need me to help decide what to do with this exceptional person?"

Hino leaned forward, speaking softly, but emphatically. "It cost me £30 million to prise Barker free from the comfort of the corporate behemoth. A million upfront in cash to him; I didn't want him fretting about financial matters when he should be concentrating on innovation. Another million to his team. Five million as a pre-emptive settlement to Rumixit; the scientists would be of no value if their years with me were spent preoccupied with litigation. The balance was in working capital to build a business. To build Xanotek into a going concern."

"What was the plan?"

"My brief to them was summarised in just one line: Please, create something amazing for me."

"What happened?"

"The numbers first. It took them two years to breeze through the cash and come back to the well. I'd been a hands-off financier to that point, but after the refinancing I introduced some tighter controls. More regular reporting, sign-off of major capital commitments, the typical disciplines."

"None of that sounds unreasonable. Many would argue they were lucky to have a free pass for so long."

"The operation is more sizeable now, so even with the controls, their burn rate is faster. I'm projecting the cash runway will be exhausted long before we see another New Year's firework fanfare light up the Thames."

"That's seven months," said Craig. "How about the underlying product development?"

Hino dabbed his finger twice against the tablet screen and invited his guests to view the carousel of images that rotated into view. Grainy photographs of an ill-lit laboratory interior. Hand-illustrated diagrams of polymer microstructures. Documentation of test results. Each flipped by too quickly for Craig to make out the details, but that wasn't the purpose. Hino had demonstrated there was copious information available for further study.

"Our time is almost finished," said Hino. "And I'm interested in your objective view, uncoloured by my perhaps ill-informed perspective. I'd like you to meet with the team. Probe, challenge, ask questions. Then we'll all gather for, what do you call it, an executive retreat. That's when we can make some decisions about the way forward."

Before Craig could respond, there was a slight cough from the direction of the padded door. The maître d' had nudged it ajar, and was poking his head through the gap like a peacock straining for food through the bars of a cage.

"You asked for an alert at quarter past," he said. "Something about urgent business in Yokahama that needs your personal attention."

"I'll be on my way," said Hino.

The maître d' retreated, deferentially.

"But there is still much to agree," interjected Marcelle. "I'm sure you're aware that Craig's services are in high demand, and his diary is…."

"I appreciate your passion for the formality of a negotiation," said Hino. "But I really don't have the time or the inclination. I have ear-marked seven hundred thousand pounds for Mr Richards to meet with the team, lead the retreat, and provide me with an honest assessment of his conclusions. I am not expecting the assignment to require more than a few days of his attentions. In fact, time is very much of the essence."

"That's very generous, but…" Marcelle began.

"I understand it's customary in these circumstances to remit half the fee as an upfront retainer. Here is my card. My plane is able to receive messages while in transit. It would give me great peace of mind if you could confirm that arrangements are acceptable before I reach the Urals. Then I can order the transfer before my arrival in Japan. You're welcome to use this room in my absence; it's rented for the full day. Now, I really must bid my farewells."

Craig offered an outstretched hand, but Hino had already gathered his belongings and was headed toward the exit. It was a trait he had noticed among many financiers - the fastidious ability to compartmentalise the working day into discrete segments of time, during which extraneous material is blocked out. The 'Craig' segment had apparently now concluded, and Hino's preoccupations were upon other matters. Moments later, through the window, they saw him striding across the tarmac, bounding up the mobile steps two at a time, and disappearing into the bowels of the Gulfstream.

With its engine fired up, and the aircraft taxiing noisily away from the apron, Marcelle finally felt liberated to indulge in refreshment more potent than mineral water. She found a bottle of Merlot towards the rear of the drinks cabinet, and filled one of the larger crystal goblets lined up alongside.

Turning to Craig, she said, "Don't even think it, about consenting."

"You must agree it's intriguing."

"It's been a rule since day one only to work with people who are known and trusted. You don't throw that

30

rule out of the window for the first stranger to throw wads of cash in your face like a demented gambler."

"It's not an entirely cold approach. Don't forget the connection through Brent Tuxworth."

"Who died last year off-piste at Val d'Isere. And what's this with almost a million pounds to attend a few meetings? That's double the maximum rate I ever extracted from Voast, when I'd been haggling for days like a Marrakesh carpet seller."

"You didn't find anything in your searches to suggest impropriety. No spells in jail, no sworn affidavits, not even a penalty for late tax filing. You'll need to check out Barker's bona fides, of course, but on the surface he seems very credible."

"Listen, Craig. You and Patricia were a great team. But now I'm the only one left to tell it candidly, as I see it. And my instincts are screaming blue murder on this one."

Craig winced at the mention of his ex-wife. Her sharp cunning, and Kenyan upbringing, had been vital ingredients during the pinnacle of his adventures as an advisor in sub-Saharan Africa. Work in the continent had been both arduous and scarce since their split.

"You're being over-cautious," he muttered.

"I can't see it ending well. That's just my opinion, and you pay me a great percentage based on my opinion. But it's your call."

"Marcelle, it's like being paid to have a beating heart. I can run an executive retreat on autopilot. After a few hours, I'll ensure they converge around some key principles to guide the next few years. They'll go away happy, I'll be able to cover alimony for the foreseeable future, and you'll have some extra funds for your pet causes."

"I still don't like it, but you're the boss."

"Any signs of deception, I walk away. Any signs of bad faith, I walk away. If you uncover proof that Hino heads up the yakuza, I walk away. Now don't you have to skip over to Heathrow for your Mumbai departure?"

Marcelle shrugged. She couldn't fault Craig's logic. Perhaps she was hypersensitive to the unconventional nature of the approach, and maybe Hino's conduct was typical behaviour for a lion of the financial jungle who was accustomed to seeing his every whim pampered and his every edict enacted. In looking after Craig's affairs, she hadn't yet acquired a fraction of Patricia's experience. Let Craig follow his impulse; meanwhile, she would monitor everything, double-check everything.

The Strategist was already powering up his mobile ready to email Hino with the requested confirmation, so Marcelle rifled through the paperwork for her flight – passport, airline tickets, Mumbai taxi voucher, hotel confirmation – and knocked back the final half inch of full-bodied Bordeaux delight.

Craig's email began, *"Dear Mr Hino. It was a great pleasure to meet you earlier today at London City. I am greatly looking forward to my coming involvement with your business interests in the United Kingdom..."*

Chapter Two

Located in:
Saki Naka, Mumbai
and
The Chandansar Orphanage

The fly was buzzing around the cracked wall clock like a toddler on a sugar rush. Marcelle had been observing its sorties for around half an hour, a brainless way of letting the time pass. It seemed trapped in an insectoid Groundhog Day, arching its thorax as a signal of aggressive intent, assaulting the clock face from multiple angles, resting momentarily on the edge of a nearby wall socket, and then embarking on a precise repeat of the entire exercise. Marcelle wondered whether it was possible for a fly to experience boredom, or whether its memory was so fleeting that each new charge felt like an expedition into the unknown.

She was sitting in a small anteroom on the first floor of a suburban police station in the Saki Naka neighbourhood of eastern Mumbai. It was a tiny oasis of calm at the heart of one of the most frenetic, rowdy districts of India's most bustling city. On the far side of a solitary, dirty window was the notorious traffic junction that connected the residential quarter to Saki Naka's landmark industrial zone. The sound of car horns was incessant, and almost rhythmic, like an eternal symphony. Pavements were non-existent; the roads blended into sandy tracks where cyclists and pedestrians, hawkers and the homeless, all jostled with one another in a fevered waltz. When she had arrived for her appointment, Marcelle's taxi had almost collided with a makeshift stall selling assorted car parts. And in the short time that she'd been waiting, she had overheard on at least two occasions the frenzied shriek of accusations following a narrowly-averted accident.

To the right of the clock, a Panasonic television hung precariously on a wall bracket. Marcelle feared that the slightest graze as she passed would be enough to rip it violently from the plaster and send it crashing onto the patterned linoleum that had been spread across most of the floorboards. The TV was locked onto CNN, where an anchorman was staring at the camera with a practised intensity. The volume had been muted, but the news ticker was providing the essential facts of the breaking story. It seemed unrest was spreading in the northern Africa breakaway republic of East Phoenicia. Appeals for calm from the newly installed president were proving counter-productive, and a number of students had been killed in clashes with the military police. Just a decade ago, the outside world would have carried on its business in ignorance of such developments, privy only to snatched and disputed second-hand reports. Now, within moments of trouble breaking out, a dozen bystanders were capturing events on their camera-phones and uploading striking digital images to servers with a global reach. *If it bleeds, it leads* goes the hyperbolic journalistic credo, and CNN had certainly embraced that principle in the case of East Phoenicia.

"Worrying, isn't it. Sudan was bad enough a few years ago. But this is a territory where the superpowers have all declared a strategic interest."

The police officer had entered the anteroom a few moments before, just behind where Marcelle sat, but until he ventured his political commentary, she had not registered his presence. She rose to greet her erstwhile sparring partner, a diminutive and slightly overweight gentleman with a caterpillar moustache.

"Superintendent Jhaveri. How good to see you again, sir," she said.

The officer indicated for Marcelle to follow him the length of a windowless, ill-lit corridor. She whispered a silent farewell to the fly, now poised to renew its incursion on the clock face; a degree of affinity with this kindred, tormented spirit had welled up while she waited, and she felt a pang of sorrow that, trapped indoors, its destiny was likely a fast-approaching encounter with a can of Raid.

At the end of the corridor, Marcelle was ushered into a spartan meeting room, furnished with just a steel table and a smattering of stools. It doubtless doubled as an interrogation chamber. Jhaveri used both hands to grip the table as he lowered himself onto his seat; he had been walking with a pronounced limp, acquired a few years beforehand in the call of duty. The injury had been the catalyst for a rapid series of promotions that took him far from the frontline. For many years, he had been conscious of impish chatter among his former colleagues that the effects had been conveniently exaggerated in service to the career ladder.

"How is your knee?" enquired Marcelle. "You seem to be walking more easily without your stick."

"I am well, thank you, Miss Williams. But this business with Mr Richards is not easy to handle. What is your timetable?"

"We are hoping to return to the Ansa Complex later this year. It will be two years since Mr Richards' last strategy review with Sagar. It was always intended he would return and give an independent view on the progress they've made in that time."

"My duty, Miss Williams, is to look after the honour and interests of the Indian people."

"Superintendent, do I need to remind you? Mr Richards' work was instrumental in attracting nearly half a billion dollars of international investment capital. How many jobs has that created? Well-paid jobs that otherwise would have materialised in Korea or the Philippines. What greater interest is there than that for the Indian people?"

"But these issues with Mr Richards are not straight-forward. They are hard to overlook."

Marcelle shifted her posture but retained an impenetrable facade. Inside, she was squirming with discomfort as she recalled the shock of the midnight ordeal that so tarnished her last visit to the region. It had been her first venture overseas with Craig, and just a few hours before he was scheduled to present to a specially convened meeting of the Sagar board of directors. The chairman, a former governor of the central bank, was flying in from Delhi for the occasion, and intended to issue a formal notification to the National Stock Exchange of Sagar's new direction within moments of the meeting concluded.

Then, without notice, Craig had gone off the radar. Surrounded by draft slides, speaker notes and box files, Marcelle waited like a jilted teenager in the hotel's business suite. She had been vaguely aware of hushed talk about Craig's interminable battle to supress his darker side. That was the evening she realised the true scope of her role; that his suave charm belied inner demons. Seared in her memory was the moment when, shortly after leaving yet another message on Craig's voicemail, she took an incoming call from his number. But not from him.

Jhaveri had retrieved a manila folder from his attaché case and was fanning the contents across the table for maximum visibility. Marcelle recognised every item. A mug shot of Craig, bleary-eyed and unkempt, staring into the police camera like a common criminal. A panoramic photograph of the public area in a seedy basement bar, where upended furniture and broken bottles hinted that an outbreak of hostilities had not long passed. A series of photos of cocaine in ziplock bags with police evidence stickers attached. At least a half dozen witness statements. A set of fingerprint impressions. And a typed inventory of damages.

"What am I meant to do with all this material, Miss Williams? It is a big problem for me. This isn't Knightsbridge, you know. Here, the authorities regard these matters most seriously."

"I would ask the authorities to take a broader view. It was a troubled period for Mr Richards. But it won't happen again. This visa is important, not just for us, but for the many thousands of staff at Sagar. Their livelihoods, and their families' livelihoods, will greatly benefit if Mr Richards is permitted to return."

"I recall that last time you were very active in demonstrating your support for Indian livelihoods."

"Yes," said Marcelle. "Of course, I'm prepared to make the same offer again."

Jhaveri collected up the array of documents that had been spread the length of the table, and returned them to the remote seclusion of his file, which he sealed with a jumbo sized paperclip.

"I can assure you, Miss Williams, this folder has not been outside the safe in my office since the last time we sat together. And nobody knows the combination number except for me and Shiva."

"Let's keep it that way, Mr Jhaveri. I checked the details on the way out. Last time I pledged thirty thousand dollars to the Chandansar Orphanage, of which twenty thousand dollars was paid through your nominee account, to be dispensed and distributed at your sole discretion. I can make a similar transfer tonight, if that's an appropriate gesture of goodwill."

"India has changed since our last meeting, Miss Williams. There are more bureaucrats. Auditors are everywhere. The banks report certain transactions to the regulator. The risks are higher, and honest people can lose everything when the state, on a whim, turns its cannon fire towards them."

"Your point about risk is well made," said Marcelle. "Of course, you need to be compensated for that risk. That's reasonable, and I respect your request. If Mr Richards is able to enter the country without fear of arrest or reprisal, if he's able to complete his work without interruption or delay, and if he departs with his good name intact, then of course the orphanage should benefit. A fair amount this time could be fifty thousand dollars, with forty thousand paid into the nominee."

"That is a generous offer, Miss Williams. The children and staff will be most appreciative, I am sure. They are so very dedicated. But, Miss Williams, it will not be possible to wait until the end of his visit before the transaction is completed. The fifty thousand should be paid before the wheels of his plane leave the Heathrow tarmac. That, I think, is fair."

Outside, there was a sudden barrage of horns as a packed school bus misjudged a sharp corner and narrowly avoided toppling. As the vehicle lurched from side to side, two young boys who had been balancing on the rear bumper were shaken loose, and landed unceremoniously at the feet of a startled commuter. The children remonstrated with each other, all jabbing fingers and wild accusations, before realising that during this vital time the bus had recovered its equilibrium and sped across the junction. Meanwhile, Superintendent Jhaveri crossed his arms, resting them atop his ample potbelly, and allowed a broad, toothy smirk to break out across his face. The expression of a victor, of one revelling in the supreme assurance that unflinching negotiations were on the brink of paying lavish dividends. This, reflected Jhaveri, has been a worthwhile hour. Most worthwhile indeed.

The taxi was still parked at an artless diagonal outside a hardware stall, exactly where Marcelle had alighted. The driver's light nap had become a deep sleep. He had long ago disabled the car seat's hinges, allowing the back to recline until almost horizontal, way beyond the preset positions. The driver's feet were propped nonchalantly on the top of the dashboard, mud-encrusted soles exposed to the world. A dying cigarette drooped from his lower lip, but somehow – despite the comatose state of its owner – it had not yet toppled into his lap.

Marcelle clambered over a pile of boxed-up pistons and valves next to the car part stall, and squeezed into the back of the taxi before rousing the driver with a vigorous shake. He rubbed his eyes with his knuckles, yawned loudly, and patted down his shirt pockets in search of the car keys. "Chandansar next," Marcelle reminded him. "The orphanage."

"Yes ma'am," said the driver, grimacing as he twisted the ignition key. At the third attempt, the engine fired up. As the driver accelerated through some red lights, dodged some scaffolding being used to erect the city's new elevated metro line, and turned onto the expressway, Marcelle scribbled some thoughts onto a notepad. It was time to brief Craig on developments, she determined. With a difference of five and a half hours, he was likely awake and active, but still aboard *The Angola*. The perfect moment to catch a few words.

"It's been a productive morning over here," she said. "I'm confident the Sagar review is a go. It wasn't cheap, but there's still margin in the job."

"Spare me the details. Nothing to make me feel queasy," said Craig. "I'm trying to make the perfect scrambled eggs."

"I know, I know. I worry about this stuff so you don't have to. I'll swing by the Sagar offices this afternoon, and work out the logistics for the meeting."

"I assume you'll also be swinging by Chandansar. To check whether your money's making a difference."

"Don't worry, boss. It won't interfere with business."

"Sagar is more like an obligation than business."

"There speaks the man with the world's worst attention span. When it's novel and fresh, it's a delight. Anything else is a chore. How are we meant to develop long-term client relationships with that philosophy? Thank God you weren't born as Kenneth Branagh. He's returned to play Hamlet on about five different occasions!"

Marcelle often gained a quiet pleasure by weaving classical references into everyday discourse, but she didn't have time to enjoy her reference to the Prince of Denmark because her driver abruptly slammed on the brakes. It seemed he was familiar with just two speeds: fast-and-furious, and standstill. He had been careening wildly towards the sole bridge connecting Salsette Island, home to Mumbai's suburbs, with the Chandansar District. At the last moment, he had spotted the snaking, near-motionless tailback of vehicles approaching the bridge. With the taxi now stopped, and resigned to spending a large chunk of her day in its cramped interior, Marcelle composed herself and resumed her conversation.

"Wait a moment," said Craig. "They're coming out a rich and glowing yellow. An impeccable breakfast! Let me turn down the gas, and then tell you warts-and-all about - what was your phrase? - the *screaming blue murder project*."

"I'm guessing you've already visited Xanotek?"

"You'd be guessing right. At the start of the weekend, it was just another name bumbling along in the lower reaches of the *Sunday Times*' list of murky start-ups. Yesterday, they treated me like I was a visiting monarch. Even the carpet was red!"

"My instincts still say *beware*."

"Marcelle, I'll be on guard. I promise. But there was nothing to fault yesterday. Even the coffee was exquisite and how often can you say that?"

"Be careful, ok."

"If they so much as short-change the chocolate sprinkles on my cappuccino, I'm calling a scam. But let me give you the highlights. Barker was exactly as Hino described him. Genius scientist, more degrees than a thermometre. If you understand one-third of what he says when he's in the zone about polymer technology, you're doing well. And an unapologetic, 24 carat geek. On the rare occasion he stopped evangelising about tensile strengths and melting points, the only other topic which got the faintest look-in was something called *Blake's Seven*."

Craig used a series of quick fire motions to arrange his personal notes alongside company and product documentation on his tablet display screen. As he gathered his thoughts, he scooped the last vestiges of scrambled egg from the pan and onto the thick sliced granary toast. Then, he zoomed in to the management account data that had formed the basis for his two-hour afternoon meeting with Xanotek's finance director.

"Adrienne Dodier looks after the books," he explained. "She's a Hino appointee. You get precise answers to precise questions, but nothing gets volunteered unilaterally. You can almost see the barriers closing around her if you get within twenty feet. Barker hinted at some tragic backstory, but I got nowhere near it. As far as the numbers go, the burn rate is frightening. Everything is still in R&D, so there are no revenues and no imminent prospects of revenues.

"But in the meantime, there's a test plan that looks like one of those timelines you see of the universe's history from the Big Bang onwards. That means, there's a lot in it! And every slightest module of the test needs cash. Equipment, experts, you name it. I tracked one test, of combustibility, and the all-in costs ran easily into six figures."

"Testing what?" asked Marcelle. "What are they actually inventing? Craig, what's the product? Hello?"

The phone emitted a stuttering, wheezing sound and Marcelle found herself speaking into emptiness. After a couple of futile shouts into the void, she restarted her device, but at every attempt to secure a fresh connection, she encountered a robotic voice informing her in a staccato tone that she was out of network coverage. This was the inevitable consequence of her journey northwards. In the business district around Mumbai harbour, the nerve centre of Indian commerce, cellular reception was on par with the standard expected in any global gateway city, but quickly grew patchy beyond the city limits.

No problem, thought Marcelle. *There will be plenty of opportunity to catch up when I'm back at the hotel.* She eased into her seat, and spent the next two hours of her trip transfixed by the dazzling cacophony of sights and sounds of this fast-emerging region. Two blocks before the bridge, she marvelled at the elation etched on the faces of two elderly worshippers as they shuffled towards a small Hindu temple, their arms laden with offerings that had been meticulously wrapped in banana leaves.

On the banks of the Vasai creek, she saw young mothers washing richly coloured garments in the river by rhythmically hitting them against the water surface, and then laying them out to dry as part of a growing patchwork of saris and shirts adorning the steep limestone steps. In Navghar, the masses surged through the single entrance of a local rail station as an announcer signalled the arrival of the next express train into the city. She watched actors engage in stylised combat atop the sun-soaked pavilion in the lush park in Kaman, the melodramatic climactic scene of a forthcoming Bollywood blockbuster. And, everywhere, the overpowering presence of food: children wandering the streets with plates of naan balanced on their heads; street vendors hawking spices, herbs, nuts, and samosas; cyclists ferrying their cargo of live chickens for slaughter; and diners in open air cafes plunging their fingers into earthenware pots overflowing with ground meat and rice, as they contemplated their next chess move. A land pulsing with energy and ambition.

The taxi parked some distance from the orphanage, in a narrow side street under cover of a canvas awning. Within moments, while Marcelle was still collecting her belongings, the driver was already stretched out and once again snoring shamelessly.

The orphanage was a sprawling complex that had been built as a fort during the Gupta dynasty, but had endured many of the subsequent centuries in a progressive state of disrepair. The grounds were overgrown with shrubs and jujube fruit trees, some as high as fifteen feet, and Marcelle spotted one young boy, no more than five, scampering up through the maze of drooping branches to seize a plum from the spreading crown. At the end of a cobbled pathway stood the orphanage itself, two storeys of weathered sandstone, with concrete posts on either side of the entrance to which children's bikes had been tied. The building had been restored with an excess of enthusiasm in the middle of the last century, and the façade was now adorned with gilded stucco and lavish fresco and tile decorations. Each first floor room boasted a generous balcony that had been added as part of the restoration. Only the ancient watchtower remained dilapidated. Funds had been running low towards the end of the refurbishment programme, and the patrons had been unable to find a practical purpose for it.

Marcelle was greeted by the orphanage supervisor. She was an ebullient expatriate and lapsed Catholic named Stella Weseldine, who had been appointed by the trustees at the turn of the century when she felt her stuttering faith made untenable her previous position as matron of a religious institution near Hyderabad. Marcelle had met Stella briefly during her previous visit, but the pressure of Craig's itinerary on that occasion had prevented any opportunity for small talk. It was a relief finally to learn about the orphanage's mission at a more leisurely pace.

The women spent the next hour chatting expansively over tea and digestive biscuits in the gatehouse, which had served as the staff quarters since the restoration. Stella talked about their outreach programme; every year they had capacity to admit another fifteen or so residents, which barely scratched the surface of the country's endemic curse of homeless, illiterate and hungry children that persisted, regardless of the pace of economic growth. She spoke about the typical life stories that awaited her charges. Once the children had acquired a basic level of education and social competence, many were ready to be fostered by well-heeled local fami-lies. Others remained at the orphanage until their late teenage years. Inevitably, some were unable to resist the draw back to the slums and shanty towns. But a majority under Stella's tutelage had progressed to college, and, she added proudly, the proportion was increasing every year.

"Not least because of the computer room we were able to furnish on the back of your last donation."

"It was very important to me that the money should help with that type of visible change," said Marcelle. "The sort of programme that's hard to finance out of day-to-day budgets."

"Your initial ten thousand covered the basic hardware," said Stella. "The local Toshiba representative was flattered to be asked, and provided two banks of desktops at cost, with the latest Windows package installed on each. We've used your subsequent personal donations to purchase additional applications, and introduce high speed broadband connectivity. We now feel part of the modern world."

"Just keep them away from Facebook," smiled Marcelle. "Back home, it's become a teenage addiction. There's no time left for kids to complete their homework, or even leave their bedrooms, because they've got to update their status every ten minutes. It's wrecking their education and I'd hate for that to be my legacy over here."

"I can't speak for the rest of India," said Stella. "But luckily, with my children, we're still at the stage where they adore absorbing knowledge. As soon as they learn to read, you can hardly keep them away from online news and encyclopedia sites. It's such an adventure."

"And hopefully your staff are up to date and can assist where necessary?"

"Most of the time, it's not necessary. In fact, I've been meaning to introduce you to somebody."

Stella led Marcelle to a narrow pine staircase just beyond the dining room. On the next floor, the stairs opened into a compact dormitory room, where – in the absence of air conditioning – the balcony doors had been hooked open to allow a light afternoon breeze to circulate. The mid afternoon sun was edging lazily into view, drenching the room in light, and highlighting even further the gaudily painted furniture: three bunk bed units, a free-standing wardrobe, and a pine chest overflowing with cartoon character pajamas.

Nestled in the corner of the room was a teenage boy, sitting cross-legged with a laptop balanced on his knees. He was staring at the screen, blinking only occasionally, oblivious to the two women who had just entered the dorm. An onlooker might have assumed he was in a semi-hypnotic state, but Stella had nurtured the boy for nearly a decade, and knew better. The child had been rescued, malnourished and distraught, at about the age of seven (no birth records were ever found) from a filthy village hospital in a northern province. Among his contemporaries on that ward, the boy uniquely avoided making his exit in a coffin. Since that day, he had exhibited almost superhuman powers of concentration; an ability to block out the superfluous and the distracting, his mind focused upon the task of the moment like a sniper training the crosshairs upon the scalp of an enemy combatant.

"Meet Dimala Naidu," said Stella. "We call him our prodigy."

Marcelle crouched next to the boy. His eyes were large and captivating; gigantic pupils swimming in a vast sea of perfect whiteness. His silky complexion was almost pre-teen, although the clumps of stubble on his chin and neck betrayed his true age. Consciously, Marcelle mustered the most kindly expression she could conceive, and lightly touched the boy's hand as he speed-typed the latest keyboard instructions. The screen was currently hosting a twelve mega-byte database, and the boy was flicking between tabs, occasionally lingering on a particular cell to inspect the formula.

"Do you enjoy doing this, making calculations?" asked Marcelle.

Finally, Dimala registered the presence of others in the room, and raised his head to meet Marcelle's gaze. He nodded steadily.

"Did you teach yourself to do this?"

Another nod, and then the boy resumed his work.

"By the time he was ten, his expertise was way beyond anything we could teach him," explained Stella.

"When he was twelve, he created a programme for the management and administration of the orphanage. Because of Dimala, we finally dispensed with our index cards of donor details, and double entry book-keeping ledgers. And when he was just fourteen, we had the first of two visits from government officials."

"Why would the government be taking such an interest? I imagine they've already computerised most of their finances."

"The first time, Dimala had cracked the security firewall of the Hyderabad Tourist Office. A few months later, it was the Regional Development Administration. I think they were concerned the orphanage was a front for an international hacking operation, or perhaps in league with Pakistani Intelligence."

"Well, you're still here. So I'm guessing you managed to convince them their suspicions were groundless."

"Fortunately Dimala hadn't downloaded any confidential documents. He hadn't used any spyware or planted any bugs. Nothing that would have brought the state to a shuddering halt. He clammed up when they started to interrogate him, but it seems he'd simply been tracing his roots. Searching for any information about his immediate family."

"Perfectly understandable in an inquisitive child with his turbulent history."

Although the women were speaking openly about his life story, Dimala remained detached from the conversation. He was once again preoccupied with his database, following cross-references from one worksheet to the next and testing assumptions and scenarios. Out of the corner of her eye, Marcelle was trying to follow the boy's endeavours, and decipher the topic that had him so utterly immersed.

"Fortunately for all of us, there's been no repeat of his hacking adventures," said Stella. "These days, he spends his time researching subjects that intrigue him, and writing the most thoughtful and well-crafted essays. His subversive period is behind him. The Indian authorities can rest easy on that score."

Perhaps, thought Marcelle. Or perhaps he's simply better able to cover his tracks.

"Tell me," she said, "The children can't stay in these magnificent surroundings forever, can they? Adulthood means cutting the Gordian Knot. With the timeline you gave, I'm guessing Dimala's days are nearly finished."

"If we could, we'd love to keep them forever. But we need to free up beds for the next generation. Plus, they need to learn independence, and sometimes that's hard when they're cloistered away."

Marcelle was no longer paying attention to Stella's exposition on the logistics of social care. Instead her mind was racing over the inventory of assignments in which she'd been involved since Craig had recruited her to his side. She was tallying the copious funds that had been consumed by third party analytical support of dubious rigour. She was reflecting on the projects where their impact had been diminished through reliance on data modelling undertaken by client personnel. She was contemplating the step-up they might achieve through adding to their team the standard of technical wizardry that, armed with nothing other than a mass market laptop and off the shelf software, was already savvy enough to outwit government servers.

"I think we can find a role for Dimala in the UK," she ventured.

She noticed Dimala flinch slightly. He might be able to block out most of the ambient noise, she thought, but that suggestion had definitely registered. What she didn't know was that, at the same time, Dimala was uploading his database to the distant folder from whence it had been temporarily retrieved. The state's budget for educational outreach into the deprived communities north east of Mumbai had just been subject to an upward adjustment of a smidgen over four per cent. And no-one, however accomplished their powers of detection or audit, would ever uncover the fact. He powered down the laptop, and closed the lid.

"Is recruitment really that easy?" asked Stella. "What about visa issues? Immigration checks?"

And what about Craig? mused Marcelle. He had always resisted incremental headcount whenever she's raised the prospect with him. We're not in the corporate empire business, he had argued. On the other hand, he had increasingly urged her to take responsibility for all items, of whatever type, so long as her activity didn't impinge upon client advice. She now seemed to have been delegated authority over large swathes of what occurs behind-the-scenes, and Craig had occasionally been exasperated when she brought routine decisions to his attention rather than resolving them using her own initiative. If she sought his blessing for Dimala's appointment, she risked being refused. Far more expedient to present it to Craig as a *fait accompli*, reassuring him that she would personally take care of the boy's induction to British life, and ongoing supervision.

"Leave that to me. I should be able to get any notes of his youthful online indiscretions erased from the record," said Marcelle.

It might be necessary to further enrich Superintendent Jhaveri's personal account, but that was a matter of price not feasibility.

"And with UK officials, I've always found that persistence trumps substance. I'll harry and hassle until they're fed up with me. They'll soon realise that approving his visa is the only fast way to get me out of their collective face."

Stella knelt close to Dimala. "Have you been following Miss Williams' ideas?" she asked. "Does that option appeal?"

At which Dimala spoke the last words he would ever utter in the orphanage dormitory.

"Ma'am, I understand everything. I will have a new life. And I will be dutiful. Thank you."

Stella insisted that Marcelle accompany her as they completed the orphanage tour. They sat at the back of a classroom where a visiting lecturer was explaining sedimentary strata and rock formation. Stella proudly introduced her guest to a music room, recently endowed with a grand piano she'd elicited from a local philanthropist, and showed her a billiards room where the children could relax in the hour before lights out. But Marcelle was no longer paying attention. Her mind was racing through the list of tasks she could assign to Dimala as soon as his clearance formalities had been processed. And the fact she must still make an appearance at Sagar before her day's work was complete.

But it was the urgent need to acknowledge a text message that had arrived halfway through the lecturer's account of the erosive properties of ice sheets that worried her most. The SMS said bluntly, *Xanotek offsite now confirmed. Malkin Castle, 16 September. Clear your diary. Craig.*

Chapter Three

Located in:
Ministry of Defence headquarters

The pinstripes and bowler hats had gone, but in other respects the early morning rush in Whitehall was unchanged throughout the generations. Civil servants spilled from Westminster Underground Station and strode towards their departments, avoiding eye contact with the hordes of tourists and school parties descending on London's landmarks. The crowds surged tsunami-like across the road junctions, treating the traffic signals as guidance not instruction; only instinct prevented them from being scythed down by the taxis and cyclists which sped around Westminster Square, like unicorns on a fairground carousel. Many worker bees were paying more attention to their watches than their surroundings, obsessively glancing at the latest time, and quickening their pace lest they be a few moments late at their desks.

Amidst this maelstrom, a freckled youth in sweat-pants stood opposite the Cenotaph memorial, trying to catch the attention of passing commuters. His shoulder bag was packed with copies of the latest *Big Issue* magazine, newly published that morning, and business so far had been brisk. The front cover image seemed to have caught the mood. A church ablaze against the jungle backdrop, gunned down bodies lying on blood-stained steps, and the headline screaming: *Africa at war?*

A short walk south of Whitehall stood the imposing headquarters of Britain's Ministry of Defence. The main building could have been designed with the sole intent of striking fear and trepidation into the hearts of enemies of the realm, exuding power, confidence and grandeur. Two imposing statues, Earth and Water, flanked the northern entrance on Horse Guards Avenue. Each weighed over forty tons, and together they symbolised the territories over which British might could be projected. Every corner of the magnificent entrance hall was used to showcase military victories through the ages; in the centre were a series of glass cabinets containing uniforms, munitions, despatches, illustrations and photographs, from as far afield in time and place as Blenheim, El Alamein and the Falklands.

Beyond the security cordon, away from public view, the Ministry's imperial majesty faded rapidly. The building was a warren of soulless grey corridors that lacked both signage and natural light. Occasionally, one would pass through an open plan area, and notice how a decade of downsizing had taken its toll. Banks of desks lying vacant, the decimated remains of a typing pool where the few surviving secretaries gazed listlessly at the screens of their ancient PCs, retired generals with permanent expressions of harassed anxiety muttering to one another around the coffee machines. At regular intervals, framed photographs had been left propped against the walls, awaiting the day someone could summon the energy or inclination to arrange for a hook to be hammered into the plaster.

A few weeks beforehand, the Ministry has been temporarily energised by the appointment of a new Secretary of State, Katherine Foster, Britain's first female defence chief. The scope of her responsibilities meant the Secretary of State was often away from the Ministry, participating in parliamentary business, or travelling to the Pentagon or NATO headquarters to plan and coordinate joint military engagements, or undertaking morale-boosting visits to troops deployed in legacy conflict zones. On the rare days her diary permitted time at the Ministry, Foster was based on the third floor, in a corner suite of offices overlooking the Thames. Significantly, much of the rest of that floor was occupied not by planners, concerned with ongoing operations, or by officials responsible for recruitment and training, but rather by forensic accountants plotting the next round of budget cuts. Nevertheless, Secretary of State Foster was popular with the rank and file. Her previous Cabinet position in charge of Culture, Media and Sports had ended amidst rancour when, legend had it, she had defied the Chancellor's zealous budget axe and commissioned analysis of the beneficial impact to the nation's coffers of investment in the arts. It was widely rumoured that the Prime Minister, impressed by this spirited resistance, had moved her to the Ministry of Defence to provide a feisty counterweight to the Treasury's continuing attempts to pare back defence expenditure, somewhat arbitrarily, to the European average.

But Secretary Foster's office was only the second largest in the corner suite. Separated by less than the length of a cricket wicket, an area reserved for the Cabinet minister's cabal of inexperienced but enthusiastic political advisers, was located the vast, ornate office of Permanent Secretary Hugo Cunningham, an MOD insider now notionally supporting his fourth Secretary of State. Cunningham's office, off limits to all but a handful of trusted confidants, bore testimony to the culture clash between tradition and modernity engulfing much of the armed forces. Behind Cunningham's desk, shelf upon shelf of military memoirs – leather bound first editions piled so high that many can only be retrieved using mobile library steps. And facing Cunningham, a bank of four widescreen monitors, each one programmed for multiple purposes – whether to stay abreast of world affairs, to speak securely via live video links, or to display critical operational information.

Cunningham tapped the end of his custom made Mont Blanc against his gritted teeth. He was contemplating a lengthy briefing dossier, and scribbling a few final amendments in the margin. The dossier was entitled *East Phoenicia – Peace Conference – 30 August.* Secretary Foster had specifically requested not only a summary of the facts of the conflict, but also the judgment of intelligence sources about the negotiating position of each of the participants, especially the Americans, the Russians and the Chinese. Three to four pages had been drafted about each delegation.

Cunningham scanned the section on the Chinese, probably the most inscrutable of the participants, but emerging as the most influential power broker. The document provided for them, as for each of the other delegations, a profile of the attendees; a record of their public statements; an assessment of areas where they were expected to display intransigence; and a list of other areas where flexibility and compromise were more likely. Cunningham finished his marking-up. He had indicated a few statements that needed to be emboldened, and tightened up wording he felt had been a little pusillanimous. He pressed the intercom and barked to his personal assistant that urgent amendments needed to be finalised so he could arm Secretary Foster with the complete report.

While Cunningham's corrections were being processed, the Permanent Secretary switched on a monitor to catch the latest breaking news from the region. Protesters were gathering outside the East Phoenician presidential palace in a show of force, holding aloft a sea of placards with grainy images of maimed and dead children. The cameras were dwelling on a group of women who had been pushed to the front. One was yelling with uncontrollable emotion, holding up to the world's press a picture of a young boy, no older than four, wrapped in a thin blanket. His face was beautiful, calm, and flawless except for the bullet hole above his left eye, the size of a small coin. In black ink, she had scrawled across the photograph: "My son, victim of a fascist state." Members of the presidential militia stood just a few feet away, nervously fingering their rifles.

Five minutes later, Cunningham was with Secretary Foster, selecting highlights that merited particular attention from the updated dossier. The Secretary of State preferred to keep departmental meetings formal. The two sofas and drinks trolley stationed in the corner had been inherited from the previous officeholder, who had cultivated a more relaxed management style, but since Foster's promotion they had been gathering dust. Whenever Cunningham was alone with his Minister, he made a point of sitting bolt upright, addressing her by her title, and dispensing with small talk.

"The American position is most unpredictable," he said. "For many years, East Phoenicia has operated effectively as an independent state, although it has never been recognised as such by the United Nations. The US has given tacit encouragement to its ambitions to break away from the Republic of Phoenicia. Publically, the neo-cons have asserted that its population has the right to decide its future democratically and without undue outside influence. Of course, the fact an estimated eighty per cent of their oil reserves lie untouched might also be a factor. But they don't trust the new president, Tshuma. He has made a number of provocative statements, and seems to be cooler than his predecessor on the issue of severing ties with the motherland and seeking full independence."

Cunningham was lacing a cigarette between his fingers. *When was it,* he thought, *that MOD apparatchiks got better at enforcing the absurd indoor smoking ban than protecting the realm?* To make matters worse, international tensions could not be rising at a more inconvenient time. Having spent – wasted? – the entire weekend reassuring his wife that her creeping arthritis wouldn't affect their future together, he had hoped for at least a couple of days of sanity and order.

"The media are making him out to be a hot head," said Foster. "Firstly, he's been inflaming tension with reckless comments, and then he's been trigger happy in quelling any protests that arise. The Americans have pressed for any transition to be orderly and on the basis of wide support. Tshuma's inflammatory approach, they argue, puts all that at risk."

"Then we have the Russian delegation," continued Cunningham, handing over a picture of four balding men in ill-fitting suits standing on the steps of a Mikoyan MiG fighter jet. "You've already met Secretary Zavrazhnov, but honestly the entire group could be straight out of KGB central casting. They've no strategic interest in the oil; they already produce over 10 million barrels a day, much in Siberia, whose landmass – if removed from Russia – would still make it the biggest country in the world."

"When I spoke with Zavrazhnov, he was very preoccupied by the ringleaders for separation in East Phoenicia. He said they were unsavoury characters. He said they had nothing in common with the wholesome freedom fighters that *Panorama* chose to depict."

"I have some sympathy with that assessment. The rebel campaign has been opportunistic in drawing support from a number of quarters, but that's left it vulnerable to criticism. There's been some infiltration by groups linked to al Qaeda, and the Russians don't want to leave behind a breeding ground for future Chechnyan fighters. My guess is the Russians will want to see Tshuma's position guaranteed."

"The Americans and Russians at loggerheads. Does it get any better?"

"Over the last decade, we've massively improved our intelligence gathering capabilities in China. It's not yet foolproof, but it's increasingly reliable, and that's been vital as China becomes more active and self-assured on the global stage."

"And what are your sources telling you?"

Cunningham slid the unlit cigarette into an inside pocket. Probably just as well. Elise Underhill, his assistant of ten years, had an uncanny ability to detect the faintest tobacco on his breath, and never hesitated to berate him for his indulgence.

"I received an encrypted document last night that was, to be frank, quite a revelation. Financial institutions controlled by Beijing have funded over sixty per cent of infrastructure development, in both Phoenicia and East Phoenicia, over the past twenty four months. Only one third of the money has been relatively transparent, advances from Chinese banks, or investments made by its Sovereign Wealth Fund; the rest has been channelled through opaque networks."

"You're telling me the Chinese won't be a passive observer of developments. They have a major economic interest in the region, and I'm guessing they'll want to protect and enhance their interests ruthlessly."

"That's my interpretation. It certainly makes the situation more nuanced and multifaceted than in my heyday, when all the scenarios we modelled were neatly two dimensional. Us versus the Soviets. Balance of power or mutually assured destruction, depending on your personal peccadillo."

Secretary Foster flicked though the rest of the dossier. There was a useful set of appendices which needed to be fully digested before the Peace Conference – maps of the region, a chronology of the recent history, a socio-political analysis of Phoenicia with IMF statistics on everything from the mortality and morbidity rates, to the frightening quantity of armaments in circulation.

She hadn't needed to cram like this since her university finals.

Foster had only been four days in the job when a thumping memorandum had dropped into her red box from the Chief Secretary to the Treasury, demanding another billion pounds of budget cuts spread over two years. In excruciating detail, it itemised the prime candidates for potential savings, such as fewer tanks, a squeeze on allowances, and the merging of regiments. Her instinct told her this was foolishly short-sighted. The so-called peace dividend mistook the end of the Cold War for the end of history. With trouble spots bubbling away on three continents, no government should bank the assumption that it would never be called upon to run simultaneous missions on a number of fronts. It was the ultimate in short-termist wishful thinking.

"Let's discuss the British position," she said. "With three superpowers arriving at these talks oozing testosterone, what's our play?"

"British civilians," said Cunningham, without missing a beat. "We have more of our own people working in the region than anyone else. A few aid workers, but primarily those employed in or allied to the petroleum sector. Geologists, hydrologists, mining engineers, chemical engineers, plant managers, oil brokers and so on. Over five thousand by my latest estimates. The joyous legacy of some extremely shady treaties signed by the last government."

"Are we expecting the Foreign Office to issue any advice?"

"The oil companies are pressing us to avoid precipitate action. If we encouraged all personnel to evacuate, the plants could be sequestered by local militia and the investment written off. We've hosted a roundtable at our embassy on enhancing security at the various sites, but otherwise I'm expecting the mood to be let's all sit tight."

Foster grimaced. While Cunningham was emphasising due process, her political antennae were foreseeing the flurry of tabloid attacks should events spin out of control. *Ministers paralysed as Britons perish*, that sort of thing.

"Within twenty four hours, I need a report on how a worst case scenario might unfold," she said. "I don't want to find we're dragged into intervention because we've failed to plan for all eventualities."

Cunningham sighed. Another awkward conversation with his wife beckoned. Another forlorn attempt to persuade Rebecca that the nation's needs took precedent over her own.

"What's your concern, Minister?" asked Cunningham.

"We're in a 24 hour news cycle. Each one of those five thousand will have loved ones – parents, husbands, wives, neighbours. At the first hint of trouble, they'll have paparazzi on their lawns, media advisers in their lounges, and microphones under their noses. The cry will go up, *Something must be done.* So we'll do something. Then, they'll turn full circle. The first setback, the first collateral damage, and it'll be *Bring our boys home.* I'd like to be remembered for something more than body bags, if it's all right by you."

Cunningham rose, leaving the dossier on Foster's desk, and tucking his notepad under his arm. "I'll see it done, Minister," he said, unable to contain a brief sigh of exasperation.

As he departed, he lingered at the door, glancing at the oil painting of a brooding Viscount Palmerston that hung just to the left. That was the era of uncompromised magnificence, he reflected. When leaders did not quake in fear of an over-mighty media. When a prime minister could pledge to Parliament that he would never "abandon a large community of British subjects at the extreme end of the globe to a set of barbarians", and mean it. When the mildest insult to the British flag by a Chinese commissioner resulted in the merciless shelling of the transgressor's compound. *What chance,* he thought, *I might live to see the steadfast rejuvenation of such pride and glory.*

Secretary Foster buzzed her assistant to cancel her appointments for the next forty-five minutes. Within two days, she would be holed up with the Foreign Secretary and other colleagues, in a secure estate just outside Vienna, where they would offer the British government's opening remarks at the East Phoenicia Peace Conference. This was the first international gathering at which she would have a leadership role. Her counterparts were all veteran schemers, while she was very much the rookie in the class. She was determined not to appear out of her depth.

Back in Parliament Square, half a dozen activists were crawling from their tents. Their next few hours would be spent dispensing polemic leaflets to bemused passers-by, and hurling invective at senior ministers as they arrived at the House in their distinctive chauffeur driven jaguars. The elder statesman among the campaigners was a grizzled Australian ex-patriate, whose baseball hat was festooned with badges he'd collected from assorted protest marches. One of his companions was a prematurely bald young man, possibly his son, whose bloodshot eyes glared with contempt at a loitering police officer.

Together, they unfurled a banner which they hitched to the railings with sisal rope. The elder statesman carried out a couple of minor adjustments, to ensure the message was displayed visibly and in its entirety. Over the next few hours, discerning commuters might notice that the lettering had been changed overnight. What previously had read *No to war in Syria,* had been updated to reflect world events. The new plea, adorned with a crude illustration of bombs raining down on groups of children, was: *No to war in Phoenicia.*

Chapter Four

Located in:
Angeline's Restaurant
The Tamahaq Refinery, East Phoenica
and
Ministry of Defence headquarters

Hino's time-keeping was beyond reproach. Craig had been waiting in the private upstairs bar of Angeline's, a discrete French restaurant nestled in an affluent residential neighbourhood around a mile from Malkin Castle. He had left Marcelle with the castle's hospitality director, reviewing catering schedules for the next two days. Hino was footing a substantial fee, and if the financier's office called to request a short notice rendezvous, that was entirely his prerogative.

The fifteen minute stroll from the castle had been pleasant enough. The estate shut to the public shortly after five, leaving the grounds deserted but for the skeleton staff and overnight guests, and Craig had appreciated the chance to enjoy some fresh air after a day when the world seemed to consist of nothing but laptops, flip charts and notepads. Leaving the keep, he had crossed over the expansive moat, where a groundsman was mooring a pair of elegant punts near the drawbridge. Beyond the moat, the grounds were a rolling collage of themed gardens and woodland trails. Craig passed through a tranquil grove where peacocks roamed freely. Accustomed to the presence of crowds, they hopped and strutted around oblivious to Craig's arrival. To his right was a south-facing landscaped English garden, where the low box hedges allowed full view of a profusion of exotic blooms. The richly coloured roses, poppies and lupins provided a vibrant backdrop to the peacocks' iridescent plumage. A red squirrel stared at Craig from an overhanging branch before scampering away into the woodland's darkening embrace.

The entrance to the estate consisted of a small Visitors Centre, retailing an assortment of overpriced castle merchandise, alongside towering oak gates with wrought iron strapwork and latticework bracing, and three medieval statues of anonymous but gruesome warriors. The security guard confirmed Craig's status as an overnight resident, and unbolted the gates to allow safe passage. Autumn rains had left the paths beyond the castle grounds pockmarked with shallow dirt puddles, but Craig persevered through the splashes. By the time he reached Malkin village, the streaks of drying mud across his shoes looked like the tired remnants of a drunken game of noughts and crosses.

The village's outer properties were a half-dozen semi-detached homes, set back from the road by a tree-lined verge. Architecturally, there was little to distinguish them; yellowing mortar with exposed brick-work around red-painted front doors. The exception was the final house in the parade, where the entire façade was smothered in a complex array of Christmas lights. Elves in exaggerated poses besieged the porch. Above the first floor windows flew a flashing red and white Santa, drawn on his sleigh by a fleet of reindeer. And, parallel with the roofline, the message Happy Christmas was surrounded by a stars and moons ensemble, blazing into the early evening September air. It was the first yuletide greeting of Craig's year, although the homeowner's enthusiasm was explained by the electronic signage latched to the chimney: *Ben Kilonback, Lighting Professional.*

Craig put aside these casual reminiscences the moment Hino ascended the restaurant's staircase.

"Thank you for making time," said the financier.

He seemed more agitated than during their previous encounter. Tiny beads of sweat had formed on his upper lip; every time he brushed them aside, they reappeared like critters in a game of Whac-A-Mole.

"It's my pleasure," said Craig. "The big tasks have all been buttoned down for the workshop, and my team are finalising the details. At this stage, they're most effective without my interference."

Hino cleared his throat. "I'd offer you a glass of champagne."

Craig was about to acquiesce when the financier continued: "But I've travelled here direct from a full day of meetings in Canary Wharf, and I've not eaten since breakfast. Let's order first. I'm told their *Clapassade* is exceptional; one of the few specialities from Languedoc that have made their presence felt in Tokyo. Excuse me," he turned to a young waiter standing by the door, alert but impassive, like a Wimbledon ball boy.

"What is your name?"

"Riccardo, sir."

"Riccardo, please can you show my colleague the options?"

The menu was unfussy, freshly typed that morning, devoid of images and illustrations. Its only concession to those who lacked fluency in French was to offer an italicised translation of each dish in a font so small it was scarcely visible. Craig started to scan the options, but had barely reached the second line of the hors d'œuvre when Hino coughed again.

"Decide quickly, my friend," he said. "We need to discuss business."

Craig plumped for the safe choices, a creamy bisque followed by a beef stew. Before Hino could mention his preferences, the waiter pre-empted him.

"Your assistant has already indicated your selection, sir."

Then, astutely recognising the diners were unlikely to welcome over-zealous attempts to build rapport, the waiter withdrew back into the shadows, leaving Craig and Hino to converse alone. The champagne, or indeed any type of alcoholic refreshment, remained a distant prize.

With rapid fire efficiency, Hino outlined his agenda.

"Firstly, now you've had an opportunity to meet the Xanotek team, it's time for us to share observations on the personnel. Secondly, I'd like to get more specific about my concerns for the business. Thirdly, I'm intrigued to know your proposals for leading discussions over the next two days, and how you'll ensure we walk away with the deliverables I need."

"That covers the bases," said Craig. "I've now spent around four full days at their Crowborough offices. Additionally, my team has analysed the financials in some depth and conducted confidential interviews with other players in the sector. I think I have a decent handle on the issues."

"Barker is my main concern. No-one can question his intellect, but he's struggled to make the transition from the worlds of academia and R&D. My greatest successes have been when I've backed decisive leaders. Perhaps his genius is his flaw. He sees both sides of every question."

Craig's conclusions supported Hino's concerns.

"All our research confirmed he has an exceptional mind. Under the surreptitious guise of a buying agent, Marcelle has talked her way into board level discussions throughout the garment and accessories sector."

"And what did she find?"

"Barker's name came up in at least two meetings, where she was across the table from materials scientists who had studied under him. There are rumours about why he's become so reclusive.

"Is he on the verge of an innovation that will force the world to take notice, or is he suffering the exhaustion of a burnt-out comet? Those are the questions being asked. Which brings us to the one-to-one discussions I had with him."

This was the crunch issue. Hino was engrossed with a surgeon's assiduity upon Craig's observations. For the first time since his plane had touched down, he was finally able to focus his concentration. Until that point, he had found himself dwelling with unnerving regularity on the qualities of the air hostess who had attended to his needs throughout the overnight flight. He must remember to compliment the agency. Ukrainian girls could be so delightful.

"During every visit, I made a point of topping and tailing the day with at least half an hour in his company, probing his intentions. He can find it difficult to put his testing programme into layman's terms. There could be a sinister explanation, or perhaps his mind just operates on a different plane. In any event, he seems to have spent the past two years in pursuit of the world's most perfect, unassailable new polymer. But he never seems to pause to make the commercial enquiries. Is he building excessive cost into the product, and how will the incremental spend realise a superior return?"

Craig paused to allow the returning waiter to adjust their place-settings with the requisite cutlery, and deposit between them a basket of crusty rolls laden with caraway seeds. Scooping at the butter dish, he wondered whether the dazzling whiteness of the knife handles was evidence of an illicit trade in ivory.

More immediately, the wine list remained notable by its absence, so Craig resolved to force the matter.

"One other matter, Riccardo," he began.

But Hino had already waved away the waiter so as to continue his unburdening. The wine choices would remain unscrutinised for a while longer.

"I've had some exposure to the financial issues from Adrienne," the financier explained.

"She has my complete trust. Before I placed her into Xanotek, she was finance manager of an Infrastructure Hub I owned near Baku. She uncovered serious, endemic embezzlement. The managing director to whom she notionally reported had hidden family ties to organised crime, and had been abusing his position.

"Not only did she identify the fraud, which was concealed behind a byzantine series of front companies and fake invoices, but she alerted me in defiance of any personal risks. That's why I was sympathetic when she asked for her next posting to be as remote as possible from Indonesia."

"I spent two hours of my first day drilling into the capital expenditure history," said Craig. "She is in full command of the records. The legitimacy and stability of every major supplier was audited in depth before contracts were signed. And she has instigated systems to track inventory, especially of items of middling value which can be most prone to wastage."

"I'm not surprised you spent such time with her," Hino allowed himself a rare smile. "She's easy on the eye, wouldn't you agree?"

Craig blushed slightly, recalling Adrienne's huge brown eyes gazing at him through a gently wafting fringe of auburn hair, as they worked through the spreadsheet columns of a budget schedule.

During the decade when Craig had been establishing his reputation, he and his now-estranged wife, had been regarded by their clients as an inseparable partnership. Patricia had accompanied him to all major events and meetings, and fiercely negotiated the terms of his engagements. Without her omnipresence, Craig was more alert to signs of flirtatious behaviour. So, yes, he had spotted Adrienne's coquettish nature.

"You'd be unwise to read too much into things," continued Hino. "She's learnt how to conduct herself in a male workplace to get noticed. People open up to her, and perhaps share more than they ought. It's part of what makes her effective. But, if she harbours secret thoughts of anyone on your team, they will be about Marcelle, rather than you."

Craig nearly choked on a chunk of crust, but managed to convey unflappability as he rewound the conversation to an earlier stage.

"It's clear she's a brilliant forensic accountant. Her memory for numbers is almost photographic; she calculates complex ratios in her head; and she challenges her colleagues robustly about line items. But it was awkward to engage her in a broader strategic discussion. Suddenly, her penetrating comments dissolved into vagaries. Her intuitive sense of financial risk doesn't carry over into commercial matters."

"I've learnt that's part of her personal defence mechanism," said Hino. "She'll never lose the scars from Paris, as a teenager in the fifth arrondissement, the Latin Quarter. She flinches from any situation where she's not in complete control. That's always worked for me. I need someone to guarantee the books are in order. If I can't rely on the accounts, the rest is fairy dust."

"What happened in Paris?" ventured Craig.

"Gentlemen, your first course," announced Riccardo.

With the flourish of stage actor on opening night, he placed a low two-handled cup before Craig. The thick soup of sautéed crustaceans and roasted vegetables trembled but didn't quite spill over the brim. As he leant forward, the waiter's nose protruded into Craig's personal space as he savoured the rising aroma of the bisque one final time. Hino's choice of toast with liver pate seemed bland in comparison, but the financier was unbothered. His hunger was finally satiated, and he folded the slices into his mouth with alacrity. The moment to probe into Adrienne's past was gone. As, with the waiter summarily waved away by Hino, was any opportunity to order a glass of chilled chardonnay.

The first slice of toast digested, Hino asked: "Have you formed a view about Chad Spillane? He seems to me to be part of the problem."

Spillane was responsible for running Xanotek's production operations, under Barker's supervision. Despite his premature baldness, Spillane was still in his twenties, and the youngest member of the firm's management team. He had been invariably cooperative, and even effusive, in Craig's presence, but to the strategist's seasoned eye, cloying eagerness wasn't an untarnished virtue.

"It depends what you're looking for," said Craig. "A psychological profiler would label him a *doer*. An action man. A person who gets things done. He will block out distractions in his drive to complete the tasks he's been set. If *getting over the finishing line* is at the expense of food or sleep, Chad Spillane is your man."

"I'm anticipating a *but*," said Hino.

"He's there to get done what Barker tells him needs doing. But he won't challenge Barker. He won't resist, or offer alternative routes. If Barker wants to spend a quarter of a million pounds adding a fraction of a percentile to the polymer's integrity, Spillane will deliver that fraction. But he won't turn around and tell Barker the whole endeavour is muddleheaded."

"Is that immaturity? Is that his nature?"

"It doesn't help that he has a young family and had taken on a big mortgage. Also his visa status makes him dependent on Xanotek's success. If he loses his job, the authorities will permit him a couple of months to secure a new source of income. Then, it's back to Michigan. Either with his wife and daughter, or alone."

"You must have spoken to him about potential applications?"

"He's an all-American kid who plays baseball on the weekend and bakes turkey at Thanksgiving. His wife is a former cheerleader. So any discussion about the new polymer heads, inexorably and predictably, down one particular avenue. A better make of blue jean."

"And what do you think of that?"

"My thoughts on Spillane reflect my wider observations. For all his undoubted strengths, Barker has created a culture of busy fools. An author of my acquaintance once wrote about the scatterbrained temperament of his pre-teen sons, who, depending on the day of the week, describe their perfect career as either that of astronaut, inventor, footballer or movie star. I see the same lack of direction in Xanotek. Strategies are not shopping lists of ideas, let alone wishlists. I see a bewildering Aladdin's cave of potential treasures. But no-one who can identify which lamp in the mound of artefacts contains the genie."

Hino had long nurtured this suspicion, a troubling doubt that had prompted his original approach to Craig. Yet having it spelled out in blunt terms was still unwelcome. The sweat returned to his lower lip. He lent across the table, his tie brushing against the crumbs that remained on his plate. Between them, with aquiline grace, had stood *Angeline's* personalised salt and pepper pots, but Hino pushed them aside like forfeited chess pieces, so that he could stare unimpeded into Craig's eyes.

"So what, Mr Richards, is your recommendation?"

He gripped the side of the table so intently that his knuckles bulged.

"I've structured the workshop into two phases," said Craig. "Tomorrow is all about opening up everyone's mind to the issues and possibilities. I'll run a number of exercises with the central aim of achieving consensus about the challenges ahead.

"The day will end with the team shortlisting a number of attractive options. Options that pass baseline criteria - they capitalise on our strengths, they mitigate our weaknesses. But I won't be asking the team to make the hard choice between these options tomorrow. That's for the second day, once people have internalised, reflected, and perhaps obtained some new insights. Day two is about being decisive about the road ahead, and again I'll introduce exercises to force the matter. In the jargon, from divergence to convergence. From everything on the table, to most stuff in the trash. The output will be a clear vision, a maximum of five strategic objectives, and some priority activities to make it happen. That's my ambition for the programme."

Hino nodded calmly. He released his hold on the table and flicked his tie over his shoulder to rescue it from its hapless encounter with the leftovers. At long last, he plucked a copy of the wine list from a perspex holder on the window ledge, and beckoned the waiter to return and take note of one further request.

"Your finest white burgundy. Grand Cru. Ideally 1991 vintage," he said.

Then he turned back to Craig.

"So, Mr Richards, tell me more about these exercises."

Craig mused, *Perhaps I won't need a dose of my favourite powder tonight, after all.*

The assault began shortly after dusk. A lorry carrying catering provisions had approached the main gate of the Tamahaq refinery. The vehicle and its driver were familiar to the guards, and despite the heightened state of security, they proceeded nonchalantly with their inspection duties. Driver unarmed, check. Paperwork in order, check.

Everything seemed routine until the guards approached the rear doors to check the cargo. The twist of the door lock triggered the activator switch of an improvised explosive device in excess of 5,000 pounds. The spontaneous chemical reaction led to a massive build up of energy. For a few seconds, there was no perceptible physical effect; then the charge sent a shock wave through the explosive materials at high speed, forcing detonation of the payload. The lorry erupted with the fury of a furnace. The thermal wave inflicted catastrophic injuries on the guards immediately around the vessel.

A dozen civilian workers further inside the compound were hit by flying debris, including nails, ball bearings and rocks. By the time the shock bubble collapsed, the area around the blast site was littered with corpses and body parts. As the sound of the explosion faded, it was replaced with the shrieks and cries of the maimed and wounded.

There was no time for the refinery management to implement a considered response to the aggression. Before anyone could weigh up whether to reinforce the defences, or to initiate an evacuation, the offensive shifted into the next gear. Heavily armed forces appeared from all directions, pouring from the cellars and attics of nearby properties like a swarm of locusts intent on demolishing everything in its path. Snipers perched on rooftops fired at any refinery workers who had not yet retreated under cover, while the first party of soldiers to reach the main gate despatched any guards who had survived the initial attack.

The refinery was a sprawling complex of offices, processing units, cooling towers, depots and warehouses. The advance party was spreading from building to building, peppering each one with gunfire, inflicting chaos and fear and denying the occupants any chance to regroup. One specially trained unit had been tasked with securing the crude oil distillation unit, three hundred yards to the left of the main gate, where the incoming petroleum was stored, preheated and desalted. No grenades or munitions were used in this operation, which relied entirely on small firearms. The intent was clearly to take control of the plant, rather than to wreak the maximum havoc.

In the Control Centre, Ted Milner watched with mounting terror the grainy images of the assault on the bank of monitors. Around thirty minutes beforehand, he had finished the day's duties in the alkylation unit, where he had been producing high octane compounds for gasoline blending, and had dropped into the centre to grab a coffee with his old friend Frank Griffiths. Frank and Ted had studied chemical engineering together at Imperial in the nineties, three unforgettable years sharing apartments, experiences and occasionally girlfriends. It had been Ted's persistence that had finally tempted Frank to take up a posting in East Phoenicia. As the political tensions had risen in the region, Ted had become quietly nauseous about the matter, but despite their camaraderie had never felt sufficiently bold to raise his feelings of guilt, even by way of jocular apology.

"We're safest here. They're going to want hostages as well as carcasses. If they make it this far, it's hands up. Nothing that could be interpreted as aggressive intent," Frank shouted, trying to make himself heard above the wailing alarm.

The siren was as irrelevant as the age rating on a Seagal movie. Everyone on the compound was aware of the assault, and the deafening sound merely accentuated the atmosphere of panic.

On the monitor, the body count was rising. The accommodation block was now ablaze, agitated flames rising high into the cloudless evening sky. And still more soldiers were sweeping through the gates. An onrushing tide that had powered through the levies and would not abate any time soon. A battalion of fighters had already crossed through the perimeter.

Then, Frank and Ted heard the sound of troops ascending the stairwell towards the Control Centre, yelling sporadic orders and responses in one of the many Arabic dialects that neither man had ever felt the need to master. The distant gunfire was slightly more restrained now. Perhaps passions were subsiding, thought Frank. Perhaps they've realised they'll need experts to help with site operations? Whether intent on continued production or immediate decommissioning, qualified engineers on-point could have some value.

"Wish me luck," said Frank to Ted, as he shuffled towards the door, his shirt thick and bloated with perspiration.

Moving into the outside corridor, with arms held aloft in surrender, he spoke into the darkness: "I can help. Don't shoot. I can help."

For a moment, silence.

Then, the sharp crack of a solitary bullet being discharged, and a crimson geyser burst from the back of Frank's head. For a moment, time stood still. The red spray seemed to defy gravity, hovering in mid-air, with Frank's expression fixed in a gasp of incredulity. Then, his light frame collapsed to the floor, eyes wide open and staring blankly towards Ted. Just below the hairline a neat red circle oozed blood.

An inner voice was screaming at Ted to run. But his body was transfixed with shock, unable to act. He sat ashen-faced on his swivel chair, blinking wildly in the unconscious hope that the scene before him might dissolve like a ghastly nightmare.

But this was no delusion. He snapped back when two soldiers, clad in full combat dress and wearing distinctive Phoenicia berets, strode into the room with their weapons pointed directly at his chest. Ted looked up but said nothing. Frank's attempt at surrender had provoked retaliation, so perhaps more muted behaviour might yield a better outcome.

"What is name?" barked the taller of the assailants in stuttering English, a hulking sergeant, whose frazzled neck-beard exposed his acne-ridden chin and jawline.

Before Ted could respond, he pointed his pistol at the floor. Ted noticed the pool of blood around Frank's body was spreading, like water leaking from a tank. Soon the man with the neck-beard would be able to parade his reddened boots like a grotesque trophy.

"Now kneel," he ordered.

Secretary of State, Katherine Foster, and Permanent Secretary, Hugo Cunningham, watched breaking news of the evolving crisis with mounting concern. The Peace

Conference had been a farce – a series of staged speeches by grandstanding politicians whose focus had been assuaging their domestic audience rather than seeking a substantive solution. Since their return, Foster had relegated the East Phoenicia unrest to the lowest rung of her in-tray. As an ambitious politician, she gravitated towards topics where there were clear cut solutions with predictable outcomes and widespread support. Phoenicia offered none of the above.

"What's your assessment?" asked the minister.

"That the Phoenician government has decided to cut off the life-blood of the separatists. The independence movement in the eastern provinces is only possible because of their access to petro dollars through their oil exploration and production sector. Deprive them of that, and you've deprived the hydra of its final head."

"But to target western interests so brazenly...."

"Not strictly western interests, minister. The Tamahaq Refinery is essentially run by ourselves. British management, British investment, British engineers. Perhaps they calculated we have no appetite for the fight. After Iraq and Afghanistan and deliberately relegating our military muscle to the lower second division..."

"That's enough, Hugo," said Foster. "Surely the Russians won't countenance this outrage?"

"I'm sure they had no advance knowledge, Minister. And I'm sure they'll express diplomatic displeasure. On the other hand, they won't be disappointed to see the Phoenicians taking a more belligerent stance."

"We need to set up a call with the PM and Foreign Secretary," said Foster. "Speak to their offices."

Cunningham nodded in stern acknowledgement. But as he rose to kick start procedures, the news anchorman, who was fronting the coverage, cut away from his filler interview with a banal foreign policy placeman from the Clinton era, and in sonorous tones advised viewers that CNN would be taking a live feed from Al Jazeera for the next few minutes. Foster motioned to the Permanent Secretary to retake his seat.

"Let's watch this," she said.

The screen was dominated by the terrified features of a battered man in his late thirties. His cheeks were raw from repeated rifle butt punches, and the skin had split into a jagged gash below his right eye. His lips were swollen to twice their normal size and a front tooth was missing. The injuries were dramatised by an intense beam of light that shone directly into the man's face from off screen. A couple of girders were vaguely visible in the rusty background darkness, but it was hard to make out any details of his surroundings.

"My name is Ted Milner," spoke the captive.

He was quivering with fright, and his words tumbled listlessly, falteringly.

"I live in Banbury in England. I have a wife, Sarah, and two young children. I have been working at Tamahaq for the past three years. I recognise the Phoenician government has authority over these entire lands, and my role here has given unwitting succour to its enemies."

"That's not good," said Foster.

"Not at all," muttered Cunningham. "So much for Peace Conferences."

Chapter Five

Located in:

Malkin Castle
and
Roeborne Woods

"To get us underway, I'm going to invite you in turn to join me at the front. Let's start with you, Jeremy."

Malkin Castle's Upper Hall was the only area of the estate available for commercial hire during visiting hours. It was one of three rooms that abutted the rear landing, and was reached at the summit of the grand staircase, a feature so wide and sweeping that a middle railing - complete with creepy bronze cherub atop the finial at the end of the balustrade - had been installed during the last refurbishment.

The hall itself was long and narrow, with a vast bay window overlooking a courtyard. At one end was a stone-lined hearth with a cracked and skewed overmantle displaying an elaborate coat of arms. At the other was a raised dais, where much of the hall's antique furniture had been lodged to make space for the workshop. The room was overlooked by a minstrels' gallery, jutting out above the dais. For a couple of the participants, who were already nervous about the day ahead, the gallery added an unsettling frisson, as if the ghosts of ancient musicians were lurking behind the balustrades, poised at any moment to burst into a haunting requiem.

The tables had been laid out in horseshoe fashion. This was Craig's preferred arrangement for smaller events. It made it more difficult, he felt, for reluctant delegates to disengage, and so encouraged an open flow of ideas. Compared with a conventional boardroom style, it also enabled him to prowl around more freely. Commanding the room like an evangelist preacher was mission critical.

At the open end of the horseshoe, Craig was surrounded by the jungle of visual aids that Marcelle and Dimala had assembled the previous day, including three flip charts, a touch sensitive interactive whiteboard, and a mobile widescreen display monitor. Given the dubious acoustics of a castle hall, and to heighten his authority over the meeting, Craig's team had even taken the precaution of fitting him with a tiny lapel microphone connected to two wireless speakers on either side of the horseshoe.

For Craig, an effective workshop relied upon theatre as much as content. His goal was to transport the delegates away from the hustle and preoccupations of the typical day in Crowborough, and open their minds to a realm crammed to bursting with beckoning opportunity. Doubt and disbelief must be suspended; the prevailing mood must be about shaping and creating, setting aside problems and obstacles. Many of the tools Craig employed were designed to displace his audience far from their current concerns, fostering a spirit of adventure and generating a thrilling, edgy buzz.

They had largely been developed by Patricia, in the innocent years before their relationship had dissolved amidst recrimination and hostility. Countless evenings throughout her childhood had been spent back stage in the West End, at the behest of her father (in the opinion of *Variety* magazine, the foremost producer of his generation). As Shaftesbury Avenue's finest performers worked themselves into a physical and emotional frenzy, their sinews alive with exertion, Patricia had often peered through the theatre curtains to behold the ocean of awestruck faces in the stalls. She had learnt about the power of music, lighting and colour to engage and inspire, and had cajoled and badgered Craig from the outset to incorporate them into his routine.

On arrival in the room, the Xanotek team had been greeted by fragments of Patricia's undying legacy: the exhilarating strains of Johann Strauss' *An der schönen blauen Donau,* as used during the lunar docking sequence in the movie *2001: A Space Odyssey,* and the waft of lavender in the air. Craig's continuing use of such motifs meant her lasting influence was never far from his mind.

96

"And can we have a rousing round of applause, please, as Jeremy takes centre stage?" Craig continued as Barker, with some trepidation, moved to the front.

In total, there were eight Xanotek delegates seated around the horseshoe. There was Barker himself, the finance manager Adrienne Dodier and her deputy Marco Elderfield, the head of production Chad Spillane and his deputy Daniel Fricke, and three scientists who worked directly for Barker on computer simulation, specification and testing: Adam Peralter, Victor Jones and Kim Drahem. The only notable absentee was their investor, Nobuyuki Hino. He had checked in to the castle's accommodation wing, but had already advised Craig and Barker that other pressing matters demanded his attentions. He planned to drift in and out of the sessions, and would certainly be present for the wrap-up, but regrettably it would not be practical for him to attend the workshop in its entirety.

Craig continued: "What I'd like to do for the next few minutes is invite you to forget about polymers. Don't think about Xanotek at all. Cast aside the day job. What I'd like you all to do is tell us about an organisation, outside your sector, that has genuinely inspired you. Perhaps you used to work there. Perhaps you have family or friends employed there. Perhaps you are a customer. Or perhaps you've simply seen media coverage of them. In any event, tell us their story. What have they done that's been so exceptional? What's been their spark of genius? And please don't limit yourselves to household names and FTSE companies. In fact, your examples don't even need to be companies. Any organisation that has a clear mission and has delivered a superior result may carry a lesson for us today."

Barker collected his thoughts and decided on a relatively safe choice.

"The National Health Service," he said. "It's a unique institution. It offers cradle to grave care, free at the point of use. My mother spent her last few weeks on one of their wards, and although she grew depressed and frightened towards the end, the staff never allowed her to lose her dignity."

With a blue marker pen, Craig wrote 'NHS' in the middle of the flip chart.

"And it seems that, for you, the inspiration is partly its distinctive identity – I think you used the word unique. Partly its central mission, which stands unchanged over the decades. Partly its focus on its customers, it doesn't forget who it's there to serve. And finally the touch points between staff and customers."

Craig drew a circle around the letters NHS, and added emanating lines until the sketch took on the shape of a squashed beetle. At the end of each line he wrote one of the words that captured the essence of Barker's tribute: 'Unique', 'central mission', 'serve' and 'touch points'.

With Barker's example complete, the marker pen was passed to Adrienne. For her inspirational case study, she chose Pellegrinelli's, a family owned bakery close to her home.

"They started up in the teeth of the recession, and that took guts," she said.

"The bread is baked in open stone furnaces and tastes wonderful. They use all natural ingredients, and source their flour locally, from British mills. And they fended off an attempt last year by Starbucks to usurp their location on the High Street and turn it into another outlet for overpriced and rather rank coffee."

There was a muffled chuckle from someone in the room at Adrienne's caustic closing remark. Craig added Pellegrinelli's name to the flip chart, and further expanded the proliferating web of key words with 'guts', 'transparent production', 'supply chain', and 'resisting predator'. The pen was then given to Adam Peralter.

Over the next ten minutes, the chart filled up with a diverse assortment of examples. Apple, Virgin and Disney all received their inevitable mentions, as did the real estate advisory firm, CBRE, which had assisted Xanotek with its fit-out, and the Chartered Insurance Institute where Elderfield had qualified. There was one charity on the list, the Royal Society for the Protection of Birds. And the illustrations were completed with Victor Jones' selection of the Chinese Communist Party.

"In the last twenty years, they have created more wealth, and pulled more people out of poverty, than the rest of the world combined," he argued. "They have transformed a nation with a billion-plus population."

There was now sufficient material for Craig to deliver some plenary remarks for the workshop. He always preferred to structure his observations around organisations that meant something to the participants, rather than arrive with a truckload of pre-prepared business school case studies. It required him to think on his feet, but the impact and resonance was magnified. Looking at the names that had been offered, he drew three conclusions.

Firstly, he said, the safe option was not necessarily the most sustainable. Apple's greatest triumphs were delivered when it put aside past successes, and took a bold step into the unknown. Secondly, the customer is the most important stakeholder. If CBRE had arrived at Xanotek's door with a technically wonderful, but wholly inappropriate solution, cut-and-paste from one client and reused for a data centre or a marina, they would not have made it past first base.

And, finally, delivery. The world was awash, Craig asserted, with a legion of failed politicians with the rhetorical gifts to promise and beguile their electorate with visions of a world that is wealthier and healthier, the perfect fusion of El Dorado and Shangri La. But while the big beasts of opposing parties from Washington to Westminster lock horns with a flourish, the Chinese rulers were getting stuff done. They know that, in the long term, success is forged not just by fanciful aspiration but by tangible achievement.

As Craig spoke, Marcelle recorded the three crucial phrases on the whiteboard: 'bold not safe', 'customer the crucial stakeholder', and 'get delivering'. Craig turned to inspect these three themes.

"Let these messages be our guiding star over the next two days. Let us imagine in a hundred years that another group of entrepreneurs are conducting a similar retreat in a similar venue. Let us dream that, when asked to nominate an exemplar of best practice, one of their multitude suggests Xanotek. Because you *thought boldly*, knew exactly what your *customers were seeking*, and *made it happen*."

Craig knew he had captured the attention of the group. That was a necessary but not sufficient achievement. The Xanotek leadership had joined him on the platform, and were expectant about the journey together. But some were still encumbered with the mindset of the passenger, somnambulant in a rear carriage, while Craig, as boilerman, stoked the locomotive's engine. Psychologically as well as physically, they needed to be with him at the front; fully invested in shaping the journey's itinerary.

"What I'm going to do now," said Craig, "is ask you to envisage you're living in 2025. But first, allow me to describe some features that will be different in your environment. By 2025, demographic structures will have transformed. Around 35 per cent of the population in Europe will be aged 65 or over, and wonder drugs will have created a militant base of centenarians. Nearly 60 per cent of the workforce will be female, as true in the boardroom as on the shop floor. London will have doubled in size, and the entire South Bank will look like a surreal dystopian cityscape, with its soaring skyscrapers and labyrinthine mid-air walkways. Increasingly dextrous robots will be prevalent everywhere - from the kitchens of restaurants to the cockpits of planes. Generally, living standards will be comfortable, and the typical office worker will operate from their garage or attic, digitally connected with multiple remote employers. The most popular consumer electronic gadget will be a head-mounted computer. Footballer Roy Keane and singer Adele will both be senior members of the British Cabinet."

As Craig developed his portrayal of this world beyond tomorrow, Marcelle was projecting a whirlwind series of complementary images to the room through the widescreen. Pie charts packed with socio-demographic data, extracts from reports issued by futurist institutes, a brief clip from the 1927 movie *Metropolis*, and a mocked up photograph of the hypothetical government benches of the future, packed with its mishmash of B-list celebrities and worse.

"And, of course, not all change counts as progress."

Marcelle flicked up an image of an apocalyptic frozen northland.

"Youth unemployment in the North-East will be catastrophic; the entire area will have been devastated by freak climatic events. Armed guards will be posted at all ports to deter escapees fleeing from the sclerotic, imploding Eurozone economies. Social unrest will be rife, as the unskilled and unfortunate defy the exploitative behaviour of the financial elite. On some days, the air will be barely breathable."

Appearing on the monitor, a graph representing the extrapolated rate of mortality from respiratory disease over the coming decade.

"That, ladies and gentlemen, is your world in 2025," said Craig, smacking his fist into his open palm to add emphasis to his conclusion.

He then handed over to Marcelle to set the next task for the group. She asked each of them to put themselves in the shoes of the chief executive of the "inspirational organisation" they had nominated a few moments ago.

As part of the role-play, each delegate needed to consider how their organisation should best shape up for the era Craig had depicted. In what respects are they already well-placed? Where should they wind down activities or withdraw from markets? What new opportunities could be leveraged? Where do threats loom?

"Here's a model you might use to structure your thinking," said Craig. "It's colloquially called the Boston Box."

He circulated a foolscap printout of a 2x2 matrix, in which the four quadrants were named respectively *Cash Cows, Stars, Question Marks and Dogs*. Briefly explaining the theoretical basis of the Boston Box, he encouraged the executives, during their role-play, to use this device to classify the activities of their chosen organisation.

"For example, with greater longevity, do certain functions of the National Health Service become defunct? What do cheap and powerful robotics herald for the seemingly unstoppable rise of China? Does Disney need to shed asunder their wholesome American image for a grittier and more troubled world? The choice is yours."

Craig sat down as the delegates worked through the challenge he'd set. He was hoping to achieve a number of objectives. By the end of the opening hour, he anticipated, the temperament within the room should have perceptibly shifted from obsessing about the here-and-now, to visualising a future state. All those present would have had the chance to unchain their powers of imagination and fancy. And they will have envisaged themselves in the hot seat of a renowned enterprise, making vital decisions with far-reaching implications for the lives of staff, customers and financiers. This, thought Craig, was essential and pressing preparation for the journey that lay ahead.

During the first coffee break, Hino slipped into the Upper Hall through the buttery door, and despite the financier's effort to remain inconspicuous, Craig sensed a slight stiffening in the body language around the room as the delegates responded to his presence. It was the first time Craig had seen Hino in such casual attire – open necked shirt, cashmere v-neck, even designer jeans.

Until then, he had wistfully assumed Hino tended to the garden dressed in a three-piece business suit.

"Please, continue as you were," said Hino calmly, to nobody in particular. "I'll stay quietly in the corner."

He lifted a stool from the dais and sat on it, legs crossed.

Marcelle reconvened the workshop with a second blast of Vangelis, and Craig flicked on his mic to introduce the next stage of the discussion.

"Our focus now shifts to your own sector. And, within that, to your own firm. But here's the deal. Let's not lose sight of the principles we've drawn from the first session, from our exploration of outstanding firms before us that confronted and prospered from the swirling forces in their path. The trick for you will be to apply these precepts to your own particular situation. And how better to introduce this topic that hearing the very latest from the Xanotek lab. Jeremy?"

"Actually," said Barker, "I've asked Kim to provide a technical briefing. I'll then comment on the development programme ahead."

Kim Drahem had, until this point, been the most quietly spoken of the group. She approached the front of the room with baby steps, as if excessive pressure would cause the stone slabs to disintegrate and send her, tumbling downwards, into some perilous yawning cavern. Her slight build was evident even through the generous layer of wool that comprised her carefully buttoned cardigan. Her pinprick eyes glared into the middle distance through horn-rimmed spectacles. She was trying, almost too hard, to avoid eye contact with any one individual, as she addressed the workshop ponderously but precisely, in the clipped manner of a station announcer.

"We all experience polymers throughout our daily lives; I'm sure we've all encountered many of them today," she said.

"There are many examples of natural polymers, such as wool and cotton and some types of rubber. There are also synthetic polymers, such as polystyrene and silicone. What they have in common is their large molecular mass relative to many other compounds we study in science. The microstructure of the polymer, in particular the size and length of the molecular chain, determines many of its physical features, and often has an exponential effect. For example, a tenfold increase in chain length, in many cases, leads to a thousand-fold rise in viscosity."

Kim's complexion had reddened as she spoke, so she paused to control her breathing and compose herself. She used the opportunities to select a folder on the widescreen, and open a series of image files of different polymer architectures. Using a pointer, she highlighted one or two distinctive features of each, and made some obscure scientific observation. She knew she must strike a balance between (on the one hand) making her content intelligible to the half of the room that last sat through a science class in mid-school, (on the other) not patronising the other half. This was a near impossible task, and she feared her failure was abject and complete.

"The issue of degradation has perplexed polymer scientists for centuries. This is the vivid change in the properties of many polymers under the influence of heat or light or chemicals. Very quickly, there will be scission, or what you'd term breakage, in the bonds of the molecular chain. The tensile strength, colour, shape and weight of the polymer can all degrade with startling rapidity. Although this has some practical side effects, for example when recycling, generally it means anything from swelling to discoloration, and from inflammation to excessive wear and tear."

To illustrate her point, Kim showed a video compilation of various everyday products undergoing degradation at an accelerated rate.

"The waste and cost to society, and to families, is almost literally incalculable," she concluded.

"Thank you for that analysis, Kim," said Barker. "You've provided the perfect segue for me to summarise our task at Xanotek. For the past two years, the focus of the research team's efforts has been to address the issue of polymer degradation. To find a solution which means that, essentially, the tensile strength of the molecular architecture is fortified without any detrimental side effects elsewhere within the covalent network. Until recently, this was an unrealisable dream. However recent breakthroughs in plasma polymerisation, supplemented by the use of proteins, has bought the dream within touching distance."

Craig thumbed through the briefing document prepared by his team after the initial on-sites with Xanotek. The issue of polymerisation technology had comprised most of the first page. It was now four weeks since Dimala Naidu had left the Chandansar orphanage with a warm parting embrace from Miss Weseldine, and experienced for the first time the inside of a jumbo jet. The visa arrangements had come through so expeditiously there had been little chance to prepare a proper induction to London living. His time was split equally between a corner desk in Craig's unnecessarily palatial office suite near Covent Garden, and a spare room in Marcelle's apartment. Almost every waking moment of Dimala's four weeks had been dedicated to researching the field of polymerisation, its key players, and the commercial profile of potential applications.

"During our first nine months, every moment we felt close to a discovery, but the solution fell apart under testing. Theoretically, particle physics tells us that polymer degradation is not an inevitability of nature. But in practice the route to a compelling, provable answer remained elusive. We tried alternating copolymers with monomer residue, without success. The same when we artificially raised the crystalline melting point through injection of a protective membrane. In each case, tensile strength rose, but at the expense of other vital properties.

"But then, our breakthrough insight. We synthesised a new protein by transcribing genetic DNA information through multiple enzymes. The result has been a fabric polymer with all the familiar attributes of cotton yet which suffers no permanent deformation under extremes of heat or impact. It seems virtually invulnerable."

Hino had been recording a few comments on his tablet device, but looked up at this last statement. "So you actually have something that works? And is ready now?" he said.

"I'm a cautious, taciturn scientist, Mr Hino," said Barker, fiddling with a clump of florid hair that continued to sprout intact on his otherwise bald scalp.

"Two more months of simulated testing to cover a handful of outstanding variables, and then I can give you a confident affirmative. But, it's true, every indicator is currently positive, and that didn't happen with our earlier experiments. We're not anticipating disappointment."

"So, ready soon," said Craig. "Begging the question … ready for what?"

The air conditioning had never worked properly, at least not since the end of the warranty period. Firstly, the dealer's servicing team had simply replaced the refrigerant. Then they pulled out the compressor. Finally, and several hundred pounds later, it was the entire radiator unit that needed to be replaced. Yet still, no matter how much the controls were prodded and poked and hammered, thirty minutes of the mildest AC would leave the rear of the truck feeling like a pantry in an igloo. And this particular truck, a four cylinder Isuzu Reach, had already been occupied for most of the day.

The truck was parked along a little used nature trail in Roeborne Woods, just at the foot of a steep and muddy incline. Since dawn, only a couple of ramblers, a cyclist and a hatchback had passed by, but nevertheless the truck's driver had manoeuvred it on arrival to prevent any risk of road blockage, and the side of the vehicle was pressing firmly against two copper beech trees. As if in retaliation, the trees had been releasing a steady downpour of scaly dead leaves which now smothered the truck's roof like the overstretched woollen hat of a moody teenager.

Neil & Neil The Sewage Specialists was painted in restrained lettering on the side of the truck, next to an outline illustration of a septic tank, and the three words *Clean, Fast, Value*. There was no indication anywhere of the address or location for Neil & Neil, but a mobile phone number was provided, in barely readable light blue typeface. In the unlikely event one of the passers-by had the urge to dial this number, they would have been curtly asked to leave a message by an automated answering service.

With the exception of the questionable air condit -ioning, the interior of the vehicle was conducive to extended occupation. The walk through configuration allowed both driver and passenger to enter the cargo area without exiting the vehicle, and the slip resistant vinyl floor meant work could proceed without the unsettling movement of objects and persons. The generous headroom had been a particular boon to the truck's passenger, who was taller than six feet by a couple of inches. The cargo area's height – around eighty inches – also meant an array of equipment had been installed without impeded mobility or seating arrangements.

Both driver and passenger were dressed in baggy navy coveralls. The garments were adorned with gratuitous features: a brass zipper the size of a penknife, hemmed sleeves, and at least eight pockets. But despite this finery, the tailors seemed strangely to have omitted anywhere for name tags. If either workman had been asked to produce some type of official documentation, the paperwork would have revealed the driver was named Neil Ward, and his accomplice Neil Shaw. In this lazy, near-deserted stretch of woodland some distance beyond the perimeter of Malkin Castle, neither Ward nor Shaw were currently troubled by the risk of such an interrogation.

The two men could scarcely present a greater contrast in either their features or disposition. Ward had the furtive twitch of a street fighter. Even within a locked truck, he kept glancing around for any signs of oncoming trouble. As he adjusted a dial on the workstation, he absentmindedly stroked his cauliflower ear as if to reassure himself it had not further deformed. Shaw had the urbane languor of a General de Gaulle. While Ward fidgeted, he sat entirely motionless, hands rested on his knees, staring at the displays. His still physique belied a mind that was alert and active.

The men were discussing a recent season of the television drama, 24.

"Do you think it's ever occurred to Jack Bauer that all the most significant terrorist plots he's ever foiled were wrapped up exactly twenty-four hours after he first got involved?" said Ward.

"Or how odd it is that moments of heightened drama always seem to occur when the clock's counting down to the top of the hour?" added Shaw.

"At least he knows when to time his bathroom breaks. Twenty-past and twenty-to are always quiet periods. For us, we know it's the ads. For Jack, everyone's on a go-slow."

The equipment bank stretched the entire roadside inner wall of the cargo area. The centrepiece was a panel containing three CCTV monitors and two receivers for covert voice and data transmissions. Alongside was a secondary unit comprising Bose speakers, a multi-band cellular signal detector and a scrambler. At the far end were two aluminium shelves on which night goggles, transmitters and listening devices had been neatly arranged. In front of the monitors and receivers, there was an audio mixing console. Ward was fiddling compulsively with the digital channel controls, buffering the input signal to erase background interference and amplify the vocals. At this time, after nearly three hours of surveillance, he was still trying to boost the mid-range frequency to its optimal level.

"We can already make out almost every word," said Shaw. "Let's concentrate on what we've got."

"I didn't appreciate how much the castle walls might affect the acoustics," muttered Ward. "But some of them are two metres of solid stone, and that's assuming no curtain walls packed with limestone mortar and stuff. I suppose it's remarkable we pick up anything."

"We're certainly getting enough material for our mission. With all this, we needn't worry about non-payment. Not this time."

"I've almost cracked it," said Ward.

He slid the volume control for one of the channels, and cocked his head in acknowledgement that the background static had finally diminished to almost nothing. The arrows on the auxiliary output metres, which had been darting around, settled at the nominal level.

And from the speakers, came the unmistakable sound of Craig's probing voice, echoing the length of the Isuzu. "So, ready soon. Begging the question ... ready for what?"

Chapter Six

Located in:

The Palace of Westminster,
Malkin Castle
and
Roeborne Woods

"**D**ivision, clear the Lobby," stammered the ageing Commons speaker, and the division bell rang out across the Parliamentary estate.

Like drones under macabre telepathic control, members rose in unison whenever they heard the wailing sound, and abandoned their paperwork, meals, drinks and lovers in their stampede towards the chamber. All in order to vote on some amendment to the Schools Admission Reform Bill, which the prime minister had somehow commandeered into a trial of his authority over the backbenches.

Katherine Foster was one of the first ministers through the Division Lobby. She had been on the premises for a brief meeting with the chairman of her constituency association, who was keen to raise residents' concerns about greenbelt development, and welcomed the opportunity to escape before he had extracted from her anything other than pious sympathy. She was neither familiar with, nor convinced by, the intricacies of the amendment, but recognised it was her duty as a member of the Cabinet to show leadership on one of the legislative showpieces of the current session.

As the tellers counted the votes, Foster intended to loiter around the Lobby, engaging in small talk with parliamentary colleagues. But any such hope dissolved when she felt a hand resting on her shoulder. It belonged to the Foreign Secretary, Roger Neilson, one of the longest serving occupants of that position in the past century, and despite his ruddy complexion and unrivalled collection of garish ties, he was widely spoken of as a future party leader.

"We need to discuss potential scenarios that affect us both," he whispered calmly.

The two colleagues sidled over to a corner of the Lobby where the risks of eavesdropping were reduced.

"What is your latest intelligence from Phoenicia, Roger?" asked Foster.

"The Russians have doubled the number of special forces on the ground," said the Foreign Secretary.

"At first, their role was low key, perhaps some military training or technical advice. But our latest intercepts suggest they've stepped up a gear. They seem to be shipping artillery to the government in defiance of the embargo. And also working with the Phoenician authorities on the timing and logistics of specific campaigns."

"Roger," gasped Foster, "You're not going to tell me they planned the Tamahaq assault."

"There's no evidence that was the case. And of course Moscow has issued a pro-forma diplomatic appeal for calm. On the other hand, we believe the Phoenicians would call back their troops if given the unambiguous instruction by the Kremlin."

"I had some dealings with Secretary Zavrazhnov at the Peace Conference. I wouldn't trust him to run a whelk stall. The fact they're using weasel words speaks volumes."

"So what are our options, militarily?" asked the Foreign Secretary. "I need to brief the PM on the possibilities."

"I've had my top officials looking into scenarios," said Foster.

"Could we let matters take their natural course? The region is inaccessible and dangerous. The British civilians in situ knew the risks. And our best troops are already deployed in other fields of combat. Ten years on, and Afghanistan is still home to the greatest concentration of British fighting expertise outside Sandhurst."

"Haughty distain might have been the solution until *that* happened," said Foster, gesturing towards a mounted TV screen which showed footage of hostage Ted Milner in a repeating loop.

"I'm not sure that's practical when the lives at stake include a named family man, pleading for our help."

"So what else did they come up with?" asked Neilson.

"We assume ransom money is off the table. Officially frowned upon, we don't pay off terrorists, yadda yadda. It's been done before, and I'm sure it'll be done again. But we can't evacuate half a continent."

"And we don't want to encourage copy cat attacks a year from an election. Nothing that could label us weak and listless."

"Neither would it be straightforward to block off their funding. The perpetrators aren't random insurgents. This is an officially sanctioned government operation to further a territorial power play. With the Russian involvement stepping up, I suspect access to finance is not their number one headache."

"So onto the military scenarios?"

"We could mount an aerial campaign. Send over the Lancers to bombard and degrade their capabilities. Support with cruise missiles. The challenge is the vast numbers of civilians from all corners of the globe who are living in Phoenicia. A few strays, and we'd have every single member of the United Nations calling for our heads."

"I'd sooner end my career in more auspicious surrounding than the dock at The Hague."

"Finally, boots on the ground. A rescue mission, or perhaps something more proactive, taking out the terrorist leadership. Cunningham has led the analysis and I expected to be horrified at the risks. Usually you can re-wallpaper Chequers with the lists of pitfalls and horrors. It makes the legalese in a share prospectus for

119

the latest tech fad seem benign in comparison. Personnel risks. Equipment risks. Outdated schematics to key installations. And the inevitable backlash when the body bags return, complete with flags and guards of honour and military salute."

Neilson nodded. His florid cheeks had grown ever more flushed since his elevation to high office, a combination of stress and his legendary inability to resist the claret when entertaining dignitaries from the Commonwealth.

"However, in this instance, Cunningham's report was more nuanced. Military engagement would need a dip into the contingency reserves; after all, the armed forces have borne the brunt of recent budget cuts. However, he proposes to catalogue the inventory of re-equipment that military adventurism would entail."

"We mustn't scrimp on protecting our boys," said Neilson. "I'll tell that to the PM. I've seen too many nineteen-year-old corpses whose flak jackets were as much use as a goldfish's bicycle against a well-hurled hand grenade."

In the chamber, the Speaker was announcing the Ayes and Noes tally. Nail-bitingly close, but the records would show another victory for the Prime Minister.

"We're creating a thing of beauty. But, if we want it to bloom magnificently, we're going to have to feed it and protect it and ensure the light is good," said Adam Peralter, one of Barker's principal scientists.

He deposited in the centre of the table a small mud-encrusted Haddonstone urn. Rising around three feet from the soil was a peace lily in full bloom. Its elongated, creamy white flowers dangled among the lance-shaped foliage like festive lanterns. A few minutes beforehand, it had been an average ornamental plant, one of the dozen or so that formed a fragrant procession either side of the castle's main entrance. Adam had carried it to the room with such an air of nonchalant affection that he had remained unchallenged by the bemused castle guides. His vision had been partially obscured by his cargo; fortunately, a young mother and her son were alert enough to skip out of his path and avert an awkward collision.

Adam's contribution was in response to the latest task set by Craig for the group. Sensing that a change of pace was needed in order to recharge mental batteries, he had dispersed the eight workshop participants with instructions to explore the castle, and return with an object that encapsulated some element of the Xanotek vision. He was now inviting each executive to present their selection. Together, the items would create a type of diorama, a sculpture of the absurd that Craig would leave on the table for the remainder of the workshop, a perpetual visual reminder of eight aspects of the task that were binding them together.

Barker was next to place his piece before the group. "I found this rock, lying by a wall in the courtyard. And it set me thinking about a number of features of our company's adventure. It was born of fire and fury, formed through the cooling and solidification of magma. It is durable; it will have witnessed the dawn of man, and its appearance will be largely unchanged from prehistory. And its power is formidable. Look at that sharp edge, with the stratified iron oxide bands. If that smashed against your car door, or your lab desk, or your skull, you'd certainly know about it."

The rock was laid alongside the urn.

Adrienne Dodier rose. Her object was to be the smallest in the arrangement; in fact, for a moment, some members of the group assumed she had declined to cooperate. Reaching into a pocket in her trouser suit, she produced a crumpled slip of paper. After careful straightening, it too joined the eclectic assortment on the table, with one corner tucked under the base of the urn. It was a discarded entrance ticket to the venue.

"And there, just above a few legal words, has been printed in large, bold lettering, the statement: Adult Price £20. So that's my contribution. Never let us forget that, amidst all the great ideas and even greater intentions, we're a business. We're here to make money."

She caught Hino's eye, and he nodded approvingly.

Next was a mobile phone, courtesy of Marco Elderfield.

"This is to remind us about innovation," he explained. "Thirty years ago, the product didn't exist. Most families had one telephone to share, with those ridiculous rotary dials, and there were red phone boxes on most street corners.

"The only people with portable communication devices that they could drop in their pockets were the officers and crew of the *Starship Enterprise*. And then, within a generation, mobiles became ubiquitous. Possessed by almost every person in the country, from pre-schoolers to grannies. In fact, with the technology advancing so quickly, if you don't replace yours every couple of years, it's an antique. Visionary engineers saw a need, met the need, and made their solution indispensable in the modern world."

He waved his device around the room, tapped an application for dramatic effect, and looked at the screen with mock rapture. Then, he balanced the phone on the rim of the urn.

"It'll stay there until tomorrow," he said, "but it belongs to me, so no framing the display behind toughened glass for posterity, if that's OK. My mother likes me to call at least once a week."

Over the next few minutes, the rest of the group added their chosen objects. By the time it was finished, the collection resembled the type of multifarious assemblage that could win a prestigious arts prize at the Tate Modern. It included an overmantle mirror in a shabby chic gold plated frame that Chad had temporarily relieved from the wall of a corridor ("To remind us that Xanotek's success depends on us. None of the actions from this workshop will happen by magical osmosis. The people around this table must step up and deliver."). A castle guidebook adorned with a glorious aerial photograph and packed with information about the building's history, construction, and contents, which Victor had purchased from the giftshop ("We must be a reference for the industry. Our customers must turn to us to inform and enable."). A walnut coat and umbrella stand with a traditional ball top, courtesy of Daniel ("We require focus not clutter. Distractions are what we don't need. They should be put aside, like a drenched barbour after a countryside ramble."). And completing the array was perhaps the most idiosyncratic item of all: a draft excluder, purloined by Kim ("Problems will beset us like the cold drafts beneath an ill-fitting door. We should block them out, and stay positive.").

The group surveyed their creation. Magnificent ambition, durability, profitability, innovation, personal accountability, customer value, focus, positivity. Eight concepts that would be used as the benchmark to test the rigour and ambition of their strategic purpose.

Craig seized the moment to ram home two concepts that, from his vantage point, the group still found elusive.

"I once lived in the American Midwest," he said. "The how and why is not important." (And, he thought, would get me in endless trouble if revealed.)

124

"But there's a reason for mentioning it now. Shortly after my arrival, I realised the entire country, from coast to coast, seems possessed by this crazy, infectious optimism. A belief, often flying in the face of the evidence, that tomorrow is a better place, and that America reigns in all things but especially apple pie, Hollywood and baseball."

Like a biblical prophet, Craig realised the power of metaphors to bring to life abstract principles. He had a knack of selecting examples that intrigued his audience. Sufficiently familiar that they could relate to his message, but sufficiently distant to take them on a journey of learning and discovery.

"There was a baseball team in Nebraska called the Lincoln Legends. Very minor league, but with a head coach who, if he was here now, would set the room alight with his enthusiasm and passion. I remember sneaking into the training ground one Wednesday evening to watch him preparing the team for their next encounter. He was a small, stocky man called Chuck Gral, and he stood on this battered wooden box so he could at least address his players at eye level. And, wow, could he motivate. His arms flapped like an over-excited eagle, his voice bellowing across the field, perspiration flying through the air as he wiped away at his sodden brow. I figure he saw himself as a wanabee Martin Luther."

Craig placed his palms against the edge of the table, and with one effortless motion clambered onto the table top. Standing next to the diorama, he picked up the umbrella stand and held it aloft, above his head.

"Yet the coach had a blindspot," said Craig. "A single flaw, but it meant the Lincoln Legends languished at the foot of the state league, battered by teams from towns and villages with a fraction of Lincoln's population."

He was now using the umbrella stand as a dynamic prop, jabbing it towards each member of the group as he approached his crescendo.

"He had *no focus*. He wouldn't leave stuff out to dry. Daniel, you spoke about eliminating the clutter. If only the Lincoln Legends coach could have heard your voice."

Craig remembered gate-crashing a pre-season coming of age party for the Legends' star pitcher. Against the backdrop of a swimming pool chockfull with inebriated, raucous, splashing skinny-dippers, he had queued patiently for the barbeque, and taken the opportunity to probe team tactics with assorted members of the playing squad and management. Every person spoke convincingly of the team's central mission and purpose. And yet no two tales were the same.

"I got talking to an up-and-coming new recruit to their playing roster, a gaunt and gangly young man called Eric. He assured me, quite vociferously, that their ethos was to attack and entertain. If their opponents scored a dozen, that wasn't a major problem – they'd chase a dozen plus one. Caution is for wimps, the spirit of adventure must reign. It all sounded wonderfully persuasive."

Craig swung the umbrella stand violently, as if he was Joe DiMaggio slugging for a home run. Adrienne ducked, but still felt the air rush from his lunge over her head.

"Or at least it did until I got chatting with the physio, who told me an entirely different story. A team of such modest capability, he said, couldn't rely on derring-do. There was no place for risky flamboyance that might crash and burn. Steady plodding, no catastrophic errors, and occasionally squeezing a victory while their opponents were napping. That, he said, was the Lincoln Legends way."

Craig held his hands aloft in exasperation.

"Two different world views. Each valid in its own right. Each one has shaped successful sports teams down the decades. But they are entirely incompatible. Incapable of co-existing peacefully within one enterprise. A schizophrenic squad may delight the armchair spectator with its sheer unpredictability, but it won't be lifting any trophies at the end of the season."

"I get the point," said Barker. "We need to work out what's important and stick with it. I like to think our R&D programme has been reasonably well focused. We know we're about polymers. We aren't diversifying into some funky new type of linen for the bedroom valance."

"That was my thinking too," said Spillane. "Are you saying we lack that laser intensity? I'm not sure your analogy is fair. We're not a middle ranking squad of baseball has-beens and never-will-bes. Jeremy is top drawer."

Marcelle sensed the mood of the room turning against Craig, and felt the urge to come to his rescue.

"I think what Craig was trying to say is…" she began. However, her doubts were misplaced. Craig was taking his audience on a journey, and used their muted but growing resistance to segue into his most powerful point.

"Yes, but focused on what?" he demanded, his eyes darting around the room.

"On the things that excite you intellectually? Or the things that matter to those who will part with money in exchange for your goods and services?"

"If we make it really well, I have no doubt they will come," said Barker.

Craig had his opening. But he chose to bide his time, to savour the full effect. He could afford to be patient.

"So let's continue our trip towards the Pacific Rim," he said. "Imagine we're in our brightly coloured tour bus, and we're heading due west from Nebraska towards the coast. And with an occasional twist along the route, we'll eventually hit California. I mentioned Hollywood, didn't I? So form the scene in your mind's eye. There we are, the Xanotek leadership, disembarking on a humid summer's day into the scorching heat of downtown Los Angeles."

"I have absolutely no idea where you're headed with all this," said Barker.

"My friend wanted to break into the movies," continued Craig. "He used every trick short of extortion to persuade a glitterati of moguls and bigwigs to privately fund his venture, and – because he had a fast mouth

– he assembled a cash pile sufficient to attract an Oscar-nominated screen writer, hire a production crew, book out one of LA's finest lots for two months, and sign up Trevor Slattery for the lead role.

"He had this unique vision for the end product – an epic biopic romantic comedy in the style of a Western caper, set aboard the supply ship to an intergalactic cruiser en route to the third universal war. Packed with pathos and bathos, with unbearable tension, with threat and recovery. An emotional rollercoaster. Extraordinary costumes, wondrous backdrops, an operatic score, plot twists galore."

Craig paused for breath.

"And…?" said Adrienne, puncturing the silence.

"And no-one went to see it. Almost literally no-one. Less than a hundred thousand dollars gross takings during its first three weeks on general release. The cash flushed away, beyond recovery, beyond redress."

"Because the problem was…?" prompted Marcelle.

"Because the problem was," said Craig, "it wasn't *for* anyone. The geeks couldn't fathom the romance; the chick lit brigade weren't into the war story; the adolescents out for a laugh hated the sci-fi.

"My friend had failed his most basic duty as a story-teller, as a producer, as the custodian of someone else's money. Which is to have at the forefront of your mind a clear image of your intended audience."

Craig plucked the castle guidebook from the array, and waved it above his head like a South African soccer fan parading a vuvuzela.

"You speak of being the reference for your customers, of being the people to whom the public turn. But do you understand your customer? Can you describe them? Precisely not with vague generalisations. Describe them as if they were standing before us, in this very room, just next to the fireplace. What do they want, what do they need, what can they not currently obtain? Crack that question, and only then do you deserve to be labelled top drawer!"

The jet of steam billowed up the spout until it was funneled into the narrow hole at the start of the whistle. At this point it abruptly contracted, forming a small pressure pulse as it hit the second whistle wall. The physics of the pulse caused the exiting steam to form vortices, and generated the wailing hiss of a tortured banshee.

Or, more prosaically, announced the kettle had now boiled, and coffee could be served.

Ward collected two mugs from the upper aluminum shelf and spooned Nescafe Gold Blend into each. With the boiled water added, he took a tupperware container from a nearby drawer (the fading black ink scrawled on the container lid spelt out 'sugar'), and shovelled the contents into the first cup until it accounted for at least one third of the brew's volume. He knew the fastidious

Shaw preferred his coffee unadorned. But Ward himself needed the energy kicker. Surveillance involved lengthy stretches of tedium, very occasionally punctured by a significant action or comment from the target. And their work today had certainly involved an excess of the former.

"I still don't get the meaning of the numbers in *Lost*," he said.

"I don't think there was a definitive explanation. But they sum to 108, and I remember from my time in Asia that number is important in Hindu and Buddhist mythology."

"It still doesn't work. Why do the numbers bring such misfortune and suffering to Hurley? He's one of the good guys so it can't be karma."

"Maybe it's the ultimate *deus ex machina*."

"The ultimate what?"

Shaw was blowing gently across the surface of his drink to cool the temperature, but years of indulgence had hardened Ward to the effect of boiled water, and he had already wolfed and slurped his way through most of the mug's contents, at which point he exhaled loudly.

"Lots of coffee. Can be the best part of the job," he mumbled to nobody in particular.

He glanced down at his notepad. During the past half an hour, he had recorded only a handful of comments. Across the top of the page, he had scribbled the items retrieved from around the hotel at the commencement of Craig's latest task: urn, rock, ticket, cellphone, mirror, guidebook, umbrella stand, draft excluder. Elsewhere he had recorded any comments that might carry meaning or relevance. *Lifting trophies and movies – intended audiences* had both been jotted on the page, with a couple of wavy lines connecting these concepts to items in the diorama.

"That's why I didn't go into business. It's bad enough having to listen to this nonsense, without having to say it," he said. "Let's hope the higher-ups find what they need from the tapes."

He looked over to Shaw for affirmation, but his colleague was otherwise occupied. A pair of ramblers was sauntering into view from further up the track, and Shaw was watching their progress with unblinking eyes.

The elder of the two was setting a brisk pace, despite the burden of an oversized backpack. His companion, possibly his grand-daughter, was struggling to keep up, and from the transparent nature of her sighs and glares seemed to be reflecting on the long list of alternative ways she could be spending an autumnal afternoon. As they drew closer to the van, the grandfather accelerated almost to a canter. He was now a full minute ahead. Shaw crouched down, so that neither rambler would be able to tell the van was occupied. The elderly man was now peering over his spectacles to make out the words on the side of the van.

His grand-daughter yelled at him in a belligerent, sarcastic tone. "Sewage specialists! And there I was hoping for an ice cream."

The elderly man was now tapping on the side door of the van.

"Is anyone there? We just need to check directions. Hello?"

Shaw and Ward were silent, motionless, save that Shaw eased back the safety catch on his pistol. Both of them balanced on their haunches like wild tigers waiting for the perfect moment to pounce on a zebra herd. They knew they had to protect the mission without compromise or scruple. If that means a couple of hikers ended the day in a shallow grave, that would be an unfortunate outcome, but neither partner would feel obligated to dwell on the philosophical or legal issues raised.

"Is it open?" asked the girl. "I'm so thirsty. If no-one's there, perhaps we can look around for a drink... "

"Locked tighter than your mother's purse," said the elderly man, straining to look through the side window. "Sure seems to be a lot of hi-tech stuff going on for a sewage van."

The girl scowled with the contempt felt by every frustrated teenager throughout the millennia at the incompetence of their elders.

"Next stop, you owe me a Pepsi," she cursed, as the man tightened the fasteners on his back pack, and turned to continue the trek. "And not just one."

As he hauled himself back into an upright position, Shaw clapped his hands against his midriff in relief. Bullets fired at close range were such a sloppy business. Ever since Tripoli, he'd had an allergic aversion to clean-up duties.

Chapter Seven

Located in:

Malkin Castle

"So let's recap the progress we've made during our first day," said Craig.

It was now dusk and the team had been grafting for over ten hours. The Upper Hall has been transformed from a room of sombre grandeur into a place of frenetic energy. As the work had intensified, jackets had been removed, ties loosened and sleeves rolled up. And the room's walls were now obscured by a morass of flip chart pages.

Each sheet contained essential information that had emerged from the discussion. On one or two, important numbers had been transcribed in massive script, sometimes underlined and with an exclamation point for emphasis. Others showcased graphics about the company or its marketplace – a pie chart here and a line graph there. And others highlighted key insights or conclusions in annotated form using bullet points. Craig and Marcelle had been busy throughout the sessions with multi-coloured marker pens to ensure nothing substantive was overlooked.

Craig knew the importance – in workshops as in movies – of a powerful ending. The opening day had been intense and occasionally uncomfortable. At times, he had sensed the barely contained jitters among the participants about where it was ultimately headed. Sometimes the conversation had veered from one opportunity to the next like a rampant bull as Craig had interjected with a wild challenge. The concluding slot was his chance to corral the miscellany into a coherent shape. To present a potent summary. His task now was to bring together numerous random strands of thought and forge a memorable crescendo. Marcelle hit play on the music system, and the opening chords of *An der schönen blauen Donau* once again drifted around the room, lending added drama and emotion to Craig's remarks.

Craig jumped onto a chair so he could tower over the group. He breathed in deeply in readiness for his oration, barely able to contain his excitement. It was for moments such as this that he lived. His forehead was awash with beads of sweat. He paused for a moment to allow expectations to build, like a headlining actor revelling in the moment of his entry onto the stage. The glare in his eyes commanded attention. His raised his hands fractionally to indicate he was about to commence his remarks. That was sufficient. His charisma infused the hall and there was no need to gesticulate wildly like a street preacher berating Saturday morning shoppers.

As he began, Marcelle lowered the volume of the background music, but decided not to mute it entirely. The harmonies created a haunting, atmospheric backdrop that lent even more authority to Craig's commanding tone.

"What a journey we've been on together today," said Craig. "We've studied inspirational organisations and marvelled at their courage, their obsession with customers, and their determination to deliver.

"We've looked at the nature of our society over the years ahead, and contemplated the shape of the world in 2025. We've explored the technical factors that make your new polymer so potent. And we've selected eight objects with properties that should guide Xanotek's future, properties which Marcelle has listed on this first sheet so they remain at the front of our consciousness: magnificent ambition, durability, profitability, innovation, personal accountability, customer value, focus and positivity. Those were our conclusions this morning."

Craig hopped down from the chair and moved to the back of the hall. The Xanotek team followed him diligently, as obedient European tourists move in unison behind their guide during a whistle-stop tour of the British museum. He was now adjacent to the output from their most recent sessions. The delegates gathered into a semicircle so each had an unobstructed view of Craig. Kim Draham was carrying a small spiralbound notepad, and was furiously scribbling key words from every sentence he uttered.

"We spent this afternoon immersed in the market information my team has been gathering about the use and abuse of polymers throughout the world. This first sheet segments the market into all its constituent parts and contains estimates of the dollar potential of each one. And the numbers are mind boggling – just look half way down the list. Sports shoes: $900 million, suitcases: $700 million, seat belts: $55 million. These are not even your major marketplaces, yet the polymer potential in western Europe alone quickly approaches $3.5bn."

The next sheet contained a depiction of the supply chain in each segment, developed – under Craig's facilitation – during the central arc of the afternoon's session. Each segment of the market had been split into the stages of the chain that turned raw materials into a marketable end consumer product. The parties playing in this sandpit were legion – firms that focused on fibres, fabric, weaving, garments, draperies, wholesaling, distribution, retail. Craig's researches in the lead-up to the event had revealed and quantified how disparate players were vying to maximise the advantage of their position at the expense of those earlier or later in the supply chain. One firm was basing its future competitive strength on buying up niche rivals in order to exercise greater control; another was investing heavily in automation, driving out costly and unreliable human labour. Repeatedly, the message had been heard that margins were tight, innovation rare, and competitive differentiation near impossible. Firms without a clear direction were being squeezed out. The legion of leaders flying too close to the sun, and crashing back to earth amidst tangled wreckage.

"And over here we have profiles of the half dozen companies which have sustained the greatest levels of success since the turn of the century," said Craig.

"As we saw, my team has delved into the accounts far enough to analyse margins and productivity at a product line level. And here are the firms that have delivered the greatest value creation over the period. Not the household brand names who have been undercut by Asian competition. But firms that have displaced an incumbent powerhouse in a discrete sector with a superior offer. Like Chaudhri Global Solutions which is now the dominant supplier of benchmarking tools to the transport sector, or New Zealand's Garwood-Morgan Corporation which pioneered online property search with unparalleled interactive features.

"The entrepreneurs behind the Garwood-Morgan success story each made nearly a billion dollars at the time of flotation and now own a cluster of Caribbean islands where, according to rumour, the global elite can flee for twenty four hours of uninterrupted debauchery with all mobile devices securely stored in a grade five safe at the point of disembarkation."

Craig wandered over to the far wall, where he had earlier suspended a banner just below the beams proclaiming the words *SWOT analysis*. The Xanotek executives dutifully followed. This time, before continuing his remarks, Craig clambered up onto a window ledge and used a lead pipe that ran horizontally just above the arch's keystone for balance. The window was central to the wall; all around him hung flip chart sheets summarising the 'SWOT' discussions.

"I'm sure you'll all remember the conclusions from our closing session," said Craig, the perspiration now sliding down his neck and starting to discolour his collar.

"Strengths: we identified four areas where we excel, where we are so far ahead of the sector that no amount of investment by others would close the gap in the near future. And foremost among these is a polymer that, as tests prove, is almost invulnerable; that's a genuine step change ahead of even the most durable alternative available anywhere else in the world. Weaknesses: three serious constraints that complicate or impede our progress. And top of that list is scale. We simply don't have the muscle or manpower to fully exploit every good idea that's within our sphere of influence, and we don't have the appetite to recruit in a hurry lest we find ourselves infiltrated by any agents of the opposition, who might have got wind that we're on the verge of something exceptional."

Craig swung around so he was facing the wall on the far side of the window. As he built towards his peroration, he was no longer gripping the lead pipe. He needed both arms available so that his entire body could be deployed to give emphasis to his remarks. Each assertion was now being reinforced by the trademark banging of his right fist against his left palm. At last, he had released that street preacher spirit, and given it full voice.

"So we turned to the opportunities," he said. "And here are shown the five that ranked highest according to the criteria we agreed. Five opportunities where there seems to be a large and growing marketplace. Where the current suppliers are vulnerable to a new entrant. Where our polymer offers an advantage that will be highly prized. Where the customer will be willing to pay a premium for products made using our technology. And where, if we execute our plan robustly, we could be shipping product within three months. These are all serious, credible opportunities which have the potential to turn this business from a bystander to a champion. We should all be standing that little bit taller for being part of the team that, at last, articulated them."

Craig pointed at Victor Jones. "Victor, remind the group. What was the first opportunity?"

"Extreme sportswear," announced Victor.

"You bet-cha," replied Craig. "New generation outfits so that skiers and sky divers and deep sea adventurers can pursue their dreams with clothing that's finally fit for purpose. Possible sales of $70m in the next eighteen months. Next?"

"Hospital uniforms," said Marco.

"Better protection for patients and staff against the spread of infectious diseases in the operating theatre. Finally a solution to the paranoia about conditions on the wards. Possible sales of $300 million."

"The military," shouted Adam.

"At last our soldiers can be sent into combat with suitable protection. No need for Kevlar vests that impede mobility and comfort. The outer garments themselves will be enough to reduce the rate of body bags at Brize Norton to almost zero. Also $300 million sales potential."

"Camping," said Chad.

"Tents as safe as houses. Camping equipment no longer a sub-set of the throwaway society. Buy a great looking tent with the peace of mind that, ten years and a few dozen muddy fields later, it will still look as great. $35 million."

"Luggage," offered Kim.

"Release at last from that nagging sense of dread every time you check in at Heathrow. It doesn't matter whether the ground handlers throw your cases or use them for darts practice. They'll still look pristine on the conveyor at the fare end. $80 million."

Craig jumped down from the ledge.

"Five opportunities, all rooted in consumer frustration, that meet a genuine need for a better and bolder solution. And five opportunities where we have the operational and manufacturing capability, with Chad on-board, to turn concept into finished product without ceding our IP."

He was now standing almost toe to toe with Barker, staring at him intently and without blinking. Barker shuffled uncomfortably; if Craig had suddenly grabbed him by the lapels and shaken him violently, he wouldn't have been surprised. He tried to look away, but was unable. He was captivated by the uncompromising force of the strategist's gaze.

"This is where the role of the chief executive comes to the fore," said Craig. "Forget about the paperwork and compliance routines. This is where you, Jeremy Barker, make your mark. It won't be possible to deliver on all these ideas, not in the next one or two years.

"The demands they'll make on your organisation are too disparate. But I'm confident you can deliver one of them. You can bring to market a product for which your customers will pay a premium price. And Jeremy, you and everyone else in this room, will one day wake up extremely wealthy men and women. That's the goal."

Craig smiled broadly and scanned the room so that every participant felt he had personally eye-balled them.

"But the selection must be made carefully, deliberately. Punters who study the form book and know the odds are more likely to win big on the Grand National than casual gamblers who pluck out the runner with the most eye-catching name. Tomorrow we will scrutinise the form book. We will analyse the odds. And, colleagues, we'll make sure you win big and seize the proudest prize. That's when I'll introduce you to the *Power Of Three*: like Ceasar announcing his victory in Zela to the Roman Senate with the words 'veni, vidi, vici', let's see if we can encapsulate your objectives in three pithy statements. As the psychologists tell us, if you want to have impact, if you want to be memorable, then *think in threes*."

As Craig drew to his conclusion, he stretched out his arms in a simulated embrace. "My friends, it's been a memorable day. Our Eureka moment. Our Battle of Agincourt. Our V Day manoeuvre. Our landing on the Sea of Tranquillity. And for these reasons, I say, simply: Thank You."

For a brief moment, there was hushed silence; nobody dared utter the first sound. And then, led by Barker, vigorous and hearty applause. Even Hino, who had been loitering against the far wall, joined in. For the first time, he thought, the team seems emotionally invested about the road ahead. Not only that, they finally seemed to be alighting on a road that would take them in a valid direction.

Beyond the castle's perimeter, inside the *Neil & Neil* truck, Ward ended the recording at the outbreak of clapping. "Battle of Agincourt indeed," he muttered. "I've not heard that mentioned since I was in fifth grade."

"I'm sure you caught the reference to the military option?" said Shaw. "The boss will definitely want to be alerted to that particular development."

Craig rubbed his hands together at the prospect of tucking into the John Dorey with buerre blanc sauce that had just been placed before him by an impeccably mannered waitress who, but for the oversized ring protruding from her nostril, could have walked straight off a Downton Abbey production set.

Two hours had flown by since the conclusion of the day one workshop. Craig was sitting next to Barker, at the head of the vast uncovered oak table that dominated the castle banqueting room. Barker was already on his third glass of 2007 *Grand Cru Bourgogne Pinot Noir*, which was being downed a trifle too quickly for comfort. By contrast, Craig's only compromise with temptation had been to request a slice of lemon in his mineral water. He was pacing himself carefully, aware that his preparations for the second day had barely begun, and he would be requiring an energy boost involving at least 200 milligrams, possibly three or four, to get through the hours ahead.

"Tell me, how did you get into this business?" enquired Barker. "It's not really a line of work that they teach at school."

Craig deadpanned, with well-honed inscrutability. "Strangely, the connection came more from the world of theatre than the world of business," he said, neglecting to reference his debt to his ex-wife. "You may have noticed, but many of the concepts I've been using today trace their roots to producers and directors such as Cameron Macintosh, David Merrick and Mannie Azenberg. I was fascinated by the ways in which they draw in their audiences and fire up their imagination. Broadway shows only sizzle when the audience is one of the cast, when it's prepared to give as well as receive. That has always struck me as the essence of a great business event."

Craig leant towards Barker to allow the waitress to serve up generous portions of Jersey royal potatoes, asparagus, wild mushrooms and baby carrots.

Barker couldn't wait until his plate was full; he was already carving viciously at his filet of beef and smearing béarnaise sauce onto every morsel before sucking it down his throat. Such was the relentless pace that, inevitably, some food got caught at the back of his throat, and he abruptly partook of another generous swig of Pinot Noir to release the blockage.

"Sorry," he muttered, as he spotted Craig gazing quizzically at his behaviour. "The surroundings remind me of college, where it was a question of eat it or lose it."

Craig waved away the matter as being of little consequence.

"Tell me," said Barker, "Hino mentioned something about your involvement with Clifton Oil. I remember one of the engineers in my study set taking a job with their Nigerian operation. Did your remit extend that far?"

Craig winced slightly. His work at Clifton Oil remained subject to robust non-disclosure clauses, and he was already uncomfortable that Hino had obtained the information. Moreover, it was still hard, despite the passage of time, to shake the memory of his bodyguard's twisted corpse, gunned down in broad daylight to "send a message", blood pouring from his shattered neck into Patricia's lap with the ferocity of water from a burst dam.

"I try to ensure my work is a learning experience for my clients," Craig's tone was wistful and non-committal. "And on some projects, it's also a learning process for me."

He paused, unsure whether to continue. But, like a kamikaze pilot, once in flight he found that turning back was not an option.

"In Africa, I learnt that protecting my team is my greatest responsibility. I swore never to place them again in harm's way."

He glanced across to the far side of the table. Marcelle looked divine this evening, and he was proud of the effort she was making to impress their client. She had changed into a layered and flowing off the shoulder evening gown of shimmering crimson velvet. With the low cut of her bodice, Marcelle's newly acquired amethyst pendant necklace was exposed in all its magnificence as it rested against the smooth skin. She was engrossed in an animated conversation about some aspect of current affairs with Adrienne Dodier. The two ladies speaking with such zest and fervour, they were practically falling over one another's words. As Adrienne, the more serious of the two, launched into her next stream-of-consciousness observation, Craig noticed she was gently stroking Marcelle's arm. Marcelle giggled but did not flinch. Craig promised himself that he had learnt from the catastrophe of his break-up with Patricia. Marcelle had shown him unstinting loyalty since coming on-board. No matter the perils and uncertainties of future assignments, he would not – would never – expose her to danger as a result of his own insatiable predilection to stray too close to unknown fascinations, like a moth around a candle flame.

At Adrienne's suggestion, Marcelle was looking upwards, high above the banqueting area, towards the timeless figure watching over the group like a renaissance sentry. Painted by Gainsborough using confident brush strokes and vivid oils, the portrait of the Duke of Argyll cast a disturbing aura across the room. The upper part of the canvas was now obscured by deep shadow, but the brilliant whiteness of the Duke's eyes still pierced undimmed through the gloom, dominant and eerie. As a teenager, Adrienne had regularly escaped from her uncle's violence by hiding within the corridors of the numerous museums along the banks of the Seine. Days spent wandering through the Louvre, squatting on her haunches for an hour at a stretch before the kindly visage of some medieval monarch, seeking solace in the wisdom of the ages. Sharpening what Hino had described as her personal defence mechanism.

"For all its faults, our forefathers bequeathed to us a world worth living in, filled with beauty and order," she said. "I hope that, in another two hundred years, people will look back at our generation and say the same."

Marcelle noticed that a single tear was welling in Adrienne's eye and took a tissue from her sequinned clutch handbag to gently brush it away.

Under the Duke's unflinching and protective gaze, the companions spoke of history and ambition and social change. Marcelle described her pride at witnessing the flowering of Dimala Naidu since she had taken her youthful prodigy from the Chandansar orphanage. Adrienne hinted at the macabre brutality she had suffered in her youth, opening up more fully than ever before, more even than with the fifth arrondissement psychiatrists after the police had busted her uncle's apartment. All the while, Marcelle – like Craig – refused every offer to replenish her wine goblet. Like Craig, she was conscious that, as soon as the festivities were over, and the Xanotek team began to withdraw to their state-rooms, she had duties to perform in preparation for day two.

"Aha," announced Daniel Fricke, patting his ample belly. "Dessert at last."

Panna cotta with a raspberry coulis top, chocolate torte in a shot glass, white coffee ice cream with a hot chocolate sauce; the final course consisted of three mini-desserts on one plate for each guest, with a personal jug of double cream on the side. Marcelle scarcely knew where to begin. Gingerly she scooped a mouthful of the chocolate torte. She noticed that Fricke had adopted a different approach. He had tipped each of the mini-desserts into the middle of the plate, and was using his spoon like a rotating blade to blend the three compositions into a single amorphous mass. Adrienne stared at the concoction with scarcely disguised loathing.

"What?" said Fricke, "It's the combination of flavours that's so explosive!"

In time, the longcase clock rang out its midnight chimes.

Marcelle looked around the dwindling company. Barker had shared his postprandial comments. Fricke had departed hastily to deal with his misbehaving stomach. Adrienne had thanked Marcelle for her attentive listening and expressed her fervent desire one day to meet her protégé Naidu. Craig had disappeared up the spiral staircase on the far side of the keep. The group was finally dispersed.

She stuffed a couple of chocolate mints into her bag and headed in the opposite direction to her companions, back towards the Upper Hall. It was her responsibility to collate the materials from day one, freeing Craig to focus on the day two agenda. He had this conception of an ideal workshop being akin to an operatic score. The pace and cadence needed to shift from the first movement, which had now completed, to the second, which would kickstart in the morning. If the pulse remained constant, it was impossible to move forward. As he had explained to Hino in *Angeline's*, the opening day was about divergence – thinking laterally, imaginatively, openly, without constraints or inhibitions. Everything he and Marcelle said and did, from the exercises to the musical selection, was geared to create this tempo. However the second day was about convergence – decisions, selection, focus.

Marcelle needed to remove the dozens of sheets hanging from the walls, and assemble them into a data pack for continuing reference. When the Xanotek team entered the Upper Hall in a few short hours, they would be transported into a different world from the one they had earlier vacated. At the moment, being in the room was like being inside the gigantic brain of a Nobel prize-winner. Tomorrow, a different mood would be nurtured - one that drew from the podium achievements of sporting superstars. Marcelle would be covering the walls with posters of Joe DiMaggio and Bobby Moore and Ayrton Senna and Joe Frazier in their prime. A flag of the Olympic movement would be fluttering from the rafters. Even the aromas and musical accompaniment would be changed. Raw herbs with a higher oil content to recreate the musty, slightly sweaty atmosphere of the gymnasium. And there would be no more Strauss. Now it was time for Vangelis' *Chariots of Fire*.

Marcelle flipped open her laptop and rested it on her knee. Microsoft Office fired up. With practised ease, she created graphs and tables and interlocking shapes to record the information that was dangling in ramshackle fashion on the A1 sheets all around her. Her challenge was to take the essentials and compose a narrative that was flowing, accessible and highly visual. Within thirty minutes, the task was complete. She scanned back over the document and tweaked a couple of points where items needed greater emphasis. Finally it was ready for encryption. Once she was satisfied the document was fully secured, she emailed it to Craig – he would by now have the running order for the second day formulated to his satisfaction, and be working up the details. Next she produced a dozen copies using the portable printer she had left on the raised dais. She had never been tempted to take the easy route of handing a memory stick to the hotel concierge to whom the print authority would be duly delegated. The work in which Craig was engaged was inevitably too commercially sensitive for third parties to warrant her trust.

Once the copies were assembled and stapled, Marcelle unfurled the Olympic flag. The beams were at least twelve feet off the ground, and she hadn't packed any scaffolding, but she should be able to reach up through balancing a side chair on top of a table. She kicked off her high heels and hitched up her evening gown – not the most appropriate garb for redecorating a large room. Somewhat precariously perched on the arms of the side chair, and at full stretch, she was just about within reach of the beam. It was now possible, given a smattering of both luck and judgement, to wrap a loop of rope around the beam, and the task would be done.

As she picked the best spot to fix the rope, the light caught an object a couple of feet further along the beam. Straining her shoulder muscles, she hauled herself up until her eye line allowed for a closer inspection. It was a fraction of the size of a mobile phone, made from nondescript black plastic with occasional chrome. There were just a couple of distinguishing features: the cap of a battery compartment, and the tiny capacitive membrane connected to its almost invisible transmitter.

Marcelle shuffled along until she could reach out and grab the object. She cradled it in her left hand and checked it from all angles. It was immediately recognisable as a medium-range covert listening device. The room was bugged.

PROLOGUE REPRISE

Inside his stateroom, Craig readied himself for the task. He was now in his element, surrounded by information and insights from numerous sources. During a break in the afternoon session, he had sneaked a moment to rearrange the room in a manner more conducive to his state of mind. Pillows and cushions had been tossed into a heap in the corner, alongside the superfluous lamps, and the mattress had been pulled off the bed, and now leant against the wall in the manner of a mutated flip chart. Over the next fifteen minutes, Richards plastered both mattress and wall with almost a hundred separate pieces of paper until it was a kaleidoscope of analysis – extracts from reports on polymer technology, meeting notes, personnel profiles, and bullet point summaries of the key issues which he and Marcelle had made at the end of every session since the early morning kickoff. At the centre of his kaleidoscope, he attached to the wall a Financial Times cutting from twelve months beforehand, headlined "Barker returns to Japan for additional fundraising."

The next hour would be crucial to a successful outcome for the event. Craig always felt a frisson of excitement when he reached this stage, and in addition now felt a slight moistening at the nape of his neck as a couple of beads of sweat bubbled out from a pore. He needed to be fully alert, nothing could be overlooked if he was to justify Hino's trust. There was no margin for casual error or misjudged conclusions.

Craig was particular about the environment that best released his creative imagination. The lights needed to be slightly dimmed; an eighteenth century symphony needed to be playing in the background (today, he had chosen Haydn's Maria Theresia). And one thing more. In his ensuite bathroom, Craig draped a towel across the floor tiles, and knelt down next to the sink. Briskly, he wiped some tissue paper across the glass surface of the vanity cabinet to ensure it was dry, and then tipped out two hundred milligrams of white powder, which he inspected carefully, removing a small section where the particles had clumped together. Using a hand mirror, he arranged the powder into two lines, each a few inches in length, and continued adjusting the contours of the lines in pursuit of perfection long past the point of practical effect. The product was remarkably fine. The lines glowed with beckoning purity, and seemed to dance like desert sand dunes in a light breeze. Finally he used a cut straw to ingest the cocaine, yelping uncontrollably and wide-eyed as the drug was sharply absorbed through the lining of his sinuses.

The effect was like an adrenaline surge; every moment of time came alive with power and significance. For a moment, Craig imagined he was an Olympic sprinter, revelling in the adoration of the spectators, lifting his arms in the middle of an eighty thousand seat stadium as every man, woman and child in the crowd rose to their feet in thunderous applause. He was the renowned Craig Richards, no less, the Usain Bolt of the corporate strategy world. As he plotted and schemed, the multitudes gazed on, expectant, dazzled, overawed.

Pumped up from his ingestion, Craig brushed the residue of powder into the sink, and headed back into the stateroom to contemplate his kaleidoscopic display. But as he turned the corner, a sixth sense told him something was amiss, moments before his ears caught the light drubbing on fingers against fabric, and his eyes made out a darkened figure seated on the camelback.

"How the..." began Craig.

"Be quiet and sit down," said the stranger, motioning towards an exposed section of hard wood floor.

"Who are you? What are you doing?"

"I'm not going to ask again. Be quiet. Sit down."

Craig ignored this entreaty and instead marched toward the rolltop desk. He had overcome his initial astonishment at the intrusion, and was now intent on seeing the perpetrator ejected with menaces from the premises. Grabbing the receiver, he was about the dial the receptionist, when the stranger rose purposely from the sofa. He was pointing a Browning 9mm pistol directly at Craig's temple.

"It's got a suppressor. So I suggest you forget about playing the hero, and do as I say. Which is to sit down," he said.

Craig returned the receiver to its cradle, and raised his hands to indicate compliance with the instructions. Finally, at the third time of asking, he sat cross-legged on the floor.

"I'm pleased we have an understanding," said the stranger. "Head shots can be so messy."

"What's this all about?" asked Craig, cautiously.

"All this nonsense you've been taping to the wall," said the stranger, looking across the room. "It all looks very elaborate. And I suppose you brainiacs need to do your stuff to justify your fees. But from now on, it's not your way any longer. From this point, you'll be doing what I say."

At which point the stranger eased the stopper from the whisky decanter, and poured himself a generous measure of 25-year-old single malt Macallan.

Being cooped up all day in a small van had given Ward slight cramp in his leg muscles. He lightly massaged the side of his thigh to stimulate blood circulation and loosen the muscle. Hollywood scripts tended to depict surveillance operations as the ultimate in glamorous detection; a ten minute wait and then bingo. In reality, it was a chore. Hour upon frustrating hour holed up in conditions that would outrage the animal rights brigade if used for the transportation of cattle. Unable to stand straight, unable to sit properly, listening to the dreary ramblings of strangers. For this he had endured the rigours of Sandhurst, seven mile pre-dawn sprints through torrential rains and biting winds. For this he had redoubled his efforts whenever Captain Phillips, his commanding officer, had berated him to tone up or get out. To spend days eavesdropping on the hesitant stutters and fatuous non-sequiturs of everyday human conversation.

"So, tell me about your day," he ventured.

"You tell me something," answered Craig. "You tell me what this is all about. Money?"

Ward snorted. "Here, please, take one," he said, holding out a second glass of Macallan. "It'll help you relax. Because here we are. Me and my buddy Craig Richards. We're just two guys, shooting the breeze like we've been acquainted all our lives."

"How do you know my name?" said Craig. "Look, if it's money, I carry almost nothing in my wallet, and I can't pay you by credit card."

Ward dropped an ice cube into his mouth and used his tongue to roll it around the inside of his cheeks as he sucked the melting water noisily from its surface.

"You're here with a company called Xanotek?" he said.

"I'm here on business, that's true," said Craig.

"Listen, I really couldn't care less about your ethics and client confidentiality and the rest of it. You're running a workshop for Xanotek. They are developing a new generation of polymers. I know about you and I know about them."

Ward was raising his voice for the first time, and to emphasis the final word *them* he crunched on his ice cube with his back teeth, shattering it into a thousand tiny shards.

Craig muttered under his breath.

"I'm not a corporate type," continued Ward.

He was no longer massaging his thigh, but on his feet, patrolling the room.

"I know nothing about your fancy strategies and programmes and stuff. I don't really care what happens with Xanotek. It doesn't matter to me if Barker and his clowns develop a supersonic hat that moonlights as the world's fastest pencil sharpener. If they sell a billion of them in Bogotá and spend the rest of their lives surrounded by silicon-implanted groupies on a private yacht in the Seychelles, well that's fine by me. If Barker's baby face smiles out at me from the front cover of *Fortune* magazine, that's dandy."

Ward was kneeling a few inches from where Craig sat, so close that the strategist could taste the sharp tang of hard liquor every time the other man exhaled. And now Ward was stroking Craig's neck with the cold barrel of his Browning.

"I want you to drink up," he said. "Because I really want you to remember what I'm about to tell you."

159

Craig did as he was bidden and sipped on his Macallan. His mouth was parch dry with the tension of the moment, and the whisky tasted like battery acid. Ward was rotating the tip of the Browning around Craig's ear as if it was a scientific instrument used for measuring the contours. Then, he jabbed it arbitrarily against Craig's ear canal to ensure he was paying attention.

"My friend, I don't care where this journey of yours ends up," he spat. "But one thing does matter very much. When it comes to the new polymers, military applications are out."

With that, Ward smashed the Browning's grip against Craig's temple. Pistol whipped, the strategist collapsed to the floor like a deflated balloon. As he toppled, the tumbler fell from his hand, and crashed against the hardwood floor. As Ward turned to leave, the pool of whisky was still spreading across the timbers, lapping against the strategist's motionless face.

Chapter Eight

Located in:

Roeborne Woods
and
Malkin Castle

Marcelle was crouching behind a low stone wall that ran parallel with the edge of the castle grounds. She was still wearing the crimson evening dress which had caught the eye of many Xanotek executives during dinner, but the folds were now caked in mud, and the material had been ripped in a half dozen places by brambles. Every couple of moments, she was checking the screen of her mobile phone. About 200 yards on the far side of the wall, an Isuzu Reach was parked by a nature trail. In itself, the vehicle was unremarkable. It seemed to belong to a firm of sewage engineers, Neil & Neil. But the truck had been motionless for the quarter of an hour that Marcelle had been monitoring it; no lights on inside, no sign of movement or activity. A works vehicle parked overnight, no different from the dozens left by their owners on any High Streets in any town and village. Except that there was no obvious property in the vicinity that might require sewage services. And also, according to the display panel of her mobile phone, it was the epicentre for intercepting transmissions from the Upper Hall bugging device.

Marcelle's immediate response upon identifying the bug had been to try to notify Craig, but her two calls had been rerouted to voicemail. This was slightly odd since she was sure he would be spending at least a couple of hours in workshop preparation. He had probably silenced his phone to avoid distractions, she reasoned. Hopefully he wasn't so pumped up with coke that the ringtone was muffled into inchoate background noise.

With Craig beyond contact, Marcelle had called Dimala. Her protégé was never off the grid, and despite the late hour he answered her call with customary reliability. Covert surveillance was not part of the fabric of a typical offsite, and Marcelle was still incredulous and slightly breathless as she explained her discovery. Dimala allowed Marcelle to vent, and then focused on practicalities. Horror, anger, fear, curiosity: these emotions were all alien to Dimala's constitution. Given an intellectual challenge, he became animated, but it was a practical and focused type of energy. It was an attitude that concentrated on getting the job done.

Under Dimala's direction, Marcelle had conducted a simple check to establish the types of tamper proofing built into the device, and then she eased open the battery case. In the compartment, barely legible alongside the spring, was an alphanumeric serial code. Marcelle texted the information to Dimala and then carefully replaced the bug on the beam. No sense in prematurely alerting the culprits that their scheme had been rumbled.

Five minutes later, Dimala had rung back.

"Fortunately the device cannot be remotely hibernated, and continues transmission until it is manually disabled. This creates a low-level ping on the castle's servers."

"I think I can guess the next bit," Marcelle had said. "Those servers have just had a visit from my favourite cyber hacker."

The silence suggested that Dimala was a bit perplexed by Marcelle's reference, so she quickly clarified her meaning. "That means you, by the way."

"I have the GPS coordinates of the equipment that's receiving the signal," he had continued. "The transmitter is short range, so it won't surprise you to know that it's being intercepted and processed less than half a mile distant."

"Send them over," Marcelle had instructed.

"What are you going to do with them?"

"I figure I may as well take a look."

The sound of a snapping twig returned Marcelle to the present moment. She looked around, startled, but there was nothing but the hind legs of a small mammal scurrying through the thicket on night time manoeuvres.

She re-checked the display of her mobile phone. She had cross-tabulated the GPS coordinates with mapping software, and there was no doubt left in her mind. The

Neil & Neil truck was the focal point of the surveillance operation. She powered down her phone and dropped it back into her clutch bag, alongside some tissues, her room key, and a half used strip of aspirins. What on earth was happening? she wondered. Why was a humble offsite for an early stage business the subject of covert monitoring by parties unknown? The bizarre circumstances of Hino's peremptory summons, and the lavish fees he had proffered, had at the time caused a degree of apprehension, bringing out Marcelle's natural scepticism before she had been over-ruled. But even she hadn't considered the need to sweep the room for hostile forces beforehand. Was this about Hino's other interests? Craig had made enemies along the way; had one chosen this moment to resurface? Or was one of the Xanotek team mixed up in some murky scheme?

Whatever the explanation, someone had clearly gone to a lot of trouble to mount this operation. Planting bugs, camouflaging a truck and setting up receiving stations, are not casual activities. Marcelle was tempted to approach the truck and gather further information, but decided on balance to retreat with the knowledge she now possessed. She memorised the vehicle registration plate, and then shuffled backwards, away from any danger or confrontation. As she moved, she lost another few velvet threads as the dense pile of a side fold caught against the thorns of a tangled rose bush.

When she returned to the castle, she resolved, she would first renew her efforts to contact Craig. If his phone still went unanswered, she'd either knock on his door, or cajole the night staff into lending her a spare set of room keys. Then it would probably be prudent to involve the police before confronting Hino or Barker. If this was somehow a response to criminal misdemeanours on the part of their client, the matter would have to be handled with extreme delicacy.

Marcelle stumbled from the undergrowth back onto the main road to the castle. She was sweating profusely, and panting as if in the early stages of an anxiety or asthma attack. She was also just a few feet away from a walker heading in the opposite direction. In the darkness, it was impossible to make out any features, but he was burly and striding as if possessed by purpose. Marcelle knew immediately that she must on no account catch his eye; just focus, steadfast, on the walkway ahead. But like the avatar in a video game, her eyes seemed possessed of a mind of their own. For the briefest of moments, her eyelids flickered, and she found herself making direct eye contact. Unshaven and with a cauliflower ear. Not one of the Xanotek party; in fact, no one she recognised at all. But he was staring back, and it didn't take him long to calculate that a pretty lady clad in a mud-stained crimson evening dress and wearing an oversized pendant who was emerging in the early hours from the woods surrounding his parked truck might be someone meriting further inquisition. He grabbed her just above the elbow.

"I'm guessing you're not a hiker," he growled.

"I just lost my way," stuttered Marcelle.

"And I'm Kate Moss."

"I need to get back to the…"

"We can talk about it later," said the burly man. "But for now I need you to shut up."

With that, for the second time in twenty minutes, Ward aimed his Browning against the skull of a strategist. Marcelle ducked out of reach and deflected Ward's assault with her outstretched arm. Her instincts were shrieking that she should flee, but Ward was blocking her return towards the castle. She dived back into the undergrowth, and her hand brushed against a couple of stones that might serve as potent weapons. Turning around, she prepared to hurl the projectiles towards Ward. But with a pace that belied his bulk, Ward was already upon her, clamping his grizzled hand across her mouth until consciousness started slipping away. Once he was satisfied that nobody had observed the encounter, Ward grabbed Marcelle by the waist, and flung her over his shoulder as a boxer might treat a towel after wiping himself down. He grunted at the extra weight but was thankful Marcelle wasn't the twin sister of the neighbour who always managed to sneak a trolley overladen with ice cream and chips in front of him in the Tesco queue.

This was a complication, he figured, but one that could be turned to their advantage. Unfortunately it probably meant he and Shaw would need to defer their planned exchange on whether or not Walter White breathed his last in the season six finale of Breaking Bad.

Craig was struggling to maintain concentration on the second day of the workshop. He was using every decision-making tool at his disposal to funnel the group's cogitation and reflection about the major strategic choices ahead. But his mind kept flipping back to the events of the preceding evening. On a couple of occasions, he had found himself zoning out entirely. He had never before experienced this sensation during an event of such significance, even during the darkest days after his separation from Patricia, when he would often stand before an executive team with his mind mangled by a cocktail of clandestine substances. For a full five minutes, he'd been staring at the Xanotek managers as they expounded on some theory of the future, watching the morphing of their lips into different shapes as the sequence of words were formed, but completely oblivious to the meaning.

"Craig, does that make sense to you?" interjected Barker, noticing the glazed expression that had settled on Craig's face.

After his encounter with Ward, Craig had been out cold for around forty minutes. He had since replayed the incident a dozen times in his mind, trying to make sense of what he had experienced. Threats, intimidation, violence. During his time in Africa, he had twice seen the sharp end of unconventional methods and reprisals, but until today they had never been part of his domestic experience. He had tipped a bucket of ice from his drinks cooler into the bathroom sink, filled the sink with water, and then immersed his head repeatedly in the freezing liquid, but still he could not fathom an explanation. He shot a line of coke up his nose with twice the usual vigour, but that too bought no clarity of insight. Even more frustrating was that Marcelle was refusing to answer her mobile. He cursed her for having the temerity to be unavailable during a high pressured workshop; she should know by now he expected her to be at his disposal regardless of the hour. Then he replayed Ward's parting shot, "When it comes to new polymers, military applications are out." On the surface, a brazen and unambiguous instruction. But Craig had a dozen questions arising, and no way of pursuing them.

Craig then worked until three o'clock on his Day Two preparations, at which point he crashed out under the cumulative impact of the head injury and his day-long exertions until the searing blare of his wake-up call. Sixty minutes elapsed before the workshop recommenced; sixty minutes during which Craig repeatedly failed to locate Marcelle. This was no longer a matter of her wilfully placing herself beyond his reach during the depths of nightfall. She was neither in her stateroom, nor the breakfast area, nor the Upper Hall. Nor the spartan room in the cellars which, on advice from an advertising agency, had been rebranded as a gymnasium after the addition of two rowing machines and some weights.

Craig could no longer allow himself to get distracted or preoccupied with Marcelle's movements. He would have plenty of opportunity once the workshop concluded to discipline her about her AWOL status. He still had to devote twenty concentrated minutes to finalising preparations for the morning's crucial discussion. He had to rehearse his opening remarks, adorn the flipchart sheets he would be using to facilitate the opening exchanges, and remind himself of the criteria and facts he would deploy to shape the discussion. Marcelle was compartmentalised for now. Her disappearance was frustrating and bizarre, but not his immediate priority.

One regulation that Craig ruthlessly enforced at workshops was the disabling of mobile phones for the duration of the event. So as the Xanotek executives filtered in for the allotted start time, he allowed himself just one final furtive glance to see whether Marcelle had attempted contact. Nothing. He grimaced, apologised to the group for his assistant's absence, and powered down his phone. In passing, he had spotted an incoming text from Dimala, but that would need to await the first break. So Craig launched the second day oblivious to Dimala's desperate overture: "Mr Richards. The room is under surveillance. Marcelle contacted me last night after she discovered a bugging device. I think she was making some investigations, and now she's beyond reach. Please advise what I should do."

"Does that make sense?" repeated Barker.

"Yes, yes," said Craig. "I'll write up the main points. Eh, perhaps you could just summarise in a few words?"

"Fine. You see the 'opportunities' sheet, the one that itemised extreme sportswear, hospital uniforms, the military, camping and luggage."

Craig shimmied over to the list.

"We have been looking through the data pack that your team prepared on each of these sectors, and there's some fascinating information."

Adrienne took over. "I have a bit of a reputation in present company for being obsessive about details," she said. "Whoever compiled these documents has managed to obtain a lot of information that's not easily available, and certainly not in the public domain. Some of the net sector spend statistics would almost have required direct access to the general ledgers of the main players in the marketplace, including government procurers. Are you sure you haven't employed a software hacker on your extended team?"

Craig shook his head sheepishly. In all honesty, since Dimala's arrival, he had delegated the market analysis in its entirety to Marcelle's supervision, leaving him somewhat remote from both the methodology and the sources. His edicts had simply been, firstly, to get the job done, and secondly, to make sure he looked impressive. Hopefully, with the enthusiasm and naiveté of novices, neither had overstepped the mark?

"Anyway, a number of us have been struck by the vast numbers involved in the military arena. I guess we're so accustomed to talk of peace dividends and new world orders and the closure of British regiments that we've lost sight of the big picture," said Adam.

"There's also a big picture in camping and luggage," stuttered Craig awkwardly, nervous about the direction the debate was taking.

"Look at this on page seven," said Marco. "I think you need to put this on the chart. $1.7 trillion spent every year on armed forces around the world. And that isn't even one of your unsourced statistics. That's direct from the Stockholm Research Institute."

"I think we also said that at least a $100 million is spent on extreme sportwear," Craig pointed out. "It might not be $1.7 trillion, but it's enough to guarantee each one of you a comfortable retirement."

It dawned on Craig that authority in these sessions was hard won and easily forfeited. His earlier lapse in focus was now haunting him. He was powerless to resist the group's momentum, even had he been so-minded. He felt impotent and puny. Now that the group had latched onto the military option, there was no prospect that Craig might engineer a change of direction. He might as well stand in the end zone of an American football field, urging an oncoming stampede of attacking players to turn tail before achieving touchdown.

"It's been a jaw dropper for me," said Marco. "I understood Japan was virtually pacifist since Nagasaki. But they spend over $50 billion. And they still barely make the top ten in terms of defence budgets."

"Now obviously a lot of the spend is outside our sphere," said Victor. "Nuclear warheads and aircraft carriers and munitions and the like. But look at this information here. There are about ten million soldiers on the planet. Add in fighter pilots, the navy, reservists, field engineers and medics and so forth. You've soon got almost fifteen million personnel needing protection."

Craig could hear a siren voice at the back of his cranium, chanting "military applications are out" as if it was some ancient ritualistic incantation. To hell with that, he figured. I'm a professional. I'm being paid to give the best advice and assist them reach the best decision. That's how I've built my reputation. I can't abandon my integrity at the first sign of peril; even young chickens fight to the last breath when there's a fox loose in the hen house. On the other hand, neither am I being paid to lie prostrate in a pool of whisky with a raw swelling on the back of my head. And what if Marcelle's disappearance is connected? Even if I take risks with my own wellbeing, is it right to jeopardise her safety?

He tried to reassert structure and control. "My role here is to ensure your assessment is within an analytical framework. Market size is a good start, but it's just one among many criteria. Let's see if we can identify the spectrum of other factors that are pertinent. What else informs the process of comparing and contrasting opportunities?"

He wrote *criteria 1 – market size* on the chart.

"I guess *future growth rate* should also be on your list – so is that number two?" said Marco. "No sense investing in a market that's about to fall off a cliff."

"Good point," said Craig. "If your business was horseshoes, then the invention of the internal combustion engine was a disaster for you. It didn't matter how great your craftsmanship; your market had just disappeared."

"With all the news from East Phoenicia, I don't think soldiers will go the way of horseshoes for a while longer."

"What about a strong reason to buy?" said Barker, loosening his collar. "Yesterday, Mr Strategist, you were telling us about how difficult it is to switch customers from an existing supplier. Unless, that is, you are offering something new and demonstrably better. Cheaper, more durable, more reliable. If you're not making a step change, inertia reigns. Buyers, you said, are too busy with their priorities to embrace the hassle and risk of changing horses unless they have to. But if you offer them a strong reason, it's happy days. So put *criteria 3 - customer motivation* on your paper."

"And you don't get much better motivation than this," said Daniel.

He held aloft a page of recent press clippings that Dimala had included in the data pack. There was a front page headline in the Daily Mail: 'They didn't equip my son for combat – now he's dead', a thundering Times editorial on the callous disregard of the frontline by Whitehall bureaucrats, and some heavily censored photographs showing the aftermath of an improvised explosive device that had been triggered by a teenage suicide bomber when unwary troops had arrested her in Helmand.

"No politician wants the press labelling them as murderers. Our polymers offer an escape from the anger of the braying tabloids. It's like liberation!" continued Daniel. "It's hard to think of a better motivator than: Buy our product. Or else you'll have the paparazzi at your front door. Before being sent off to Alcatraz."

"And the technology will work to perfection," said Barker. "When we've refined the polymer and customised it to be woven into service uniforms, they will be all but impervious to shrapnel and bullets. If the politicians aren't convinced, wait until the mothers find out. You'll have never seen a lobby group like it!"

Craig needed a rain check. Matters were moving too quickly, and he felt devoid of a coping strategy. He was like a raft, buffeted about by the elements, and his occasional interventions were feeble to the point of irrelevance. He must try, once more, to locate Marcelle; what on earth did her absence symbolise? He needed to weigh up last night's threat; was it just a warning shot, would it really be followed through? Was it perhaps – conceivably, hopefully – an hallucination, and his throbbing temple was in reality the result of a graceless and blundering fall? Did he trust Hino sufficiently to share with him the gunman's caustic remarks – and, if he did, how would Hino react? Would that expose the entire group to a higher level of personal jeopardy, and did he have the right to make that call on their behalf? He could not plot a coherent way through this maze while simultaneously trying to moderate the most salient stage of the workshop so far. A quiet room, with the support of either strong herbal tea or maybe something more illicit, should bring a degree of clear-headedness to the confused morass of issues and scenarios.

"This is good progress," he announced. "So let's call a halt at this point. I'm bringing forward the morning coffee break so we can celebrate this substantive milestone before we contemplate the next stage."

And with that he bounded out before any of the delegates had time to frame an objection.

After a moment's silence, Barker said "Maybe the John Dorey disagreed with him."

Craig was sitting cross-legged at the blocked-in summit of the castle's easterly turret. He had vaulted over a permanent railing adorned with the message *Danger Do Not Cross* in large scarlet lettering, so he figured he was sufficiently secluded for the next quarter hour. The prospect of interruption, either by a castle guide or a Xanotek executive, was remote.

What to make of the morning's developments? Even if he wanted to, and employed barrister-like cunning and powers of advocacy to argue the contrary view, it would be hard to stem the emerging conclusion that military applications were technically and commercially an attractive route. Dimala's data pack presented persuasive testimony that the market was meaningful, appropriate and receptive. His best course would be to hope his unwelcome visitor remained ignorant of the outcome for some time. He might be able to bluster something about "interim conclusions" and "further research needed". Craig had no intention, especially after last night, of allowing his workshop moderation to develop into a prolonged engagement. Xanotek would be a lapsed client by the end of the week; a part of the tapestry of his personal history. With luck, he could put a credible distance – of weeks or months – between his team and this event. So that by the time the wider world grew aware of the intended application, he and Marcelle would long ago have achieved escape velocity from the company's hazardous orbit.

Thinking about Marcelle reminded Craig of the urgent need to track her down, one of the other pressing tasks nagging at him. He fired up his mobile, which had been inactive since early morning, and shifted closer to an arrow slit to maximise reception through the thick stone walls. There was still nothing from Marcelle, which was perplexing. If she'd been taken ill overnight, she would surely have left him a communication.

But there was, he finally noticed, a text from Dimala. A text informing him that – what the Hell? – there was a bugging device in the Upper Hall. That, presumably, every cough and stammer from the morning's proceedings was now digitised for posterity at some remote location. That hostile personnel had been poring over the twists and nuances of their latest conversation. Craig felt the perspiration break out on the back of his neck, and swept it away with a quick motion of his open palm. He stared at his hand; it was almost saturated. So much for the option of keeping his persecutor in sweet and dreamy ignorance about Xanotek's 'military option'.

He called Dimala. "I don't have much time. Any word on Marcelle?" he barked.

Dimala hesitated. "Mr Richards," he said. "I have not heard from Marcelle. But there is something else that demands your attention. It happened a few minutes ago, and I don't know what to do."

"What do you mean?" asked Craig.

"Mr Richards, where should I begin...?"

Dimala had not left Marcelle's apartment since their midnight correspondence. Hours after dawn, the blinds were still drawn and a makeshift tent had been erected by draping his bedsheets over the furniture and securing the corners with anything he could locate that was sufficiently solid – a transistor radio, a heavy duty stapler, a paperweight. Ensconced beneath the coverings, he felt safe; concealed from an environment that suddenly was awash with uncertainty and menace. Ignoring hunger pangs that had intensified during the morning, Dimala was resolute. He would stay concealed from unknown marauders until he could be confident, without prevarication or question, about the safety of his environment. Until then, like a galactic explorer returning from the outer reaches, it was uncompromised lock-down. Quarantine.

"Dimala? What's wrong?' Craig spoke into silence.

"Mr Richards. Is it true that someone at Xanotek thinks the firm is like 'a peace lily in a stone urn'? That they are creating a thing of beauty, that it will 'bloom magnificently'? Was 'magnificently' the word they used?"

"That was Adam Peralter's contribution," said Craig. "I set them an exercise to mind shift away from immediate obsessions, and define the characteristics of the organisation they're creating over the longer-term. But how do you know about that?"

"And Mr Richards, did someone else say they are like 'a twenty pound admissions ticket'? Because 'they need to make money'?"

"That was Adrienne. Dimala, where are you getting this stuff?"

"And a coat and umbrella stand? And a draft excluder? And a guidebook? Mr Richards, did all that happen?"

"Yes, those were objects they selected. Dimala, stop telling me what you know. Start telling me how you know it."

"Mr Richards, sir, everything you discussed during your workshop yesterday has been transcribed and loaded onto the internet. It's being replicated from one server to another. I'm looking at a message board in South Korea and there are already three dozen comments."

"Comments? Like what?"

"At the top of the list, sunhwa78, says You're meant to be serious business people. Stop acting like you're in kindergarten and get back to some proper work. 214 likes."

"And you're seeing this on the public internet. Not away from general view in some secure or esoteric corner of the web?"

"It's worse than that, Mr Richards. I'm afraid you've gone viral."

Chapter Nine

Located in:

Ministry of Defence headquarters,
The Angola
and
The Wheatsheaf

The report was densely typed, packed with technical information and almost no space for annotations. Since her appointment at Defence, Katherine Foster had repeatedly asked her civil servants to use double spacing and wide margins when preparing material for her red box. And as a minister with almost no previous experience of the armed forces, who had spent her years on the green benches dodging questions about military policy, she had pleaded for jargon to be red-lined, or cross-referenced to an accompanying glossary. Just another in a legion of petty examples of how officialdom routinely ignored the wishes of a senior Cabinet minister. Sometimes she figured politicians were no more than media-savvy spokespeople for their bureaucrats. A couple of weeks ago, she had spent thirty unnecessary minutes sitting in stationary traffic when her driver made a poor choice at Trafalgar Square, and she whiled the time away doodling titles for her memoirs on the back of an ATM slip. *Don't worry just sign here* was the most apposite so far.

Foster reread the executive summary. In passionless prose it laid out a series of indicators that quantified Britain's military capability and effectiveness. Each seemed to have diminished rapidly since the last election. In common with hordes of fresh-faced backbenchers, she had been somewhat overcome with euphoria at the unexpected victory on polling day, and hadn't appreciated the brutality of the armed forces cutbacks announced in the small print of the Chancellor's emergency budget. Troop numbers, munitions, supplies, transport; nothing had been spared his axe.

"It would have been even worse if I hadn't called in some favours from one of HMT's senior financial analysts," said Cunningham. "You remember the mood. Markets panicky, Chancellor wanting to demonstrate his mettle. And how much easier to chop soldiers, who are trained to obey orders and get the most unreasonable jobs done, than teachers or nurses who are psychologically disposed to kick up merry hell?"

"It certainly limits our options when a crisis pops up like Phoenicia," mused Foster. "Zavrazhnov's spies will have been all over our expenditure programmes. They will smell our fear of confrontation."

"Public opinion is fickle," said Cunningham. "They may be wary of foreign engagements, but national pride runs deep. Humiliation on the world stage is not taken phlegmatically. The mood can turn on a sixpence."

Foster was studying the numbers intently. The names of regiments and categories of provisions meant little. But there was no mistaking the trend. Nor the weight of the 'disadvantages' that had been catalogued by the report's author against each of the non-military options. This would not make for an appetising conversation with the PM.

Cunningham paused to allow the Secretary to absorb the report's headlines. He filled the time with preparing some tea. The Ministry was notorious throughout Whitehall for its old school approach to beverages. The hot water was scalding, in steadfast defiance of the forest of plaintive memos that were circulated weekly by the department's neglected Health and Safety team. Steam rose like a delirious geyser from both teapot and cup. Cunningham sat across the table from Foster, rhythmically plunging an assam tea bag into the darkening brew. But he wasn't looking at his handiwork. He was gazing directly at the Secretary as she read. Out of her peripheral vision, she was conscious of his stare. Not the first time that Cunningham had intimidated her through his passive aggression.

The silence was broken by a light tap on her office door. "Madam Secretary," said a waifish official, "Can I switch on your screen? Another broadcast from the refinery is about to hit the internet." Foster nodded calmly.

The person on the monitor was immediately recognisable as Ted Milner, but this time the camera had been set to shallow focus, allowing more of the surroundings to intrude into view. He had been secured to a cheap low-back office chair using steel cables, and his legs had been bound together with rope. Cuts and bruises – the signs of sustained mistreatment – were visible on his naked arms. Every few moments, he would spasm, but his eyes contained no signs of hope or defiance. Instead they gazed, haunted, into the middle distance. The captive had the abandoned, resigned visage of cattle in an abattoir. In contrast to earlier appearances, the new footage would not be granting him a speaking role: a filthy rag had been shoved into his mouth and was being held in place with both horizontal and vertical stretches of duct tape.

Off-screen, a narrator was reading a script with broken, second-language articulation. "The days of Western Imperialism are over," he announced. "The West is weak while we are strong. It wallows in its fast food and pornography while we rise and conquer. It flaps like a butterfly while we pounce like a scorpion. The future belongs to the resolute. To those who are prepared to make sacrifices and do what is necessary."

Milner's eyes were tightly shut now, his head tipping to one side as if the strain of keeping upright was too daunting for his weary neck muscles. Only the tautness of the cables prevented him from collapsing in a desultory heap onto the dusty grey floor.

"The person you see before you. We are told he is a good worker. A loving husband. And a proud father. But he is an intruder in our lands, plundering our resources without concern for the oppressed citizens of our lands. Which is why we do what is necessary and what is necessary is this."

The narrator's last utterance was slow and deliberative, as he extracted every ounce of emotion from the syllables. The camera panned slightly to the right, bringing him into view. Tall, thin, dressed in camouflage fatigues, with a tightly-wrapped scarf partly disguising his face. And with a Soviet NR 43 combat knife in his clenched fist.

Other sounds were now audible, like the yelps and howls of braying dogs. Only after a few moments did Foster realise with horror the true nature of the noises. As the narrator brandished his weapon, there was a rising cacophony of off-screen encouragement, steeling him for the task ahead. Shouts and chants and now a slow handclap to build the tension of the moment. The moment when Milner would be sacrificed in open view of a worldwide audience. A Sydney Carton for a hi-tech era.

Foster looked down at her report, averting her eyes from the awful denouement. But Cunningham was transfixed. The narrator was standing behind Milner now, grabbing a clump of the engineer's red-brown hair like a farmer might yank at a bail of straw. As he raised his hand, he lifted up Milner's head, exposing the neck to the camera's glare. One final brief pan around the room, and then an unremitting close-up of the victim as the fatal moment approached. His breathing was in short bursts now, his nostrils flaring and twitching as he inhaled oxygen for the final time, his Adam's apple pumping like the baton of a frenzied conductor. And then the grisly climax. The serrated edge of the narrator's blade pierced the skin, plunged into the flesh, and slashed the windpipe in one sweeping motion. The assassin held aloft his bloodied weapon as his victim convulsed and gyrated in terrible death throes. Foster gulped hard to stifle rising vomit. Despite her efforts to avoid directly watching the unfolding drama, the sound of the killing left precious little to the imagination. A British civilian, whose wife and children had been a staple of news reports since the crisis had broken, lay dead and his government had not lifted a finger to deter his captors. Foster knew immediately that matters would not be allowed to rest there. This had been the first day of the defining period of her term.

The waiflike official was once again peering nervously around the door. "Madam Secretary, I have the Prime Minister on the phone."

"Put him through," said Foster, her voice laden with acid. "No pleasantries this time. It's straight to business."

In the background was the Bethesda Fountain, framed by elliptical balustrades, its magnificent bronze angel gesturing her wholesome blessing at the clear water spouting into the upper basin of the sculpture and then cascading into the surrounding pool. To the side, a few teenage climbers were scrambling up an outcropping of glaciated rock. And, dead centre, the big cheesy smiles of Craig and Patricia and the then five-year-old Natalie. Central Park in Autumn. Situated in the heart of one of the world's most aggressive, bustling, hustling cities, but forever an oasis of calm. Happier times.

Craig held the photo up to the light, just a few inches from his nose. The more he stared, the more the details of the scene came flooding back. The diamond and pearl encrusted chandelier earrings that his wife had been wearing that day. The constellation of freckles on his daughter's button nose. The way they looked. How they felt to touch. Their scents. He stroked Natalie's shoulder length hair in the photograph, imagining he could lift up the blonde strands, and twist them gently through his fingers just one more time. His thumb still carried the trace of a tear he had wiped away, and it created a light smear on the surface of the picture.

Craig imagined Patricia next to him in the houseboat, chiding him about his behaviour, berating him for his impetuous nature. "You were told to avoid that assignment," she scolded.

In his fantasy state, even Natalie was unforgiving. "Daddy, you should be more sensible," she chided. "What on earth did you think you were doing?"

Patricia again: "Of course it's never the great strategist who suffers the consequences, is it? Yet again, we see it's those around you that are hurt. It happened to me, now it's happening to your new assistant."

"I love you daddy," said Natalie. "You're my hero. But you're not a superhero."

He slid the photograph back into the rustic wooden frame, and propped it carefully against the arm of the sofa. He stared up at the light fitting. A moth was hovering within its orbit, flapping its wings wildly. The creature seemed confused and distressed. In his imagination, the moth was growing to five times its usual size, then ten times. It was the godzilla of moths. It turned to face him, rasping, hissing, eyes bulging, its wings beating with increasing fury. Craig squinted in wonderment. Then, the moth evaporated before his eyes, transformed into vapour that wafted reluctantly out through an air conditioning vent.

Craig took a glass vial from his trouser pocket and unscrewed the cap. For a few moments he stared adoringly at its contents. The emotional surge – yearning, desire, fear, regret – was almost indistinguishable from the feelings that, a few moments before, had possessed him as he reflected on his estranged family. Then he smoothed some aluminum foil onto the work surface, and tipped a helping of white powder from the vial. With a razor blade, he started to arrange the cocaine into lines ready for ingestion.

"This is a disaster." The high-pitched proclamation of Jeremy Barker resonated through his brain, bouncing around his skull like a squash ball in play.

"An embarrassment." The voice of Chad Spillane.

"And you came with such an unimpeachable reputation." This time, Nobuyuki Hino.

"We certainly didn't expect our laundry to be hung out before the laughing world." Barker again.

Craig studied the lines, finessing the contours with the care of a model railway enthusiast. The lines were like long, thin, undulating Scottish highlands. Two picturesque ranges, with their peaks and valleys and lakes. He imagined a couple of tiny hill walkers with their backpacks and compasses, tackling the challenge of his cocaine munros. Rising at dawn, measuring the gradients, setting out in all weathers to traverse the low-lying passages and attain the summit.

"And where's your assistant?" Spillane was in his head once more.

"She's been absent all morning." Adrienne.

"Has she been leaking our secrets?" Barker.

"What kind of misbegotten operation are you running?" Spillane again.

"If you've betrayed us, you're finished." The last word, inevitably, was Hino's.

What use do I have for the Scottish highlands? thought Craig. They are a fleeting pimple. What I need is the Himalayas.

Leering and determined, Craig emptied the rest of the vial onto the foil, tapping its end to ensure not a single grain of powder was clinging to the inside. Then he remolded the highlands into mountains, gargantuan edifices with soaring elevations and sweeping glaciers. Higher and higher he shaped the peaks. And at the centre of the line, his Everest. A glorious imposing mound of cocaine, dominating the horizon with majesty and grace, until that triumphant, satisfying moment when it would be sucked skyward into the nasal cavity of its master. Craig's eyes were already dilating in anticipation of the moment. Then, with alacrity, his fulfilment. The powder hit him with the force of a Gleasons welterweight. Energy surged through his sinews. No more maudlin preoccupation with bygone years. He was once again Craig the Confident. Masterful. Preeminent. Unchallengeable.

Impatient for new adventures, Craig threw the empty vial into the sink, grabbed his trilby from the cupboard, and – without bothering to lock behind him – exited *The Angola*. He leapt onto the towpath with the exaggerated drama of an Olympic medal winner. Wide-eyed, he surveyed the environment. A few cottages. An abandoned village shop. An old-style red telephone box. Overflowing litter bins. A family of scampering squirrels. And, on the far side of the green, The Wheatsheaf. Without a momentary glance back towards his boat, Craig set off with purpose in the direction of the pub. To his winner's podium.

The Wheatsheaf could have materialised directly from the Casting Central encyclopaedia of traditional village pubs, complete with thatched roof and lightly swinging, hand-engraved signage. Craig barged through the main door, barely conscious of the retired vicar he bulldozed from his path. The pub was already abuzz with early evening activity. Three tradesmen were sitting by the roaring fire in the saloon, exchanging stories after eight hours without a break on a commercial building site elsewhere in town. Waitresses were balancing crockery on improbable parts of their bodies as they navigated towards the dining area. From the corner jukebox, Tom Jones was crooning plaintively. Behind the counter, an overweight barman with unkempt sideburns was fighting a thankless battle to keep his guests simultaneously replenished with ale and entertained with anecdotes.

Craig cursed loudly as he smashed his head against one of the lounge's many low oak beams, but he would not be deterred. His goal was neat double vodka. And the only thing separating him from his shot was the horde of patrons competing for the barman's favours.

At the counter he stared unblinking at the selection of vodkas on display. My God, he thought, they looked thirst-quenching. He felt his torso shiver in anticipation of the alcoholic onrush. His hands shook as he took a £50 from his back pocket and waved it like a chequered racing flag in the barman's face.

"Please wait your turn, I'm busy," said the barman.

"My good gentleman," he pronounced with accentuated pomposity. "Serve me next, and I'll buy a drink for everyone else here assembled, and let you keep the change."

A part-time accountant at the far end of the bar, who had been due to finance the next round, decided the mantle of group spokeswoman fell into her lap. "I don't know who you are," she said, "but that's an offer that works for us."

"Double Smirnoff on the rocks, no tonic," said Craig.

"Seems like you're someone escaping from something," said the barman, as he poured out two measures of liquor and added an extra splash for the hell of it.

"Aren't we all escaping something, sideburns?" said Craig. "It's only a matter of whether you're escaping *from* or escaping *to*."

"I guess so," mumbled the barman. Then, more loudly, "I've not seen you here before. Are you new to town?"

"Just passing through. But it's not about me. Let's talk about you. Is this place yours?"

"You might put it like that. Or at least, you could once I've paid off another eleven years of commercial mortgage."

"Don't think small," announced Craig. "Don't think inside the box. My man, with a product like this, you could have an international reach. Listen to Tom singing *It's not unusual to go out at any time.* So here's the plan. Where? – I think sub-Saharan Africa. Great colonial legacy, an entire continent awakening from its dark ages, a wall of Chinese investment buoying its economy. And when? Don't procrastinate, I say! It's time for the G-force, to be valiant and bold. This is no time for faint-heartedness. It's the day to release your inner Genghis Khan and conquer your demons. Wheatsheaf International

Corporation, listed on the NYSE, sponsor of the next Presidential inauguration, the world awaits."

"I value the opinions of all my customers. But I'd better get back to the pumps if you don't mind."

"Like I said, it's not about me. You think about my words. There's no charge. But another double please before you resume your duties."

With his tumbler duly replenished, Craig surveyed the characters gathered around the lounge, like a pickpocket sizing up his targets. A group of executives who had escaped the tedium of the office for personal downtime before hurrying back to their suburban homes and immaculate lawns. Gawky teenagers on a first date. A loud-mouthed cabal slurping light ale while waiting for the Champions League coverage to commence. Senior citizens chewing down their steak and chips under the mistaken impression that tonight was quiz night. And the three tradesmen.

"Aha," thought Craig, "time to get better acquainted." He tucked a leg of his stool under his arm, and sauntered towards the fireplace to greet the group.

"You planning on joining us?" asked one of the tradesmen as Craig thumped his stool onto the slate floor tiles to announce his presence. The speaker was the youngest of the three, with an uneven fringe cut just above his eye line. His broad Glaswegian accent made his words almost indecipherable.

"I am indeed."

"Do we know you?"

"I think not. But I have need of your services."

With this hint of a commission, the other two companions took more interest in the conversation.

"We're always looking out for people who need our services," said the leather-skinned man to the left of the Scot, as he noisily licked his yellowing teeth.

"You got money?" demanded the third.

"Yes, I have money."

"So what will it be? Plumbing? Electricals? Carpentry? We got you covered."

"I'm on a mission. And a captain needs a crew," said Craig.

"You a developer? Or halfway through a renovation and you've realised how much needs fixing?"

"If the price is right, count us in. And if it's a good site, we can work for the minimum wage and take the rest in cash."

Craig swallowed his remaining vodka shot and leant forward. "I'm not looking for half wits or people that leave their work half-complete. I'm looking for the best. In fact, the best of the best of the best."

"So what's the project?" said leather skin. "Because this doesn't sound like any job I've ever sorted before now."

"It's about a woman," said Craig.

"You say what?" said the Scot.

"She means a lot to me."

"Are you serious?" the Scot was almost yelling now.

"She's missing and it's my fault. And I need some guys who are gutsy and heroic and will never give up. I need people to help me find out where she is."

"Do we look like Amnesty International to you?"

"You look like doughty soldiers. You look like the type who never abandon a cause. That's why I've chosen you."

Leather hands looked up from his half-finished pint. "Is this a set-up? Are we on candid camera?"

"When I called you gutsy, I've never been more serious. And I've never been more desperate than I am at this moment."

"Enough with this lame-brained baloney," spat the Scot. "I've seen your type around the Easterhouse Estates. You use longer, posher words. But I recognise the signs a mile away. The runny nose, the manic eyes. You're a junkie, pure and simple."

Craig was momentarily speechless. The exchange was not progressing as he had pictured in his addled, fevered mind.

"So don't you come in here, interrupting us, telling us your smackhead lies in your piteous smackhead voice."

The Scot kicked out at the leg of Craig's stool and the crack of the strategist's hip bone against the floor reverberated through the lounge.

As he rubbed his pelvis, Craig snarled, "I thought you were gutsy soldiers. That's what I said. Now I see you're nothing of the sort. Non-entities. Cowards. Glasgow's prize coward, that's your name."

Deep within his subconscious, a shrill tiny voice was imploring Craig, where are you going with this? What are you hoping to achieve? But the cry of reason was overwhelmed by the red mist that engulfed his faculties. He staggered to his feet.

Now the barman was re-entering the fray. "In the corner," he roared in their direction, from behind the Thornbridge pump. "I don't know what your problem is. I don't care. Just take it outside."

Craig shouted back, "It's not my fault if you've no ambition."

The Scot had now seized Craig's lapels and was escorting him across the room. "You heard what the man said. We're going outside."

Craig was struggling manfully, but the Scot's clench was vice-like. The effect of the cocaine accentuated the emotion of every step as he was ushered towards the exit, passing by crowds of patrons as if they were the denizens from *Dante's Inferno*, and every yard was another circle towards Hell's vestibule. Treachery, the ninth circle, beset by giants on every ledge, and Satan, waist deep in ice, weeping prodigiously from each of his six eyes. Yes, treachery was all around. From one patron who was kicking him in the shin, sending sharp jolts of pain throughout his body, to another who was calling out, "C'mon, Steve. We need to watch this. It'll be a lot more fun than seeing City lose again."

On the Green outside The Wheatsheaf, Craig put up a half-hearted show of resistance. He waved his fists around in front of his chest, and begged a final time for assistance.

"Marcelle. She's been taken. I have money and I need to find a crew."

But the Scot was pumped up with rage of his own.

"Who's Marcelle? Your junkie girlfriend?" he demanded. "She's better off a long way from you!"

With that he smashed Craig with a perfectly executed jab. The strategist reeled but did not topple.

"That one was for wasting my time," he announced. "And the next one is for saying that me and my buddies are cowards."

The Scot shifted his hips to the right, dropped his rear hand, and bent his knees ominously. Then, without further warning, he thrust his fist in a rising arc at Craig's chin. The uppercut connected with a crack. Craig was lurching now, and only resisted collapse through sheer force of will.

"And this last one is because I just don't like the look of your junkie ass," said the Scot, whacking his cranium against Craig's cranium with the force of a small rock.

As Craig succumbed, he saw his daughter Natalie weeping uncontrollably on the far side of the green, oblivious to the comforting motherly arm draped around her shoulder. She was holding Froggie, the bright lilac cuddly toy that had been her constant companion during times of distress. *That's our bond, our Froggie,* thought Craig. *You and me and Froggie, what a team.* But Froggie was more furry than usual, and more … brown. In fact, more like a bear than a frog. And Natalie was more like a … small boy? Who wasn't actually crying, but gawping, wide eyed and incredulous, at the scene – transfixed with morbid fascination like a front row spectator at a public execution.

Craig grunted, an involuntary response to his pain and confusion. Then he collapsed, unconscious. A toppled scarecrow spreadeagled on the wet grass. His tormentor punched the air in exultation.

"Nearly thirty, and I ain't lost it yet," he chortled.

Behind the melee, the barman had emerged from the pub's side entrance and was engaged in an animated talkfest with a participant who was newly arrived at the scene. Despite his boyish complexion and greasy teenage hair, the newcomer's attire – jet black trousers, reflective jacket, and head gear – indicated he was a member of the local constabulary.

"I'm advised there has been a disturbance," he said, approaching the group.

"I don't think so, Officer," said the Scot, aiming a final discrete kick against the small of Craig's back. "Not here. No problem at all."

Chapter Ten

Located in:

Harpenden
and
A mooring near Windsor

Hugo Cunningham bit into the evergreen Sevillian olive and allowed the peppery juices to trickle across his tongue. He then settled the fruit inside his cheek, and chomped and sucked until he was satisfied that all the nutrients had been extracted, at which point he spat the stone across the lawn and into the rose bushes. He then stretched out across the hot tub, checking the assortment of delicacies on offer, before stabbing at another olive with a toothpick and offering it to his wife.

Rebecca was sitting beneath the tub's waterfall feature, where the jets were the most powerful. It had originally been installed for its massaging properties, which she hoped would mitigate the arthritic back pain which had been her constant companion since her forced retirement from competitive athletics. She now used it compulsively, sometimes for hours at a stretch. It was rare that her husband would return home from Whitehall and not find his wife submerged in forty degree water, her head bobbing on the swirling surface like a football in rapids, barely visible amidst the columns of steam ascending into the night sky.

"Divine," she said as she finished her olive, and allowed herself to be drawn gracefully back into the silky, spongy head rest.

Cunningham laid the toothpick by the control panel, and depressed a couple of buttons. There was a delayed reaction of a few seconds, and then the muzak faded and the jets quietened to a trickle.

"I'm sure you've seen the news reports, that tensions are rising again in Phoenicia," he said.

"I saw the ghastly killing of that poor oil worker," said Rebecca. "There's been nothing else on television since this morning."

"Over the next few weeks, I'm going to need you to be patient. I'll be heavily involved in the British response. Some nights, like today, I won't be home until nearly midnight. On other occasions, I'll need to stay in town, and you won't see me at all."

Rebecca winced at the sharp stab that shot up her vertebral column. This was a sensation she often experienced when the massage jets were turned off. It was as if her pain was a miniature infantry regiment located within her body, and had been waiting to charge forth the moment her defences were down. One of the specialists at the local hospital had tried to persuade her that the problem was psychological rather than physical. It was nonsense, of course. The charlatan should try living in her body for a day; that would show him.

"You work so hard," she said. "You have so much responsibility. And we have so little to show for it."

Cunningham knew where this conversation was heading. When he was invited to join the civil service fast track, around a year before their wedding, both he and Rebecca had assumed their financial worries were over. How different the reality had been over the past ten years. Nearly half his take home pay was swallowed by mortgage payments, and there were still twelve long years remaining before he owned his four bedrooms, free and clear. They had spent a fruitless summer visiting the open days of the half dozen outstanding prep schools within the vicinity of Harpenden, but abandoned the exercise when they realised there was no prospect of affording the exorbitant fees. Rebecca's people carrier was now an ancient seven years; it was costing more to repair each year than to run. And their one indulgence, the hot tub, had become the source of vitriolic wrangling between them when the quarterly energy bill hit the mat.

"We can't think like that," said Cunningham. "Most of the population would look at our lifestyle with envy. In any event, public service is a vocation."

"Most of the population, but not your Cambridge contemporaries," scoffed Rebecca. "Where on earth was your head when everyone else was heading to Wall Street and Madison Avenue?"

"Please, can we leave this discussion to another day? I need a clear head for the next week. I've got an inexperienced minister who can't see beyond the next day's headlines, and a PM who thinks this could be his Falklands moment. And I'm stuck in the thick of it."

"And there you'll go again saving the world. But once it's rescued, there won't be any military bands welcoming you home. Just a pile of bills. You know, sometimes I hide behind the curtain, physically quaking, when I see the postman at the gate."

Cunningham scooped the final two olives from the bowl and placed the largest directly into his wife's mouth. He held the remaining one a couple of inches in front of his eyes, and studied the tiny sediment flecks as if they held the solution to his financial quandaries.

"Just trust me for a little while longer," he said. "Things are underway, and this could be the moment everything comes together to our advantage."

Rebecca nuzzled closer to her husband, and ran her finger along the bridge of his nose. "I've trusted you this long, I might as well give you the benefit of the doubt one final time," she said coquettishly.

Cunningham returned her gaze, watching the shimmer on her skin as the tub's lights progressed through their colour mood cycle, from azure to crimson to white. He had always relished power over money, but with discretion during the current turmoil it might be possible to realise both simultaneously. Like the bridge champion whose innocuous early gambits are only revealed as tactical masterstrokes as the game approaches its climax.

The tranquility of the moment was interrupted as the ringtone on Cunningham's personal mobile sang out through the partially ajar lounge doors and across the patio.

"I should take that," he said, landing a parting peck on his wife's forehead.

Rebecca made no objection to his departure; she was relieved to once again have sole authority over the jet controls.

Cunningham grabbed a towel, and then took his phone from the lounge to his study, which he bolted from the inside. Beyond the reach of potential eavesdroppers. The *bridge* philosophy must now infect every aspect of his behaviour. In tense games, casual errors can multiply with triumph in sight. The moment before victory is frequently the time of greatest peril. As Cunningham organised his hand and prepared his tricks, nothing – absolutely nothing – must be left to chance.

He sat behind his pedestal desk and accepted the incoming call.

"A day of developments for us both," he said into the phone, his voice barely above a whisper.

"I saw they killed Milner," came the reply.

"You can imagine the reaction in Whitehall."

"I could. But I'm not paid to imagine."

"Good. Thorpe asked too many questions. That's why I don't work with Thorpe any more."

Despite perfunctory efforts to towel himself down, a pool of chlorinated water underneath his chair was spreading rapidly across the linoleum.

"Let me give you today's mission highlights," said the caller. "It's important you're aware that Craig Richards let us down badly. From the moment they resumed, all the momentum was towards militarisation."

Which would have been disastrous for Tizett, thought Cunningham.

"We couldn't allow that to happen. So we didn't. Using a fake ID, we uploaded some of the most embarrassing material we picked up through surveillance, and then employed source code algorithms to ensure it went viral."

"I'm guessing Xanotek doesn't look good?"

"They're a laughing stock. If you hadn't been holed up at the Ministry all day, I'm sure you'd have been snickering, along with the rest of the country. Craig's credibility with Hino and Barker has been ripped to shreds; in fact, they are blaming his assistant for the leak. And Xanotek will be too preoccupied with salvage operations to even think about polymer technology. Honestly, I wouldn't be surprised if Hino pulls the plug outright."

Cunningham was pushing aside the clutter from the middle of his desk. His vintage Sholes & Glidden typewriter, one of many beautiful but impractical family heirlooms, was brusquely deposited onto a side table. Once he had carved out enough space, he scribbled the date, 17 September, at the top of a lined sheet. He added some cryptic references, all would be meaningless to anyone but himself, folded the sheet and slid it underneath a model warship.

Below, each leg of Cunningham's chair was now standing in water. But the civil servant didn't notice. He was too possessed by this unalloyed good news.

"Any problems I should know about?"

"Just one. Richards' meddlesome assistant couldn't keep her nose out. We had to take her in."

"Take her in?"

"Best you don't know the details."

"What are the options?"

"We just need to know one thing. Should we press our advantage?"

"Yes. We need Richards completely out of the picture. If that's easier with a captive, get it done. The usual invoicing reference."

Cunningham terminated the call, and gazed out through his study window. Rebecca was using her fingers to supplement the massaging effect of the tub's jets on her bare shoulders. Her eyes betrayed a fragility, a sadness that the book had closed on her days as a revered sprinter, a suppressed terror that her once lithe and toned body was now a source of such agony. Since the turn of the year, she seemed to be wincing more often from the effects of her arthritis. *Hang on there, baby,* thought Cunningham. *Just let me get everything sorted with Tizett. Perhaps then your life will be one long paradise of luxury therapy. Or perhaps we'll bring your whining to a different conclusion.*

Under cover of dusk, Craig had taken *The Angola* far down river from the pub. His bruising was most severe on the right cheek, where the flesh was darkening and swelling as blood escaped from the broken capillaries under his skin. He had lost a chip from one of his incisors, and the rest of the tooth was wobbling, loose and tender. Not his proudest hour.

The boat was moored on a secluded stretch of river west of Windsor. Inside, Craig was preparing scrambled eggs for his newly arrived guest. It had taken him a couple of hours to coax Dimala to abandon the security of the makeshift compound he had constructed in Marcelle's apartment. But he needed every asset at his disposal if he was to make sense of the debacle of the past forty-eight hours. His immediate concern was to locate Marcelle. He was also conscious of the need to implement a damage limitation exercise before the disintegration of his Xanotek workshop entered the lexicon of consultancy mishaps, imperilling his hard-won reputation.

Fear had made Dimala ferociously hungry. Craig had assumed they would talk while they ate together in the galley. However, by the time he had set out cutlery and condiments, the boy had already devoured the entire contents of his plate, and wore the forlorn expression of someone hoping for (but too anxious to request) a second helping. Craig relit the stove.

"Let's check over every detail, one more time," he said. "There must be a clue somewhere, I'm sure of it."

Each word that had passed between Dimala and Marcelle on the fateful night when she uncovered the surveillance was etched into the boy's near-photographic memory. He recalled the precise description of the device she'd located, the words that had passed between them, and the coordinates he'd provided. Of course, there was no evidence in the woods that any vehicle had been recently parked there, let alone its make or model. They would need to identify some other method to trace its origins.

Dimala recounted his narrative from the beginning. Craig prodded at certain elements in case there were further details to uncover. But at the end of the retelling, the main elements were as obscure as ever. Who had planted the bug? How was that connected to the intruder in his stateroom? Why were the hostiles preoccupied with the semi-random brainstorming of an early stage polymer firm? And what had befallen Marcelle in the fateful period after she had spoken with Dimala about her discovery? At this stage, there was no guarantee she was still alive. No, Craig quickly corrected himself. We're a long way from venturing down that particular route.

Marcelle had been a muse and inspiration during some of his darkest moments. After the collapse of his marriage, he had thrown himself into his work, but without care or focus. Many of his long-established clients had threatened to pull their business unless his engagement was more professional and reliable. Marcelle's first week had been spent organising his delivery machine; understanding who he was supporting, the terms of reference, and the upcoming schedule of output. However her value went much deeper. As she apprehended his dark side, she initially sought to vanquish the monster. That, she soon recognised, was a forlorn ambition. The monster could be caged and curbed and put on tranquillisers. But vanquished? Never.

Dimala was welling up in distress at Marcelle's disappearance. It was just over a month since he had departed the shelter of the Chandansar orphanage, swapping a life of familiarity for realms unknown. Marcelle had been the one constant during that period. She had started his long induction into London's culture and practicalities; she had provided a place of refuge; and she had been available, without consternation or complaint, whenever he had stumbled. Without the umbrella of her protection, was he now at risk of deportation? More immediately, he could not shake the sense that he was responsible for her disappearance. If only he had been less eager to please, and had exercised caution before sending her after ghosts during the depths of night time. If only...

"Back in Mumbai, Miss Weseldine's lectures often spoke of the virtue of persistence. She taught us the worst stains survive the first washing. That, she said, is no reason to capitulate. It is a reason to try again. To redouble efforts."

"I don't care if it costs me everything, Dimala," said Craig. "This won't stand."

The next serving of scrambled eggs was almost ready. Craig tipped the pan at an angle, and prodded the meal with a spatula. The ideal texture – moist with a creamy constituency. He beckoned Dimala to make a selection of ingredients; he chose anchovies and chives with a sprinkling of cheese. And then the colleagues sat down yet again to recite every stage of the ordeal in search for anything they'd overlooked.

"I take that to mean you don't want to discuss any other instructions?" said Dimala. "I've got a stack of client messages. The CEO of Westhaven insisted you call back before he leaves the office."

"No. That's my choice and damn the consequences."

Craig and Dimala made a curious couple as they furrowed their brows, staring across the galley into the middle distance for inspiration. The established strategist with a global reputation, and the technology prodigy plucked from obscurity. A gulf separated them in so many ways – so vastly different in their stature, age and wealth. But in other ways, there were growing similarities. The same tufts of stubble sprouting from unshaven chins, the same bleary shadows underneath their bloodshot eyes, the same unkempt clothing. And the two increasingly united in their undiluted resolve to track down their missing colleague.

Their concentration was interrupted by a heavy banging on the outside of the boat. Two, three, four times against the side of the cabin. Craig peered out through a window. After the Malkin Castle episode, he was reluctant to engage with strangers, and certainly not to grant safe passage onto the boat. It was a single woman, her features obscured in shadow. She had arrived on the scene on a mixed terrain touring bicycle, which had been propped, unfastened, against a tree. It was a wonder of cargo-carrying efficiency, with a generous front mounted basket and synthetic panniers attached to the rear. The flap atop one pannier had been left open. Craig assumed it had been used to transport the laptop which the woman held under her left arm. Her right fist was still banging against the elm timber of the boat's exterior, and her knuckles were starting to redden with the impact. Craig marvelled that a woman of such slight build could muster such aggression.

In the absence of a response, the woman walked along the side of the boat, looking in through the windows. Taking no chances, Craig and Dimala crouched down, out of view. Recent events had made them so paranoid they were convinced that, if their presence was confirmed, hostiles would surge from the undergrowth like Viking marauders, devoid of pity and mercy.

One of the boat's windows was resting on its locking catch. The woman crouched down on the bank, alongside this point of vulnerability, and swivelled the barrel of the catch away from the centre of the window so she could ease it further open. The window's aluminium frame creaked softly as it submitted to her pressure. It wouldn't release far enough to enable the woman to squeeze through; however, if was sufficient for her words to be heard clearly as they echoed throughout the boat's interior.

"I'm looking for Craig Richards, the famed strategist," called the woman. "Are you here? Please acknowledge."

The slightly dropped 'h'; the exaggerated dipthongs, the rising lilt. The sultry accent left no doubt about the identity of the speaker. Adrienne Dodier – the trusted finance manager Hino had helicoptered into Xanotek. She'd been content to spend much of the Malkin Castle workshop prowling discretely in the background. But now, here she was, brazenly encamped on his proverbial doorstep, very much demanding attention.

"This is Craig," he replied. "I'm here with my analyst, Dimala Naidu."

"Aren't you going to invite me inside?"

"Who knows you're here? Did Hino send you?"

"This is a freelance mission. I'm here alone, representing nobody but myself."

Craig unclipped one of the boat's screen doors and nudged it to the left. The rollers moved noisily along the track.

"Please, come onboard," he said.

"It's certainly cosy," said Adrienne, ducking to avoid an overhang as she descended from the bridge.

"Welcome," said Dimala, offering a somewhat apologetic handshake.

"I'd invite you to make yourself at home. However, we're quite busy. And I imagine this isn't a social call," said Craig.

"It's about the retreat," began Adrienne.

"The implosion was farcical," said Craig. "An abomination. But if you've come to slap a writ on me, it'll be resisted. I'm as much in the dark about the leak as anyone else."

"I promise, no writ today," said Adrienne. "And I'm not here about the retreat in general. I'm here about Marcelle. I think I was the last person to speak with her before her disappearance. I don't believe she was responsible for the upload; I think it's more sinister. I have certain skills in financial detection. I'd like to help."

Chapter Eleven

Located in:

A mooring near Windsor

Every spare surface inch within *The Angola* was now commandeered to support the search effort. Any objects that might interfere with the mission – magazines, crockery, a couple of paperweights – were unceremoniously dumped into storage containers. At under three hundred square feet, the boat's interior might be cramped. But Craig thrived in concentrated space. He felt it aided concentrated thought.

Adrienne was charged with seeking leads in the defence sector.

"The intruder had no interest in any of the other polymer applications we identified," said Craig. "He didn't even mention hospital uniforms or camping equipment. But he was very agitated by the fact defence applications made the cut."

"Got it," said Adrienne. "I'll start with Europe's top thirty military contractors and take it from there."

"See the counter top by the sink," indicated Craig. "That's your workstation for the day. I'll put the printer on my berth."

"I hope you've got plenty of paper."

Within minutes, the cabin was filled with the perpetual background whirr of a printer in action. Articles of association, statutory reports, stock exchange announcements – anything that might provide an avenue for further pursuit. Adrienne scanned each document and categorised it according to potential interest. Where connections were spotted, papers were bundled together and placed into piles, such that within a couple of hours one corner of the cabin was resembling the Manhattan skyline. Where the information merited further study, papers were taped to the inside wall. A thick turquoise marker pen was used to highlight numbers or facts that piqued Adrienne's curiosity.

Adrienne was particularly fascinated by the ownership structures of many contractors outside the top, publically listed behemoths. In many cases, there seemed to be a web of nominee companies, shell companies, non-trading entities, and cross shareholdings. On her laptop, she built a basic database to record and model the most intricate links.

Adrienne's corporate analysis was just one of the lines of investigation. In total, Craig was setting in train eleven parallel activities, each one listed in permanent marker on the shower room door (absorbed in the

219

moment, and wracked with concern for Marcelle, the activities had been inscribed directly onto the veneer).

"This is how we'll be working," he said. "We'll each toil away independently for a thirty minute sprint. Then we'll reconvene and share progress. Then another half hour burst. That way we can keep track of the progress being made, spot connections, and re-channel our energies if the evolving evidence warrants."

Craig asked Dimala to take ownership of the second task on the list. He needed profiles of all the workers at the castle, from the chief executive to the cleaners. Dimala was to ferret out their back stories, searching for the untoward – unexplained gaps in their resumés, criminal convictions, undesirable networks, suspicious extracurricular interests; any hints of a darker side.

Craig himself was developing theories. Everything from a disaffected former co-worker, to blackmail, to duplicitous behaviour by Hino; even mistaken identity. For the time being, no potential explanation was left out. Each hypothesis would then be rated in light of *supportive information* and contra information, giving an overall conclusion. As Sherlock Holmes had commented in *The Adventure of Beryl Coronet*, "When you have excluded the impossible, whatever remains, however improbable, must be the truth." A valuable maxim for their current investigations.

But Craig was struggling to block out a troubling and recurring image. He kept imaging Marcelle, terrified, perhaps tied up in the trunk of an abandoned car.

Perhaps tortured. Perhaps abused. Perhaps dead. He smacked his forehead to banish such thoughts from his consciousness. *Let's focus on what I can influence,* he told himself. *Anything else is a council for despair.* The vision started to blur, Marcelle's face morphing into Patricia's and back to Marcelle, until he was unsure which was which. An amalgam of the women he'd disappointed, who had suffered because, for all his great intellect, there was so much he couldn't control. That was an image incapable of banishment.

After their first sprint, the three compared notes. Lots of data, but precious little that was meaningful. Adrienne's research had yielded a dozen impenetrable balance sheets, bullish statements from identikit chairmen that could have been (and probably were) drafted by the same PR advisers; and reams of notes on matters such as executive remuneration and lease obligations. From Dimala, nothing more than youthful high jinx and long-past drunken indiscretions. The castle prided itself on continuity of service. A number of its supervisors and guides had been in unimpeachable employment since they left high school.

"We must look harder, and go deeper," said Craig. "Dimala, let's switch direction. I want you to gather whatever you can within a two mile radius of the castle during the twenty four hours before Marcelle disappeared," he instructed.

"Anything and everything that was happening. You've got roads, a village, shops, walkways. Think tweets, posts, Facebook updates, CCTV. And get it time-stamped wherever possible. If a rat fell from a tree, I want to know about it."

Turning to Adrienne, he asked her, "Where do you think this should go next? There must be something screaming out an alert."

"I really would like to get under the skin of the ownerships," she responded. "The numbers are out there in the public domain. But three or four of these companies have exceptionally complex shareholdings. That says to me they're trying to hide stuff."

"Maybe shy about the tax authorities?" asked Craig.

"That's probably part of it. But I've set up structures for Hino in Thailand and Malaysia that were effective at mitigating taxes. Nothing as byzantine as I'm finding here. I think there's something else going on."

"I agree," said Craig. "As for me, I'll be uncovering the dirt about the shakers and movers in the defence world. Not just who they are, but what makes them tick. How they spend their money, where they eat on special occasions, what they do at the weekend. If it's out there, it'll be in here."

He pointed his two index fingers at the centre of his head.

"Let's pick up tools again. It's time to crack on with the next sprint."

Again, the printer whirred. More skyscrapers dotted around the Manhattan skyline. More sheets and notes and corporate structures wallpapering the sides of the cabin. Dimala staring intently at the layers of data on this screen while his fingers pounded the keyboard with the dexterity and speed of a Rubik's Cube maestro. He was now customising advanced search software so he could apply it across multiple data sources. He tested a number of parameters, linking the program to open source websites and databases featuring aspects of the Malkin hinterland. The results were browsed and filtered using algorithmic logic and judgement. The most innocuous results were discarded, and plenty fell into that category. Pictures from a jumble sale at the school fete, details of three speeding tickets issued by an automated camera, and a handful of credit card transactions he had managed to hack. All looked run of the mill; stories of a nondescript day in a nondescript village. On a second screen, Dimala maintained a holding folder in which to dump any content that seemed unusual. Thirty minutes on, the folder remained empty.

And so the cycle repeated. Every half an hour, the team regrouped, compared notes, determined the next priorities and moved on, working their way through the list of tasks that Craig had immortalised on the shower door. Like the Mount Sinai commandments given to Moses on stone tablets, the task list was now stamped onto their consciousness, a perennial fixture, a reminder of how far short they fell of achieving a breakthrough.

Noone noticed the passage of time. Noone suggested they break for lunch or supper. Black coffee and chocolate biscuits replenished energy levels from time to time, and that was the extent of the gastronomic delight. The frying pan languished unused in the sink, still bearing the detritus of the most recent scrambled eggs. Assorted takeout menus from local pizza parlours and burger joints hung unread from the noticeboard. Food was an interference. There would be time aplenty for luxury, Craig reasoned, once Marcelle had been found.

Occasionally, Adrienne would yelp in surprise when stumbling upon some new nugget. And Dimala would ask Craig to review information he uncovered that didn't fit the larger patterns. Almost invariably, these proved to be false leads; just examples of the natural variability in human existence rather than signs of a larger, more sinister plot.

The absence of any breakthrough was becoming almost intolerable for Adrienne. In frustration, she was muttering a stream of French obscenities. She tore her analysis from the wall and screwed the sheets into little balls. She stabbed her pencil against her thigh. Craig was too engrossed in the scenarios he was running to offer any comfort; his emotional intelligence count today was not at its highest. So it fell to Dimala to offer gawky words of comfort. He patted her on the shoulder, a gesture he'd learned from the movies. But he was also burning up inside with concern for his mentor, the person who had taken the risk, after talent-spotting him in a Mumbai orphanage, of offering him a new life. As every hour passed, she was fading further into the distance. Like a mountaineer toppling off a cliff edge, time moved slowly while they stretched to grab a flailing hand. But eventually the moment would pass. Gravity would win out. The mountaineer would tumble beyond reach, the rescuers left powerless except to watch in harrowing despair.

As dusk approached, Craig craved a fix. This was awkward. It was critical that neither Adrienne nor Dimala had the remotest intuition of his appetite. Even in normal times, Marcelle aside, none of his circle suspected his proclivities. And today was no normal day. His makeshift team saw him, he knew, as a role model. His presence had a galvanising, motivating effect. If they suddenly observed him snorting away like Al Pacino in *Scarface*, would they become confused, upset, and unreliable? Their challenge was not simply finding a needle in a haystack, but also locating the haystack itself. The risk of failure was high, even given maximum performance. He needed both Adrienne and Dimala to be smashing it out of the park; operating with the mentality of a Michael Phelps or a Freddie Mercury, obsessed by the making of history, not beset by doubt or trepidation. If performance fell below that of champions, if he allowed disarray or bickering to fester, they might as well forfeit any prospect of success and vacate the stage.

Craig sidled into the boat's tiny washroom, jammed the door shut, and lifted a small cocaine sachet from his trouser pocket. Not much left, but sufficient to last the next few hours. But there was something else that caught his attention: a red blink, reflecting in the transparent plastic. The indicator light from his mobile phone. The phone whose number was known to just four people. Craig had been so preoccupied, hours had passed since he'd last checked for messages.

With a few rapid fire clicks, Craig deleted a couple of spam messages that had, notwithstanding his secrecy, somehow reached his handset. But, when he saw the one remaining message, he froze. It was as if a mad cartoon villain had suddenly drained all warmth from the atmosphere.

Your woman is alive. If you want to keep her that way, remember what I said. Now finish the job you were given. Do not reply to this message.

Craig reread the text. No hidden meaning, no room for interpretation. Marcelle was alive and he sighed with relief. But the reassurance ceased after the first four words. Thereafter, every letter oozed menace. For this reason, Craig resolved to keep the communication hidden from his companions. There was not a lot that would encourage, and much that would play on their minds. And not even Dimala would be able to trace the text to its origins; he had no doubt that, by now, the phone had been cracked in two and was resting on the bed of a large lake. *Far better to carry the burden on my own shoulders,* he thought. Like the schlep in a horror movie who checks out the rasping sounds in the basement, rather than wake up the rest of the group.

At three in the morning, with human activity at its nadir, the sounds of nature around the waterway were magnified. The river lapping against the bank, the strident chirping of distant crickets, even the rustle of leaves on swaying branches. For much of the day, these would be drowned out by the cacophony of argumentative voices and screeching tyres. With people asleep, and vehicles garaged, the natural world came alive.

Three in the morning was also the time that Craig decided the sprints were producing diminishing returns, and they must move to a new phase. No more half-hourly catch-ups; more substantive probing was now required. Dots needed to be joined. Patterns needed to be defined. Connections made.

"I'm sure the answer's here, so let's find it," he asserted, as much to convince himself as his colleagues. "Anything untoward, let's all see it. Whatever time it takes."

Dimala had prepared a timeline of the day in and around the village. Thirty-one people had left some type of electronic footprint during the period, and in many cases he'd been able to track movements from one time slot to the next. Adrienne was both aghast and amazed. Within ten minutes, she'd totted up over a dozen breaches of data protection legislation. *Just as well,* she thought, *that the ends justify the means.*

Dimala relayed every detail he'd uncovered about the thirty-one. Mrs McDermott was a retired secondary school headmistress. She visited the village shop in

mid-morning and purchased a daily newspaper, breakfast cereals, and packaged meats. Later, she'd spoken
with her daughter in Spain. In the afternoon, she'd
surfed for cut-price Hornby carriages on eBay, and
submitted bids in two auctions. Then she'd caught the
bus to the nearby district general hospital, where her
husband was recuperating from a biopsy. Next on the
list was Monsieur Daviau, owner of *Angeline's* restaurant. He had signed to accept a consignment of meats
and vegetables shortly after breakfast, and then received
a series of young visitors, presumably candidates
for a vacant waiting position. In the afternoon, he'd
approved sundry credit card payments – insurances,
subscriptions and so forth. The rest of the day was spent
on-site, supervising the restaurant's operations.

The third and fourth people tracked by Dimala were a
couple of ramblers, an elderly man and his grand-daughter. They'd entered the village in late morning, when
their blurred images had appeared in the background
of one of the speeding camera's shots, and they briefly
dined at *Angeline's*, where their charge was settled by
credit card. Dimala had used the name on the card to
search for any other electronic residue left by their trek,
and had come across three photographs uploaded to the
Cloud from a mobile within the specified coordinates.
One of these was a selfie of the ramblers standing atop
a steep incline. Behind them was a nature trail, winding
its uneven way through a forest of copper beech trees.
And in the distance, at the foot of the hill, was parked

a small truck bearing the name *Neil & Neil The Sewage Specialists*.

Dimala was equally methodical with the remainder of the thirty one. By the end of his inquiries, every Malkin villager and visitor who had engaged in a transaction, or completed an upload, or made use of public transportation, had been catalogued for reference. Craig had long been aware of the revolutionary implications of so-called Big Data, but even he was struck at the insurmountable hurdles now facing anyone who, like the furtive creatures at the bottom of the jungle food chain, tried living a life in the shadows.

When Dimala had completed his report, it seemed nothing material could have occurred anywhere close to the castle without being captured on his timeline. But there was no evident breakthrough, no unmistakable sign pointing to a culprit. Nevertheless, good foundations.

"Adrienne," said Craig. "You're up next. I'm hoping you can help the pieces fall into place."

Adrienne waved her hands across her tapestry of corporate charts.

"I think this is probably the most comprehensive overview available of who controls what in the defence sector," she said. "You'll recall I started with just thirty firms. But the trail has let me through a maze of over five-hundred separate legal entities. With some of the businesses, you need to track through over four jurisdictions to find where the real power lies."

"We spoke about whether this was for tax efficiency, or whether there may be other motives?" said Craig.

"Here is what I found fascinating. Forget the bottom half of my display. Concentrate on just these two firms, *Tizett* and *Sterling Arms*. Both are household names, so to speak, within the defence world. They employ tens of thousands, and their active export licences could fill up an encyclopaedia. And yet…"

"And yet what?"

"Once you trace the shareholding back far enough, you arrive at shell companies within a block of each other."

"Which is where?"

"The Tyreso Municipality, on the Sodertorn Peninsula. About an hour from Stockholm. I've printed out some pictures of the landscape."

Craig looked at the photograph. "Nature reserves. Lake systems. A few hundred million Christmas trees," he said. "And not a killing machine in sight."

"And both buildings owned by the same man, Thomas Pohl. A virtual recluse for the past decade. I couldn't find any photographs, or public statements, since the turn of the century. No known relatives, no parking violation. If not for his name on a few title deeds, you wouldn't know he still existed."

"And before 2000?" said Craig.

"A Royal Marine. Awarded the Conspicuous Gallantry Cross for close-quarter fighting when encircled by insurgent terrorists in Mozambique. His men were low on ammunition, and reinforcements were hours away. He was decorated for single-handedly saving the day."

"Cover fire? Calling in air support? What did he do?"

"The public records are subdued about the details. So I checked the blogs. Luckily, it seems ex-army types are prone to having too much time on their hands. They retire early on generous pensions, and pass their days hankering after past glories. Even when the posts get deleted, which often happens, their signature remains. And a lot of those signatures involve Pohl's valour in Mozambique. Here's the most explicit example."

Adrienne rotated her screen towards her colleagues. "This is from a fellow ex-Marine who developed a talent with the paintbrush," she said. "They say a picture is worth a thousand words. And here's his picture of the scene. If it wasn't already obvious, that's Pohl, dead centre, wearing the crazed expression."

Adrienne hadn't been kidding about Pohl's expression. Eyes bulging fit to burst, nostrils flaring, jaws locked in the tormented scream of a soul being sucked through the gates of Hell. Pohl was standing knee deep in a dark putrid swamp, his torso bathed in a miasma of browns and reds as a result of the violence of his struggle. His right hand was plunged into the gaping stomach wound of his first opponent, cartoonishly overweight. Pohl had grabbed hold of intestines as if they were lengths of cable, and was yanking them out from the flailing body through the tear. His left hand was digging into the face of a second terrorist, a younger man with devotional tattoos on his exposed forearms. Two fingers were gouging out eyeballs, two others were snapping the nose. In the waters beneath, corpses lay face down, sundry body parts floating alongside. The title of the piece was simple: *My Hero, Captain Pohl.*

"It's fortunate I have a strong gut," said Craig.

"That's not all," said Adrienne. "Let me scroll a bit further down the page."

Three paragraphs of text had been written to sit alongside the painting. Amidst the expletives, which at times seemed to outnumber the regular words, it was clear the tableau was intended as a paean of praise to Pohl. Despite the passage of years, the author remained awe-struck by Pohl's audacious heroism, with no trace of doubt about the bloodlust.

"But that's not the most interesting thing," she said. "Look here. The name of the platoon."

Adrienne indicated the final line of the second paragraph, and both Craig and Dimala craned their necks forward for a closer look. In the tradition of the Marines, each platoon had a pet name that was part jocular, part macabre.

"My God," said Craig, realising for the first time how it felt for one's jaw to literally drop. The name of Pohl's platoon, like the inscription on the Neil & Neil van, read: *The Sewage Specialists.*

"That doesn't seem like a coincidence to me," said Dimala.

"No it doesn't." Craig was acerbic. "And I think I've found another gem which is no coincidence either."

Adrienne folded away her laptop and watched as Craig laid out almost a hundred one-page profiles he'd prepared.

"You could call this crowd the illuminati," he said. "If anything is happening in the military arena, these are the men and women who are making the decisions."

Adrienne and Dimala scanned the faces.

"You'll find all of humanity in this crowd," continued Craig. "From the eldest, Retired General Bartington, to the youngest, Rory Steranko, an MOD high-flyer. Mostly white, but nearly twenty-five from other ethnic backgrounds. Soldiers, spies, engineers, politicians, military planners. Some are the first generation in their lineage to answer the call of duty, with others it has been passed down from father to heir. You'll find people who have made great sacrifices in the service of their country, losing their health, or a limb, or forfeiting a comfortable family life. As I said, you see the gamut of society."

"If it's all of humanity, there's a villain somewhere," said Adrienne. "You'll always have a villain in any selection of one hundred people."

Craig took one of the pages, and moved it to the centre, right between where Adrienne and Dimala were squatting.

"And here is my nomination for villain *du jour.*"

In the corner of the profile was a passport-sized photograph. It was of a balding man in his fifties, thin lips and deep set eyes, sitting bolt upright and staring confidently into the camera. A man used to exercising authority and seeing his demands enacted. The rest of the page was a patchwork assembly of information that Craig had been able to piece together from different sources. Some had been obtained through digging around forgotten corners of the internet; a resumé the man's office had provided for delegate packs at a conference where he was plenary speaker; interviews granted to specialist publications and the MOD's in-house journal. For other sources, Craig had relied upon Dimala's technical assistance to break behind firewalls. The result was a fascinating insight into the life and times of a senior Whitehall official.

It seemed the gentleman had been married for nearly twenty years, although his wife had recently suffered debilitating and near-endless health problems. The couple lived in the Home Counties with two teenage children. Their spending patterns suggested they were reasonably frugal, financially secure without being wealthy. And an impeccable credit rating, although one that reflected the man's employment within the Civil Service First Division, rather than his ownership of a magnificent nest egg.

"Seems a decent family man," said Adrienne. "Where's the villainy?"

234

"Look there," said Craig, with the flair of a magician ripping away the covers to reveal that his severed assistant is still intact. His finger was jabbing at some abbreviated text at the foot of the page.

"And kudos to Dimala for designing a bit of malware – it fooled Europe's integrated air passenger database into believing I was as a benign EU government making routine security checks."

Adrienne studied the information. The gentleman in the profile, having never previously had cause to visit Sweden, made six separate trips in the preceding thirty-four months. All trips to an anonymous regional airport on the outskirts of Tyreso.

"Not only home to your two shell companies and the mysterious Captain Pohl…" said Craig.

"But also somewhere an MOD high-up is choosing for his vacations ahead of Val d'Isere or Tahiti," Adrienne finished Craig's sentence.

Outside the boat, the gentle night-time sound of wildlife was still discernible. But the invertebrate orchestra lost one of its percussionists. A bush cricket was swallowed whole by a stalking frog, and the amphibian seemed almost to smack its lips in satisfaction at its nutritious repast.

Back inside, Craig was also licking his lips. Hours of retrieval, correlations, fuzzy logic and data pairing had yielded its first fruit.

"I think it's time I paid a visit to this particular gentleman," he said. "Permanent Secretary Hugo Cunningham, here I come."

Chapter Twelve

Located in:

A basement room
and
Ministry of Defence headquarters

Marcelle blinked as she struggled to adjust to the sudden light. Without her watch, it was hard to keep track of time, but she figured this latest stretch in pitch darkness had been at least seven or eight hours. A hazy figure was hunched a few feet in front of her. She didn't need to wait for his features to come into focus. She had already been interrogated twice by her abductor, the man with the cauliflower ear.

She had been straining against the polypropylene rope that dug into her wrists for any hint of loosening, but had only succeeded in drawing blood. Now, the rough strands of material were chafing against the exposed wounds. A stabbing sensation shot the length of her arm. She bit the inside of her cheek to distract from the agony and prevent herself from welling up. She was not going to give the abductor the satisfaction of seeing her tearful.

Ward inspected the rope and grunted with smug pleasure that it was still holding fast.

"It's a constrictor knot," he explained. "It won't work loose. The more you fight it, the more taut it becomes. Wonderful creation, knots."

The room was dank and dusty. Building materials were stacked against the far wall: half used bags of cement, rolls of thermal insulation, assorted masonry and a couple of steel beams. In the corner were a couple of steel storage shelves, piled high with boxes of wartime rations, yellowing maps and coloured pins. Large pools of water were visible across the floor, thick with oil, and blending into one another like miniaturised Great Lakes. From the floor above, Marcelle made out the noise of construction workmen going about their daily grind, barking orders, hauling boxes, banging one item of equipment against another; the sound had been an anchor to the outside world during the hours of loneliness. And beyond that, the hypnotic vibrations of internal combustion engines. Her senses were in overdrive, sifting through the information for any obscure clues that might give an inkling of her whereabouts.

"I still have my little list of things I need to know," said Ward. "Are you ready to play?"

He freed Marcelle's gag and let it hang around her neck. She glared at him, unblinking, unresponsive.

"One. I need to know exactly who you spoke with after you discovered our little bug. Two. What research did you undertake for Xanotek on military applications, and how close did you get to an entry plan? Three. Most importantly, I need to know about Mr Richards. His mandate from Xanotek, what he might do next, his drug addiction? And any validity in the rumours about his demons?'

Marcelle continued to stare.

"We know all about the cocaine, Miss Williams. No sooner was he back at his stateroom, he was snorting away. Not so much as a *by your leave*."

"I can give you my name, rank and serial number."

"This isn't a war, Miss Williams. Not yet anyway. And it's certainly not a game. But here's what I don't understand. You have everything going for you. Great qualifications, looks, talent. So what are you doing with that waster? Come in from the dark side, Miss Williams. He'll only drag you down into his slough of depravity and tragedy."

"You're wrong about him."

"I get it. He brings out the maternal instinct. You must be stronger than that. He has no sense of responsibility, no empathy with those he harms. You owe him no further allegiance."

Marcelle relaxed her arm muscles and then, tensing sharply, pulled against the knot. If sheer force of will was sufficient for it to release, she might have stood a chance. As it was, another few layers of epidermis rubbed away, but her status as forlorn prisoner was unchanged.

"This is helping no one," spat Ward. "We're on a schedule, and you really don't want to spend more days festering with the cockroaches and rats. Let us help you, Miss Williams. Tell us what we need to know. Will Richards quit the field of play? If not, will he respond to … certain incentives? Is that worth trying?"

"Try going to Hell."

"I've been there, I assure you. Or at least to Kandahar, which is its twisted and evil clone. When you've looked into the face of a teenage Afghan mother carrying a baby in each arm so you don't suspect there's a suicide bomb beneath her burqa, this job is like a Lego tea party."

"You're a bloodthirsty savage and Craig Richards is a brilliant man. That's all I'm saying," said Marcelle, averting her eyes.

"It's such a shame we got off on the wrong footing," hissed Ward. "You have me figured out all wrong. I'm a gentleman and a scholar. Who knows the music we could've made together in a different life."

He turned away.

On the floor above, a team of builders was discussing the various tasks involved in demolishing a partition wall. The supervisor was preoccupied with how many clay bricks needed to be smashed out, and how they would be transported through the Courtyard Rooms without causing damage to fixtures and fittings. Apparently, their wages would be docked to cover the cost of making good any scratches along the walls or gouges in the timber door panels.

Ward was rummaging noisily through a canvas hold-all, like an alcoholic searching through the weekly shopping basket, desperate to claim the bottle of gin. After dismissing a couple of items that were unsuitable for his purposes, he clucked with delight at laying hands on his chosen object. It was a fibreglass rod, a couple of feet in length. At one end was an insulated handle attached to a rectangular battery pack; at the other, two electrodes embedded in a bronze tip. Holding the rod tightly in his right hand, Ward patted it repeatedly against his calf, like an absent-minded policeman with a truncheon. But Marcelle recognised immediately that this was no truncheon.

"It looks like an everyday cattle prod," muttered Ward. "In fact, it's called a picana. A wondrous invention courtesy of an Argentinian police chief in the 1930s. Because of its high voltage and low current, it can work over a prolonged period without causing loss of consciousness. Up to 16,000 volts and yet the current is less than a thousandth of an amp. Isn't it splendid what some unhinged minds can conjure up?"

Am I in a dream? thought Marcelle. *Can someone really be threatening me with a South American torture device in the early twenty-first century?* She desperately wanted to spit in his face, but her throat was dry with terror. She tried to scream, but Ward was forcing the gag back into her mouth. He pushed it hard behind her teeth, making it impossible to breathe except through the nose. In this surreal moment, Marcelle found herself grateful for the small mercy that, despite allergy season, she was not a habitual hay fever sufferer.

242

Ward touched the electrodes lightly against Marcelle's lower lip, and her upper body convulsed in torment. The acrid stench of burning flesh momentarily engulfed her nostrils; in front of her eyes, she saw the faint wisp of smoke rising, billowing from the point of impact, like the first airborne particles from a November Guy atop his pyre.

"I'm not a callous man," said Ward. "That's why we've started on the lowest level. Think of it as your sampler course. Now I'm going to give you some time to think about co-operating. I'm very confident our next session will be more productive."

The door shut with a screech that echoed around Marcelle's chamber. A few seconds of silence, and then the harrowing finality of two dead bolts dropping into place. In the black velvet darkness of her seclusion, a solitary sliver of light was able to cut through just above the hinges. The illumination it provided was near useless. Just sufficient, in fact, to make out the slightest trace of crimson as a drop of blood tumbled from Marcelle's wrist like a high diver from a springboard, and entered the watery embrace of one of the wannabe Great Lakes, where it balanced on the surface for a few moments, precarious and defiant, before succumbing.

A police cordon had been in force around Parliament since dawn. Westminster Bridge was closed and traffic rerouted along the South Bank towards Vauxhall. A heavily manned barricade blocked the Whitehall exit from Trafalgar Square. As a result, gridlock reigned. Mother-of-three Nicola Everill was now late for a crucial meeting in the City to sign off a flotation prospectus, but her people carrier had barely moved for ninety minutes. Her frustration boiled over when she started to recognise diners leaving the pizzeria; she had been in the identical spot when those people arrived for lunch. Overhead hung a speed restriction sign, exhorting her not to exceed thirty miles an hour.

"If only," she grumbled, wondering – not for the first time – whether she should abandon her vehicle by the roadside and suffer the consequences later.

Police activity had been stepped up due to the emergency recall of Parliament. Inside the Chamber, politicians were debating the heightened crisis in Phoenicia, and whether to grant authority to the government to initiate a military response should tensions escalate further. Secretary of State Foster was making the case that Contingency Funds should now be accessed to reinforce military preparedness in the event of conflict. Stock market analysts around Europe hung on every word, listening for any hint that rhetoric might shortly spill over into action. A quarter of a mile away from the despatch box, *Stop The War* demonstrators were assembling along the Mall. The more excitable student ringleaders were hurling vitriol at the police line that was preventing them from marching towards the seat of democracy itself.

On the Embankment, overlooking the Thames, a temporary security point allowed safe passage inside the cordon for anyone on official government business. Visitors were required to ascend a steel ramp into a mobile unit for immigration-style checks. A dozen armed guards surrounded the unit, poised like highly sprung Jack in the Boxes to pounce on the slightest inkling of confrontation. Inside, those claiming legitimate business behind the cordon underwent thorough vetting. After fingerprint authentication and a mandatory pat down, it was necessary to pass through a millimetre wave 3D body scanner before exiting the unit. The security procedures were ubiquitous; no dignitary or civil servant, no matter how esteemed, could bypass the process.

Of course, the inspection protocols only kicked in once visitors had established their credentials. At the top of the ramp was the first line of vetting. A security officer was barking "Please state name and business" at anyone approaching the unit, and then checked the answers against information on her tablet. Although in her mid-twenties, the officer was overweight almost to the point of being rotund. Her head seemed to blend into her shoulders, with her neck submerged behind rolls of fat, and acres of flesh were spilling out from her tight-fitting uniform. Craig imagined an experiment in which he pushed her into a deep ravine and watched her falling, spinning head over heels, before ricocheting against the distant rock and bouncing back to where she started like a rubber ball. No wonder she needs to sit all day, he thought, two minutes chasing criminals and it would be off to intensive care.

"We have an appointment at the Ministry of Defence in thirty minutes," Craig explained, handing over his passport.

The officer squinted at the photograph through her horn-rimmed glasses. Her tiny eyes were starting to recede away, lost inside the corpulence of the rest of her face, but for now just about functional. Satisfied that the person matched the documentation, the officer placed Craig's passport in a tray to her right, and turned her gaze upon his two companions.

"My colleagues Miss Dodier and Mr Naidu," he said.

The officer tapped away at her tablet for a near eternity. Even Dimala, for all his stoicism, felt the rising urge to grab the device from her clammy grasp, and demonstrate how it should be used efficiently. Eventually, she located their names in the appropriate files, and handed back their identification. Without any glimmer of enthusiasm or humour, as if granting permission was to her everlasting regret, she mumbled, "You may proceed."

Just a few hours beforehand, Dimala had been seated on a park bench close to the Angola, wracked with self-loathing and indecision. During his early years at the orphanage, he had pleaded with Stella Weseldine and her staff for information about the fate of the other children – including his younger sister – at the northern hospital where he had been found. He had grown accustomed to their averted gazes and clumsy ruses to change the topic to a more congenial matter. However, the staff had only been able to delay, not eradicate, this knowledge. Dimala's first off-the-radar cybersearch had established in graphic detail the truth of his origins; the brutality of the rivalries in his remote village that had made victims of an entire generation. And Dimala still had not come to terms with his survivor's guilt. For a year, he had treated the Chandansar staff with contempt, resenting their selection of him alone, from the hospital ward, for rescue. How dare they play God; what gave them the right? Dimala's guilt placed a burden on his shoulders that was almost unbearable. He felt he was carrying the torch on behalf of twenty-three others – twelve boys and eleven girls, he knew every name – who were denied his good fortune. When he cowered for fear of his life in Marcelle's apartment, the fear was not on his own behalf; he was terrified the torch would be extinguished for his generation, for the twenty-three.

On the bench, he had swayed back and forth for an hour before sunset, muttering *They must never know, they must never know.* Marcelle must never know that he was unworthy, so unworthy, of her blessings. The orphanage must never know that, ten years on, he was still plagued with the same seductive bitterness towards them, that an inner voice would rejoice if, one day, he learned it had been reduced to rubble by bulldozers. Craig must never know that, at any point in their mission, his demons might surface and jeopardise their work. And

247

the twenty-three must never know the cavalier manner in which he had connived with this audacious scheme, once again placing in peril not only himself, but the precious legacies he carried, the flickering spirit of those innocent and ill-fated brethren. When Dimala crept back aboard *The Angola*, having renewed his commitment to aid the rescue effort, Craig and Adrienne were crashed out, oblivious to their colleague's extended sortie. *They deserve their rest*, thought Dimala. And, once again: *They must never know.*

Given leave to proceed by the officer, Craig was elated but retained his composure in the manner of a seasoned poker player. He gazed around the security room, apparently with nonchalance, but in fact memorising its access points in case a rapid exit was later demanded. Outside, the noise of the protestors was reaching fever pitch; they were now chanting about the Prime Minister's parentage with imaginative and gratuitous invective. He noticed how one or two of the guards were stiffening their posture, ready to respond should the barricades be broken. Behind the front ranks, one of the officers was minding a steel container labelled 'riot equipment'. Craig assumed that, if the situation deteriorated rapidly, all types of water cannons and pepper sprays and electroshock tasers would be mobilised. For the time being, his priority was not to be distracted with thoughts of crowd control and police kettling tactics, but to retain the pretence of calm normality. Dimala had assured him that he left behind no suspicious electronic signatures when he hacked into MOD servers and registered three additional 'official visitors' that morning. Craig figured Whitehall's cyber-defence was as impregnable as any in the developed world, and until they had been ushered through the scanners it was impossible to shake a lingering doubt that detection was imminent. Followed, no doubt, by summary arrest and the death of their mission.

The trio walked briskly passed Cleopatra's Needle on Victoria Embankment and then through two more security checks into the bowels of the MOD headquarters. Adrienne took inspiration from the sight of the giant Egyptian obelisk so close to London's corridors of power. In her youth, when her abusive uncle was out of town, after roaming the shores of the Seine in an erratic, desultory fashion, she would often sit on the verge close to Paris' own 'Needle', L'aiguille de Cléopâtre. For hours she would gaze upon the hieroglyphics, overawed, wondering whether they contained any messages for her, sent down the millennia by Luxor craftsmen. She felt humbled at the trivial nature of her own afflictions when set against the vastness of history. How symbolic that today, of all days, the Needle once again appeared before her. *Pharaoh Ramesses II* was a man without fear, it seemed to intone; *so feel no fear today.*

Once inside the main building on Horse Guards Avenue, Craig indicated that it was time to separate. In line with their pre-agreed plans, he would head to the corner suite on the third floor, while Adrienne and Dimala descended to the basement communications hub.

If any of them was unable to proceed with their mission, either through physical resistance or verbal challenge, it would be time for hurried excuses and rapid departure. If arrested, they must exude the aura of a maverick lone wolf. No attempts to regroup until safely back on the other side of the cordon.

Craig had committed the floor plans to memory. Cunningham's office was left out of the elevator, at the far end of the corridor, overlooking the Thames. If he strode with sufficient purpose and authority, avoiding eye contact and grasping his manila folio as if it contained the secrets to global peace and tranquility, there was an evens chance of reaching his target unimpeded. Secretary Foster would be in the Commons for the Phoenicia debate with her entire ministerial team, meaning that Cunningham was likely to be either at his desk catching up on paperwork, or in meetings with junior officials. Outside the lift, a wall sign usefully pointed the way towards the Executive Offices. His information had been faultless. There was a fighting chance that, within the next two or three minutes, he would be face to face with the Permanent Secretary himself.

Four floors below, Adrienne watched from the shadows as a junior engineer pressed four digits in rapid succession onto a numerical pad. The code would allow them through the tinted Plexiglas doors and into the landlines exchange. To be unobtrusive, it had been necessary to keep some distance from the engineer; however, she deciphered the sequence perfectly. 5-7-0-5. *If Hino gets wind of my freelance operations and I'm summarily dismissed for my split allegiances,* she thought, *it seems I can always fall back on a career as an ATM thief.*

The exchange still occupied the same cavernous acreage it had required when hordes of switchboard operators spent their days plugging ring cords into jacks. Of course, manual service had long since been overtaken by automation, and the room now comprised a handful of unmanned machines, and a lot of empty space. At its height, the exchange had created employment for over forty people. Now, only two MOD staff members looked up to acknowledge Adrienne and Dimala's arrival: the junior engineer, who was preoccupied with rewiring some ceiling cables, and a wizened and balding gentleman who, according to his identification badge, was Fred Humphreys, Exchange Supervisor.

"We're here for the software configuration upgrade," said Adrienne.

Humphreys slurped a mouthful of coffee then emitted a half-stifled belch. "Don't know anything about that. This is the weekly schedule, and there's nothing happening today."

"We're on a tight timetable. Can my colleague get to work while we sort out the forms?"

"No work without paperwork. That's been my motto for thirty years."

"Can you show some flexibility, just once? I'm under a lot of pressure."

"Not my problem. Get your paperwork in order next time."

Adrienne exchanged nervous glances with Dimala. All he needed was a few moments at the far workstation, where the most secure lines were administered. It was time to switch to the contingency plan. She unbuttoned the top of her blouse. Then she unfastened another button for good order.

"Can I have a look over the schedule?" she said, leaning forwards towards Humphreys. "The upgrade might have been logged in the wrong place."

Humphreys coughed and handed over his clipboard. Half a dozen sheets were held in place by the clip, and Adrienne slowly cast her eyes over each one.

"You seem a very intelligent man," she said, switching on her coquettish routine. She ran her index finger along her lower lip which, Humphreys noticed, was gently quivering. "Tell me about yourself. Are you married?"

Over Humphreys' shoulder, Adrienne noticed Dimala was maneouvering himself into position, ready to commence his assignment. She nodded imperceptibly, and the young Indian acknowledged the message being signalled. *I can hold his attention for the next few minutes. Time to get started.*

"My wife and I, we don't speak much. Not any more," Humphreys stammered. "Why do you ask?"

"I like a man who keeps himself trim," Adrienne replied. "Look at you, not an inch of pot belly. Not an inch."

252

She patted the elder man's stomach, allowing her hand to linger long enough to turn a platonic gesture into something more suggestive. "I'm assuming you work out."

"I have a set of dumb bells at home," he said. "Twenty minutes every morning for the last fifteen years. It's good for muscle tone, they say. And you seem to have nice muscle tone as well."

Without asking for permission, Humphreys slid Adrienne's sleeve a few inches up her lower arm, and ran a leathery finger back and forth along her exposed flesh. She smiled again, this time licking her front teeth until they glistened with saliva. *Hurry up, Naidu,* she thought. *Even if he was younger, even if he was magically more female, I'm really not one for impulsive affection.*

Fifteen phone lines in the exchange had been selected for maximum security protection. All voice and data transmission was subject to four levels of encryption using coding and decoding formulae that were programmed to evolve without the need for human intervention. Encoded messages were then relayed through virtual pipes that occupied the dark spaces on dedicated servers. The lines were allocated to the Secretary of State and the Ministry's ten most senior officials with the remainder reserved for staff on special projects, who needed to communicate with the intelligence services or foreign powers. Naturally, Cunningham's line was one of those fifteen. It had taken Dimala three hours of probing to realise that only on-site intervention could thwart the security measures and enable, for however short a period, eavesdropping of the Permanent Secretary's communications.

The fifteen secure cables each fed into a unique section of a KL-43 cypher and cryptologic box, like the interweaving appendages of a mechanised alien robot. Each connector was labelled with an alphanumeric reference that spanned two lines, but with a unique middle sequence that corresponded to the private line concerned. Bingo: the third section related to Cunningham. Even better, it seemed the line was not in current use. There had been a risk that Dimala's work might send out the electronic equivalent of a massive red flare, alerting Cunningham of suspicious activities that merited investigation. But, in fact, he could now proceed without the embarrassment of disconnecting conversations mid-flow.

Suddenly, Dimala froze. His legs started to give way. His mind was ablaze with the voices of the twenty-three, as raucous and contradictory as the shrieks and cries at a fairground.

What are you doing, Dimala? Get out of there! Come back home!

When you do great works, Dimala, you act on behalf of us all.

You abandoned us to our graves. None of us were even ten, and you abandoned us.

We love you Dimala; if you cannot do it alone, use our strength to complete your task.

In his mind's eye, Dimala could picture the girl who spoke these last comments. It was his younger sister, just five when she passed away from her injuries and malnutrition. But every detail, every contour, of her face was visible to him. Her wide bright eyes, her snub nose, her generous fringe. When she mouthed the words *We love you Dimala*, he was certain these, and not the calls to cease and return, were the collective sentiments of the twenty-three.

Taking careful hold of the secure cable, Dimala eased the ethernet plug away from its socket in the KL-43. He then inserted between the cable and the device a small ferrite cylinder, which he clipped firmly into place. The cylinder contained software he had written the previous evening which could intercept data from Cunningham's office prior to encryption and provide a parallel onward route. He rested the cylinder towards the rear of the ledge, where it was largely obscured by the maze of other cables. Unless a counter-espionage technician was specifically looking for such an intercept, it was unlikely anyone would uncover it within the next forty-eight hours. Hopefully that would be sufficient to determine whether or not Cunningham possessed information that was relevant to their pursuit. Dimala pushed shut the door to the KL-43 cabinet and gave a thumbs-up signal in Adrienne's direction.

Meanwhile Humphreys was on a roll.

"There's a place in town where I sometimes stay. It's a small guest house near Paddington. I've known the owners for years. Perhaps I could give you my number and we could…"

"Yes, that's an excellent idea," said Adrienne.

But while her words seemed to endorse the proposal, her body language was no longer flirtatious. She was rolling her sleeve back to its full length, her blouse was suddenly re-buttoned, and in an instant her concentration had switched back to the clipboard and away from Humphreys' rheumy eyes.

"And your other amazing suggestion was that I should get proper authorisation for the upgrade. I think that was spot on. Why don't I head back upstairs with my colleague and sort out the signature?"

Feeling defiled by the elder man's seedy attentions, it would take a couple of hot showers to shake off the sense of grimy contamination. Before Adrienne left, she couldn't resist a parting gift. As Humphreys took hold of the clipboard, she slipped a tiny capsule into his half-consumed coffee. *That'll give him something awkward to explain to his poor long-suffering wife,* she thought.

Humphreys spent the next five minutes visualising the series of erotic Paddington encounters which seemed imminent. They would awaken the neighbourhood with their carnal passion! Only when his fantasy reached triple-X proportions did he realise with dismay that, despite her enthusiasm, Adrienne had not after all taken a note of the number. At which, the supervisor sank back into his chair, his complexion once again an anaemic grey. The joy of a few moments reliving the excesses of

256

his wayward youth. But the resurgence had been temporary. He was now, once again, a faded light, destined to return every night to a loveless home, shackled by an ever-present temptation to stray which was satiated with increasing rarity.

In the corridor outside, Dimala whispered to Adrienne, "The cylinder is active. No-one was on the line, so the cylinder is active."

There was a simple reason Cunningham had not been using the line at the time Dimala was reconfiguring the KL-43, and it could be found back in his suite on the third floor. He was facing off with an enraged Craig Richards, who had smarmed and charmed his way through two anterooms, and was now separated from the Permanent Secretary by no more than the width of an antique Wooton desk.

"Listen to me for two minutes. Don't think about buzzing for security until you've listened to me for two minutes," said Craig.

"I recognise you. I've heard of you," said Cunningham as he jabbed a finger at the interloper. "You're that strategist, you used to be on television all the time."

"After my two minutes, I will walk out of here calmly. I expect to leave this wing, this floor, this building without being bundled away by strongmen with arms the size of tree trunks. In your profession you'll be familiar with the principle of mutually-assured destruction. So be assured that, if my exit is impeded, even by the tiniest iota, today won't end well, not for either of us."

"You can't walk straight into my office without being noticed. My private staff all know this is an unscheduled appointment."

"You lie for a living, I'm sure you can find a lie for our heart-to-heart. I don't know, just say I'm a diplomat with the FCO and we've been discussing areas of mutual concern. You'll think of something."

"I could. But why would I? And, by the way, you have ninety seconds left."

For dramatic effect, Cunningham straightened his pocket handkerchief, embroidered with its stampeding herd of bright green African elephants. It had taken a few moments, because he wasn't accustomed to strangers marching on his private office; but his composure was now restored.

"I don't care about your ties to Tyreso. Or Tizett, Or Thomas Pohl. I'm not interested in upsetting your nice little domestic arrangements with your picture perfect wife and picture perfect children. But you've taken something – correction, someone – who means a lot to me."

"I have no idea what…"

"Her name is Marcelle Williams. She pays her taxes, she obeys the law, she's done nothing to harm you. So keep her out of your schemes. Tell your men to let her go."

"This is preposterous. I'm a Commander of the British Empire and a confidant of…"

"My two minutes are up by now. You didn't offer me a drink, but I can overlook that. Think about what I said."

"And?"

"Get in touch. You run the country. You'll figure out how."

The manila folio that had accompanied Craig throughout his journey to the heart of government had been for show, not to transport any incriminating documents. All it contained were a selection of sports magazines and random pages ripped from *TurboCharged Strategy*, a recently published bestseller brimming with management tips for entrepreneurial firms, social enterprise organisations, and professional bodies. Craig tossed it onto the Wooton.

"Have this. I don't need it any more. You might learn something." And then, pirouetting on his brogues, he turned his back and was gone.

Cunningham fumbled for a cigarette and lighter. At times like this, the smoking ban was the least of his concerns. Then he noticed his assistant, Elsie Underhill, peering around the door.

"I need a few minutes alone," he said. "Don't worry about anything. That was just a ... a fellow from the Foreign Office. Joint programmes, enhanced cooperation, that sort of thing."

Elsie nodded silently, and withdrew.

Finally alone, Cunningham ignited the end of his cigarette and gazed at the shredded tobacco leaves as they smouldered like a well-lit barbeque. For a couple of minutes, he was virtually motionless, transfixed by the burning embers and the occasional ash that fell gracefully to the carpet. Then, leaning forward, he inhaled. An inhalation that almost knew no end. The tobacco smoke filled his lungs with the therapeutic effect of air inflating a tyre. And still he inhaled, indulging in the sensation of every slightest whisp, every vapour, of toxin within his system. Surely when, in Norse mythology, the god Thor almost consumed the oceans through his drinking horn, even that feat had not been as satisfying as this luxurious nicotine fix.

After two more deep breaths, Cunningham snapped back to reality. He had spent his career solving problems, and Richards' challenge was just one more for the list. He reached for his secure phone and stabbed out an eleven-digit mobile phone number.

"Ward," he snarled into the receiver, "It's time for me to speak with the girl."

Chapter Thirteen

Located in:

A basement room
and
Crowborough Business Park

When she heard Ward re-entering her cell, Marcelle feared the worst. The thud of his hold-all being dropped to the floor, the sputter of the zip being pulled back, the click of the picana being switched on. She winced with apprehension. How could the expectation of pain be so agonising, she wondered, not for the first time during her days of captivity; how could it be almost as disturbing and intense as the reality?

But Ward, normally so deliberate, was today in a hurry. He deposited his hold-all alongside the ration boxes on the shelf, and strode to where Marcelle sat bound.

"There's someone who wants to speak with you," he said, holding his mobile up to her face.

"You don't know who I am. And you don't need to know who I am," said Cunningham at the far end of the secure line. "But the man holding you answers to me. So

I'm going to ask you a few simple questions, and I would be very grateful for honest and full replies."

"I have quite a few questions of my own. And I need to speak to Mr Richards," said Marcelle.

"Maybe in another life, Miss Williams. In this one, I'm in control. And I suggest you comply, or next time you spot a man peering at your face from across the street, it will be for all the wrong reasons."

Marcelle weighed up the options. Defiance, silence, collaboration, evasion. None seemed especially appealing.

"Please don't sulk, Miss Williams. You are our guest. We don't like to fight with honoured guests. We like to make them comfortable."

"I hate to break it to you. But this hellhole isn't exactly like being in church," Marcelle laced her tone with as much sarcasm as she could muster.

"If you can help our enquiries, I'm sure we can arrange some home comforts. Perhaps a proper meal, or a shower and some fresh linen."

"What a charmer."

"Firstly, let me establish some facts. Your name is Marcelle Williams. You trained as an economist in New York and Frankfurt. You sat on the board of Scholarship Outreach until 2012, promoting the role of education in developing countries as a route out of poverty. Since which time, you've been working with the strategist, Craig Richards."

"So you know how to use Wikipedia. You win the Kewpie doll."

Cunningham inhaled from his cigarette one final time. He held the smoke in his mouth until it had cooled and the flavour taken on the slight stale taste that he relished. Then he drew the vapour through his lungs and expelled it from his nose. The smoke tickled his mucus membranes, and he rubbed the side of his nostrils to clear the irritation. Since any sight of an ashtray on his desk would have sent compliance into apoplexy, he chose a special forces coaster on which to stub out the cigarette.

Richards had been allowed to walk free from the Ministry a few moments ago. Cunningham's instinctive circumspection and caution had obliged him to take the intruder's threats seriously. The man's demeanour was unpredictable, almost unhinged. It would not advance Cunningham's longer term purpose to have somebody, however capricious, languishing in custody and lobbing outlandish allegations in his direction. Surely it would be more prudent to take him out, to despatch him from the board, at a time and place of Cunningham's sole choosing.

"Let's cut to the chase, Miss Williams. You're familiar with Mr Richards' movements. If I wanted to track him down, say this evening, where should I begin looking?"

"Why so interested?"

"As we've established, Miss Williams, I'm the one posing the questions today."

"Try the top of the hill. With Jack and Jill. And I hope you break your crown as well."

"Don't make us do this, Miss Williams."

Ward had now retrieved the picana from his hold-all and he was stroking it rhythmically against the nape of Marcelle's neck. Since her abduction, she had been experimenting with a series of mental ploys to disassociate herself from the imminent peril. The most effective was to imagine herself in spirit form, released from her corporeal body, floating without impediment through the labyrinth where she was trapped. In this construct, she would be soaring between floors, following rafters and girders as if they were routes through a maze. Her spirit form was able to linger above the construction workmen on the floor above, witnessing their frenetic endeavours, observing their camaraderie. She had repeated this exercise with numbing regularity, catching snatches of conversation each time. Piece by gruesome piece, Marcelle had been able to use overheard remarks such as yesterday's casual reference to Courtyard Rooms, alongside evidence from her immediate surroundings, to build a clearer picture of where she was being held.

"I have a clear message," said Marcelle. "You've made this a war. And in this war you may think there's room for many victors – yourself, your cronies, whoever's pulling the strings at the top. You may have heard of Craig Richards. But I've worked alongside him. And there aren't many rooms in this war. There's one room. And Craig Richards will occupy it. Now do your worst."

This time, when Marcelle stared at Ward, there were no signs of agitation or dismay in her expression. Instead, she exuded a new-found resolution, a gutsy calmness. Ward even detected the stirrings of a smirk playing at the corners of her mouth.

This time, uncertain and slightly ashamed, it was Ward's turn to avert his gaze.

The Crowborough Business Park had been established in the boom years of the early 2000s as Blair's answer to Silicon Valley.

Funded with over £500 million of pump-priming public investment siphoned from the National Lottery, almost no expense had been spared to create a futuristic environment fit for the United Kingdom's hidden army of potential technology billionaires. Nearly a quarter of the seed money had been used to attract Suiren Zhi, the award-winning architect whose stamp was on the skylines of a dozen of the most commercially aggressive Chinese cities, to relocate his team to the garden of England for eighteen months. The result had been startling. The sleepy town of Crowborough, nestling on the edge of Ashdown Forest, and largely anonymous since illustrious resident Arthur Conan Doyle had penned the *Sherlock Holmes* stories, was now firmly back on the map. The business park dominated the town, towering over its narrow streets, playing fields and town hall. Two hundred thousand square feet of brushed chrome, mirrored windows, interactive displays, and exotic indoor plants. Ambient temperature, general cleanliness, and air quality all maintained around the clock to within a percentile of the target levels by Europe's most sophisticated artificial intelligence.

The boom had turned to bust and Crowborough Business Park was yet to produce its first billionaire alumnus. Three of the seven earliest beneficiaries of Blair's largesse had spectacularly folded, and occupancy had never since exceeded seventy per cent. Essential AI upgrades had been foregone, and it wasn't unusual for the temperature to be stifling for an entire morning while engineers figured out where the coding had gone awry. These were just a few of the reasons behind Jeremy Barker's ablility to secure favourable two year rent-free terms for a suite of offices and a secure laboratory when he'd been searching for a suitable incubator for his Xanotek start-up.

The Park's atrium was more like an upmarket aviary than a reception area. The soaring glass ceiling focused the midday sunlight onto a three-tier stone fountain which ejected great shoots of water in tempo with the background muzak. The back wall doubled as an IMAX-standard digital screen on which roving scenes from the tropical rainforests of Central and South America were projected. The reception desk was not a desk at all, but a fully automated toughened glass screen with inbuilt voice recognition capabilities. New arrivals were invited to address the screen with the nature and purpose of their visit, at which point, assuming a glitch-free session, the visitor management software took over.

It was three or four minutes since Craig had made himself known. He had joined two other visitors in the waiting area, where the only seating comprised a series of solid marble blocks that made up with their wow factor what they forfeited in comfort. Opposite him sat a nervous teenager in a goth cloak, with around eight studs through nose and ears.

"They've kept me waiting here over an hour for their sucky job," she grumbled to nobody in particular. "And they can't even provide a cushion."

Craig was spared these indignities. He had called ahead to ensure Barker was available to receive him. While the Goth glowered and simmered, Craig found himself once again face to face with the Xanotek founder. The lab coat and *Blackadder* pin badge were cheerily familiar. However, this time, they were accompanied by an air of menace. Barker offered no handshake, no smile of recognition lit up his face.

"I wasn't expecting to meet you again. You'd better follow me." At which point, without a single backward glance, he marched the width of the atrium towards the building's primary stairwell.

Xanotek's offices were at the far end of the business park, straddling two floors. Barker directed him into the boardroom, in which Craig had conducted a number of his pre-Malkin meetings with members of the management team. One side of the room was a floor-to-ceiling window, overlooking the firm's polymer laboratory.

Although the illumination was poor, with the lights dimmed and the external windows permanently shielded, Craig saw that scientific activity was continuing. The central vat was churning away, and on the far wall a dozen display monitors recorded various readings from the chemical reactions being catalysed.

"I've laid off two of my best staff since the Malkin fiasco," said Barker. "We haven't shut down entirely, but that's no thanks to your so-called support."

One of the chemists opened the top of the vat and drew out a measure of liquid in a volumetric pipette for separate analysis.

"They are good men; hand-picked men. Some I've known for fifteen years. Some I'm proud to call my friends," said Barker.

"I appreciate that," said Craig.

"They have families and mortgages. Do you ever stop to think of the repercussions of your ham-fisted efforts on these people...my friends?"

"I didn't come here expecting a bouquet of your finest roses," said Craig. "And please don't think I'm chasing my fee. That's not what this is about."

Barker seemed inexplicably larger than during their previous encounters. Where he had once faded into the corner of a room like *Chicago's* angst-ridden Mr Cellophane, swallowed up by the enormity of his surroundings, now his posture was more upright, his bearing was more domineering.

"How dare you set foot in this building again. If not money, what are you after? And you'd better be quick, because Mr Hino will be calling us in the next few minutes. And he's not carrying flowers either."

"The past week has been crazy," said Craig. "But it's not my fault. My team didn't leak the workshop online. Marcelle hasn't gone rogue."

"I'm a little squeamish, Mr Richards, and I'm allergic to grown men begging for forgiveness. You'll have to do better than this in front of Mr Hino."

"I think we've stepped onto a mousetrap. And it's a very big mousetrap and there's a ton of money sitting where the bait should be. And it might even be a government mousetrap."

"Please speak in riddles in the privacy of your own home," said Barker. "I don't know anything about any mousetraps. Me and my team, we're just trying to make an honest living."

Craig cursed inwardly. The conversation was not going in the anticipated direction. Understandably, Barker felt that he'd been failed by those who were meant to support him, and he was neither in the mood to listen nor to compromise. If Craig was unable to make progress with Barker, then he suspected Hino was a lost cause.

In the laboratory, Chad Spillane was drawing a flowchart on a whiteboard to illustrate the next stages of production. Adam Peralter was reviewing computer simulations on a widescreen. What joy, thought Craig, like worker bees in a hive. They buzz around, fulfilling their duties, assembling stuff, and doing what bees do. They are shielded from the bigger picture. All the mayhem and chaos that I deal with, that's a whole world far beyond their horizons. What pleasure there is in simplicity.

His reverie was ended by a sharp knock on the boardroom door. Adrienne entered with a pile of finance reports. Barker took hold of them and whispered his gratitude.

"I'm sure you remember Adrienne, our numbers girl, from the workshop," said Barker.

"Of course," Craig nodded, giving Adrienne no more than a passing acknowledgement.

Neither wanted to risk Barker suspecting their acquaintanceship ran deeper than cursory encounters at Malkin. As far as Barker was concerned, Craig recognised Adrienne as one of eight delegates at an ill-fated workshop, nothing more.

"It's time to call Mr Hino," said Adrienne. "Don't forget, he's the one who pays me, and he doesn't like to be kept waiting."

"Let's find the telephone," said Craig.

"Not necessary. Just remember, you're in a technology centre."

Adrienne's next remarks were addressed not to the men in the room, but to the centre of the boardroom table. With clipped enunciation that accentuated every syllable, she instructed it to "Please phone Mr Nobuyuki Hino."

In acknowledgement, the table lit up, its surface a sea of colours like the floor piano at FAO Schwarz. Craig swore the furniture was purring in graceful acknowledgment of Adrienne's request. A few moments later, gears could be heard shifting beneath the centre of the table, and a thin beam of light projected upwards through a small triangular hole. The light flickered twice, and then a holographic image of Mr Hino's upper body shuddered into focus, hovering in mid-air like an attack helicopter.

"Are you able to hear us, Mr Hino?" said Adrienne.

"Perfectly."

"Where do we find you today?"

"I think we've just passed the Petronas Towers of Kuala Lumpur, a couple of miles below."

"Sir," said Barker. "I mentioned that Mr Richards asked to come into our offices today. He's with us now, and I understand there are a few points he's hoping to make."

"Mr Richards," said Hino. "You need to come into view of the camera. Let me see you."

The holographic projection was dazzling in its precision. It magnified every pore and mark on Hino's face. Yet the financier's skin was remarkably blemish-free, with no trace of stubble breaking through the surface, and precious few wrinkles across his forehead. *Yet the man is almost a Mick Jagger contemporary,* thought

Craig; *I'm guessing botox, diet, lifestyle, or a combination of all three.*

"Mr Hino, I'm obviously sorry about the castle last week. But events have moved on rapidly. And there's a lot I need to tell you."

"Mr Richards, I know you're a talker. You talk for a living. You can be eloquent and persuasive. But for once I'd like you to sit down and open your ears, not your mouth."

Craig followed Hino's bidding. He sensed the financier would cut the line if he displayed any provocation or rebellion. Better to retreat and stay in the game.

"Firstly, I've made my decision about the future of Xanotek. Miss Dodier, how much cash remains in the business?"

Adrienne had no need to refer to the balance sheet; she had photographic recollection of the data.

"£1.27 million of cash. £111,000 in loans to staff on preferential terms. Around £50,000 in inventory. A similar amount held in escrow for trade purposes."

"And how much to close the business, assuming no ex-gratia payments beyond the legal minimum?"

"Assuming six weeks average severance per employee, that would be just shy of £200,000. Add fifty per cent on top of that for other trading liabilities."

"Thank you, Miss Dodier. Mr Barker, you reached the end of the gangplank last week, I'm afraid. Effective immediately, Xanotek is to enter into no further contractual commitments. Effective immediately, every member of staff will be served notice. The business is now in run off. Where investment can be salvaged, do what you must. Where it must be written off, do so expeditiously. Based on the numbers Miss Dodier has supplied, there should be a surplus of at least £1.1 million when the process has concluded. And I'll be looking for at least £1.25 million, since I don't expect all obligations to be met to the letter. Negotiate where you can. I doubt many of the creditors have deep pockets or Magic Circle lawyers. I expect they will be susceptible to compromise agreements."

Barker was visibly trembling. He had assumed the belt-tightening of the past few days would satiate his financier's lust for sacrifices to be made. The end of his dreams, he hadn't seen that coming. In weeks, days even, the laboratory that was now bustling with assiduous enterprise would be another empty shell. Papers would be boxed up for incineration; machines would be packaged up for the insolvency auctions alongside impounded goods and the fruits of asset seizures. It was almost too much to bear.

"Just another few weeks, Mr Hino," he pleaded, tears welling in his eyes. "I really think I can turn this around."

"We will never know," said Hino. "You will never have that opportunity. And you have Craig Richards, renowned strategist, legendary consultant, to thank for your ignominious demise."

Barker lifted an empty water jug from the side table. This wretched man, this so-called guru, had bought him nothing but anguish and despair. Adrenalin was pumping through his sinews, and he felt the urge, almost irresistible, to smash the jug on the side of the table, and shove the broken shards into the disgraced strategist's face. But he was a man of science, not a man of violence. He wrote papers and led ground-breaking research. How could a man such as he stand in the dock on trial for common assault? So he dropped the jug to the floor and collapsed back into his chair, head in hands, sobbing uncontrollably.

"The man's a fraud," he wailed, "And it's the decent people who suffer."

Hino was now leaning towards the camera, so close that the tip of his nose pressed against the lens. In the boardroom, this meant the hologram assumed frightening proportions, as if a vengeful deity was amongst them, rooting out miscreants, showering the world with punishment on account of its wayward nature.

"So now my decision regarding Mr Richards. The closure of Xanotek was taken with a heavy heart. That was business, pure business. But this, Mr Richards, this is pleasure."

"You're being over-hasty. There are leads I'm following. If you just let me have a moment."

Hino muted the incoming sound.

"There's no time for more lies. Barker has cost me money. But you have cost me something even more precious: reputation. My name appeared in those viral leaks, and Mr Richards that is an unforgivable sin."

Adrienne looked across at Craig. She longed to comfort him; to express support. But Hino had entrusted her with the closure of Xanotek, and what could jeopardise that responsibility?

"This is my easy promise. Your career as a strategist is over. You can forget your turnaround projects and your million dollar retainers. I know too many people. And the people I know, they know people. Whenever the name Craig Richards is mentioned as a possible adviser to the world's game changing corporations, your name will be erased from the shortlists. I hope you're adept at washing dishes, because you're now a minimum wage serf."

Behind Hino, off screen, two distant voices exchanged aviation formalities. It seemed his plane was starting its descent. Hino's hologram fluttered in and out of clear resolution as the pilot retarded the throttle and directed the aircraft's nose on its downward trajectory.

"It looks like I must sign off now. So let me leave you with a closing thought. One does not stay at the peak of Japanese commerce without encountering some rather unsavoury individuals along the way. I'm referring to people who would slit their own parents' throats like cattle in an abattoir if that's the purpose of the mission. And one day, perhaps when you're retired, perhaps when you're playing model railways with the grandchildren, perhaps when you're walking a labrador along the seafront promenade, they will come for you too.

"So be alert for that slight rustle in the hedges, for the tourist whose stride takes them a little closer than usual. And when it comes, don't bother to fight it. Stop, put aside anything you're carrying, lean back your head so your throat is fully exposed, and recite your final prayers."

As Hino's menaces grew more graphic, his voice quietened, until at *final prayers* it was barely above a whisper. The financier eased back into his leather recliner. A Ukrainian stewardess was on hand to pull his seat belt across his chest and ensure it was securely buckled. As she left to replenish his drinks, Hino glared one final time into the camera. No words, but his stare convinced his boardroom audience that his threats were deadly serious. *This is my solemn promise,* was the unspoken post script.

Hino had left no room for doubt about his intent. This was not something Craig could fend off with a jocular quip. His hands were folded in his lap like a much-chided kindergarten pupil. *After this,* he thought, *will my life ever be the same?*

Chapter Fourteen

Located in:

Tyreso Municipality near Stockholm
and
A Thames tributary

"**R**ook to queen six," said Mikhael, the words barely decipherable beneath the thick Russian accent.

Of course Mikhael wasn't Russian at all. His birthplace has been in the industrial belt around Seoul, and for the past three years he had resided in Sweden. Pohl had chosen to configure him with the Russian cadence in homage to grandmasters from Kasparov to Yakovich. There was a certain frisson in pitting his skills against such chess luminaries, even if he knew that Mikhael was in fact a highly sophisticated assemblage of integrated circuits and simulated intelligence, able within seconds to analyse the minutiae of over fifty million games stored within its memory.

Pohl studied the board for a few moments and then slid a bishop forward three spaces. At the midpoint of a match, it was not unusual for Mikhael to have a numerical advantage, to have more pieces still active.

It was only as they approached the endgame that its limitations became apparent. With over thirty moves available in any typical position, the computer would become increasingly predictable in its choices. Pohl knew this was the moment to strike. A rash, creative, counter-intuitive choice would upset Mikhael's calculations, yet it was unable to respond in kind. That was the time at which to press home an advantage.

Half of the board was bathed in fierce sunbeams. There were around two hours of daylight left, and as the sun descended towards the distant hillsides, it radiated across the water and through the gargantuan windows that adorned the west face of Pohl's sprawling lakeside bungalow. It was from this remote location that Pohl wielded invisible control over his military empire. Even connoisseurs of the Tyreso region's tracks and trails were oblivious to his presence. It was possible to walk within two hundred feet of Pohl's front door, and see nothing through the dense coniferous forest except for pines and spruces.

Mikhael communicated with Pohl through a wafer thin screen suspended on the wall like a piece of original artwork. Its next move was demanding more contemplation than usual. A vertical white line was flashing hypnotically on the screen as the AI processed thousands of scenarios. Only after a full thirty seconds did Mikhael decide on its strategy. As Pohl had forecast, the most audacious options were discarded. Instead, Mikhael advanced his knight's pawn by a single space.

"I am very sorry if I am interrupting anything."

The voice belonged to Joakim. Despite having worked over half a decade for Pohl, Joakim still felt intimidated and overawed in the older man's presence. The apologetic nature of this opening remark was typical of the manner in which he broached any new conversation.

Pohl raised a hand to signal that Joakim should be patient. The game had reached a pivotal point, and the next move might be crucial to the outcome. There were a couple of options; he could advance his forces down the right hand of the board, which had nicely opened up; or he could start a bold but risky pincer movement against Mikhael's queen, which was somewhat isolated from the pack. The decision could not be rushed.

While Pohl worked through the options, Joakim stood almost motionless. He knew any sudden movement might ignite his boss's ferocious temper. Over the years, he'd often been on the receiving end of unprovoked vitriol, sarcasm, threats and occasional violence, and the experience was chilling. Every time, he bore the punishment with stoicism. His pay, while meagre, supported his ailing parents, and could not be jeopardised. Once or twice, he fantasised about retaliation. He imagined Pohl in a frenzy, his complexion puce with rage, until he – Joakim – landed a punch between the eyes and sent the elder man staggering backwards. But, of course, this was the stuff of imagination, no more than that. Joakim had suffered from bone growth disorder since childhood. At full stretch, he was a little over four feet, although his head was large in proportion to his trunk, and his forehead was particularly prominent. Even if his filial duties were disregarded, he would last no more than seconds in combat. Pohl had, after all, been awarded the Conspicuous Gallantry Cross while in the Royal Marines, and even in retirement the first two hours of every day were dedicated to pumping iron in the basement gymnasium. If the berserker rage took hold, Joakim figured Pohl could snap his neck without a moment's remorse.

So Joakim stood and waited. Pohl's overfed guinea pig Rex sniffed at his feet. Joakim's toes were exposed to the air by his rope sandals, but even when the rodent started to lick his skin, he didn't flinch or fidget. He was his master's servant, and that was how matters must remain.

Eventually Pohl selected his move. His knight leap-frogged from its contained position behind the ranks of white pawns to join the fray. The assault on Mikhael's queen was underway. Pohl felt an adrenalin surge. The AI was likely to choose caution over valour, enabling him to press forward.

Pohl turned to his hireling.

"I assume you are bringing me news that cannot wait," he said.

"I believe so, sir."

"And what is the subject?"

"Developments in England affecting your Tizett business, sir."

"It seems that it's all happening today," muttered Pohl to himself.

Most of the afternoon had been spent in communications with the factions in Phoenicia. He had been displeased with the summary execution of Ted Milner. The man's eventual death was probably inevitable, but the situation had been brought too quickly to its climax. Another week of media hand-wringing would have exacerbated the psychological impact still further. Moreover, his officer training had immersed him with a very straightforward view of military discipline. Frontline troops carried out orders; they did not embark upon unilateral ventures. Command and control was incompatible with solo adventurism. During numerous conversations with parties on both sides of the conflict, he had reasserted propriety and procedure. East Phoenicia was a tinderbox. The players were circling around one another, just like the pieces on a chessboard. With care, the arms race would be reborn, but it required both sides to be wrestling with the fog of uncertainty. A quick resolution was not, absolutely not, in his interests.

It had taken most of the morning to establish the identity of the commander who gave the execution order. Pohl had exercised leniency, and allowed the man to live; however, he could not afford to be seen as weak. He had instructed the man, live to camera, to sever the hands of his youngest child, a daughter still a few years from puberty. Even as he was delivering this sanction, the commander was tearful with fawning gratitude towards

Pohl for his clemency. Thankful to be mutilating his own progeny, thought Pohl; such is the lasting power of the arms trade.

"There are things happening in London," said Joakim. "I heard from Ward."

"He shouldn't be calling here directly," said Pohl with scorn.

He and Ward had once been blood brothers, but much had happened since then. That was one of the frustrations with the Services. Too many Marines felt they were entitled to a lifelong bond. Watching comrades blown apart by your side, sharing secrets that could land you before a war crimes tribunal, those experiences were hard to eradicate. But it was time for Ward to remove Tyreso from his speed dial. Pohl could no longer cover-up for his erstwhile colleague, or troubleshoot every dicey complication.

"There's a chain of command."

"I know," said Joakim. "But this sounds serious."

"Give me the guts of it."

"As you know, Ward has been monitoring a number of potential threats to your interests, including this polymer business in South-East England. Covert listening, communications intercepts, that sort of thing. I'm not sure of the details but it seems that, as a result of a recent operation, he took into custody one of the subjects of the surveillance."

"Capture not kill?"

"She's now under advanced interrogation. Before termination, Ward wants to establish the extent of her knowledge, and who else is involved."

"So far, so operational."

"I agree, sir."

"So why the hell is he calling here? What aren't you telling me?" Pohl smashed his fist against his desk, toppling two of the chess pieces. His opponent's queen dropped onto her side, and careened towards the edge of the board.

Joakim looked at the floor. It was always prudent to avoid eye contact, he felt, when the red mist fell upon his boss. Rex was no longer loitering by his feet. The guinea pig had been playing with a seagrass ball at the foot of a side table. Yet at the sound of Pohl's fury, Rex too turned away, scampering towards the corner where it crouched on its hind legs, squeaking softly, and licking its fur.

"He's concerned about Cunningham's behaviour, sir. Apparently the Secretary called a few hours ago demanding to speak with the captive. Ward couldn't think of a reason to refuse."

"If anything gets traced back to Cunningham, the project could unravel," said Pohl.

He had hoped a senior civil servant, of all people, would be able to maintain composure. "We can't afford for him to act impetuously."

"What would you like me to do?"

Pohl picked up the black queen just before it rolled off his desk. He curled his fist tightly about the object until the veins on this back of his hand were protruding through his flesh. A parade of earthworms could have been on the move beneath the skin.

"Surveillance operations getting revealed when, above all, they should be discrete. A woman in chains who may have figured out the scheme. A Permanent Secretary who could blow his cover any moment. Can I trust nobody to do their job effectively? I'm paying them a small fortune, is it not enough to at least expect reliability?"

"Yes, you have the right to expect it, sir."

"So why must I do everything myself?"

Rex let out a poorly timed chirp, and, enraged, Pohl thrust the chess piece in the direction of the hapless creature, bellowing as he released it from his grasp. The queen hurtled through the chill air, spinning around like an unhinged car at a fairground waltzer, and seemed almost to accelerate along its trajectory at it neared its target. A split second later, the guinea pig lay lifeless on the stone floor, its bloody brain matter scattered behind it in a V-formation, with the lower half of the chess piece jutting from the corpse and the remainder embedded in the seagrass ball. Pohl's anger was temporarily sated and he could now focus on practical steps to resolve the predicament.

"Arrange for transportation to London," he snapped at Joakim.

"Sir, are you certain?"

Joakim knew many things about his master, and foremost on the list was his reclusive nature, his yearning for privacy. Pohl had not left the region for two years, nor the country for five.

The mogul did not answer directly. He glared at Joakim with a barbaric power that screamed *How dare you question my authority, you oaf? Did you not see what befell the rodent?*

Joakim nervously patted down the flaps of his jacket pockets.

"I mean, you are certain. Of course you are certain. I'll arrange things right away."

Craig turned up the heat until the butter melted across the flat bottom. Then he poured the mixture into the pan, and allowed it to sit, unstirred, for almost half a minute until the underside was tinged with a light crispness, at which point he lifted and folded parts of the scrambled egg to create the perfect blend of foam and runniness. Dimala was by now accustomed to the signature dish served on *The Angola*, and held out his plate expectantly, like a pitiful Dickensian child.

Over the past five hours, Craig had steered the boat into a little known tributary of the Thames, as safe as possible from detection, and moored it in a stretch of waterway blessed with abundant, lavish foliage. He could not risk that Hino's threats were sham braggadocio. In all aspects of their dealings to date, he had seemed a man of earnest authenticity. His promise of vengeance could not be dismissed. For the time being – perhaps forever – Craig was a man on the run.

Exhausted, Craig had crashed out as soon as the boat was secured in its clandestine location. However, his reverie had not lasted long. After thirty minutes of troubled sleep, he had been woken by an excited Dimala, shaking him by the shoulder and repeating "You must hear this" in an ever higher pitch. Craig was still so groggy that he smashed his head on the top of the door-frame as he walked through into the cabin, and even twenty minutes later blood was still trickling from the cut. But as soon as Dimala explained his discovery, he knew that his full attention was required. Hence, the need for eggs. So much easier to concentrate without a groaning stomach.

While Craig had been navigating *The Angola*, Dimala had been listening to hours of tedious conversation recorded by the ferrite cylinder implanted in the bowels of the Ministry of Defence, and transcribing the bulk of it into notes, on the off-chance it might carry value. He was now well-versed in the committee structures of the defence bureaucracy, and the ways in which minutes of meetings between ministers and officials were drafted and filed. With waning interest, he stuck to his task, listening as one caller after another obfuscated, hedged bets, and shifted responsibility for budget over-runs or missed deadlines. After plodding through over 24 hours of recordings, he had finally struck gold. He had worked his way back to the very first call that Cunningham had made after Craig's intrusion into his private office. On a clammy Friday afternoon, half a world distant from the people who had raised him, he heard words he would never quite shake from his consciousness. The words spat by an incensed Cunningham into his supposedly secure line, and then the words offered in response – subdued, but recognisably spoken by Marcelle.

"Dimala, you genius," said Craig. "She's alive. You've proven she's alive."

Over the next hour, the strategist and the analyst replayed the recording a dozen time or more, until they knew by heart every syllable, every cadence, every pause. The entire conversation was written out in long hand, across three sheets of foolscap, each word that passed between one of the most senior officials in the country and their beleaguered colleague. Their hypothesis had not, after all, been some paranoid delusion. Criminality, and perhaps worse, had penetrated to the highest echelons of power.

Even after an hour of repeat listening, the dialogue still made Craig sweat, from Cunningham's opening remark, "You don't know who I am," to Marcelle's climatic "Now do your worst". She was clearly in imminent peril; surely there must be a clue, somewhere in the recording, that might help mitigate the danger.

"What are you thinking?" asked Dimala. "What should we be doing?"

There was no obvious course of action. Craig's thrill at their discovery, at this proof of life, was tempered by uncertainty about how best to proceed. Forwarding the evidence to the police was a non-starter. If those implicated included a member of the ruling elite, working at the heart of the government machine, the tentacles of venality could stretch far and wide. How could he place Marcelle's fate in the hands of the local constabulary, who might be equally culpable in the deception and lies? Better to trust nobody than to prematurely alert Cunningham of their intentions. He could take some small satisfaction in the knowledge that Marcelle was still living. But if Cunningham or his cronies got wind that he was escalating matters, it might panic them into reckless measures. And that could be fatal for Marcelle. Far better, in the near term, to keep the circle of insiders to those whose loyalty was beyond suspicion.

Craig's current assumption was that the population "beyond suspicion" was limited to just two individuals: himself and Dimala. Even Adrienne was too conflicted to enjoy his unquestioned confidence. She had been indispensable during their recent infiltration to the bowels of the MOD. But she was still on Hino's payroll. If it came to the point where she had to protect his interests, or theirs, he could not be entirely certain which way she would leap.

So, if there were any signs or hints in the recordings, he and Dimala would need to uncover them alone. And that was why the pair had barely moved from their seats for the past hour. Dimala had adjusted the settings so that each loop was slightly different. In the most recent, the two voices were almost inaudible; he had modulated the frequencies so that the background noise was dominant. But there was nothing that could be pinpointed to a particular location – no hints, for example, of an aircraft firing along a runway, or a railway station announcer in full flow. Just the occasional sound of a hammer or drill, the generic noise of construction that could be happening in any of a thousand sites across the land.

"This time, I'll try phasing out Cunningham, so we can concentrate purely on Marcelle's words," said Dimala, adjusting the amplification to block out the Secretary's distinctive pitch.

The recording was blank for the first few seconds, corresponding to the period when Cunningham introduced his agenda. And then Marcelle came in. Her opening seventeen words already searingly familiar: *"I have quite a few questions of my own. And I need to speak to Mr Richards."*

"That's what I don't get," said Craig. "Why does she say that? She must know there's not a snowball's chance of being patched through to me."

"Yet still she makes the demand," said Dimala. "It does sound strange, abrupt."

"It's almost like she's talking directly to me," pondered Craig, "and not to Cunningham at all. How could that be?"

"It's not impossible that's exactly what she's doing, Mr Richards."

"Because?"

"Since I arrived in London, she and I have spoken for hours, days even, about fringe elements of the digital world. She saw some of the ways I was able to use predictive coding in India, and was intrigued at the broader potential. She knows there's hardly a security wall that can't be breached with targeted programming. It wouldn't take an enormous leap of faith for her to conclude there might be eavesdroppers, two in particular, on her call with Cunningham."

"If you're right, we need to trawl back through the rest of her answers. Perhaps Cunningham wasn't the audience for a single remark she made. Perhaps every word was addressed to us."

"We have to believe it."

Throughout the conversation, Marcelle spoke one hundred and thirty-seven words. Each of these was now typed separately into a computer programme, and sorted by a number of parameters: chronologically, alphabetically, by letter count. The various results were displayed side-by-side on the screen. Craig studied the lists, looking for anything unusual – a bizarre pattern, a stray connection, any signal of hidden purpose or intent.

"Let's ignore the definite and indefinite articles," said Craig, "Then the personal and possessive pronouns. Stutters, they can go too."

"That's removed about half the content," said Dimala.

"Next eliminate any repetitions, and the times she uses my name. What have we got left?"

"It's there, displayed for you."

Craig lent forwards. "Come on, Marcelle, what's this all about?" he mumbled. "What are you trying to tell us?"

The script had been pared down to just twenty-one core terms: Questions – Speak – Break – Hell hole – Church – Charmer – Wikipedia – Kewpie doll – Interested – Hill – Jack – Jill – Crown – Message – War – Rooms – Victors – Cronies – Strings – Occupy – Worst. Dimala enlarged each word to the largest sans serif font that would fit to a page, and printed out twenty-one separate sheets. Craig spread them around the floor of the cabin. Whatever Marcelle was trying to communicate, it didn't seem to be a twenty-one word sentence. However they arranged the sheets, they couldn't generate a specific message or instruction.

"It must be hidden deeper," said Craig. "We need to delve further."

To one end of the cabin, they grouped the verbs: *Speak – Break – Occupy.*

"There was the Occupy London movement a couple of years ago," said Craig. "Overnight, they set up an encampment on the steps of St Paul's. The area was a gaudy mass of weathered tarpaulin set against austere Portland stone. Could that be it? Is she held in the far reaches of the Cathedral Crypt, perhaps?" said Craig.

Dimala mulled a few other options – "Spring *Break*? Prison *Break*? Weekend *Break*?" – without reaching any breakthrough insight.

"What about the brand names: *Wikipedia, Kewpie doll*? Dimala, see what the free encyclopaedia says about dolls, where they were invented, where they're sold. Perhaps that's it?"

"According to this page, it seems their origins were in Waltershausen, Germany, but they went into mass production in Missouri."

"Neither seems an obvious location. It wouldn't have been easy to transport her out of the country, especially across the Atlantic. And it might have set alarm bells ringing if she'd blurted out such an obvious clue. What about the nouns?"

"A couple of Christian names, *Jack* and *Jill*. Otherwise, let's start from the top. First on the list we have the word *questions*."

"We're not short of those. What we really need are answers," said Craig.

"Then we have *hellhole*; is that a noun or an adjective?"

"Dimala, just step back for a moment. I think I'm seeing something here."

"What is it Mr Richards?"

"Sentence two, she says this isn't like being in Church. So, it's not *Church*, she's established that much. But what? And here, in sentence six, we must try the top of the *hill*."

"So let's do what she says, and try the hill instead."

"Instead, Dimala. Or perhaps as well."

Craig picked the two sheets from the floor and taped them to the window.

"Church hill. Churchill!" read Dimala.

"Exactly," said Craig triumphantly.

"So what does that mean? Do we look where Churchill lived?"

"Perhaps Chartwell. Or places associated with his achievements, like Yalta?"

"Or some of these places named after him?"

Dimala typed the key terms into the Google search bar, but Craig was already rattling off the possibilities.

"There's a Churchill College, Cambridge. And Churchill Place in Canary Wharf. HMS Churchill, the submarine. A few schools dotted across the country. Damn it, we need to narrow the search parameters. What nouns do we have left?"

Dimala read from left to right the sheets still spread across the cabin floor.

"Crown. Message..."

"Dimala, look at this."

Craig attached a third sheet to the wall. "*War.* Sentence seven, she couldn't signpost it more clearly. She tells Cunningham, or rather tells us, *I have a clear message – you've made this a war.*"

"Churchill War..."

"And then, look at the rest of the sentence. Three times she uses the word *room* or a derivative. *Room for many victors.* There aren't many *rooms.* There's one *room.* She knows about my obsession with *The Power Of*

Three when it comes to breakthrough strategies. I guess she wanted to make certain we didn't miss the jigsaw's final piece."

"I'm sorry, Mr Richards. I've been living in your country for just a few weeks, and I'm unfamiliar with much of the culture and history. What does this mean?"

"What this means, my friend, is that nobody – not Hino, not Cunningham, not Tizett, not the Devil himself leaping into my path from the hottest circle of his inferno – nobody is going to sabotage an appointment I'll be arranging for a few hours from now."

Craig slammed shut the lid of his laptop. The time for analysis and word play was over. He was now on a mission of revenge.

"This very evening, a few minutes after sunset, a block away from Downing Street ... in the Churchill War Rooms."

And a hundred miles away, her wrists purple from the bite of the polypropylene rope, her face pale from interminable confinement in a grimy and dank environment, Marcelle allowed herself a moment of hope.

"I figured it out," she whispered to herself. "Please God, Craig. I hope by now you've figured it out too."

Chapter Fifteen

Located in:

St James's Park
and
The Churchill War Rooms

The poorly lit and ventilated basement complex now known as the Churchill War Rooms operated as the command centre for the British government for the duration of the Second World War. With hostilities between Britain and Germany rising throughout 1938, the decision was taken to convert an inauspicious warren of store rooms under the Office of Works and the Board of Trade, into a refuge for the War Cabinet and Chiefs of Staff.

For six years, it was both home and office to the country's war leaders, its existence kept secret beyond a tiny coterie of senior officials and ministers. Discretion was vital for all concerned: the rooms remained vulnerable to collapse in the event of a direct hit. They were chosen as convenient improvisation, not as an impregnable bunker. A massive detonation, or a poison gas attack, or infiltration by enemy parachutists, could have cut off the country's military head, and dealt a potentially fatal blow to Allied morale. Its covert status remained intact throughout the conflict; in over seventy years, scholars of the SS archives have uncovered not the faintest trace that the Nazis suspected the existence of this hidden refuge.

Since the 1980s, the War Rooms have undergone repeated cycles of renovation and reconstruction. When it became apparent that the dry, dusty basement conditions were causing irreversible damage to historic documents, the complex was converted into a functioning museum, open to the public, and meeting exacting standards for temperature, humidity, lighting and pest control. Many of the civil servants who had risked vitamin D deficiency through long periods underground, working amidst the fug of cigarette smoke and the stench of appalling sanitation, joined Churchill family members and other dignitaries for a celebratory opening event in 1984. In 2003, the museum was expanded to include a suite of rooms used by Churchill, his wife, his bodyguards, and other associates. In 2005, after further development, the ajoining Churchill Museum was added, a large room – also underground – dedicated to retelling the story of Britain's most maverick and revered Prime Minister, and containing many of the objects most closely associated with his rollercoaster political career.

A few months before the eruption of the crisis in East Phoenicia, building works had once again been commissioned at the War Rooms. The Imperial War Museum, the body now responsible for the site's administration, had finally unearthed evidence of a tunnel connecting the War Rooms with the Prime Minister's official residence at Number Ten Downing Street. This passage had been long rumoured but all efforts to confirm its presence had hit a wall of obfuscation and delay. Only due to dogged perseverance and an uncharacteristically enlightened ruling by the Information Commissioner was the tunnel's existence established as fact. The museum's trustees, in discussion with the Ministry of Defence, had recently approved a modest fund to complete some basic works on the tunnel. Rotten timbers needed to be replaced, mould treated, and waterproofing clay injected where the rocks were most porous. Once these were complete, it had been provisionally agreed that a stretch of the passageway, perhaps a few dozen feet, could be opened to visitors and incorporated into the overall War Rooms experience.

It was the connecting tunnel that provided Craig with his opportunity. Direct access to the War Rooms was vigorously controlled; there hadn't been a single instance of unauthorised entry in thirty years, and the most battle-hardened criminal, let alone a novice trespasser such as himself, would struggle to bypass the country's finest protection protocols without triggering swift detection and incarceration. However the security of the tunnel was unproven, and Dimala's ingenuity had offered a way in. The renovation work was being completed by Mexel, a fast-growing private contractor from Hereford. Mexel was widely admired for its quality procedures and meticulous approach to staff selection.

It was proud that its ethos and values commanded the confidence of government procurement officers, and strove daily to justify that trust. Unfortunately for Mexel, its policies and practices suffered from the vice of predictability. They were no match for Dimala's more intuitive and lateral psyche. It had taken him just twenty minutes to bypass their firewalls and crack precisely how their workmen gained access to the tunnel every morning.

The War Rooms were open daily including weekends, but visiting hours ended at 6pm. Craig allowed another hour for the curators, tour guides and cleaners to complete their duties and leave. During that time, he strolled around St James's Park, just across Horse Guards Road from the expanse of Whitehall that housed the War Rooms. In many ways, his future hinged upon the next phase proceeding without a hitch. But that wasn't the concern playing on his conscience like a screeching toddler. Marcelle's well-being, and potentially her life, were also at stake. Any mis-step, and she could bear the consequences of his failure. That was the outcome he was desperate to avoid.

As he wandered around the park, Craig steeled himself for his rescue attempt. From the bandstand, he watched the colony of pelicans being fed by a party of French schoolchildren. But still his limbs were shivering with trepidation and self-doubt. He plunged his hands into the waters of the Swire fountain, hoping the cool crystalline sensation would neutralise any shaking. To fortify his resolve, he focused on particular individuals that passed before his eyes – a skateboarding Jamaican teenager, a City worker cycling home in a three-piece suit, a hawker of replicas and trinkets – and imagined a life story in which each one overcame hardship and emerged in triumphant glory. In his mind's eye, he pictured them together on stage, bathed in the glow of a dozen spotlights, basking in the audience's wild applause, each one holding aloft a trophy to their towering accomplishments. *That's my destiny today*, he urged himself.

But he needed something else. Discretely, in the shadows of a scarlet oak tree alongside Birdcage Walk, he tipped a mound of white powder the size of a small acorn onto the back of a credit card, furtively glanced around him lest the eyes of any nearby park-goers had meandered in his direction, and snorted it up his right nostril. *That felt better*, he told himself, as if a fist-pounding motivational psychologist had taken up residence inside his head. *I can do this thing! I'm the man!*

It was now past seven. Craig could no longer prevaricate, like some latter-day Prince of Denmark. He checked again the instructions that Dimala had texted him and committed them to memory. Then he set foot towards the Clive Steps – the passageway between the Treasury building and the Foreign and Commonwealth Office. A workmen's pit had been constructed at the top of the steps. It was located just behind the statue of Major-General Robert Clive, the eighteenth century officer and politician who secured India for the British crown. The pit provided temporary access to the War

Rooms tunnel for Mexel's engineers and builders, and the lid was operated through a fingerprint recognition monitor. If Dimala's cyberspace exploits lived up to their billing, a scan of Craig's thumb and forefinger should be sufficient to trigger release of the deadbolt.

As Craig approached the Clive Steps, two police motorcycle outriders hurtled into Horse Guards Road from the direction of Westminster Palace. The outriders were followed by a convoy of government limousines. Craig had been following the news reports closely enough to make an educated guess about the identity of the passengers. The Phoenician crisis had already caused the government to shower unprecedented largesse on its defence preparedness, raiding contingency reserves built up over half a decade. Now, senior ministers were meeting with the leaders of NATO, the EU and the United States to forge a collective response, and determine the circumstances under which an armed response might be considered. In the second limousine, through tinted windows, Craig vaguely deciphered the silhouette of Defence Secretary Katherine Foster. *If only you knew,* he thought, *how the crooks running your department spend their time as soon as your back is turned.*

"I'm talking to you."

A gravelly voice a few feet behind Craig interrupted his contemplation. It was a uniformed police officer, Special Constable Martin Thorpe according to the insignia on his sleeve. Short and slightly overweight, he was

305

swirling a leather wrapped truncheon as if he was Bruce Lee with a chain whip.

"So pay attention."

Craig played the naif. "Sorry, I was distracted. Can I help you, officer?"

"You certainly can. You can help by getting out of Central London."

"I don't understand. I'm simply…"

"This park is for tourists. And families. And law-abiding people enjoying the Princess Diana Memorial Walk."

"I've got no problem with that, officer."

The officer jabbed his truncheon into Craig's chest.

"So don't confuse this park with Junkieville High Street. I know what you were doing by that tree. What sort of man sniffs his nose into oblivion when there are kids and their mums all around?"

The sort of man, thought Craig, *who was both proud and disgusted at the spontaneous explanation he once concocted for his daughter.* Natalie: Daddy, I wanted you to see my new party dress. Craig: It's very … red, and … very dresslike. Natalie: Daddy, what are you doing on your knees? And what's the matter with your eyes? Craig: I'm using sugar to build a tower. Natalie: But why are you building it in the bathroom? Craig: I'd like it to be a surprise for mummy. You won't tell her, will you? Natalie: Can I help you, daddy. I'm used to making things at school, but I think you'd need some paper and glue to make the tower stay up. Craig: It'll be the Richards Tower. One day, maybe we can all go and live there. Natalie: You'll probably need more sugar, daddy. Craig: Why don't you fetch some from the kitchen? And darling, don't walk in again without knocking, you know how I feel about that. Natalie: Can I taste some, it looks very … soft, like a cushion. Craig: Keep awa… Nat, I think we're going to have to wash your hands now. Nat, don't tell mummy, remember? Not until it's finished.

"Count yourself lucky this time. I didn't get a good enough view to be certain," continued the officer. "And the PM's emergency meeting means I'm too busy for stop and search. But, if I see your sorry butt anywhere in Central London in the next 24 hours, you'll know what it's like going cold turkey in the back of my van. Is that clear?"

The officer's belly wobbled like blancmange at the intensity of his lecture.

"I will leave town," said Craig. "You won't see me again."

Of course, Craig had no intention of being blown from his course. For a couple of minutes, he pretended to be heading towards Victoria Station, with all the urgency of a cup final footballer protecting a one goal lead in the last seconds of the match. But all the time he was watching the Special Constable march off towards Downing Street, various parts of his body waddling in tandem.

The moment the officer disappeared from view, Craig doubled back. No more distractions, he resolved. Like Hamlet throwing off his antic disposition, there must be no further obstacles to his precious mission. Near the

Blue Bridge, a dozen young Americans were standing in a large circle throwing a frisbee around; Craig walked right through the middle of the group.

"Dude, that's uncool," said one of the group, his dreadlocks dancing on his shoulders and his ZZ Top T-shirt sweat-soaked from his work-out.

Oblivious to the catcalls, Craig continued in a direct line towards the Clive Steps, even as the frisbee arched a few inches from his temple.

At the entrance to the workmen's pit, Craig took a hard hat from his rucksack and clipped the chin straps into place. The hat's purpose was not so much for protection (he would remove it as soon as he was in the War Rooms); rather, to hide his features from any CCTV surveillance, and to reassure any casual observer as he descended into the pit that his business was legitimate. Then, he pressed the extremities of his fingers against the digital recognition monitor, and held his breath, half expecting the distinctive wail of an emergency alarm to ring out. A light twice flashed red as it processed the fingerprint data, paused momentarily, and then reappeared as luminous green. Dimala's work had been impeccable. According to the instructions on his phone, Craig now had sixty seconds to gain entry to the tunnel or the opportunity would be relinquished.

Access to the pit was through a cast iron removable plate, similar to a manhole cover. With the deadbolts released, Craig took a hook handle tool from his rucksack and inserted it into the pick holes. He was then able to lift the plate on its hinges, raising it to an angle of around fifty degrees, sufficient to squeeze through. He sat on the lip of the hole and dangled his legs until they knocked against a metal ladder attached to the side of the pit. As he lowered the plate behind him, he whispered silent thanks to Dimala's resourcefulness. *If I get out of this intact,* he promised, *you and I are headed for the most authentic three hours of gastronomic indulgence available in Brick Lane.*

The day's renovation work on the tunnel had finished mid-afternoon, when the array of temporary spotlights had been killed for the night, so Craig was forced to advance in near total blackness. The only meagre illumination was provided by an app on his phone, and the seeping into the tunnel of illumination from the distant War Rooms, but none was sufficient to speed his journey. And with construction work ongoing, every step held danger; debris and pick axes and half-erected girders littered his path. Most importantly, Craig had no way of knowing whether Cunningham's henchmen might be active in the War Rooms at this hour. Any careless slip, any yelp of agony as stray steel pierced his side, and they could be upon him. Until he had properly assessed the scene, stealth was the only viable option. With such vigilance and deliberation, it took nearly forty minutes for Craig to complete the short route from workmen's pit to the tunnel's opening.

The tunnel joined the War Rooms at the end of one of its narrow arterial corridors. Immediately next to the intersection, a room had been set aside for use by the renovation supervisors, and it was from this room that Craig heard the beat of laptop keys in use. The nature of the tapping suggested he was not listening to a professional typist at work; the key strokes were ponderous, with regular pauses as the operator searched the keyboard for a particular letter. The typist was facing away from the door. As Craig peered into the room, he saw the back of a closely-shaven male head and the contours of a cauliflower ear. He did not know yet, but would soon discover, that the room was only partially dedicated to the oversight of Mexel's tunnel excavations. With the MOD's privileged role in the War Rooms programme, Cunningham had been able to commandeer it as an occasional base for covert purposes at his personal discretion.

The typist's room, as with all rooms in the basement complex, was sparsely furnished in keeping with the austere diktats of war-torn Britain. Further along the corridor, Imperial War Museum curators had recreated a series of bedrooms as used by dignitaries throughout the combat years. Each room was the size of a supplies cupboard, which in many cases had been their origin, stocked with a standard civil service bed, table, chest and chair. The bleakest prep school dormitories would be more inviting. Yet Ward's military tutelage long ago exorcised any need to be surrounded by frivolities and luxuries. In any event, tonight he was fixated upon one over-riding purpose: to complete his report. Thomas Pohl was en route to London, and would expect a pithy update on matters, so Ward was determined that his own perspective, devoid of bluster and bluff, would be the first in Pohl's hands. His personal loyalty and his instinct for self-preservation dictated this course.

From the rear view, the typist was nobody Craig recognised. But any interruption would compromise his mission. He tiptoed past the room in almost complete silence. Just once did the side of his shoe scrape against an unevenly-laid flagstone. Ward looked up from the keyboard, as if sensing something was amiss.

"Strange," he mumbled. But he did not turn around. Even underground, London provided an incessant hum of scuffs and knocks. It was probably nothing more, Ward figured, than the night watchman making his final rounds.

Having navigated his way past Ward, Craig hurried past two hundred feet of exhibits and memorabilia. Marcelle could not, of course, be captive in any of the public areas of the War Rooms. The Map Room, the Conference Room for the Chiefs of Staff and the Broadcasting Room were all visited daily by throngs of school parties, tour groups and independent travellers. However, Craig and Dimala's research had revealed these accounted for less than half the venue's total floorspace. Numerous ancillary areas were restricted from general access. Having discounted those where museum staff could readily gain admission, and anywhere soundproofing was minimal, one intriguing part of the complex remained, fixedly in his sights.

The Dock was the disparaging name given to the shelter's cramped sub-basement by Churchill's junior staff in 1941. It was a warren of low corridors and rooms, made available as overnight quarters to those whose rank did not entitle them to accommodation in the basement proper. Insects, rodents, the lack of flushing toilets and numerous other deficiencies meant most War Rooms personnel preferred to take their chances with the random terror of Nazi bombing raids than suffer its squalor. But for others the indignities outweighed the peril. For six years, the Dock was an integral part of the bunker's functioning.

A single steep staircase led from the basement into the Dock, but this was blocked by an inch-thick sheet of toughened glass. Public visitors were able to crane their necks and gaze through the glass, witnessing the first few feet of sub-basement corridor, but that was all. A couple of guides were approaching the tenth anniversary of their employment, yet despite a decade spent recounting statistics and anecdotes to inquisitive guests, even they had been no closer than the glass sheet to entering the Dock. It was strictly off-limits. Which meant it was an ideal place to stow a hostage.

The glass sheet was held in place by eight hex cap screws. Craig already knew the specifications from his earlier reconnaissance, so he took a wrench from his rucksack and fixed it to the first screw's hexagonal head. To his delight, it rotated easily. This confirmed that, quite recently, somebody else had been using this route into the sub-basement. If the screws, so contaminated with the rust of ages, had resisted his efforts, he might have needed to revisit his hypotheses. But then, he thought, his confidence fuelled by cocaine and adrenalin, I wouldn't be worthy of my global reputation as the Strategist.

The air within the Dock, while breathable, had the fetid aroma of a primordial swamp. Craig stifled a cough, and his eyes started to water, as the pungency hit the back of his throat. Small wonder Churchill's back room staff had not exactly leapt at the chance to savour its embrace on a more permanent basis. But he had no time to worry about its historic inadequacies. He needed to search every corner of the Dock's network as quickly as possible. Until his mission was complete, anyone passing through the War Rooms would notice the displaced glass cover. Was there an hourly security patrol? Or perhaps every thirty minutes? Craig had no idea. But there was only one way out of the sub-basement, meaning escape would be impossible if his incursion was discovered.

The first room in the Dock provided no answers to his desperate search. Dusty puddles, a pile of broken bricks, a scurrying rat. The second and third were the same. However, as he turned a corner, and descended a few more steps, the rooms were somewhat more purposeful. One contained a metal table on which were strewn – as far as he could tell from the light of his mobile – yellowing 1940s books and magazines, perhaps kept for light relief at the end of a shift by members of Churchill's typing pool. In a second, the table was piled high with a mountain of rolled-up maps. Craig correctly surmised these were untouched for seventy years. The War Rooms, and other bastions of allied command across the country, had worked their way through hundreds of thousands of maps of different parts of the globe during the long years of the Second World War, sketching on them the latest intelligence about casualty numbers and marginal changes in the curvature of the frontline. Many of the scrawls were no more than ill-informed footnotes, and only a handful of maps had been preserved as artefacts of lasting historical significance.

Then, in the third room, Craig heard movement. Another rat, perhaps? Or perhaps more? Pulling back the deadbolts, he eased open the door. His heart pumping, he realised he was hearing more than movement. There was the muffled sound of a female voice calling out through a tightly-bound gag. He turned the light of his phone towards the room's interior. Bound in the centre of the room, victim of Craig's swaggering vainglory, of his impulsive commitment to an assignment of which she was rightly wary, was the one person who kept his demons in check. The cryptic message had been accurately interpreted after all.

The last time they had been together, at dinner at Malkin Castle, she had been the epitome of sophistication and refinement. Now, she looked wretched, like a medieval street urchin so battered by calamity and misfortune that any residue of hope had vanished from her distraught gaze.

Craig could only guess at the psychological or perhaps physical brutality she had endured. But at the moment, none of that mattered. Just a few feet away, the dim glow from his mobile screen illuminated his muse.

And all the while, ten feet above, and two hundred feet due north east, Ward was still pummelling away at the keyboard. He was a man of actions, not words, and his task did not come easily. Every now and then he grimaced in frustration at a paragraph that failed to convey his chosen meaning, and he held down the delete button as the text was erased. But slowly, incrementally, his report was taking form. Ward clenched his teeth determinedly. There was no other option; it must be in good shape before Pohl arrived in town.

Chapter Sixteen

Located in:

The Churchill War Rooms

"**Y**ou're late," wheezed Marcelle, her voice hoarse from the acrid basement air.

Craig smiled grimly as he untied the rope.

"Someone chose to set the world's most enigmatic clue."

Marcelle put her arm around Craig and hauled herself to her feet. Her leg muscles had suffered atrophy from the lack of physical activity during her days in captivity, and it was hard to find her balance. She lent awkwardly on Craig as she recovered her orientation. Without his support, she would collapse under her own weight, like a fifties tower block imploding during demolition.

"Someone's got to give you a new challenge," she said.

"We had a bit of help from the other side," said Craig. "I think you've gained an admirer."

318

"Admirers are good," said Marcelle, a faint smile playing on the corner of her lips.

She kicked out her right leg with as much energy as she could muster, trying to stimulate renewed blood circulation. But she was still desperately weak.

"We'll need to talk all about your ordeal," said Craig, brushing the dirt from her forehead. "But the first priority is to get out of this place."

As Craig's words sank in, Marcelle jolted.

"Listen," she stammered. "This is important. Are the War Rooms empty, or did you notice anybody on your way in?"

"There was almost nobody. I just passed one guy. He was typing, and had his back to me. Why?"

"Did he have a boxer's ear?"

"I think so. He had his back to me. Is he the person who's been…"

Marcelle shook with the involuntary spasm of unalloyed fear, as if she'd brushed against an electrified fence.

"We need to move fast. He's a thug and a sadist. He mustn't find you here, or we'll both regret it."

Craig hooked his arm around Marcelle's waist, and, in stumbling, juddering fashion, led her along the basement corridor. She was clinging to him so tightly her fingernails were digging deep into his skin, drawing blood. *No danger of Stockholm Syndrome with you*, he thought. *So hold fast. Hold fast and don't let go!*

Marcelle was wincing as they inched along the corridor, passing the Dock's side rooms. During her days in

319

captivity, this route – the only connection between her cell and the world above – had taken a painful hold in her mind's eye. She imagined it to be an interminable, meandering track cutting through desolate wasteland. A track which, every few hours, reverberated with the squelching noise of boot against stone, a sound which was magnified as it echoed against the silence. In her fancy, whenever Ward approached, the corridor transformed into a hideous birth canal, awash with swirling demonic colours as it ushered up her tormentor. Bustling with terror and foreboding, this was the path along which Craig now encouraged her.

Instinctively, she was glancing into every other side room, dreading the revelations that might be offered up. Another woman, perhaps? Maybe the skeletal remains of a captive unable to endure? Or a legion of handcuffed children, their skin turned albino from light deprivation, their expressions vacant and resigned. In fact, the rooms were uninhabited, every one of them, but still Marcelle felt tears streaming unbidden down her face, in empathy with those who might have been here. The ghastly parade of fellow victims had comprised her sole, imaginary companions these past long days.

Ascending the steps was a daunting physical trial after so long spent virtually immobile. It seemed to demand greater reserves of stamina and willpower than any of the charity half marathons she had completed in her teenage years. On those occasions, the exercise was the culmination of weeks of preparation and training, and the streets were lined with onlookers whose enthusiasm pumped up any flagging spirits. This time, there was no banner proclaiming *Finishing Line* once the course was run. On the contrary, having climbed the steps, she knew they faced the real prospect of worse to come.

Craig was crouching at the top of the steps, grasping her hands, pulling her upwards with the stubborn will of a deep sea fisherman refusing to let go his prize catch.

"Are you OK to continue?" he asked.

She nodded silently, her nails still searing into his flesh. But her body was barely responding whenever she urged herself onwards, and now the light of the War Rooms upper floor was assaulting her senses. Disorientated, she staggered and knocked against the glass cover that had lent against the stone wall ever since Craig had released the hex cap screws.

Craig grabbed Marcelle's arm lest she fall back through the trap, and held her as her breathing steadied, adjusting to her new environment. But that meant he was unable to do anything about the glass cover itself. It slipped from the wall, and skated across the floor in defiance of friction and physics. Craig saw where it was headed, but it was too late to make amends. Like a Tiger Woods golf ball heading remorselessly towards the centre of the green, so the glass cover seemed drawn to the trap by an invisible suction device. One moment, it was accelerating across the stone. The next, it had vanished from view, replaced by an unnerving sequence of bumping noises as it ricocheted down the steps. And then, the denouement. The cover smashed against the basement floor, shattering instantly despite its chemical toughening. Marcelle sat motionless, petrified at the way the noise carried. The sounds were almost interminable; not just the smash of the initial impact, but dozens of secondary chimes as shards and slivers bounced around in the basement corridor. The endless crashing tore through the stillness like the devastating noise of an almighty motorway pile up. It was the Beethoven's symphony of sound effects.

This time, there was no chance Ward would shake his head and resume his dissertation. This time, he would need to act. Even now, thought Craig, he is grunting with exasperation, hurling his laptop into a drawer, ensuring his pistol is fully loaded. Even now, he is striding towards us. Implacable. We need to hide – and in moments, not minutes.

With Marcelle still unsteady on her feet, Craig raced with her deeper into the War Rooms, away from the tunnel through which he had entered. They fled past the Conference Room where the Chiefs of Staff had argued in sombre mood about the nature of evolving threats in the most pressurised zones across the continent, and agreed where young men would next be sent to their deaths. They turned sharply at the kitchens, where the corridor narrowed, and Craig ducked to avoid slamming his scalp against the low-hanging fluorescent strip bulbs. Even if Ward had set off instantly in pursuit, they were still a couple of hundred feet ahead; hopefully it would be possible to find an area to hide for a few minutes, and perhaps sneak away when Ward took his search down into the Dock.

Just beyond the kitchens was the bunker's Map Room, one of the largest rooms in the complex, and certainly the most cluttered. The War Room curators had been meticulous in recreating a display that matched to the finest detail the facility's appearance throughout years of war. The Map Room had been the hub of information around the clock about deployments, enemy mobilisation and casualty rates. This had been the source, every morning, of daily summaries for the King, Prime Minister and the Chiefs of Staff. Its many desks were barely visible beneath piles of books, papers, cases, and dozens of containers filled with coloured pins. A half dozen colour coded rotary telephones, used to solicit updates from field officers, occupied a raised shelf between facing banks of desks. On every wall hung charts representing key areas of the global conflagration, each depicting an area of conflict from France to Java to North Africa. The maps were punctured with tiny holes, left behind as coloured pins had been moved around the map to reflect the shifting nature of the enemy frontlines.

The Map Room was kept secure from the public by a floor-to-ceiling glass partition, but once the venue was closed to the public, the partition was unlocked to allow for cleaning and occasional maintenance. Craig slid back the partition; it was not an ideal hiding place, but it was the best shelter available. He directed for Marcelle to take refuge beneath a small rolltop bureau.

"We'll be safest if we're not together," he whispered.

Marcelle nodded in compliance.

The furniture had been selected by Churchill's officials to maximise space efficiency. In practice, this meant a working environment more suitable for hobbits than adult humans. The rolltop was perhaps three feet across by two feet deep; Marcelle needed to squeeze into the nominal leg room between two sets of built-in drawers. She forced herself back into the cavity, and drew her knees up to her chin. Another inch or two of height, and it would have been impossible to complete the manoeuvre. But unless Ward was looking face-on directly at the underneath of the desk, there was a fighting chance her concealment would be effective.

For Craig, there was nothing quite so convenient. In the middle of the Map Room, two thick steel columns had been installed to take the weight of the concrete slab that gave the War Rooms a measure of protection from aerial bombardment. Each of these columns was a couple of feet in width, and Craig crouched behind the one nearest to the room's largest wall chart, a map the size of a minibus, on which was labelled every town and city in Europe from the Atlantic to the Urals. He was acutely aware of his racing heart and laboured breathing. It was astonishing how, no sooner did silence become life-critical, then his body seemed to transform into a chuntering mass of organic sound, as deafening as the pounding rhythm of a nineteenth century satanic mill.

Out of the corner of one eye, he spotted an elderly gentleman, with a pronounced stoop, shuffling towards the Map Room. This was not Ward. Craig had only seen Ward from behind, but this man's build and posture was of a different order. As he approached, the elderly man was peering towards Craig's column.

He had been the War Rooms' night watchman for long enough to recognise every inch of its interior. When something was amiss, be it the faintest shadow of a foreign object, or an exhibit slightly out of place, the night watchman was the man to notice. And, thought the watchman, there is certainly something strange about the contours of that column. Craig raised his index finger to his lips, urging the watchman to keep calm and avoid any precipitate commotion.

Ward was now upon the Map Room. He burst through the connecting door from the kitchens, waving his pistol from side to side with his outstretched right arm as he scanned for potential threats.

Damn my thumping heartbeat, thought Craig, *How can he not hear it? How is it not alerting the whole of Central London?*

Ward then trained his firearm directly at the watchman.

"What was that crashing? Was that you?" he demanded.

The watchmen seemed to age a decade in the face of this aggression. His shoulders hunched up even further behind his neck. His frame retreated in upon itself, like an ageing sun collapsing into its core. Cowering, then shaking. Cowering a bit more, then shaking a bit more.

"Not me," he stuttered. "I was coming to investigate the same thing, it sounded like breaking glass."

"If it wasn't you, then who?" shouted Ward. "Have you allowed anyone else in here tonight? I need to know now."

Craig was still indicating for the watchmen to stay discrete, but with a dwindling degree of hope. Slowly, the watchmen raised a bony finger, until it was level with his eye line. Avoiding any sudden or arbitrary movement, he rotated on his heels until his finger was pointed directly towards Craig's column.

He mouthed the words, "Over there" at Ward.

The watchman's role was complete, but his subservience was insufficient to save his life. Ward was in no mood to risk witnesses. With the tiniest pressure on the trigger, the rim of his gun erupted with billowing cordite. And breaking out from the propellant like a fighter jet through cloud cover burst the bullet, soaring through the air, bridging the dozen feet between Ward and the watchman in a fraction of a second. The projectile smashed into the watchman's face just above his right eye, and, barely troubled by the obstacle, erupted from the back of his skull before coming to rest, deeply embedded in the far wall, surrounded by fragments of brain matter and bone. The watchman slumped to the floor, his extremities still twitching in their abrupt death pangs, a final convulsion before the onset of rigor mortis.

Craig realised he had at most a couple of seconds before he suffered the same fate. As Ward moved sideways to secure a better angle from which to take out the interloper behind the column, Craig grabbed one of the telephones and thrust it like a baseball at Ward's head. He knew that, if his aim wasn't true, it was probably the last action he would ever complete. Instinctively, Ward raised his arms to shield himself from the missile. His second bullet fired harmlessly at the ceiling where it rebounded from a wrought iron pipe and torpedoed into a light fitting. Craig pressed his advantage. He dipped his hands deep into a tray of coloured map pins and then leapt across the table in the direction of his assailant. Ward recovered just in time to avoid the brunt of the impact. His gun went flying to the other side of the Map Room, but at least he'd avoided two dozen pins being buried in his face. Just two stuck to their target, a blue pin which dangled from the tip of his nose, and a green one deep within his chin.

As Ward removed the debris from his face, Craig recovered his footing and ran back towards the Conference Room. Ward quickly surveyed the Map Room in case his gun had come to rest in an obvious landing point. When he failed to locate it, he abandoned the search, and set off in pursuit of Craig before his quarry was lost. Left alone in the Map Room, Marcelle stayed hunched beneath the rolltop desk. Alone, that is, except for the corpse of the watchman. Toppling backward from the bullet's impact, the body had fallen just a few feet from her hiding place. His open, lifeless eyes were looking directly at her. Despite his death, the watchman's stare was as intimidating and accusatory as the most aggressive prosecution barrister at an Old Bailey trial. For all her agonies, Marcelle lived on. The watchman, Mr Phillips according to his tag, did not. An innocent in this theatre of corruption and vice.

And I don't even know your first name, thought Marcelle.

At the T-junction fifty yards from the Map Room, Craig turned away from the Conference Room, where improvisation would be difficult and advantage would inevitably lie with the more experienced fighter. Instead, he followed the signage towards the Transatlantic Telephone Room, a small room not much larger than a broom closet, from where Churchill engaged in his most secretive conversations with President Roosevelt, aided by scrambler technology provided by the Pentagon shortly after Hitler's incursions into Poland.

The centrepiece of the room was a waxwork of Churchill seated on a wheeled swivel chair. With Ward now recovered and in pursuit, Craig ducked into the Telephone Room and worked through a dozen scenarios for how he could turn the props into offensive weapons. But there was no time for exhaustive analysis. Ward's steps had quickened, and only moments remained until he would catch up.

"You can't hide for long," Ward hissed into the ether. "I've snapped the necks of Afghans and Iraqis; make no mistake, I won't hesitate to add yours to my collection."

Craig took the wheeled chair in both hands, unseating Churchill in the process, and crouched behind it like an Olympic hurdler on the starting blocks. As Ward came into view, Craig jettisoned the chair. It shot across the floor, with impressive speed for an antique, and for a moment the former Marine was caught off guard.

This was Craig's best chance, perhaps his only chance, to achieve dominance. He lifted the Churchill effigy using both arms. It was surprisingly heavy, but the combination of desperation, adrenalin and cocaine seemed to swell Craig's muscles, infusing his body with unaccustomed strength. He took a step back to maximise room for his swing, and then smashed the waxwork full-square against his foe. Ward recoiled under the blow, and Churchill shattered into pieces. Craig was still holding Churchill's legs, and with the rest of the waxwork littered across the floor, he made jabbing motions towards Ward, using the Premier's lower half like a medieval lance. Unfortunately for Craig, Ward's army training had taught him how to recover from the severest blow in just a few moments. In the Hindu Kush mountains, a second's disorientation often had fatal consequences, and while Craig was still working out his next move, Ward was seizing the initiative.

Churchill's head had detached from the rest of the waxwork upon impact. Like a rugby ball completing a majestic arch over the Headingly crossbar, it had spun in mid-air for an improbably long time, as if suspended by the gods' fine thread. As the head spiralled and twisted, Winston would firstly gaze up at the ceiling, and then down towards the battling opponents, then up once again. And as he looped, his archetypal plump Cuban cigar stayed firmly clenched between his teeth. The old warrior might have lost his body, but he was damned if the *Romeo y Julieta* would slip away so easily.

When Churchill's head finally succumbed to the pull of gravity, and came toppling back down from the roof void, Ward was perfectly positioned to receive it. His pistol might be lost, but he finally had possession of a replacement weapon. Smirking at his anticipated triumph, he thrust Churchill's head at the Strategist. With a sickening crunch, it caught Craig on the temple, sending him reeling. Before Craig knew otherwise, he was prostrate on the floor, pinned down by Ward's weight. The ex-Marine was lying on top of him, biting and punching. Craig was on the verge of blacking out.

"I know who you are," spat Ward. "I spent a day of my life listening to your rubbish."

Now his hands were around Craig's throat. *How can human hands be so powerful?* thought Craig, Ward's training enabled him to leverage the weight of his entire body so that strangulation was quick and effective. It would be easier to wriggle free from the embrace of a six hundred pound silverback gorilla than to escape Ward's throttle.

Craig coughed, but even this was now difficult; his throat was filling rapidly with alien substances. He was starting to black out. If only there was something, anything at all, he could use to strike back. He stretched out his fingers. *What I'd give for a harpoon or a bayonet left lying around by an absent-minded tourist,* he thought. *Or a machete; I've always been a backseat admirer of the potency of the machete.*

His eyelids were heavy now. His stretching out was more frenetic; he was flailing. Is this what death throes feel like? he wondered. It was only when his eyelids were sagging their last that his forefinger touched something that almost felt like a makeshift weapon. In fact, it was Churchill's revered Cuban cigar, which, with the force of Ward's blow, had finally fallen free from the Premier's gritted teeth.

They say smoking kills, he grimaced. *But it may just save my life.*

He dragged the cigar two inches towards him, just enough to curl his fist around it. He imagined every client and lover and friend and dealer and relative and mentor circling around his dying body, urging him not to abandon life just yet, cheering on a last monstrous effort. Their support was flowing through his veins like a stimulant, invigorating him with unknowable strength. It was sufficient for him to raise the cigar to Ward's face, and plunge its end into the centre of the ex-Marine's left eye. Ward's grip loosened immediately. Transparent liquid was showering onto Craig's face from behind the burst cornea. Craig squirmed out free from beneath the bigger man. He had survived the immediate threat, but Ward was not beaten yet.

Even walking was now difficult for Craig. Both legs felt like dead weights as a result of the punishment he'd experienced. Yet it was imperative that he kept moving. He needed to put distance between himself and Ward. *Nothing is as savage as wounded prey,* thought the strategist. *I'm sure that goes double for wounded Marines.*

Beyond the Telephone Room, beyond a velvet curtain, the darkened passageway led into the latest addition to the War Rooms complex: the Churchill Museum. Occupying a single large room, the Museum was organised into a dozen sections, each focusing on a particular time or theme of the former Prime Minister's life. Craig was vaguely aware of its existence from press coverage at the time of its opening, but he'd never toured it in a private capacity. *I wonder if I'll ever have the chance to return without the dubious company of an enraged mercenary consumed with bloodlust,* he reflected.

Craig had moments to decide which part of the Museum provided the best camouflage before Ward crossed the threshold. He chose a scale model of Chartwell, the Westerham estate purchased by a consortium of wealthy businessmen for exclusive use by Winston and his wife, Clementine, when it became apparent, shortly after VE Day, that Churchill had insufficient means to live independently in such a manner. Adjacent to the model was a twelve-foot high signage topped with the legend *The maverick politician*. Not a perfect shield, thought Craig, surveying his surroundings. But the best under the circumstances.

Soon, Craig heard Ward in the museum, breathing heavily.

"Remember what I said," he grunted. "In the next few minutes, I'll be snapping your neck. The longer you drag this out, the more painful I'll make it."

Craig figured the ex-Marine was trying to goad him into revealing his position. *Forget any smart aleck replies,* he told himself. *This is neither the time nor the place.*

The training for young Marines had been sadistic in its intensity. On the final day of the affectionately-named *Hell Week*, Ward had completed an Iron Man triathlon, spent thirty minutes in the boxing ring, notched a hundred press-ups in two minutes, and been parachuted into the killzone of a Somme reconstruction, all in quick succession and at the end of a week when he'd been allowed less than five hours total sleep. But it had given him the valuable lifelong ability to block out pain. Fragments of cigar leaf were still dangling from his dead eye, but Ward had compartmentalised that particular setback. He could almost hear his CO's voice lambasting him for any momentary fragility. *Call yourself hard?* he'd bawl. *My baby sister finished the course before breakfast. Now back in the mud!*

Ward had also been taught exactly how to scout a room for a hidden opponent. The first rule was to block off any escape route. He took the single key hanging by the entrance, locked shut the door, and tucked it into his trouser pocket. Next, he mentally subdivided the museum into searchable areas through which he could systematically work. Finally, he needed to replenish his arsenal. Close to the entrance was a glass cabinet of Churchill memorabilia. He smashed through the front with his bare hand, ignoring the gashes to his forearm from the force of the impact, and grabbed hold of his latest weapons – a Toby jug crafted with Winston's inimical features, and a souvenir ashtray. As part of the Museum display, both items were comically nostalgic. But in the hands of a ruthless professional, they could be lethal.

"I've got my motivation. I've got my weapons. Now, I just need to find you," he stammered.

Ward's intimidation was working. Craig shuffled uncomfortably behind the Chartwell display, fearful that his hiding place was insufficiently secure, and with no plan to defend himself once his refuge was exposed. And, disastrously, the moment of discovery was imminent. Craig's movement triggered one of the museum's interactive features. Seconds later, from a speaker just behind his head, Churchill's sonorous tones were booming forth.

"To give security to these countless homes," he counselled with statesmanlike deliberation, "they must be shielded from two gaunt marauders, war and tyranny."

With Churchill's iron curtain speech underway, and Ward marching with haste and aggression towards the Chartwell display, Craig's cover was blown. He knew from their previous engagement that he would never be able to outfight Ward. Could he outrun him?

In the background, Churchill was continuing his declamation: "We all know the frightful disturbance in which the ordinary family is plunged when the curse of war swoops down upon the bread-winner and those for whom he works and contrives. The awful ruin of Europe, with all its vanished glories, and of large parts of Asia glares us in the eyes."

Craig broke for the next display, entitled *The Wilderness Years*. Inevitably, Ward was alert to the movement. He flung the Toby jug and it collided with Craig directly between his shoulder blades. He staggered, but this time didn't fall. Yet Ward was now just feet away. And still, Churchill was muttering gravely, "When the designs of wicked men or the aggressive urge of mighty States dissolve over large areas the frame of civilized society, humble folk are confronted with difficulties with which they cannot cope. For them all is distorted, all is broken, all is even ground to pulp."

Built on the diagonal across the museum was one of its most original exhibits, a fifteen metre long Churchill Lifeline, taking the form of an interactive table. Throughout its length, the table's surface was touch sensitive, enabling visitors to access tens of thousands of documents, images, films and letters from any year or event they wish to select by a simple swipe of their finger. During the day, the table was often surrounded by dozens of virtual explorers, some tapping randomly, some pursuing tightly defined research, all benefiting from the living history made available by the museum's expert scholars.

Craig had no time to marvel at the table's extraordinary chronicles. For him, it was the best – the only – means left to escape his violent pursuer. He vaulted onto the surface of the table, and ran its length, with Ward just a fraction of a second behind. Beneath their feet, the table's entire surface transformed into a bed of red poppies, an effect usually reserved for Armistice Day. But these were not usual times. To his left, a giant reproduction of the *Evening Standard's* iconic cartoon of Churchill rolling up his sleeves in businesslike fashion, marching at the head of a procession of politicians in the direction of war. To his right, a life-size detached door whose jet blackness was interrupted by just three items of decoration: an iron knocker shaped like a lion's head, a brass letter box bearing the inscription "First Lord of the Treasury", and the number 10 (as in 10 Downing Street), with the zero – as ever – set slightly askance. And behind him, a bloodthirsty maniac, wild with revenge for his damaged eye, hell-bent with fury that Craig's neck must not survive the night unbroken.

Just as Craig was reaching the far end of the interactive table, Ward launched himself through the air. To the uninitiated, he might have been executing a well-timed rugby tackle upon an opponent on the verge of touchdown. In fact the force had a more grisly outcome. The two men went careening off the side, bound together in their lurid embrace, until they crashed into a large display board dedicated to press photographs and witness comments from the day that Churchill's body was carried in a lead-lined coffin from Westminster Hall, where it had been lying in state, up the River Thames, and on to St Paul's Cathedral for his funeral service.

The men's combined momentum sent the display toppling back, knocking into a glass and mahogany cabinet. The cabinet hovered on its rear legs, as if undecided whether to right itself or topple. But the force of the impact had been too strong. With a crunch that reverberated throughout the museum's aisles, it tumbled against the far wall. The wood tore open, as pathetically vulnerable as the hide of a gazelle downed by a lioness. And out spilt one of the museum's most valued artefacts; the Union Jack flag that was draped across Churchill's coffin from the moment it embarked upon its solemn journey, until its final arrival late that evening at the Bladon family plot.

Ward was the fastest to respond. Springing to his feet, he grabbed the flag in both hands. Craig, dazed from the fall, was still lying helpless on the ground as Ward wound it into a primitive rope.

Craig experienced the next few moments as if he was a spirit, floating free from his body, watching the scene as some disinterested spectator.

In its rope form, the colours of the flag had become a psychedelic motley of reds, whites and blues. Now Ward was wrapping the motley around Craig's neck, looping it into a knot at the top of the beaten man's spine. With his prey now stunned and impotent, the mercenary rose triumphant to his feet, towering behind Craig like a big game hunter brandishing his prize.

In his disorientated state, Craig was still imagining himself as an observer of the scene, as a bemused and disinterested bystander. Watching Ward raise his hands aloft. Watching Ward pull ferociously on either end of rope. Watching the knot slide tighter. Watching the makeshift rope digging into the flesh around his neck.

"You've no idea how much I'm enjoying this," hissed Ward with derision, his dead eye wide with the thrill of the kill, a congealing amber liquid oozing like paste from its wound. "It's like being back in Kandahar."

Finally, Craig's wandering thoughts returned to the desperate immediacy of his situation. With spasmodic bursts of movement, he attempted to fight back, clawing into the air behind him to grab hold of any part of Ward's anatomy within reach. But he had left it too late. Ward had gained the ascendancy and was not going to sacrifice his advantage. As he pulled ever tighter on the rope, the arteries around Craig's Adam's apple grew thicker and darker through the soft tissue. The garroting was now approaching its gruesome end game. Craig's face was a deep purple shade, the blood straining to burst free like a reservoir through a breached dam. His hair was matted with sweat that was now dripping down his face, the salty bite stinging his wide-open eyes.

An exultant Ward was now ready for the final stage of the strangulation. He held the rope just above the knot, and channelled every lingering ounce of strength into the decisive twist.

A *crack* rang throughout the museum. The crack of bones succumbing under pressure. A fleeting, eerie, brutal sound. Then, all was silent.

Chapter Seventeen

Located in:

The Churchill War Rooms
and
The streets of Central London

Craig gasped as the oxygen returned to his lungs. Every clutched breath felt like the most precious indulgence at the world's most exotic spa.

We're surrounded by this stuff, and we all take it for granted, he thought. *Never appreciated until it's stolen from us.*

He pawed the flag away from his neck. With astonishment, he saw it was now his adversary who lay prone, sprawled barely conscious across the stone tiles. His head was propped awkwardly against an immense canvas photograph of the young Queen and her eldest children on the steps of St Paul's, as they awaited the arrival of Churchill's casket.

Craig's vision was slowly returning. Out of the blurred shadows, the next object to take shape was a type of rod, perhaps two feet in length, floating in weird fashion in the air above Ward's torso. It was a dull grey, but the far end of the rod was glistening, and as Craig squinted, he figured out the cause. It was newly coated in a dripping crimson liquid. Ward's blood.

And now the third element of the frightful tableau. The bearer of the rod. Bathed in darkness, the bearer stood above Ward's prostrate body, like a harbour-straddling Colossus of Rhodes, *beneath which petty men could do little more than peep about in search of a dishonourable grave.* And then the bearer turned toward Craig.

The throbbing glow of the interactive table was casting its illumination far across this corner of the room. The bearer's features coalesced into focus. Female, brunette. There was no doubt. The Colossus, Craig's saviour, was revealed. Marcelle bore the rod.

"Now who took their time?" he stammered.

"You're welcome," she said. "Now wait a moment. I have some unfinished business."

Ward was slipping in and out of consciousness. Blood was still oozing from the gash to his forehead, staining the canvas, and trickling down in uneven manner like raindrops on a windscreen. The Commonwealth delegation outside St Paul's was now smeared in crimson.

In one hand, Marcelle was holding the keys she'd relieved from the watchman's corpse to gain entry to the museum. In the other, the rod. She angled it so that its tip rested on Ward's bloody gash.

"I think you called this a picana," she spoke to her former tormentor. "You said it was like a cattle prod but designed by unhinged minds. Well, after the last two weeks, I'm feeling quite unhinged myself."

Marcelle twisted the tip deeper inside Ward's open wound. He writhed in agony like a field mouse brutalised by a cat.

"Does that hurt?" she said with mock pity. "Well, let's see what happens when it's switched on."

She flicked the dial on the front of the battery pack, and the rod hummed with the vibrations caused by the alternating current. As the electricity reached the tip, Marcelle pressed the electrodes against Ward's raw laceration. For the first time, the ex-Marine was not merely shaking, but also let out a sharp scream. For such a muscled and stocky man, his howl carried a remarkably high pitch. Like a jittery pre-teen upset by a Halloween prankster.

"I don't think I mentioned it at the time," said Marcelle, her tone dripping sarcasm. "But I really did appreciate all your wonderful lectures. I remember what you told me about the picana. Sixteen thousand volts but low current, a thousandth of an amp. So I wonder what happens if we turn the charge to maximum?"

Ward's face was twisted in an expression of pained terror, and his one good eyeball was flicking from side to side in distress.

Craig stammered, "You don't need to do this; you're better than this."

"That's not your call. You've no idea what he's like."

She alighted her fingers on the dial.

"I guess it goes clockwise," she said, her timbre now matter-of-fact, as if deciphering the instructions on a kitchen appliance.

Ward was calmer now, and muttering to himself. The words were blurring into one another as he rushed to recite the complete text.

The Lord is my shepherd; I shall not want. He maketh me to lie down in green pastures: he leadeth me beside the still waters. He restoreth my soul: he leadeth me in the paths of righteousness for his name's sake. Yea, though I walk through the valley of the shadow of death, I will fear no evil: for thou art with me; thy rod and thy staff they ..."

At Ward's mention of rod, Marcelle's determination was complete. She rotated the control dial until it turned no further, using the picana to skewer Ward's head against the canvas so that, no matter how his dying body might flail and shake, it could not escape the punishment. And she held firm until she could be sure the task was complete, the power coursing up the picana handle, through the electrodes, and onwards to the entire length of Ward's convulsing frame. All the while, the grainy black and white image of the Royal family and their entourage was staring out from the canvas just a few inches above Ward's head, with the uniform expressions of serenity and contemplation.

When she was certain he was dead, Marcelle finally let go of the picana. It tumbled through the air, coming to rest on the corner of the Union Jack flag. The stain of fresh blood on the white diagonal of St Andrew's cross would not be obliterated until three of London's finest dry cleaners had made their attempts. Not that the former Premier would have minded. He had roused the nation with his immortal call to expend blood, sweat and tears. He might be honoured to know the site built in his memory had finally witnessed such a hard-fought clash of wills.

Craig was still struggling to breathe normally. Marcelle knelt alongside him, and cradled his head in her lap.

"Once, you told me that I was a lifesaver," she said. "Now you can mean it literally."

"I've always meant it literally. Because there are many different ways to save a life," replied Craig.

"I couldn't let you go. You still owe me a paycheque."

And with that, for the first time in two weeks, Marcelle smiled. Faint and nervous, to be sure, but gloriously unmistakable.

"Where did you find that ... thing?"

"He always carried around a bag of tricks. The picana wasn't the only tool he used to intimidate but it was probably the worst. I guessed it wouldn't be far away. I was right. I found it right next to his laptop, in that room he seems to use with impunity."

Craig was now back on his feet, his spirit and vitality fast returning. There would, he was sure, be time during the days ahead to reflect on their brush with death. But that was not the immediate concern.

"We must get his laptop," he ordered.

"Wait, Craig, I think I hear footsteps. There's someone coming in this direction."

The clip of shoe leather against stone came from the corridor connecting the War Rooms with the Museum. The footsteps themselves could have been innocuous, they could even have held out the promise of rescue. Except that, moments later, Marcelle heard the accompanying words. The accent was polished, with the vowels and diphthongs generously elongated, and essential consonants clipped.

"Mike, it's me, Quentin Shaw. Where are you? I saw that the guard's been shot."

"I know that name," whispered Marcelle. "While I was in the cell, someone called Shaw was often at the other end of the phone, discussing my situation with... him. I think they were partners."

Since the confrontation with Marcelle outside Malkin Castle, Shaw had stayed in the background. A man of fastidious disposition, he preferred to delegate the coarser side of the mercenary trade to others, while he schemed from afar. Interrogating captive females in dank basements was not to his taste. Not because he condemned the process; he recognised the need, but chose to limit his intervention to the analysis and interpretation of the results.

Shaw was now in the museum. He was carrying a small but powerful lithium flashlight that bathed the room in intense white light. So it didn't take him long to notice the wreckage around so many of the exhibits, and particularly the scene in the far corner – the toppled cabinet, the sea of broken glass, the bloodstains that proliferated across the funeral canvas.

Shaw focused his torch directly at the two figures at the centre of this carnage. Both were unsteady on their feet, faltering in their movement, their arms wrapped around each other for support.

"Are you Craig Richards?" he demanded, recognising the strategist's features from Cunningham's briefing pack.

The light was dazzling, and Craig raised his arm to block out the glare.

Marcelle was in no mood for a prolonged showdown. She couldn't spend a moment longer than necessary in this forsaken place. So she stepped across to the canvas, and grabbed a clump of Ward's hair in her right hand, lifting the ex-Marine like a plant from a pot.

"Don't go there," she snarled. "Just don't. This is what happened when your ally crossed us."

Shaw and Ward had been accepting commissions for over a decade, and throughout the years Shaw had held his partner's brawn and virility with unalloyed awe. Never married, there had been times, just once or twice, when he had awoken a few hours before dawn, his bed sheets damp with sweat, his mind besieged with erotic images of Ward's bulging physique. Like a thunder strike, it dawned on him those years were now closed. And this was their tragic, pathetic culmination. Ward, food for worms, his lifespan unexpectedly brought short in a moment… by this savage woman. If Ward's Herculean biceps and triceps had been inadequate against her thirst for vengeance, then he – Quentin – stood no chance. He dropped the torch, and raised his hands in surrender.

"I think this has been a mistake," he stuttered, retreating towards the exit. "Let's not argue. I'm leaving now."

As Shaw slunk away, Craig handed Marcelle a handkerchief.

"You might want to wipe off a few fingerprints," he said. "I'll be needing you more than ever from now on."

"Don't doubt that for a moment," Marcelle replied, hugging the strategist with such force that he feared his oxygen deprivation might kick back in.

"That was the most audacious mission this side of the Navy Seals' raid on Bin Laden's compound. After what we've been through, I wouldn't leave even if you threw me out of the window. I'd just bungee jump right back to your side."

Craig squeezed her nose affectionately.

"I better rewrite the first rule of strategy. Always carry a bungee cord when you're near my window. Now let's go find that laptop."

When the glass cover had crashed into the Dock, Ward had set off to investigate the disturbance with such brutal single-mindedness that he hadn't had time to power down his Toshiba. The laptop was exactly where Craig had previously seen it, beneath the glare of a single reading light on a standard issue table in the Mexel supervisors' room. With Marcelle guarding for any more watchmen, Craig searched through *Recent documents*, and located one entitled 'Pohl briefing – timeline'.

"That's my boy, now it's time to come to papa," he said, clicking to open the document.

On this occasion, however, his entreaty was spurned. It seemed that Ward had at least shown the vigilance to create a password for the document, and none of the most obvious that Craig attempted (*password, Churchill, Shaw, Xanotek*) provided a route in.

"Annoying but not terminal," was his conclusion. "Gratification delayed, definitely not gratification denied."

He removed his sweater and used it to create a protective layer inside his rucksack, before depositing the laptop inside.

"No more fights," he said. "From here on, it's no longer about you and me. It's about the laptop. Until the moment it's been decrypted, this is one computer that gets treated like a butterfly's wing."

When Craig arrived through the Downing Street tunnel, caution had trumped speed. Now the priorities were reversed. The pair made it back to the workmen's ladder in a fraction of the forty minutes he had taken to traverse in the opposite direction. At any moment, anyone with cause to use the War Rooms in the evening, perhaps for a corporate event, or an out-of-hours cleaner, or because Shaw had improbably sounded the alert, could trigger a police cordon and an intensive search of the area. An arm snagged or a knee scraped against some jutting masonry was a small price for liberty.

"How are we meant to get through that?" asked Marcelle, pointing at the cast iron plate at the top of the ladder. "Intangibility isn't my strongest suit."

"Just like I got in," said Craig, pressing his hand against the Mexel's digital fingerprint recognition monitor. A familiar green light flickered in response. "And for that, you've got Dimala to thank. That boy's a wonder."

"He sure is," said Marcelle.

While Craig had been underground, dusk had fallen across Whitehall. Central London's tourists had all but drifted away to West End theatres and Knightsbridge restaurants. Only a handful of late commuters were still around the Clive Steps, and only one looked quizzically in their direction as the pair emerged from the workmen's pit. He might have been speculating as to why a thirty-ish woman was clambering out through the manhole, her face blackened with grime, and dressed as if she hadn't changed for a month. But then he shrugged and continued his journey, his pace slightly quickened. In the scale of London oddities, said his inner voice, probably not so consequential, but best not to linger.

Craig was keen to put a vast distance between themselves and an area of Whitehall that had, minutes beforehand, been a scene of such bloodshed and peril. But Marcelle insisted on a moment's pause. She needed to savour anew the sights and sounds and smells of the surface world. Since Malkin, her only comforts had been the scampering rats and the snatched conversations of Mexel workmen. Now a million everyday joys assailed her senses. The wafting scent of greasy meat and onions from a burger van, the cooing of pigeons in formation en route to Trafalgar Square, the *Read all about it* clamours of *Evening Standard* vendors. Unremarkable, humdrum, but so wonderfully real. So just a second to relish these delights, so she could be reassured – so she could be absolutely certain – of their authenticity.

But there was something else.

"Can you hear that?" she asked Craig.

Through the cacophony of sounds, she had distinguished a hundred camera shutters in operation, less than a block away. And accompanying the cameras, a hundred voices, yelling *This way Minister*; or *Sir, do you have a statement?* or *Will there be war?* with such ferocity that vocal chords might snap.

"It sounds important."

"It's all about Phoenicia. The situation deteriorated while you were AWOL. Tonight, Downing Street hosted an international gathering to discuss military options. Half the Cabinet's been involved, ambassadors from our closest allies, NATO."

"This could be our opportunity, Craig."

"What could be?"

"Secretary Foster will surely be present. And we have in your rucksack the evidence of the treachery in her private office. Machiavelli reborn, planting seeds everywhere to rush us into war. She needs to know."

"But first, let's get you somewhere safe, clean you up."

"Craig, you're the one who taught me to seize the moment. If we can intercept Foster while she's getting into her limo, we'll have not only seized the moment, but possibly the whole year."

And so, ignoring the lure of self-preservation, the temptation to withdraw with the immediate skirmish won, the pair strode back into the fray, towards the paparazzi and international news corps. And, beyond the baying press crowds, towards the most powerful gathering of leaders and bureaucrats that had taken place in London for over a decade.

Official protocol dictated the order in which dignitaries left the premises after emergency summits. Members of the Prime Minister's Cabinet were obliged to await the departure of their guests before summoning their own chauffeurs, so they could offer tributes and goodwill messages in a fitting manner on the Number Ten steps. Some of the handshakes were interminable; *even old Blue Eyes didn't take so long to vacate the stage,* thought Craig. But the elaborate proceedings did allow Craig and Marcelle to manoeuvre to the heart of the press throng gathered outside Downing Street's imposing security gates.

"This is all the fault of the IRA," said Craig. "I remember when anyone could wander straight up to the

PM's front door, as if London was a harmless Nordic enclave. I guess those days won't be returning."

The hacks were still shouting for a snippet or sound-bite from every delegate, however obscure. Their efforts were proving futile; the best they had solicited all evening were a couple of half-hearted waves of acknowledgement. And then, with the crush intensifying under pressure from both journalists and the casually curious, and with Craig on the verge of abandoning the task, finally they had sight of Secretary Foster. A hundred yards away, the silver-haired woman of impeccable bearing, clad in a sombre purple power suit with so much padding that it created a canyon-like effect around her head. Within the next few moments the gates would part, and her official car would speed through.

"This was your idea," whispered Craig. "So what's your play? Are you going to throw yourself before the wheels like a suffragette, and challenge them to halt else you'll be roadkill?"

Marcelle had been playing with a couple of options, and was about to share her analysis when the evening took an unexpected twist. Craig had been vaguely aware of a slightly overweight man lurking behind him, whose stomach wobbled like a waterbed as it squeezed against his back. But suddenly, with a speed that belied his girth, the man grabbed both of Craig's arms, and locked tight-fitting handcuffs around his wrists.

354

"Don't bother to struggle," said the man into Craig's ear. "They don't release without the key, and that's round the corner in my van. So you'd better come with me."

Craig recognised the gravelly tone. It was Special Constable Martin Thorpe, the policeman who had spotted his cocaine use in St James Park a few hours beforehand, and threatened him with arrest unless he fled from Central London for at least the next 24 hours.

"Officer, let me explain, please. This is important."

"I'm tired, it's been a long day," said Thorpe. "So do us all a favour, and spare me your lame excuses. I made myself clear as crystal. So I don't appreciate that you're still hanging around."

Craig cursed his luck. On the verge of revealing corruption at the heart of government that seemed to permeate throughout Europe's defence establishment, and now their plans were evaporating due to a petty felony seen by a junior officer. Damn the bathos. Damn his drug dependency. Throughout his life, people that meant the most to him – Patricia, Natalie, Marcelle, and so many others – had beseeched him to clean up, or at least seek counselling. Through arrogance and stubbornness, he'd treated their pleas with contempt. And now, with the stakes higher than ever, he would be paying the awful consequence.

As he was dragged from the skirmishing crowds, he caught Marcelle's eyes. Her expression was one of foreboding and helplessness. Behind her, the Downing Street gates slid open, and Secretary Foster's limousine sped past, unimpeded by any modern-day suffragette. It turned sharply at the Cenotaph, accelerating away into the gathering London night.

Thorpe was chewing on a bagel as he escorted Craig along Whitehall. He was a couple of steps behind the strategist, confident that – with his hands securely fastened behind his back – Craig constituted a negligible flight risk. Occasionally, the officer encouraged Craig to quicken his pace by shoving him between the shoulder blades with his truncheon. He ignored Craig's transparent effort to build rapport or threaten unspeakable consequences, greeting pleas such as *Am I under arrest?* and *I know people and will be complaining at the highest level* with Neanderthal grunts.

Five minutes later, ten minutes later, they were still walking. The promise of a van "around the corner" had morphed into a trek past a succession of government institutions and onwards towards the Shangri-La of boutique hotels and shopping arcades west of Piccadilly Circus. This no longer had the semblance of a routine arrest. As they passed Carlton Gardens, and with Craig growing increasingly fretful about the officer's intentions, he threatened to stand immobile unless he was given more information. However, the Constable was insusceptible to bluff.

"I really don't think you want me abandoning you here, trussed up like Lector on day release," he scoffed.

Another five minutes and they reached a cul-de-sac near Jermyn Street. With just a single working street light, and two enormous skips, it could have been a text-book venue for an assassination.

"I told you I had a van," said the officer.

Gratuitously, but enjoyably, he prodded Craig a final time with the truncheon, with such force it was difficult for the strategist to keep his footing.

Craig was about to point out that the area was devoid of vans of any shape or size when, as if on cue, one reversed at speed around the corner, disconcertingly close to the concrete wall against which they stood. Both constable and captive stepped backwards to avoid the impatient trajectory.

As the van drew alongside them, the driver slammed the brakes. They were almost pinned in the slight gap between building and vehicle. Craig had already figured it had as much in common with a police van as his boat had with a Caribbean cruise liner. *Van* was probably a misnomer; this was a Mecedes-Benz Sprinter monster. Amongst its many distinctive luxuries was a rotating camera mounted on the roof. The camera was now trained upon him, and he observed a series of slight movements of the lens components as the operator finessed its focus.

The cameraman was evidently satisfied with the results of his scrutiny, because a few moments later the side panels of the Mercedes slid ajar. The vehicle's sole occupant was now visible. For a few seconds, neither party made comment. Craig still half expected that, with one swift gesture, a bullet would go crashing through his skull.

Instead, the occupant leant forward, and said slowly "This is a great pleasure."

The voice was male, but he was otherwise so weighed down in a trenchcoat and trilby that it was impossible even to guess at his age or features or build.

"And I must apologise for the subterfuge. I wouldn't have resorted to it were it not absolutely necessary."

From an inside pocket of his trenchcoat, the occupant took a bundle of fifty pound notes, and threw them to the floor next to the officer. Thorpe retrieved the bundle, and had started to check the quantum when the occupant fixed him with a glare of pure contempt.

"It's exactly as agreed. Now leave us alone," he snorted.

Like a humiliated dog slinking into the shadows after being castigated by its owner, Thorpe tucked the bundle into his trouser pocket, and backed away with hesitant steps until he was safely beyond both skips.

"Here, let me help you with those," said the occupant, pointing behind Craig's back. "Please turn around."

He produced a key from another inside pocket and twisted it until the levers released.

"Now, please, can I entice you to join me for a chilled Bollinger so we can talk business? I think it's about time for solutions."

Throughout the turmoil of the past six months – from Hino's emergency summons to attend the London City airport lounge, to the debacle of the Malkin workshop, to the threats of retribution while in conference at

Crowborough, and near strangulation by Ward on the floor of the Churchill Museum – it was a long time since anyone had suggested *solutions* to Craig.

Intrigued, he stepped up into the Mercedes and lowered himself into a seat opposite the occupant. The leather upholstery shifted beneath his weight, reshaping itself under the direction of the vehicle's diagnostic system until it accommodated him in the position of greatest comfort. A dozen discrete rollers were already massaging the tension out of his neck and back muscles. The Bollinger hit the back of his throat with the restorative power of an Asgardian elixir.

"Wow," he gasped.

"I understand you've had quite a day. It's the least I can do."

"You've piqued my interest," said Craig. "I'm flattered by the hospitality, even if my route here was unconventional."

"Let me declare my purpose."

The occupant was now speaking so softly that Craig had to block out any stray thoughts lest he miss a vital syllable.

"And it is this. I think it's time for some lateral thinking about the future of polymer technology."

"Polymer technology hasn't been my greatest ally this year," said Craig.

"Here are the pieces I see on the chess board," said the occupant. "We have possibly the world's most accomplished materials scientist, Jeremy Barker. We have a business that has synthesised these proteins to create a virtually invulnerable polymer fabric, Xanotek. We have a precarious world situation with governments under pressure to rebuild defence capability, and senior officials in the British government who are in a position to make it happen and dispense favours. We have incumbent defence contractors with solid relationships and delivery platforms."

"I'm aware of most of these pieces. Some required more detective work than others."

"I'd heard rumours that you infiltrated MOD headquarters. And I acclaim your ambition, your execution, your panache. That was when I realised we should be working together."

"Together?"

"I'm one of the chess pieces, Mr Richards. And, if modesty allows, I'm one of the most valuable pieces. But no chess set is functional without somebody removed from the action, figuring out how the pieces should be manoeuvred around the board. Over the past few months, I've seen the pieces engaged in nothing more than ad hoc, jerky movements, often implementing contradictory tactics. Bishops at war with knights. Rooks undermining the queen. No proper formation. No clear objectives. No overarching strategy. That is no formula for a tournament victory, Mr Richards. That's the recipe for mutual destruction."

"And I come in where?"

"I'm not talking about devising a strategy for one of the pieces, Mr Richards. Not for a start-up, struggling to bring product to market. Not for a mid-sized player preparing their great leap into the firmament. Not even for a market leader protecting its vested interest. No; this is an entire industry in need of a strategy. And I would like you, Mr Richards, to be our grand master."

"Grand master?"

"Imagine an observer from a dimension that could only view the pieces on the physical chess board. They might never see Oratovsky or Kasparov. The grand masters don't hop around from square to square. But their influence is pervasive. After your experiences, you're now familiar with the configuration of the pieces. You have the vision to direct us all into the right positions. Never conspicuous. But ever present."

"I'm sorry," said Craig. "But I don't think I caught your name."

"Thomas Pohl. I think perhaps you have come across me in your investigations. Now, if you're agreeable, I think it's time to get to work."

A dozen pigeons had been jostling noisily on a church tower in the adjacent alleyway. Now they took flight, ascending steeply as if reaching for the heavens, before banking sharply towards the Thames and then looping back in the direction of Soho. If it was so minded, the flock could view the frantic richness and bustle of modern London, laid out beneath it like a canvas.

In Leicester Square, a throng of teenage autograph hunters was straining against the security barriers, desperate for a moment's attention from the waiflike starlet being hurried along the red carpet by scowling bodyguards. On the South Bank, a speeding ambulance jumped the lights outside St Thomas' Hospital, and then clipped a post outside the entrance to the Casualty Unit as it skidded to a halt; within seconds, the paramedics were decoupling the trolley stretcher and wheeling it like sprinters on the final straight, the young knife victim already in cardiac arrest. Near Covent Garden, a minor royal sat in the rear of a pristine Audi saloon, using the window's faint reflection to adjust the knot in his bow-tie, and wondering if he would ever summon the courage to ask the Opera House management to desist from sending invitations to tedious ballet productions. A few blocks away, in Wigmore Street, a gang of intoxicated Scousers on a bachelor party were remonstrating with the doorman of a lap dancing bar, while the groom-to-be retched in the gutter, and were learning that crude insults are not the most effective tool for changing minds or gaining admittance. And in Chinatown, crowds were gathering around a street fortune teller whose latest customers, a Texan family on their annual vacation, were demanding a refund after being informed the year head would be characterised by lawsuits and infidelity.

The tour of the pigeons reached its conclusion when the birds settled on the mermaids, dolphins and tritons of the Trafalgar Square fountain, where they glowered at the hordes of pedestrians in the expectation that some might offer them bread.

It was a typical mid-week evening in Europe's most vibrant city. Yet the starlets and paramedics and ballerinas and drunks and tourists were oblivious to the decisions being made in close proximity in their name.

Oblivious that the fractious jealousies throughout Europe's defence industry would soon be displaced by a shared vision and unified purpose. Oblivious that, in an Islington drawing room, Secretary of State Foster was, at that moment, signing a raft of documents to authorise emergency expenditure to boost Britain's military preparedness, at the discretion of her Permanent Secretary. Oblivious that the beguiling assumption western governments could retreat with impunity from dangerous conflict had, these past few hours, been supplanted by an altogether more frightening and foreboding truth.

Aftermath

Six months later

Epilogue The First

Located in:
Harpenden

"Please, Mother, I know I haven't been good at calling," said Rebecca Cunningham, her mobile sandwiched between shoulder and ear.

"I can't interrupt him now. He's been downstairs since six. It's the last day of the month, and he never likes to be disturbed until the paperwork's in order and the numbers tally."

"I'd just like to wish him a happy birthday."

"I'll tell him you called. In the meantime, you'll have to make do with me."

On the bedroom side table was a lidless lacquered box and a scattering of balled-up tissues. Rebecca used one of them to dab at an obstinate tear halfway down her cheek.

"I've been thinking a lot about Munich," she said.

"We were so proud of you," said her mother softly.

For a moment, there was silence on the line, as both women reflected on their own memories of that phenomenal day. It was over a decade ago, but every second was still etched in their consciousness; the climactic moments of the European Championship thousand metre race. For Rebecca, as she entered the final stretch, the stadium's sweeping canopy of steel cabling and acrylic glass had functioned like a wind tunnel, echoing with the raucous din of an eighty thousand crowd, sucking her towards the finishing line with its all-consuming vortex. And her mother had been one of those spectators, shrieking with such euphoria that for the next three days she barely managed a croak, indiscriminately pumping the air with her fist as Rebecca accelerated up the field of runners with godlike strides. Four years of training and preparation condensed into the final unforgettable seconds.

"You know," her mother continued, "When the ribbon snapped, even Hugo was on his feet."

Stoic, sober, unflappable Hugo, the most overdressed man in the stadium. For the entirety of the outbound flight, his face had been buried in the entrails of a closely-typed government report. But at the moment of Rebecca's triumph, the barriers and inhibitions momentarily melted. He had bear-hugged his future mother-in-law with such force she feared a rib might snap. In the following morning's press conference, with a hundred microphones thrust beneath her nose, Rebecca had charmed the world's media with the announcement that she was engaged to the young civil servant.

Her Hollywood smile led the back page of every British tabloid that weekend.

"Did you hear we've been going through rocky times?" said Rebecca.

She was still attempting to obliterate that infernal tear, but the traces of wetness were too stubborn.

"Mary mentioned something, but no details."

"We've separated now. It all blew up a few months ago."

"Darling, I'm so sorry. Tell me what happened. Your father always felt he was a bad egg."

Every evening, every single evening, Rebecca was still struggling to make sense of the bewildering fragments that remained from the most tumultuous days of her life. Cold and shivering before the bathroom cabinet, fumbling with another pot of sleeping tablets. The changes had started in the week of the Cabinet's decision to send troops into Phoenicia. Hugo's schedule was unpredictable and erratic; one night, he arrived home at two, and spent the next three hours making furtive calls from his downstairs office until being collected by an MOD chauffeur before daybreak. The following night, he'd ordered three irked children to their rooms so he and Rebecca could dine alone, and devoted the next hour to a monologue of complaints about her spending habits while toying with his lasagne until it turned to mush. In an unguarded moment, he'd left a newly-acquired pre-pay phone on the table while visiting the bathroom, and Rebecca had noted down a couple of recent numbers stored in the log. The following morning, she'd been curious to find out that one was answered by the breezy receptionist of a mid-tier Cayman Islands bank.

Her final conversation with Hugo took place the day that British casualties passed one hundred, a fraction of the usual loss rate during such intense combat operations. He refused to divulge his location (in fact, he was leaning against the entertainment screen of his treadmill, looking down on the London skyline through the floor-to-ceiling window of a nominee-owned forty-first floor South Bank apartment), and kept his remarks short and candid. He had instructed lawyers to represent him in the separation. If she was compliant, he would be generous. But awkward questions would be punished with an aggressive legal response. He recommended she cooperate.

"I don't want to talk about it. I can't talk about it. I'm still not sure what happened," she said wearily.

The legal process would have drained the spirit from the most indefatigable fighter. After her first meeting with her husband's appointed solicitor, a man who deadpanned every inquiry from behind coke-bottle lenses that reduced his eyes to the tiniest marbles, she decided resignation was the only viable course. Months later, the steady trickle of arcane documents was still grinding onwards.

"If you need help, any kind of help, just let me know. If we can help with the children. Whatever you wish," said Rebecca's mother.

"I really would like to talk to Dad."

"You've seen his temper. Just let him balance the books. Now isn't a good time, trust me."

"Goodbye, Mama. Always remember that I love you."

"What do you…?"

The next few minutes passed for Rebecca like a misty dream sequence. After she clicked the *end call* button, she tossed the handset casually through the open window, and was vaguely aware of the dull sound of plastic cracking against concrete paving slabs. She rose from the bed, arthritis stabbing up her back with her sudden movement. She untied the sash of her bathrobe and allowed the garment to slide gracefully from her body. Naked, she walked onto the landing, passing the wedding day photographs that still adorned the walls, and down the stairs, using the railing for support whenever she stumbled under the soreness and irritation of her back pain.

On the patio, she lifted the cover of her cherished hot tub for the final time. Beneath it, the waters were pure and radiant; not a single stray leaf or drowning insect to spoil the immaculate surface. And so beautifully warm too. The fiery liquid enveloped every inch of skin; she felt her nerve-endings relax as the heat penetrated through her pores. And although she was curled up in just one corner of the tub, she switched on its entire orchestra of jets and pumps until a million bubbles frothed with hypnotic energy.

As she slumped beneath the tub's waterfall feature, and as the downpour cascaded and massaged her aching shoulders, Rebecca opened her right hand. The sleeping pills were piled like candy on her palm. *One, two, three* she started to count but quickly abandoned the effort. *I'll just make it plenty.*

In her mouth, each pill seemed to follow its own journey, as if possessed of an independent mind. Some dwelt on her tongue, slowly dissolving. Others romped intact down her throat, as if sprinting Munich-style for her stomach. It would not be long until their chemicals would be spreading the length and breadth of her bloodstream.

Rebecca slid deeper into the warmth. She kept both eyes wide open so she could watch the surface closing back upon itself as she sank.

Epilogue The Second

Located in:
The Chandansar Orphanage

It was the rumble of the engines of a dozen trucks that told Stella Weseldine this would be no ordinary day. She had been officiating some petty dispute between two of her charges. Apparently, Nripendra had promised to swap some Panini Cricket World Cup stickers with Jasveer and then welched on the deal. All efforts to seek a compromise had so far proved elusive, and Stella was on the verge of confiscating and torching the entire collection. Meanwhile, Saryu had tripped over in the girls' toilets and cut her forehead against the sink. So far, so typical.

The vehicles arrived in convoy, and parked themselves before the entrance to the orphanage in a precise, almost military formation. A group of children had been playing hide and seek in the shrubs and jujube trees, but now stopped to gaze at the unexpected assemblage. The equipment being transported included a bulldozer, an excavator, a concrete mixer, numerous pallets of bricks, a buzz saw, and a couple of skips. *Cool hiding places,* said the group's notional leader, a girl in a bright yellow T-shirt who had turned thirteen the previous month.

Stella was still on the building's rear balcony, seeking a Solomon-like resolution to the Panini dilemma.

"Nripendra," she was saying, "I want you to be honest with me. You remember everything we've discussed about telling the truth."

"He promised me two for one, Ma'am," said Nripendra. "You've taught us about promises as well."

Stella sighed in exasperation. Another few minutes and she would be forced to implement her drastic solution. But as she steeled herself for a final attempt at mediation, her concentration was interrupted by the booming and insistent horn of the convoy's lead truck.

"That sounds like it's inside the grounds," said Jasveer.

"I wasn't expecting anyone this morning," said Stella. "Let me sort this out. While I'm away, why not act like grown-ups and work it out together?"

"Being grown-up is so boring," said Nripendra. "It sucks to be like that."

Despite her two decades in India, Stella still found the midday Mumbai heat oppressive. En route to the entrance hall, she donned her favourite wide brimmed straw hat, which she kept on her sideboard for emergency use. Great protection from sunburn, yet as light as paper. Plus it made her feel like a regular cowboy. Infused with the buccaneering brashness of the Wild West, she strode out to confront the intruders.

A tall man, who had been riding as a passenger in the first truck, was now standing in front of the vehicle fleet, with a sheaf of papers in his hand. His cheeks were pockmarked with the lifelong evidence of appalling teenage acne, but he stood with poise and confidence as Stella approached. There was not the slightest flinch or cringe as he enquired, "Are you Stella Weseldine?"

Stella's gait hastened rather than slowed as she closed in on the gang leader. And a moment later he was reeling from the most almighty slap across his face. In shock, a couple of papers flew from his grasp. As he turned back to his assailant, one of his flunkies gathered up the documents, and returned them to his possession.

"I don't care who you bribed to get your permits. You are not demolishing this building," Stella screamed.

"If you are Mrs Wesel…"

"We are doing God's work here. We provide safe refuge for children who otherwise stand no chance against your cruel and pitiless system. So tell whoever sent you: Stella is staying put!"

Every child in the orphanage had now gathered to watch the escalating showdown. Most of them huddled together on the main steps, the older ones wrapping their arms around any infant in close proximity, as if to shelter them from an impending storm. Three children had joined Stella where she stood, dead centre in the driveway, glaring defiantly at the trespassers, trying with sheer force of will to evacuate them from the premises. One of them, young Nripendra, who moments before had been whining and lying about his cards, stood directly in front of Stella, like a human shield. His body language shrieked out, *the only way to her is through me, over my twitching corpse.*

"But Miss Weseldine, we've not come to demolish the orphanage," said the pock-marked man. "We're here to build."

"Build? Build what?" asked Stella, cautiously.

The pock-marked man snapped an elastic band from a rolled-up document, and spread it out across the gravel. Stella squinted at the drawings. They looked like schematics for a new building; a floor plan, a site plan, an elevation view and a cross section. And on a second page were more detailed drawings; one seemed to contain hardware and plumbing instructions for a series of shower cubicles, the other had measurements for a small swimming pool. And a final page featured an artist's rendering for the interior of what looked like a space age gymnasium, with banks of black-and-chrome equipment and annotations such as *airbounder* and *gyroscopic dumbbells* and *total body arc trainer*. Stella flicked back and forth through the papers. This was nothing she'd ever commissioned. And yet there, in huge lettering on the front page, were the words that made her tremble with emotion: 'Chandansar Orphanage Sports Hall Extension'.

"Ma'am," said Nripendra. "Who are these men? What will happen to us?"

The pock-marked man handed Stella an unstamped manila envelope, on which her name had been written with a broad tip fountain pen using faultless, flowing calligraphy. And inside, another note, transcribed with the same personal care: *Dear Ma'am, I have fond memories of my time at Chandansar, and will never forget your kindness. Soon after I arrived in England, I found myself the owner of a small percentage stake in a private business that has grown rapidly. It has just paid its first dividend. And I would like to use this money to offer something back. I owe so much to you, your wonderful staff, and all my dear friends. Dimala.*

"You know, Nripendra," said Stella. "I have a feeling things are going to work out just fine."

Epilogue The Third

Located in:
South Korea

The Gulfstream taxied along the final stretch of runway at the private airport a hundred miles south-east of Seoul. The pilot had executed a flawless touchdown that provided some recompense after the turbulence of the flight from Jakarta. After a couple of turns, the plane pulled up alongside the narrow, single-storey terminal building. In the cabin, Nobuyuki Hino fingered at one more roll of sushi. Recently he had adopted a new custom: neglecting to belt up for the landing. After all, one of the joys of owning one's own plane was freedom from the pettifogging rules imposed by the international aviation bureaucrats.

Hino's current delight was narezushi, or matured sushi. It seemed such an indulgence to consume delicacies that had fermented for a period of six months or more. On one recent occasion, while negotiating in Shanghai, he had sent his pilot on a roundtrip to Lake

Biwa to collect a dozen additional pieces from a small village which, he considered, to be the source of the most authentic narezushi anywhere in the globe.

The financier was in South Korea to address irregularities at a million ton capacity dry dock in which he was a majority shareholder. The facility had secured a ten-year contract to modernise a fleet of oil supertankers, but margins had been disappointing and, according to local rumour, free cashflow had been funnelled away in bribes and kickbacks. During a series of otherwise nondescript meetings, Hino would be awaiting the opportune moment to confront the local director, Dr Kwoong, with the allegations. If he was dissatisfied with the response – not so much the spoken word, but pupil dilation, voice biometrics, skin tone, even micro-expressions – then Kwoong would not see another sunrise.

"Sir, are you ready to disembark yet?" asked the Ukrainian prostitute who freelanced as Hino's personal flight stewardess.

"One moment," said Hino. He wiped some sauce from his chin and powered down his laptop.

There was another important item of business that should no longer be deferred. In fact, it had been remiss of him to allow six protracted months already to slip past. In his last dialogue with Craig Richards, he had solemnly promised that one day the strategist would suffer the slash of a Japanese blade across his windpipe. It was now time to act on that threat.

He'd been unable to shake the feeling that Craig's involvement with Xanotek had not ended that day. Over the following weeks, he'd enacted his pledge to have no further dealings with the company. Frankly, he'd been aghast at the lack of order in British business life; the chaotic uncertainties and plethora of competing interest groups. His excursion into European ventures had not been happy, and it was time to disengage, to gather his wealth for redeployment in areas of greater predictability. Unexpectedly, soon after he announced his unsentimental verdict, Barker had submitted a counter proposal: that the management team buy out Hino's interest for a nominal sum, relinquishing him of any liabilities, and allowing him to walk away with honour intact.

Distracted by the emerging revelations of malpractice in South Korea, Hino had perhaps too readily agreed this resolution. It was only once contracts had been exchanged, and he'd been archiving Barker's emails, that he paused for reflection. In one correspondence, Barker had apologised for, at times, seeming as "exhausted as a burnt-out comet." The phrase had played on Hino's mind. It was an unusual and imperfect simile, and he was certain he'd heard it before. Finally, he put his finger on it. It was the self-same phrase used by Craig to describe Barker during their Angeline's dinner the night before the workshop. Had Barker's … stratagem? … been entirely his own initiative? Or had there been an unseen influence at play? Perhaps it hadn't been the amiable transfer it superficially appeared? Had it rather borne the hallmarks of a perfectly-executed putsch, orchestrated by a mind that had spotted Xanotek's hidden value, and had strong opinions on how that value should be distributed?

No matter, muttered Hino under his breath. History might prove that, on this one occasion, his nemesis had tactically outwitted him. But history would also prove it to be a pyrrhic victory. As soon as Kwoong was despatched – in suitably violent circumstances so that the message was unambiguous to any others tempted by the easy lucre of the double-cross – then Craig would be back firmly within his sights. He vowed to entertain no fresh investment opportunities until the strategist lay cold in his grave.

Hino wrapped a silk scarf around his neck and tucked it beneath the lapels of his overcoat. He felt energised. Knowing that his greatest irritations would soon be despatched with brutal finality did wonders for his spirits, and he bounded down the aircraft steps two at a time. On the tarmac, he looked around for his local chauffeur, a young man named Konu whose Hyundai driving was notorious, even by the furious standards of the region, on account of his artificial hand.

But instead of Konu's dapper figure, Hino faced a party of four marching towards him across the apron, in perfect step with one another like cheaply animated clones in a straight-to-video sci-fi picture. Three men and one woman, each dressed drably in crumpled suits that suggested regular dry cleaning was not an occupational priority. Surely I don't require four chauffeurs today? thought Hino.

The eldest of the group was evidently the most senior. His weathered features were barely visible beneath frizzled and unkempt white hair that formed a circle around his face like the petals around a sunflower.

"Nobuyuki Hino, my name is Mr Ryu. I am going to require you to come with us," he said, his voice detached and flat.

"And who might you be?"

Hino's question was brushed aside.

"My colleague Mr Kim is armed, so please don't cause an incident by resisting."

"Surely you're going to tell me more than that."

"You are being arrested, Mr Hino, on fourteen counts of tax evasion totalling over $3 billion dollars, and another eight counts of money laundering totalling a little under $2 billion. The offences stretch back a decade, with the most recent committed earlier this year."

"This is an outrage. I'm here on legitimate business and I have a full schedule of meetings ahead."

"Mr Hino, when these offences are proven – which they will be – you won't be engaging in any business, legitimate or otherwise, for the best part of, say, two-hundred years."

Mr Ryu raised his right arm above his head and wafted it around as if to dispel a bothersome mosquito. Responding to his signal, two police cars that had been parked innocuously alongside the terminal, stuttered into activity and shunted forward towards the group.

"Now, please, can I introduce you to your new chauffeur for today. Make yourself comfortable. The cars are quite pleasant, especially in comparison with conditions at the station.

"I need to make a phone call," said Hino, scrolling through his contacts folder. "Whatever allegations have been made against me, Adrienne will be able to refute."

Mr Ryu chortled. The motion caused a slit to open in his beard, through which his yellowing teeth were visible, dancing around in time with his guffaws like drunken canaries.

"I was planning to tell you this once you're in custody, Mr Hino, but it really won't assist your cause to contact Miss Adrienne Dodier. Her witness statement is appended to virtually every indictment on your charge sheet."

Epilogue The Fourth

Located in:
Salvador, Brazil

Outside the bar, the Capoeira dancers had been kicking, flipping and spinning for over an hour, but despite their exertions showed no signs of fatigue. The unique Afro-Brazilian style, with its eclectic combination of acrobatics and martial arts, was often on display during street carnival season. Half a dozen musicians controlled the rhythm of the performance. They were currently in high tempo mode, plucking vigorously at their single string percussion instruments while holding the gourds against their bodies to create a background buzz. As the song intensified, it mutated into calls and responses which grew louder and more lusty with repetition. Finally, at the Capoeira's climax, the lead dancer cartwheeled back and forth across the cobbled street to the crowd's thunderous applause. A hundred phones were clicking away to record images of the powerful and colourful display.

Marcelle and Adrienne sat in one of the bar's upper level booths where the view of the carnival was unimpeded. As the cartwheeler soaked in the acclaim, they raised their cocktail glasses in appreciation of his performance. This time, they had opted for a caiprinha, Brazil's intense national cocktail based on cachaça, sugar and lime. Their table was littered with remnants of their many previous cocktail orders which the bar staff had not yet found time to clear away.

"I'm so pleased you could share these weeks with me," said Adrienne.

"I've always wanted to spend serious time in Brazil. I've made a couple of flying business visits, but I've never been able to relax and savour its culture and climate and food. It really is like nowhere else on earth," said Marcelle.

"I figure that after a couple of days in Salvador we might head inland. Across the peninsula and towards the rainforest. Up for that?"

"One hundred per cent."

Even now, six months later, and a hemisphere away, Marcelle found it difficult to escape the trauma of her War Rooms ordeal. Nights in Brazil were rarely silent, and she often woke two or three times before dawn when a nearby door was slammed too harshly, or passers-by yelled at one another on the street below. She had negotiated with Adrienne they would never sleep in absolute blackness; she could leave one bed-side light switched on, perhaps the curtains slightly parted.

"Hino's probably in a cell by now," Adrienne smiled. "I was told it would be some time this week. I just wish I could've seen the look on his face."

"He's got access to some canny lawyers; do you think he's nailed?"

"The evidence is overwhelming. The government is desperate to raise the tax yield. If Hino walks free after abuse on this scale, they might as well hand over the Exchequer for every crook and fraudster in the country to loot. They can't afford not to make an example of him."

"And what about you?"

"I'll take my time. Since Craig added my name to Xanotek's share register after the restructuring, it's not like I'm about to run short. It would be great to stay involved somehow with you guys."

"I've said it a thousand times. We're so grateful for your support during our darkest hour. It was a brave thing you did. I probably owe you my life; definitely my sanity."

"I know what it's like to be caged, Marcelle. I couldn't stand on the sidelines while it happened to you."

After two more rounds, the women headed towards the promenade. During their week in Salvador, they had often ended the day sitting on the Porta da Barro beach, by all accounts one of the finest in the world, gazing across the Atlantic, wondering how Craig was faring all those time zones distant. Tonight, with the crush of residents still gathering for the weekend carnival, it took over an hour to traverse two blocks, but once the crowds dissipated Marcelle took Adrienne's hand, and they strolled casually, lethargically, as if time had no meaning, through the historic centre towards the promenade. After her brutalisation by Ward, Marcelle had for weeks been terrified to let down her guard in front of another human being. She had blocked and withdrawn to such an extent even Craig had grown frustrated.

"Getting your head straight takes precedence over racing back," he reassured her at the airport.

Close to the city's oldest Jesuit church, the women stopped to view a lavish street mural created by local artist Bel Borba, and compare the different emotions the work provoked. For Adrienne, Borba's colour palette inspired a sense of hope. Instinctively she squeezed Marcelle's hand a fraction more tightly. But their calmness and reverie was about to be interrupted. Marcelle spotted it first. Out of the corner of her eye, the glint of light reflecting from the metal of a switch-blade.

"*Tudo bem,* darlings."

The mugger was dressed like a rap artist: Wolverine baseball cap, dark glasses, and over-sized medallion chain. Despite the poor street lighting, his teeth were luminescent, flashing brilliant white like a Los Angeles starlet. But there was no time to dwell on his penchant for dental hygiene. The blade was being held tight against Adrienne's throat, and the mugger's other hand was already deep in her handbag rummaging around for loot.

"You pretty girls," he said. "Look like rich girls. Let's see what you got for Paulo?"

The police response in Salvador had grown so ineffective under its thrice-elected corrupt mayor that perpetrators of street crime no longer even attempted to disguise their identities.

For half a year, Marcelle has struggled to suppress feelings of fear and rage. Hours of meditation and self-discipline crumbled away in moments. The fury was welling up and needed release, like the explosive energy in an atomic bomb a split second after detonation. The thermal wave raced through her body but the aggression needed to be channelled. And so it would be, directly at Ward's – no, Paulo's – face. She clenched her fist, and felt her biceps tighten as blood pumped through the muscles of her arm.

"This way, buster," she shouted.

The mugger turned just in time to receive the full force of Marcelle's single punch. The blow was devastating in its effect. Paulo collapsed to the floor, holding his bloody nose, and yelping in pain from the shattered bone that had lodged in his optic nerve. The mural, already colourful, now benefited from an extra splash of crimson sprayed incongruously across the tranquil nativity scene.

"That was magnificent," exclaimed Adrienne. For Marcelle, the realisation was just sinking in of the risk she'd just taken, and the terrible consequences if she'd mis-timed her jab.

The dozen onlookers, all conveniently attending to other matters while the mugging was in progress, now clapped in spontaneous appreciation of Marcelle's courage. And as Paulo slunk away, Adrienne cupped her hands around her friend's head, cradling it like a precious toy, smothering it with kisses. In moments, Marcelle's composure was returning; the taste of Adrienne's tongue inside her mouth stimulated a frisson, a rapture, that overcame her nervousness.

"That felt better," she said. "So where were we headed?"

Epilogue The Fifth

Located in:
Crowborough Business Park

Xanotek now occupied two thirds of the Business Park's entire floorplan. With its fast growth, none of the management had found the time to oversee the search for a permanent headquarters. Instead, they instructed the country's most revered leasing agent, a silver fox they had tracked down in the basement wine bars around Paternoster Square, to mediate mutually-agreeable early termination deals with most of the other tenants in the complex.

In a bid to raise its international profile, the landlord – a semi-autonomous public body established to handle the government's portfolio of residual property invest-ments – had successfully pleaded with Barker to consent to the planned inclusion of Xanotek's name within the Park's legal title. Today would witness the culmination of this agreement: to much fanfare and in the presence of a minor Royal, the gaudy new signage proclaiming *The*

Xanotek International Business Park was being unveiled in under two hours.

Many of Jeremy Barker's former colleagues had been astounded at the ease with which the geeky Blackadder aficionado had made the transition to ruthless and charismatic leader. Craig's recommendation, that a licensing model provided the most effective platform for rapid leverage of the polymer technology, had focused his choice: to step up, or to step aside. And Barker had no intention of allowing anyone else to take credit for commercialising his innovation. At a stroke, licensing eliminated many of the artificial constraints on the company's growth prospects. It sidestepped the need for heavy investment in plant and equipment, and provided a viable route to parallel expansion in multiple sectors and geographies. However, it required Barker to develop the harsher, more obdurate facets of his personality.

Firstly, their nascent manufacturing operation was mothballed. Next, his management team was restructured; the new strategy demanded different competencies. IP protection was mission critical. The most aggressive patent lawyers in five continents were now on his speed-dial. And, most importantly, he could not afford to be a pushover in client negotiations. Craig had mentored him to be cold-blooded in his choice of customers, identifying either the dominant brand or the likeliest challenger in each sector. And to never accept a profit margin below 92 per cent. Barker had steeled himself and proved unswayable before a raft of maudlin pleas to make an exception for one good cause or another. Perhaps Craig had never intended him to be so uncompromising, but Barker was terrified that, should he display any hint of weakness, the edifice of invincibility he'd erected would putrefy and fall.

Barker had appointed Adam Peralter as his Director of Licence Sales. He had interviewed many of the world's most illustrious licensors for the position, including three shortlisted candidates who flew over on consecutive days from Silicon Valley, but in the end, under Craig's counselling, had opted for somebody who understood the science inside out. Peralter had been with him from his days at Rumixit, and at Barker's insistence, had surrounded himself with licensing lawyers, business development managers, and contract negotiators. But Barker needed a subject matter expert on point to judge the shape of any deal before it was executed.

Peralter was presenting a sales update from the defence sector, where they had recorded their first – and, to this date, most remarkable – commercial breakthrough. The revenue spike was literally off the charts; Peralter had needed to compress the vertical scale to prevent the final column in the sequence from bursting across the edge of the printout.

"You've got to hand it to Craig, the old goat," said Barker. "After that debacle at Malkin Castle, I hoped and expected that he'd depart the scene. I'm still not entirely sure how he spotted the chance to build a partnership with Tizett."

"The rumour is he took it direct to Thomas Pohl," said Peralter. "I've been dealing with Tizett now for six months. Our sales are extraordinary. Yet I've never met Pohl. Hell, I've not caught a glimpse of the man, or seen him copied onto emails. I think even his intermediaries have intermediaries. Yet if you catch the right middle manager at the right moment, normally at the local lap dance joint a few hours after quarterly bonuses, that's the hypothesis they blurt out. Between shows, of course."

"I was speaking with Craig this morning, I think I was the only one in the office at the time," despite (or perhaps due to) Xanotek's success, Barker was not averse to the occasional caustic aside about the inferior work rate of his subordinates, "and the subject of a second offsite came up. My gut tells me we've reached a stage in our development where it would be useful to take stock. Of course Craig will be vital, and he's already suggested a couple of themes to explore."

"Tell me you're not thinking of..."

"Malkin Castle? For nostalgic reasons? It was quite formative in the Xanotek story. To be honest, I'm undecided yet. Maybe a fresh locale would stimulate fresh thinking. What's your view?"

"Let me think about that one, sir," said Peralter. "But I'd like your guidance on a more immediate, certainly more sensitive, matter."

"Hit me," said Barker.

"Our polymer has been a singular blessing for British forces. Enemy casualties in Phoenicia outnumber our own by twenty-to-one; that's unprecedented in a ground war involving so much hand-to-hand engagement. But the blessing is not, shall we say, untarnished."

"There's not been much to tarnish so far," said Barker, gesturing at the wall behind him. The plasterwork was barely visible beneath the rows of awards, certificates, plaques, and the growing collection of appreciative letters from high-ranking Cabinet ministers. "Any day, the phone should be ringing to vet me about the New Year's Honours List."

"And therein lies the irony. It's the very efficacy of our polymer that sows the seeds of the looming problem. You see, Tizett tell me that asymmetric warfare is unsustainable."

"Meaning…?"

"To put it bluntly, we need to be supplying both sides."

"What does that mean in practice?"

"I have had a request this morning to release the source code to Tizett's shadow factory. Strictly off the books. It supplies…"

"I don't want to know the details," said Barker. "I need to think."

He was thinking of his decades of idealist intent to shape a better world. Since school, Barker's inventive spirit had been inspired by an ambition to put food on more tables, and improve the life chances of the down-trodden. Their framework contract with Tizett had been constructed with meticulous care, allowing Xanotek's polymer to be deployed in ways that aided the survival rate of Britain's fighting forces, allowing them to project their influence in regions where citizens were imperilled by the ferocity of conflict. How could this humble idealist countenance participation in some type of renewed arms race that would only escalate the suffering and killing?

Yet, he was also thinking about how he could sustain Xanotek's defence sector growth into the next year. There would always be a ceiling on the sales potential when observing a fatuous rule about playing for one side. What other business would agree to such strictures? Would a food processor limit itself to supplying a single super-market chain, cutting itself off from the remainder of the marketplace? And what about the 92 per cent edict? Surely that was the ultimate parameter. If in doubt, chase the profit margin. That was, after all, his fiduciary duty.

Outside, a crane was lifting the Xanotek logo high above the Park's entrance gate. A posse of royal protection officers had arrived to secure the site in advance of the princely arrival. But for the moment, Barker was oblivious to the commotion. He passed the sheets back to Peralter, and uttered just two words.

"Do it."

Epilogue The Sixth

Located in:
The Angola

In mooring his boat outside the *Fox and Hounds*, Craig used a far more elaborate web of liens and ropes than was necessary for a vessel the size of *The Angola*. There were only a couple of bollards within reach, so he started using other available props: a lamp post, an oak tree, a bench. He had even had the effrontery to tap on the window of the boat moored immediately alongside, and enquire of the owner whether he could use his stern line to join the two vessels together. Craig had been a little perplexed when the other owner had answered pithily and in the negative, but the attempt had been worthwhile. He was in a belt-and-braces mood.

News had reached him of Hino's arrest in South Korea, and the struggle now underway between the tax authorities in multiple jurisdictions that each wanted to take the lead in the financier's indictment. It was possible that a rogue assassin had already been despatched, but the chance of a follow-through had dramatically receded. What type of mercenary proceeds with a commission when reimbursement is likely to prove so problematic? For the past couple of days, Craig had been notably less tense.

Since his encounter in the rear of the Mercedes-Benz Sprinter in the Jermyn Street cul-de-sac, Craig had met Pohl on just one further occasion. He had been returning from the Ansa Complex in Mumbai where he had been advising Sagar on their next generation channel strategy, and (given his history) experiencing a remarkably light touch from the immigration authorities both on entry and exit. After showering in the Executive Arrival zone, he had taken a croissant over to the corner of the lounge and sat to check emails on an upholstered cube stool. Within moments, a gloved hand was blocking his view of the screen. Speaking softly, Pohl addressed just two topics. Firstly, he wished to confirm Craig was receiving appropriate recompense for his endeavours. Then he said:

"I don't expect we'll be speaking directly again. I'm leaving Europe later this week, with my chess set of course, and I have no plans to return. I ask you to make no attempt to track my movements, or to initiate contact. Such efforts would be fruitless and simply cause embarrassment. You may hear things of me; please disregard them. Or things of Tizett; I ask the same. In return, I ask you to continue your vital grand mastery of the sector. Guide and push the pieces beyond their limits. Don't accept established boundaries. If you overstep, I'll find a way to let you know."

That evening, Craig dined alone in the pub's garden. Though *The Wheatsheaf* was a county away, he still felt a pang of guilt when he crossed the threshold of any hostelry. He couldn't help but glance furtively around in case the Scot, who once labelled him a junkie, and left him spread-eagled on the green, chanced to be at the bar. On this occasion, the patrons were hospitable. But, mused Craig, it's just a matter of time.

Refreshed and satiated, he returned to *The Angola's* cabin, where he resolved that it was finally time, three years after their *decree absolute*, to muster his courage and reach out to Patricia. He couldn't face seeing her in person; that might tear him apart. But surely a call wasn't beyond him.

"Patricia, it's me, Craig. I know it's been long. Too long. And I realise everything was my fault. But I'm a better person now. Business has been going well. And a few months ago, I saved someone's life. Things had got a little out of hand, I guess that doesn't surprise you. But there's someone walking around on this planet, someone's who's kind and wonderful and fixes things really well. And she wouldn't be doing that if…

"But Patricia, this isn't about me. How are you? How is Natalie? She must be, what, nearly ten by now. You should send me a picture. In fact, we should get together. I'll stay clean. Why not Legoland? Or Longleat Safari Park? I bet she'd like that. Just let me know.

"I think a lot about us. About what could have been. Is it possible for people ever to revive their magic? I don't know, I really don't. Maybe you've found someone else. Maybe it's just a silly dream that we might ... that we could ... Damn it, I can't even say it."

The mobile was lifeless, and Craig cradled it in his hands. Two minutes passed; then a third. At last, he switched the device on.

But no, he thought. *I'm not yet ready to make that speech to anyone other than myself. But perhaps, if I keep practising.*

He placed the mobile on the counter top alongside the pile of analyses Adrienne and Dimala had prepared, a lifetime ago, about European military contractors. The pile had shrunk slightly over the months, as key documents found their way onto the inside cabin wall, where they were being used to create one of Craig's trademark displays. Stretching almost the entire length of the vessel, the panorama was already three times the size of the display he'd been forming on the wall of his Malkin Castle stateroom at the time of his initial encounter with Ward. This time, in addition to corporate data, his display comprised annotated transcripts of intercepted communications, grainy CCTV images from Central Asia, and complex illustrations purporting to track back through multiple jurisdictions, the funds used by Cunningham for his recent extravagances.

At the centre of the montage, a sheet of cardboard – the remains of one side of a cereal box – had been stapled to the cabin wall. The sheet was connected by lengths of coloured string to the other elements of the display, fanning out across the wall like the radials of a spider's web. Just six words had been written on the card – all capitalised, all underlined, all in permanent purple marker. The six were: *Best Options for taking down Pohl*.

Patricia, Pohl, his future as a strategist. Since he first learnt of Xanotek in the innocuous surroundings of London City airport, precious little of his time had been spent advising, counselling, acting in accordance with Pohl's *grandmaster* precept. During the unfolding drama, at vital points, he had found himself a player on the board. The tapestry of events had forced him to take responsibility, to pre-empt, to take risks. Was he sufficiently emboldened to seize the initiative once again?

Perhaps some music would strengthen his resolve. Since his unusual tour of the Churchill's underground bunker, Craig had acquired a taste for the soulful melodies of war-torn Britain. He scanned the extensive library on his tablet and tapped on Vera Lynn. Soon the rich, haunting strains of *We'll Meet Again* filled the cabin.

The intensity of Vera's vocal performance meant that Craig didn't hear the *ping* of his mobile as it registered an incoming text, although his attention was caught by its flashing red light. The message read: *Craig, there's an opportunity in Rio that could be the biggest yet. We need to respond urgently. Please call. Marcelle.* But Craig wouldn't be reading the message tonight. He had just remembered what was taped to the underside of the cistern lid in the washroom.

The packet was bulging with cocaine like the belly of a cartoon snake after gorging on a particularly rapacious feast.

Keep smiling through, Just like you always do, Till the blue skies drive the dark clouds, far away.

Craig took the mirror from the washroom wall, and balanced it on his knees as he squatted in the narrow gap below the sink. He tipped the white powder into the centre of the glass, and stared at it with a mixture of longing and contempt. He had two options.

We'll meet again, Don't know where, Don't know when.

He could fill his nostrils with a lavish dosage. Where was the shame? Why was it even taboo? He'd never killed anybody while high. And amidst the carnage of his personal life, one fact stood perennial and beyond contradiction. Whenever he was pumped up, he looked with a fresh perspective on the morning that Patricia walked out of his life with Natalie in tow. That day suddenly seemed so … trivial. And as for Pohl: why shake the status quo? On balance, Craig had dispensed more good than ill from his sinecure; in any event, it would never be a perfect world.

But I know we'll meet again, Some sunny day

Or he could start making amends and rebuilding. He could take the mirror from his knees and tip every last grain of the snow mountain on a one-way journey into the depths of toilet bowl. He could try calling Patricia tomorrow. He had the speech worked out, he just needed a clear head. And then, his personal life in order, he could turn his attention to Pohl. Options scoped and scrutinised and filtered into one memorable outcome: the planet's most inescapable noose tightening, degree by degree, around its most odious target.

What would be his strategy?

With thanks

The Xanotek Stratagem would have remained a distant dream were it not for the valued contributions of many people.

Excellent comments on the draft manuscript were provided by Michele Brailsford, Stephen Dryland, Darren Garner, Kathleen Garwood, Tamsin Mills, Owen Morgan, Pamela Smith, Theresa Wallis-Smith and New Generation Publishing. Rita Sexton designed the layout with her customary panache, and Simon Collins created a distinctive and memorable front cover image. I also thank Gary Gray, Keith Lindsay, Vinay Patel and Laura Stevens for their various contributions. To each of you, my hearty gratitude. I trust you're all pleased with the end product!

chasenoble

Chase Noble helps clients survive and thrive during
uncertain times.

Consultancy
Delivering game-changing strategies for market leaders.

Research
Revealing fresh insights into the needs and expectations
of stakeholders.

Publishing
Management guides and novels exploring new 21st
century challenges.

Mentoring and coaching
Working with high fliers to achieve audacious personal goals.

Training
Practical workshops on the application of strategy principles
in the real world.

Facilitation
Interactive strategy sessions with executive teams from the
board to the frontline.

Keynote speaking
Exploring themes through a powerful cocktail of observation
and entertainment.

Chase Noble Ltd
Audley House
Brimpton Common
Berkshire RG7 4RT
Tel: +44 (0) 119 982 1074
www.chasenoble.com

Also available

The Advertising
Handbook

A Winning Approach
to Strategic Business
Planning

(co-authored with
David Wolfe)

Why Strategies Fail:
17 Bloopers, How to
Spot Them and How to
Avoid Them

ISBN: 978-0-9575092-0-7

TurboCharged
Strategy

ISBN: 978-0-9575092-0-7

Why Strategies Fail:
A PostScript for
Governments

ISBN 978 - 0 - 9575092 - 2-1

Why Strategies Fail

LAURENCE SMITH

ISBN: 978-0-9575092-0-7

"A concise guide to … delivering quickly and effectively."
Colonel (retd) Tim Collins OBE

"Strategic insight should not be this accessible and entertaining."
Graham Davies
author, The Presentation Coach

"This is brilliant. Smith's book is readable, practical and gives really good advice."
Dermot Mathias
Senior Partner (fmr), BDO LLP

"A great diagnostic roadmap."
Victoria Wallace
Chief Executive, Leeds Castle Foundation

"Failures are finger posts on the road to achievement," said the great C. S. Lewis. With this simple observation, he gave hope to business leaders who reflect on their recent strategies and ask, "Why on earth did we do that?"

Why Strategies Fail investigates 17 bloopers that are commonly made by organisations, from global corporations to local start-ups. Included in the mix are errors of analysis, application, judgement, implementation and communication. These errors are sometimes bemusing and sometimes frustrating. Inevitably, they increase the risk that strategies will fizzle, flop, flounder, fold and fail.

In keeping with C. S. Lewis' maxim, the tale cannot end with exposing the blunders. *Why Strategies Fail* is also packed with examples of firms that have defied the ruinous temptation to be second best. Complete with anecdotes and cross-references, this book is an invaluable management resource for anyone wanting not only to spot the pitfalls, but to avoid them. And instead to design and deliver outstanding strategies to the benefit of all their customers, staff and investors.

Why Strategies Fail: A PostScript for Governments

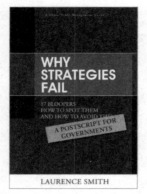

ISBN 978 - 0 - 9575092 - 2-1

Visionary politicians inspire us with their rhetoric of a beckoning tomorrow. So why, as the decades pass, does their El Dorado remain a distant mirage?

In *Why Strategies Fail*, the spotlight was shone ruthlessly on commercial organisations, from global corporations to local start-up businesses. However, many of the same themes are applicable to those who govern us.

In this short companion volume, focus turns to why the laudable intentions of successive governments so often go awry. Selecting three ingrained bloopers – Chaos Theory, Goodwill to All, and Busy Fools – the pitfalls are surveyed and possible reforms suggested to the body politic. Riotous, polemic and challenging, *A PostScript for Governments* is another must read management guide in the Chase Noble series.